VULCANA

VULCANA

A Novel

Rebecca F. John

HONNO MODERN FICTION

First published in Great Britain in 2023 by Honno Press
D41, Hugh Owen Building, Aberystwyth University, Ceredigion, SY23 3DY

1 2 3 4 5 6 7 8 9 10

A catalogue record for this book is available from the British Library.

Published with the financial support of the Books Council of Wales.

ISBN 9781912905805 (paperback)
ISBN 9781912905812 (ebook)

Cover design – Kari Brownlie
Typeset by Elaine Sharples
Printed by 4edge Ltd

To Kate Williams, strongwoman, whose story inspired me.

For Jane Vanderstay Hunt, who shared Vulcana with me.

In memory of Andrew Bullock, a strong man.

Opening Act

Abergavenny, Wales
1892
FLIGHT

The rain is a scuttling creature – moody and glancing and out to do harm. From the scant shelter of a locked and darkened doorway, Kate Williams watches it cross at a quick diagonal under the street lamps, then hasten away down Tudor Street on the wind like a murmuration of silver starlings. Where it gathers into puddles, their surfaces flecked and rippled by the insistent downpour, it soon spills over and escapes to the runnels to rush away. Even the rain does not wish to stay in Abergavenny.

Above Kate's head, a stream of raindrops collects in the broken end of a drainpipe, and proceeds to drip, with percussive regularity, onto the dome of her cranium. She has come to know herself in these terms since meeting William. Not scientifically, exactly, but ... specifically. Intimately. Cranium – twenty-one inches. Neck – twelve inches and one eighth. Neck, flexed – fourteen inches. Her body means something now. She is learning what it might be capable of.

Across the street, the gymnasium hunches in the darkness. The windows, black, reflect only the movement of the storm.

Kate knows that the door is bolted, and she resists the urge to run through the rain and put her hand to the stubborn catch of the handle and try to twist it free. She does not want to know what it feels like – the fact that William has gone. William, Mabel, Seth, Anna. Gone, without her. She takes a deep, shuddering in-breath, then exhales through her nose and watches her fury rise into fog. The air tastes of dampened woodsmoke, battered down from the chimney stacks by the weather to linger over the pavements. It is cigar-bitter. Choking. It tastes like home.

She tightens her arms around her waist – trim but sturdy at twenty-five inches – in a feeble effort to counter the cold. Her father will be sitting before the fire in their living room now, ankles crossed on the footstool, pipe clamped between his lips as he scribbles his next sermon on the back of an old hymn sheet. Her mother will be knitting without needing to count the stitches, and watching her husband as intently as he, in turn, squints over his penmanship. She will be talking about some friend or other – *Aneira will arrange the flowers, and Nerys will offer the tea* – and her husband will be grunting in response. The reverend's wife's voice is the soothing background noise to which he works, but does not listen.

Kate supposes neither one of them will miss her until morning. Neither would dare open their daughter's closed bedroom door. They are far too frightened of the mysteries that thick wooden divide conceals.

This Kate – who, at sixteen, has hips and an ample bust and ideas – is not the rose-cheeked baby they had thought to bring into the world. This Kate, who wraps her slender hands around barbells more successfully than she ever has a fiddly needle and cotton... This Kate, who already men grin at and posture for... This Kate, who has felt her pulse quicken and the unexplored place between her legs throb at the sight of William Roberts straining under two-hundred-and-fifty cast-iron pounds of bar and weights... This Kate is entirely unknown to Robert and Eleanor Williams.

And so, Kate reasons, she is at liberty to do exactly as she pleases, whatever Reverend Williams might have to say about *appearing before the judgement seat of Christ*. If her parents have no knowledge of her, no understanding of her desires, no interest in her talents whatsoever, why should she stay here and disappear under their indifference? Particularly when they have Margaret and young Eleanor and little William – who are all far more obedient than she – to find pleasure in.

When Kate's William – as she has secretly come to think of him – looks at her, she is brighter than she ever has been under God's gaze. Through his eyes, she is a pearl, gleaming from the cupped bed of an oyster shell. And she cannot give that up.

It has not escaped her attention that his name is an inversion of her father's: William Roberts; Robert Williams. Indeed, the fact has only served to persuade her that what she is doing is right. Everything she has in Abergavenny is the exact opposite of what she needs. She cannot tolerate another morning of sitting to a tea-and-brown-bread breakfast around their long oak dining table and watching her mother, her brother, her sisters simpering over her father's pronouncements. She cannot bear to see him peacocking around before his congregation, as though he is treading the London boards rather than creaking over the rotting floor of a dank old church in the Welsh hills. If Reverend Williams had wanted to be a star, she thinks, he should have gone out into the world and made it happen.

In less frustrated moments, Kate feels sorry for him. Her father is a great speaker. He might have made a name for himself somewhere, if only he'd been braver.

But tonight, Kate's frustration is a live thing. She can feel it in her stomach – a coiled rope, braided from strands of hurt and desperation and ambition and lust, and cast into a wild sea to thrash and dance. It is as though there is a rough-handed fisherman at one end and a writhing finned creature at the other, and she, the rope, is being pulled in both directions. It is the creature that will win out, she knows, eager as it is to break free and go chasing after William without the first inkling of a plan. And in truth, she does not want to stop it. She only hopes to slow it long enough to make the proper arrangements.

Though she has never acted on any such impulse before – never felt it for anyone other – she is wise enough to recognise it for what it is. She wants William Roberts as much as she covets the life he leads with the troupe. She wants him to hold her too hard; she wants to learn how his lips taste; she wants to feel herself pinned under his muscled weight; she wants to bite into him until she draws blood and can swallow the pulsing red heat of him. The remembered scent of his skin as he stood over her supporting the bar – cigarette smoke, iron, sweet talcum, sweat – is enough to thrust her into action, and, for want of anything better to do, she marches across the street and pounds a fist against the gymnasium door. She needs the indulgence of exerting her force against something solid, and the satisfaction of hearing its empty thud. She needs William.

Held in her left hand is the travelling case she had packed in preparation. She'd been planning to leave with him for weeks. It was going to be a surprise. She has timed it badly.

She hammers the door until she is breathless, then she spins about and strides away, a lone silhouette in the sleeping streets, her falling heels echoing off the mountains which sulk over the little town.

Kate Williams and William Roberts, she resolves, pushing her chin higher in defiance, though there is no one to see her, no one to counter her intentions. That's how it will be. The two of them. She is going to convince that man to show her the world.

Intermission

London, 1939

A low, insistent hum bothers her ear as she takes the long way – she has to keep her fitness up somehow through these slow days – across her city towards the letterbox. A bee, perhaps, she thinks, though the weather is wrong for it. She swats a knotted hand at the close, dank air; the noise does not subside. She swats again, for good measure, but she refuses to be irritated by it. London is as flat and grey as a bad mood today, and she is not inclined to join in with it. She is not about to start submitting to despondency now. What a waste that would be, after so much fighting for this life she wanted.

She looks across the street for the bright red pillar of the letterbox and, spotting its happy colour through the smog, pats the pocket containing the letter for Nora. Safe. The hum grows louder and she swats at the air for a third time. Indeed, she swats at it twice more before she recognises the sound: not the flight of an insect at all, but the grumble of an engine. A cab. Oh, how she had preferred them with horses. Where, she wonders, have all the horses gone? That such an elegant creature could be replaced by a bloody Austin High Lot... Beastly vehicles. So square and graceless. And always travelling too fast, like so much else these days. The declaration of another ugly war seems to have ground the country into a new gear, and she wants none of it. She has only just managed to slow down.

But she needs to slow down further, it seems, because she is breathless. There is a tightness in her chest that she would have thought impossible once. To be left breathless by a simple walk! And yet, here is the evidence of it – she is wheezing. Without checking her surroundings, she stops and closes her eyes, to concentrate not on the pain in her lungs or the fading blur of the world around her, but on the sounds, the smells. Clutches of delphiniums are pushing through the park railings to her right, and she is just able to catch their sweet, unobtrusive scent against the dirt and smut of London. Beautiful, she thinks. The small things. Slow down... But the cab does not. And she is not looking.

1892
Act One

1.

London, England
1892
THE FOG

London, she soon discovers, is filthy. She steps out of Paddington Station near mid-day, creased and smoky and itchy with tiredness, thinking to escape the blackened smut of the steam engines and breathe again, only to find that the air without is thicker than the air within. The city is a pale blear of fog.

Here and there, if she squints hard enough, the dark squares of window frames or doorways become visible. She discerns an uneven row of brown chimney pots, thrusting into the stone-pale sky, only when a raucous pair of corvids flap down to settle on them. She seeks out the curves and edges of nearby buildings, in hopes of studying the enormity of this place through its smallest parts, and eventually, after much concentration, a pitch of black slate roof is revealed, faded to grey; a pane of glass glints and then is lost; a line of rain gutter runs across nothingness like a railway track to the clouds. But these are only abstractions. They have the spiritless effect of a badly executed watercolour rather than the bold pride of an oil painting – which is closer to what she had expected of the city.

Kate can barely view the opposite side of the street from where she stands, her nostrils already blackened, her travelling case clutched between the aching fingers of her right hand, and the brim of the small felt sailor hat she borrowed from Margaret's closet pinched between the trembling fingers of her left. She has to hold firm to something. Though she hasn't stepped properly into it yet, she is already breathless with London.

'It's a bad one today,' says a plump lady who has stopped alongside Kate to set down her bags and rearrange the ribbons of her bonnet. The lady grimaces as she feels about for the bow, unloops it, and begins again, tipping the bonnet backwards and forwards half an inch until it sits comfortably. She gives off the soft scent of flour, and her blue eyes are small and kind, and suddenly Kate wants to hug her. She bites her lip against the temptation.

'Excuse me,' she says, 'but a bad what?'

'The fog,' says the lady, giving her head a little shake to ensure that the bonnet is properly secured. Satisfied, she bends to gather her bags. 'I'd keep that case close if I were you. You know what it's like in the fog – unwelcome hands all about. Here. Bring it up in front of you, like this...' She hoists her own bags up against her chest, as one might a swaddled baby. 'Wrap your arms tight around it, and keep your head up as you go. It's always worked for me.' The lady gives a friendly wink and walks away. Kate hardly knows what she is protecting – the travelling case or her own body – but, all the same, she does as she has been told as she prepares to set off. She does not yet know how to move through this strange new city, and she is grateful for the instruction.

With both hands occupied, however, she soon finds herself in want of a third – so that she might hold a freshly laundered kerchief to her nose, for the smell is brutal. Though she clamps her lips tightly shut, she can already taste it. Smoke, yes – gritty with coal dust, even here. And beneath that, a stench like wet wool drying over a fire. And beneath that again, passing traces of manure, stale beer, and something as full and briny as a caught fish.

She pictures the neat white kerchief she has folded into her travelling case, regrets not placing it in a pocket, and begins to stride away from the station. She has only one destination in mind. She has kept it on her tongue all the way from Abergavenny, so that she might ask the way.

York Road, please, she will say. *Battersea.*

She believes that the straightness of her posture and the breadth of her shoulders will dissuade anyone with funny ideas from misdirecting her. Though she stands only averagely tall at five feet and four inches, and appears nothing more than shapely in her blouse, hooped skirt, and jacket, she knows herself to be strong. Exceptionally so. She had been only fourteen when William had invited her to appear at the Pontypool fete as a strongwoman. A year younger still when she had taken hold of that runaway horse's rope and bodily hauled the skittish mare to a stop in the street – they wrote about that in the papers. She is of the steady opinion that, should any person with unwelcome hands sneak up on her in the fog, she will be more than able to fight them off.

Summoning up a pinch more bravery, she lowers her

13

travelling case back to her side, where it can swing more conveniently, steps into the white mystery of Praed Street, and begins the walk towards Battersea, where she will find her new life.

That afternoon, Kate wanders for miles. She thinks that perhaps she has never encountered so many different kinds of people. For a time, she walks through a large park – Hyde Park, the signs tell her – kept in gentle company by swaying sweet chestnuts and whispering hornbeams. But even amongst the trees, she does not find silence. Walkers pass in urgent conversation, and carriage drivers murmur comfort to already placid horses, and geese gabble like washerwomen at the water's edge. London has not yet revealed its bold strokes of oily colour, but it is growing brighter. On the countless streets she turns into and out of and into again, she dodges apple women and flower sellers and match hawkers; a fish porter, with a basket balanced expertly on his bowler-hatted head; plagues of little urchins, scrabbling shoeless and frozen for the congealed scraps fallen from the fishmonger's table; barrow boys cupping their hands over their mouths and blowing their blue hands pink again; a frightened horse, with rolling eyes and high hooves, being trotted through the crowds on a tat of rope; men in black top hats and frock coats lifting their feet to the quick rags of the hunchbacked shoe shiners; university smarts with good clothes worn purposely grubby and lofty airs; scoundrels leaning against lamp posts awaiting an easy theft; a young girl flogging a stack of magazines higher than herself. And all of them cough-coughing against the gag of the insistent smog.

At breathless intervals, she catches sight of her father, striding through the crowd towards her, his cassock flapping wildly. She hears his voice, intoning the lessons of Matthew 25:46: *Then they will go away to eternal punishment, but the righteous to eternal life.* Words which ran through their home like stitches through fabric echo in her mind. Each apparition resolves itself, eventually, into a passing stranger.

Kate wants to stop and ask them questions, to strike up conversations as she would at home, to learn more about these people's lives. Each one of them intrigues her, whether on account of the tone of their skin, or the contents of their barrow, or the unfamiliar sounds which flick from their tongues. But all she says is, 'York Road, please? Battersea?'

Until, some time near dusk, she finds herself standing on Battersea Bridge, her palms to the cold, cast-iron balustrade, staring down into the dark murk and lap of the Thames.

At her back, carriages rattle from one bank of the river to the other. The gas lamps which dot the length of the bridge have been lit and leave little orbs of luminosity on the water. Cold mists churn around the submerged granite piers. It would be beautiful, were it not for the inescapable stink of mouldering seaweed and shit. Kate thinks that perhaps all the sewage in the city is dumped into the river, to slosh away into the sea. Not wishing to watch it go, she continues across into Battersea. She had left Abergavenny with nothing much more than the name and location of the theatre where William and his troupe are due to perform their first London show: The Washington Music Hall and Theatre of Varieties.

It had sounded so impossibly romantic that she had known she must see it. She longed to stand on its grand stage, to drink in its hubbub and glamour, to listen to its stories without being able to begin imagining what they might consist of. She is sorry now – as she coaxes her aching feet through yet another cobbled mile – that she hadn't simply told William she would come with him. Perhaps some small part of her had feared that he would not allow it. *Your parents*, he would have argued. *Your father*. His gentlemanly ways would not have permitted him to say otherwise. Better perhaps, then, that she has denied him the choice. He'll be happy when she gets there. He will – whether he can show it or not. But there is a tight pulsing sensation worrying her neck and jaw which reminds her that she still doesn't feel sure he will not turn her away.

She plays through the nightmare of it, to prepare herself. *Go home, you silly girl*, he'll say. *Why would we want you here?* And then he'll slam a door in her panicked face and, with a muted laugh, shatter her heart.

Mercifully, these are not the words he does choose when, a couple of hours later, he finds her sitting on top of her travelling case on the pavement outside The Washington Music Hall and Theatre of Varieties, bone-cold and exhausted.

All he says is, 'Kate,' and Kate, her forehead resting on her knees, does not need to lift her head to know that it is him. She has never before heard her name spoken with equal measures of tenderness and excitement. The sound causes her stomach to clench, and she knows then that she will have him. She must. She cannot do without him. *When the woman saw the fruit of the tree she took some and ate it...* And when at length she looks up and sees his expression, caught somewhere between worry and joy, and his eyes, soft but sparking, and his hand, already reaching tentatively out for her, she thinks that perhaps, just perhaps, he cannot do without her either.

'It's bitter,' William says, stepping nearer and offering Kate his hand more firmly. She takes it, though she does not need the assistance, and pulls herself up. His warm skin causes hers to rise into gooseflesh, and she draws herself as close to him as she dares, yearning to catch a hint of cigarette-smoke breath through the oiled whiskers of his moustache, or to feel the shifting of his muscles beneath his swarthy skin. William is not tall – he stands only a hand's span taller than Kate – but he is powerful. His chest is forever expanded. His forearms bulge under his shirtsleeves. His thighs bow outwards, strengthened into the shape of a chimpanzee's. William bristles with an alertness that Kate senses but cannot define. He might always be ready to defend himself; he might always be ready to attack.

'How did you get here?' As he says the words, he glances about himself as though seeing the theatre, the street, the city for the first time. Kate, too, is able to consider her surroundings in closer detail, now that William is here, and she is safe, and she can begin to unclench. The theatre's upper two storeys have a clean brick façade, crowned by a row of stone parapets; the entire ground floor boasts a colonnaded entrance way, with hanging gas lamps and shuttered doors. Posters positioned beneath the gas lamps inform her that performances at The Washington proceed 'twice nightly'. She does not know, and does not question, why the building is closed now. Everything seems closed up tonight: the theatre, the row of black-windowed shops opposite, her own good sense.

'Kate?' he says again.

She remembers herself and engages her stomach muscles, straightening up from her core, as she has been taught. She lengthens her neck and lifts her chin.

'By train, of course,' she says, allowing herself a small smile. 'I knew you would come to scout the place out.' Then, after a short pause. 'Do you think I'm so useless that I can't step onto a train by myself?'

William laughs – a short, surprised sound. 'No, I don't. I think you're capable of just about anything, Kate Williams.'

'Good.' She is growing haughty now. Her confidence always swells when she is in William's presence. She cocks her head in what she considers to be a playful but determined way. 'Because I have come to be your strongwoman. Star act only, mind. I won't be second on the bill.'

William's eyebrows rise above his brilliant green eyes. 'Is that so?'

'It is very much so.' Kate brushes down her skirts, which already feel grimy to the touch, then bends to lift her travelling case. It has grown heavier by the hour, as though her fear had crept in through the seams to weigh it down. 'Now, where are our rooms? It's been a long day.'

She imagines how it might be, if she and William were to share a room to themselves, and her stomach jumps at the thought.

William hooks his arm and offers it to Kate. 'I'll show you to the rooms,' he says, 'on one condition.'

'I'm sure I'll agree to it.'

'Wonderful. I'll find some papers and an envelope and you can write straight away to your parents.'

A whine rises in Kate's throat, but she manages to quell it.

'All right,' she agrees. 'But just a short note.' She turns her eyes on him, all flutter and lashes. Her eyes – large and round and a startling rich cinnamon brown – are her greatest beauty. She does not know how to bargain with them yet, not flawlessly, but she is learning.

'All right,' William agrees, and finally she loops her arm through his and their steps fall together and Kate knows without doubt that walking down a strange London street with a man as wise and sophisticated as William Roberts is exactly where she ought to be. He really is going to show her the world, and she wants to explore it all.

'I can't see where we're going,' Kate says, pressing herself closer to William, inhaling the clean cotton scent of his pressed grey suit. Ahead, the ashy fog waits to enshroud them.

'No. Neither can I,' he replies. 'It's exciting, isn't it?'

Kate's face opens into a wide, silly smile, but she does not lower her head to hide it. She is quite happy for William to see her exactly as she is.

'Yes,' she says. 'It is exciting.'

2.

London, England
1892
AWAKENING

The next day dawns cold and splendent, and Kate wakes between clean white bedsheets, her lids heavy and a deep ache spreading across her lower back. She opens her eyes a dash, is confronted by stark morning light, and closes them again to shut out the sting of it. She straightens her legs over the cotton undersheet, then arches her spine. She is stripped to her petticoat, but feels warm enough, snugged in as she is. Pulling her arms free, she stretches them above her head until she feels something inside her pop, then slackens again in relief, her exposed skin already beginning to turn chill. Somewhere nearby, voices converse at a murmur, but she does not reach for the words: she does not want them yet. There is a drifting scent of coffee, and perhaps, though less pungent, sugared tea. Kate feels she might be in Paris. Or Vienna. Or on the other side of the globe entirely, waking to breakfast she will take on a balcony overlooking cliffs and the crashing sea. She sees herself opening a book as she bites daintily into a croissant fresh from the oven, and smiles at the presumption of the idea. Kate Williams, from Abergavenny! But, how beautifully foreign it feels, to be here and not staring out of her parents' kitchen window at a rainy rampart of fields and trees and flocked sheep.

Escape, she thinks, feels opulent.

Opulence was not permitted under Reverend Williams' roof. Prayer, charity, and study left no space for indulgences, however much she might have begged for a Sunday in the sunshine instead of watching it through a stained-glass panel. Her father's voice chimes through her mind again: *do good, and lend, expecting nothing in return, and your reward will be great, and you will be sons of the Most High*, Luke 6:35.

She stretches again, gives a groan. The sons of the Most High. What, then, of the daughters? Outside the hotel window, the city is a muted collection of unfamiliar sounds: the grind and clop of horse-drawn omnibuses; the thud and clatter of carts being loaded or unloaded; the prattling of so many people along the pavements; the shouts of disgruntlement or greeting; the ringing of bells above shop doors as customers swing through. In Abergavenny, she would wake only to the pot-and-steam sounds of her mother at the stove.

Finally, she opens her eyes again, slanting her hand over her eyebrows to shield them from the glare, and lifts her head and shoulders slightly. When William had snuck her into the room last night, she had seen nothing of it but shadows. Now, she discerns that the walls and ceiling are painted white. At the window, a pair of mustard-yellow flowered curtains hang, already pulled open and smartly pleated into their tiebacks. There are two more single-width beds, a heavy mahogany

21

wardrobe, and, on the far side of the room, a small round table at which two women sit drinking tea from small china cups.

'You're finally awake, then?' says the woman on the right. She is already neat in a high-necked cream shirtwaist and blue tweed skirt. She has not yet laced on her boots, and a stockinged toe peeps from under her hem. Her deep auburn hair falls loose over her shoulders. She is half put together and easy with it: Mabel. In the other chair – shorter, plumper, and fair-haired – Anna plucks purple grapes from a stalk and sucks them between lips pursed with amusement.

Mabel grins into another sip of her tea, swallows it slowly. 'We said you'd come, you know.'

'You did?' Kate asks, and her voice is rough with thirst. She longs to share the tea, but it feels rude to go over and help herself when she has descended on Mabel and Anna's room unannounced.

Mabel indicates the furniture with a sweep of her head. 'Three beds and two of us to share. I think William was expecting you to leave home with us.'

'I intended to,' Kate answers, sitting up fully and arranging the sheets modestly at her hips. 'I must have just missed you.'

'Well,' Anna puts in. 'You're here now.'

'Is that all right?'

In response, Anna pours from the teapot into a third china cup, adds a splash of milk, then brings it across to Kate, who accepts it from her sitting position as if she is a grand lady. Part of her flushes for the shame of allowing Anna to wait on her; another part of her enjoys it.

'Of course. Why shouldn't it be?'

Kate can conjure a thousand reasons: because she couldn't imagine two women in their middle twenties would want a sixteen-year-old trailing around the country after them like an annoying younger sister; because Kate has made it known that she intends to install herself as the troupe's star act; because she has already proven herself stronger than both Mabel and Anna in weightlifting contests across Wales, Bath, and Bristol; because she represents, doesn't she, a threat to how much of William's attentions they might receive. But then again, perhaps they do not crave his attentions as she does. Kate has never known them to flirt or fuss over him. It would seem that theirs is the business relationship it ought to be. After all, Mabel, Anna, each of the women who has passed through the troupe, know as well as Kate does that William is married.

Kate drains her tea to avoid offering Anna an answer. It is tepid and sweet and a godsend.

'That's that, then,' Mabel announces. 'Now get dressed. We're going out.'

'Won't you be wanted at rehearsals?' She is careful not to say 'we'.

'Later,' Anna confirms. 'First, we have to go to the river.'

'Why?'

Anna's face lights with child-like excitement. Her smooth round cheeks pink. 'They say it's freezing over.'

'It's not cold enough,' Kate says.

'Open the window,' Mabel replies. 'You might disagree.

23

They say it's always warmer when the fog is down, but now that it's cleared…'

Kate needs no further persuasion. Throwing back the sheets, she rushes over to the window. Without a thought for who might look in and see her exposed in her slip, she grasps the handle and pulls the thin-framed pane back into the room. The cold thumps her straight in the stomach and causes her to gasp. Laughing, she turns back to Mabel and Anna.

'Do you think it will snow?'

'No,' Mabel replies. 'We're too close to the water. But hurry and get dressed and you can check for yourself. Don't forget your gloves.'

Kate skips over to the wardrobe, beside which she had abandoned her travelling case in the dark hours before, and flips open the clasps. As she rifles through it for her gloves, she tosses blouses, petties, and stockings over her head to alight in heaps on her unmade bed.

'Gloves, gloves, gloves,' she mutters to herself as she searches.

'The Thames isn't going anywhere,' Anna laughs, eyeing the mounting pile of clothes. 'No need to wreck the place.'

Kate pays her no heed. Delight – at finding herself here, at the memory of William's hand over hers as they walked back from the theatre last night, at the brilliantly cold air swooping in through the window – is welling up inside her and she needs to be outside, under the sky, where she can run or spin or dance. Now that she has found the bravery to walk away from home, she feels that she might never stop moving.

'Gloves!' she squeals, lifting them above her head like a trophy.

Within fifteen minutes, Kate has gathered her hair up into its pins, pressed on her sailor hat, and the three women are laughing down the hotel stairs towards the start of the day.

They reach the river before nine o'clock. Though the sun is still low over the city, it throws out its light in sturdy beams, hitting the water at a shallow diagonal and illuminating the cold mists which steal over its surface. Kate can hardly believe how far the temperature has plunged. Inside her gloves, her knuckles are stiff with it. The three women's exhaled breath makes steam engines of them. The ground beneath their boots glints with frost, and Kate chooses not to look from the pavement and into the street itself, where mud gathers into furrows and skets off the wheels of passing carts and bicycles. Perhaps making the most of London, she thinks, will mean deciding where best to place one's eyes.

With no real direction in mind, the three friends gravitate towards the busiest stretch of the river. There, a troop of industrial ships – imposing black funnels and empty slicked decks – brood silently. Around their hulls, the water has already thickened and stilled to ice. Further out, in the middle of the river, a darker stream continues to flow, and along this narrow passageway, smaller wooden boats manoeuvre, though it is evident from the warning shouts of the sailors that the going is not easy.

'How can it have happened so quickly?' Kate wonders.

In answer, Anna and Mabel only stare down at the unmoving whiteness. None of them knows the patterns and peculiarities of this place yet, least of all Kate, and she is as thrilled by the lack of knowledge as she is scared.

'Look over there,' Mabel says, pointing across the river, to where three dark figures sit crouched on the bank, lacing themselves into three pairs of large black boots. 'They're going to try skating on it.'

'They're not!' Anna breathes.

'They are!' Mabel laughs. 'It's going to be disastrous, surely.'

The women lean as far over the stone balustrade as they dare to watch. The three small figures help each other to rise, then wobble tentatively onto the ice. They take a moment to gain their balance, heads bent in concentration as they test the blades of their skates with small forward pushes. They slow to a stop, adjust their coats, begin again. And it is a matter of minutes only before they are gliding over the river, hands tucked behind their backs as though they are champions of the pursuit.

As they come nearer, Mabel pushes her head forward further still and squints.

'They're police!' she shrieks.

'No,' Kate says.

'They bloody are,' Mabel laughs. 'Look at their helmets, and their matching coats. They're skating police. What a thing.'

'They must be going out to check on the ships,' Anna suggests.

'They're having a good time doing it, too,' Mabel replies, as the three men reach the last of the established ice and, gathering speed, skirt along the edge of the few feet of lapping water which still separates one solid bank of the river from the other. They speed out of sight like an arrow of black birds, launching themselves into flight.

'I want to try it,' Kate says. Never in her life has she skated over ice.

'We don't have any blades,' Anna replies.

'Not today. But one day.' She closes her eyes and pictures what it would be like, to rush along with only water to hold you up, and feel yourself so very, very free.

She opens her eyes again when there comes a disturbance to her right side: clutches of small children are clambering over the balustrades and dropping down onto the ice below with hard thuds.

'You'll fall through,' Mabel calls, 'thumping down like that.'

But the children only glance back and smile toothlessly, then take off running and sliding, their tatty clothes hardly sufficient to keep them warm even on a balmy day. Some wear flat caps; others go bare-headed. Some possess coats – either too big or too small and never just right – while others have on only dresses and shawls. Inside her thick coat and woollen gloves, Kate shivers for them. Their fun will keep them warm, she supposes, as they scatter over the ice, skipping with arms linked, or shoving each other over, or lowering themselves onto their bottoms to skid along all the faster. Based on their stature, Kate would suppose them no more than six years of age, but the flint look in their eyes persuades her that some might be closer to ten or twelve. Their whoops and cackles ring out, clear as chapel hymns on the calm air.

Two smaller children remain on the pavement beside Kate, staring wistfully out through the balustrades they cannot reach to climb over. They are perhaps four years old. They retain the round-bellied look of toddlers. Their eyes are big with sadness at missing out, and yet Kate cannot bring herself to lift them up and drop them down to join the others; it really is too dangerous. Instead, she invents a game.

'Come,' she says, beckoning to the grubby pair. They shuffle closer to her with the willingness of hungry kittens. 'Let's play trains.' And angling her arms at her sides like rods and using her elbows as crankpins, she begins to chug along the pavement, jerking her hands through a rough oval arc and pouting her lips to push out breathy white puffs. *Choo-choo-choo-choo*, she goes. *Choo-choo-choo-choo*. And the children, giggling, join in behind – the carriages to her engine.

Anna and Mabel, backs leaning against the balustrade, watch as Kate and her orphan playmates mark a wide turn around a nearby fruit hawker before chugging back in their direction. Kate sends them a wink as she *woo-woo*s past and deposits the children on the spot where she found them.

'Your friends will be back soon, I'm sure,' she says. 'Now why don't you carry on down that way, to keep warm.'

The children, grinning, keep up their *choo-choo*ing and continue the train's imaginary journey along the pavement. Kate laughs to see them go – arms orbiting, breath steaming – and ignores the stab of guilt she feels at having left her brother and sisters behind. As a small girl, she had enjoyed having siblings in a way her school friends had not. They had laughed and teased together, the Williams children. They had bent their heads over secrets that must be kept from their parents. They had invented games with rules they vowed not to share, purely for the joy of possessing something which was only theirs. And when they had grown too old for such simple pleasures and carelessly discarded them, Kate had told herself that she would one day have children of her own, and that with them she could recreate what had been lost.

Soon, the train-engine pair are lost amongst the crowds which assemble to watch the skating policemen, and the frolicking children, and the locked-in ships, and the little boats which cluster to clog the last moving rivulet of the Thames. People line the river and point out this sailor or that struggling vessel. Herring gulls swoop and caw overhead. Pigeons flap around ankles, pecking up dropped nuts and bits of detritus without distinction. Passing dogs prance, exhilarated and confused by the chill at their paws. Of a sudden, it feels as though the entire city is celebrating, and so different is this from the impression Kate had yesterday that she could roar with relief.

This is it. This is the place she imagined. Here, with a stage and an audience, she might reinvent herself. Here, she might be seen.

'I was wondering...' she says, turning back to Mabel and Anna. 'Would you show me inside the theatre?'

3.

London, England
1892
THE TROUPE

Gathered as they are by twelve noon under the high ceiling of
The Washington Music Hall, William Roberts' troupe of
strongpersons seems a diminutive group indeed.

In their day clothes, Kate, Anna, and even Mabel – despite
her height – appear as might any group of women out for a
day about the city. William, who stands on stage speaking to
the theatre manager, seems no more impressive, dressed in
the same grey suit he wore the night before and standing a
head shorter than the man to his right. There are two more
men engaged in the troupe: Abraham, 'Named for the
president,' he says, winking and clicking his fingers into a
point, though Kate is convinced the accent is affected for its
exoticism and the name an invention; and Seth, a farmer's
son, who, by comparison to Abraham, is lean and spare.
None cuts a particularly exciting figure on this bitter
November day.

As they wait for William to finish his conversation, Seth
stands with his hands linked behind his back and rocks on his
heels, like an old man awaiting the appearance of a tardy

grandchild or a fussing spouse, and occasionally tips his head back to peer up at the enormous gold sun-burner suspended above them. Each time he does this, Kate stares at the bulge of his Adam's apple and wonders why she can summon no romantic feelings for this man, who is tall, and wears the broad shoulders of a boxer, and who, at twenty-one, is much closer to her own age than is William, at nearer thirty. She knows it to be an impossibility, so frequently has she tried to distract herself from William with thoughts of Seth, but still, she can't help but wonder at it. No blushing. No churning. Nothing. The wiser option holds no appeal for Kate.

'Can you feel the heat off that thing?' he says now, though of course they all can. The sun-burner has been lit for some hours and, in contrast to the temperatures outdoors, it feels as intense as a blistering hearth fire.

The others lift their heads dutifully to the embellished gold crown the burner has been fashioned into. It looks to Kate as though it must have cost a year of her father's wages. She cannot see the need for such a piece of ornamentation when the entertainment will surely be onstage, and ought to be sufficient to keep any audience member's eyes from drifting upwards. She says as much, and is met with grins from the women and a serious glance from Abraham.

'But the girl is right,' he drawls. He has called Kate 'the girl' since their first meeting; it does not rankle her any less with repetition. 'We'll have to be more than spectacular just to compete with the walls in this joint.'

'If you don't imagine yourself any more interesting than the

31

walls, Abe,' Kate replies, 'then I don't suppose there's much hope at all for your performance.'

At this, Abraham laughs a little too loudly and the others snigger. Secretly, they appreciate his fears. The Washington is by far the grandest venue they have yet performed at. The seating – they have lately overheard the theatre manager boast – can accommodate over nine hundred persons. The furnishings, from the wood-panelled ceiling all the way down to the boards, are complementary shades of cream and ivory. The balconies are decorated with papier-mâché mouldings, accentuated with gold to match not only the enormous sun-burner but also the intricately cast Wenham lamps positioned under the galleries.

The impression is of fire and stars and the gods.

Though they are poking fun at Abraham, William's troupe know they will have to shine here.

'We've got two days,' Mabel says. 'And William says there's a rehearsal space near the hotel. The bloody walls will have nothing on us come Saturday.'

'Right enough, too,' Anna nods, crossing her arms over her bust.

Onstage, William is shaking hands with the theatre manager, who does not stand straight enough to take possession of his gangling frame, but instead slumps over his own pot belly like a man defeated. William could teach him something about posture, Kate thinks; and strength; and grace. It seems to her that William knows everything there is to know. After all, it was he who had noticed her potential, encouraged her to visit the gymnasium, first held a weight bar over her head and lowered it into her open palms. He alone has taught her what she might be.

And that, she decides, is why she really will write to her parents as he has asked.

She will say, *I am come to London to make my way in the music halls. I shan't return home except to visit, if you will have me. I am safe with William Roberts' troupe, and assure you that there is nothing shameful in this life.*

Even as she designs the letter, her mind wanders to the page torn from the *Pall Mall Gazette* which Mabel had pinned up on the wall of the Tudor Street gymnasium a year or two before. It flutters there still, faded into blankness – or had, the day before they left. Mabel had taken a pencil and circled a sentence which claimed that 'no girl ever kept her virtue more than three months' in some London theatre or other – Kate recalls the phrase perfectly, if not the location. But what does that matter? Kate will not lump herself in with all those other girls. She is to be her own woman, whatever the cost to her soul.

My mind is made up, the letter will end. *I am to be a strongwoman.*

The troupe takes to the rehearsal room almost immediately, pausing only to change into their leotards, tights, and belts. They find it decked out with all the dumb-bells, barbells, kettlebells, and Indian clubs they could need. On one side, the room has three large, high windows, through which they can see only the roof slates of the building opposite and the jackdaws which congregate around its single chimney stack. On the other hangs a wide mirror, slightly misted, in which they watch each other's distorted reflections. Within the hour, the room smells of sweat and talcum powder. By that evening, the air is heavy with their exhaled breaths. At nine o'clock, William disappears to fetch sandwiches and, on his return, they sit on the dusty floor, tired and sticky, and chew through thick cuts of bread filled with cheese or egg or salmon paste. Or, in Seth's case, sliced apple and pickles. They curse him for that choice when they arrive back early the next morning and begin again – talcing up, lifting, spotting, adjusting.

And all the while Kate watches William, and William watches Kate, and something – something she does not know how to name – begins to shift.

By dusk on their second rehearsal day, they are, all six, wet-haired and spent. Their chatter has sunk into silence. They listen to each other's joints creak as they brace and lift.

'All right,' William announces, setting down the barbell he had been overhead pressing. Kate watches a trickle of sweat meander down his temple and swallows the urge to lick it away. 'That's enough.'

There follows a murmur of dissent, but it is half-hearted, and Anna, Seth, Abraham, and Kate are lowering their weights to the floor even as they make it. Only Mabel holds firm, staring into the mirror and curling a dumb-bell with inhuman regularity: she has always been the most disciplined.

'We've got all evening,' she pants between curls. 'Tomorrow morning, too.'

'We're ready, Mabel,' William replies. 'Overdo it and the performance will suffer.'

'What do you intend instead?'

'Drinks!' Abe suggests.

'An early night and a good breakfast,' William counters, laughing and reaching out to slap at Abraham, who dodges him. 'Besides, I can't stand to look at your scowling mugs for a minute longer. Go back to the hotel, take a hot bath, sleep, and I'll see you all tomorrow morning. Thank you for your hard work. Now get out of my sight.'

When the others start to wander out, Mabel finally relinquishes the dumb-bell, raises her arms into a cursory stretch, then moves after them.

'Any help tidying up?' she asks from the door.

William, who is collecting the Indian clubs up in one spread hand, keeps his eyes to the floor as he answers. 'Kate offered,' he says, and at the words, the implication of them, Kate's head starts to pound. She has done no such thing. Colour floods her cheeks and she angles her face away from Mabel, so that the older woman does not see and question it. Ridiculously, tears are welling along Kate's lower lids. Don't be stupid, she tells herself. He could need you to stay behind for a hundred different reasons. And yet, the way he had looked at her...

'We'll manage between the two of us,' he says.

'If you're sure,' Mabel replies and, giving her customary wink, she swings around the door frame and is gone.

Kate does not know whether it is Mabel's retreating footsteps or her own heartbeat she can hear as she watches

William set five Indian clubs down on the middle shelf of the iron storage rack positioned in a far corner. The wooden clubs bump against each other, making a dulled thunking sound. William straightens up and moves across to the kettlebells. Lifting one in each fist, he positions them on the shelf below the clubs. He moves calmly and methodically, as though there is no one else in the room. He does not glance up to meet Kate's scrutiny. In fact, he seems to avoid it. He is nervous, Kate realises. And she knows it is her heart she can hear then, for it is louder than a marching band, and, to her mortification, there is nothing she can do to silence it, because she knows suddenly that William is going to kiss her. He is going to clear up the mess – perhaps he needs the time, the distraction, to ready himself – and then he is going to stride across the room and claim her. She knows it. She does not move to help him to slide the bars into the rack or roll away the mats. She only stands, and waits.

She has been kissed before. After her first weightlifting appearance, at the Pontypool fete, she had sat around in the bandstand with a group of school friends – all of them laughing at nothing and clumsily touching each other's legs or backs or shoulders to see what would happen. It seemed they had been hunkered there for hours before a quick black cloud scudded over, bringing with it a heavy downpour. The rain was cacophonous on the bandstand roof, and they had stood and shrieked about the noise, until a boy in the class above Kate's grasped her hand, dragged her down the bandstand steps, and started her running across the field towards the shelter of the trees. Beneath their slick green canopy, they soon discovered an old sweet chestnut, hollowed out, and ducked inside, where they could stand straight up in the emptied chamber of the trunk. The kiss itself was forgettable. Kate had found herself uninspired and eager to have it over with. But the sweet chestnut she remembers vividly: the dark, wet weight of it surrounding her; the tapping of the rain against its long leaves; the damp stench of the litterfall beneath her boots against the salty tang of the catkins. She had felt herself somewhere other, unfamiliar. And that was far more exciting than the fumbling boy at her lips. The world and all its beautiful possibilities had stolen in and ruined that kiss.

But with William, she is certain, it will be quite the opposite. When William kisses her, the rest of the world will cease to exist.

To signal that he has finished his task, William brushes his hands across his thighs, leaving two smears of white talc in the cotton: the imprint of his fingers makes them look like wings, feathering into flight. Then he balls his fists, rests them against his hips, and finally turns to look at Kate.

Kate is a statue. She has not moved an inch since Mabel descended the stairs and left the exterior door to slam behind her. She wonders now if she can move, or if perhaps she really has hardened to stone. She cannot think of a word to furl over her tongue, or how to impel her limbs into movement, or whether she ought really to be standing alone in an empty room in an unknown city with a man of twenty-eight, however much she might want to. Perhaps she is not ready for what might follow. She knows something of it – rumours and imaginings and the occasional stifled sound through her parents' bedroom wall – but not enough. She is not experienced. She is not quite a woman. She is not William's wife.

And yet, the longer he looks at her, the bolder she feels herself becoming. In her leotard and tights, every line of her body is visible to him, but she experiences no urge to cover herself up. Instead, she pushes back her shoulders and stands straight – not a statue after all – and wonders, unexpectedly, if the dark points of her nipples are evident through the black pull of the cotton. She hopes vaguely that they are. The idea that William might put his eyes on any bared part of her sets her stomach fluttering. What she wants – so physically that she trembles against the urge – is to tear the fabric open and reveal herself to him. It doesn't matter that she is unsure of what comes after. She wants to open herself to William. Only William. A scenario enters her mind, whereby ripping the leotard isn't nearly enough, and she begins to peel away her skin, and then her muscle, until he can peer into her chest cavity and watch her heart throbbing and tremoring.

'William,' she manages to say, finally. The word is sugar and vinegar on her tongue.

'I'm glad you stayed,' he replies. His bunched fists remain at his hips. His stance is wide, business-like. The small leather ballet slippers they all wear to train are an absurdity over his thick, knotted feet.

'Yes...'

Still, neither of them has moved. From the chimney top at her back, a jackdaw croaks out a sermon of its own – about sin, probably.

'There's something I wanted to show you,' William continues. 'It's a surprise, of sorts, but I hope you won't mind it.'

'Should I?' Kate asks. 'Mind it?'

William shakes his head, smiles just a little. 'I should hope you'll be impressed. Come.'

He indicates the door of the rehearsal room, and Kate moves towards it blindly. In the hallway, she waits for him to lock the door, then makes to descend the stairs. Back to the hotel, she thinks. Where else would they be going? But William stops her with a raised arm.

'This way,' he says, tipping his head towards another door. This one has no glass panel and she can discern no chink of light around the frame. William grabs the handle and turns it; it is not locked. Within is only darkness and the acrid smell of stale air. Kate looks confusion at William, who smiles wider.

'You don't expect me to get inside?' she asks. The disappointment she would feel at another fumble in the darkness. With William, she has already decided, it will be all light and clarity.

William laughs and shakes his head.

'Wait,' he says. He moves into the darkness and begins shuffling about. A moment or two later, he emerges, carrying a large board – perhaps four feet in height. He holds it side on, so that only its three-inch width is visible.

'Close your eyes,' he instructs.

Kate hesitates. Already, her anticipation is sinking into disenchantment. This cannot be the beginning of what she had intended. This is ... what, then? A game? She narrows her bright round eyes into dashes of doubt. Her temper is brewing. When stirred to, Kate gathers and breaks like a storm.

William twists his mouth, challenging her as a father might a tantruming child. That he is a father is a fact Kate can barely take hold of. In some dark fold of her mind, she knows that William and his wife share three peachy babies: the eldest just five; the youngest but a year old. But she knows it in the same way as she knows that there are parts of the Earth forever deep in snow, or that, whatever her father preaches, there is no being called God. William's family is a distant thing – a story almost – and it is not her concern. If it were, William would speak to her of them. The fact that he does not persuades her that William is building two separate lives for himself. One with Alice; another with his troupe. The second, she might be a part of.

'Close your eyes,' William says again.

This time, Kate acquiesces. She listens as he scrapes the board out into the hallway. Behind her lids is William's squared silhouette.

'All right. Open them now.'

She does, and finds that William has made a sandwich-board boy of himself. His disembodied head grins madly.

'Read it, then,' he says.

Kate scans the board. In tall, sharp letters is written, *Atlas and Vulcana: the World-Famous Brother and Sister Strongperson Act.*

'Who are Atlas and Vulcana?' she asks, frowning.

'We are!'

Her frown deepens.

'Or we will be. We're going to reinvent ourselves, play the characters. Star act only, you said. I thought we could share it. You and I, Kate. Atlas and Vulcana.'

'Brother and sister...' she reads slowly, swallowing an odd clag of deflation.

William shrugs. 'It's a good hook.'

'But...' She shakes her head, trying to find the direction of the conversation. 'You can't have had this made up in two days.'

'No,' he admits. 'I made an order in advance.'

'And what if I hadn't come?'

Her question is met with a beat of silence. William slides the board away from himself and settles it along the wall; it is crisp and neat against the map-like patches of flaked cream paint and grey plaster beneath. He was right about her response – she is impressed. Impressed and devastated. Abruptly, she longs to return to the hotel, and throw herself beneath her rumpled sheets, and breathe heat and fury into the dark until she falls asleep. She is ashamed of her thoughts. Ashamed of herself. Little wonder she cannot shake her father's voice from her mind when she is so full of sin. She should have come to London for the stage alone, not for this man.

William takes a step nearer and gently touches her shoulder. Kate loosens into his hand.

'I knew you'd come,' he says.

Kate's only response is to stare into his soft, almost sea-foam green eyes; at the spiny bristles of his blond moustache; at the smooth tulip petals of his lips; at the protuberant tendons of his neck. His scent – sweet talcum and rich iron – lingers under her nose: familiar yet contradictory. As she watches, his mouth opens and she hears the moist unsticking of his tongue as it rises towards his teeth, and she shudders at the hope it brings her, but he is only speaking.

'So, what do you say?' he asks.

'Say?'

'To Vulcana. Do you want her? Star act.'

'Acts,' Kate corrects him. 'Atlas *and* Vulcana.'

'Yes!' William nods. 'We'd be brilliant, you and I, Kate. I know it. We could tour the world.'

Kate gives a small nod.

'Then you'll do it?'

William bends down slightly, bringing them exactly eye to eye. His are deep and hooded. Yes, Kate thinks. Yes, to anything. Yes, to everything. A mean, microscopic shard of her fears that she might one day grow to hate herself for it, but she will do whatever it takes to stand alongside this man; to venture out into the world and never look backwards; to learn exactly who and what she, Miriam Katherine Williams, might become.

'I'll do it,' she says and, as her face opens into a smile,

William flings his arms about her, scoops her up, and swings her around and around as though she is riding a whirligig.

'Atlas and Vulcana,' she whispers and, in the growing darkness of the hallway, the words echo, like an incantation or a prayer.

4.

London, England
1892
ATLAS AND VULCANA

They are scheduled for seven that Saturday night: 'The Atlas Troupe, Headlined by Brother and Sister Act, Atlas and Vulcana'.

By six, there is a thick-waisted woman onstage, wearing a modest shawl and wide-brimmed hat, and singing friendly ditties. The Washington is packed to the rafters with all manner of people: clerks, newspapermen, midshipmen, warehouse managers, tradesmen, cotton merchants. And alongside almost every man sits his docile wife or impossibly young mistress. From the wings, Kate glances about in search of a clutch of women, come together to the theatre without male chaperones to laugh and revel, but she can spot none. It's a shame: she would dearly love to encourage other women to take vigorous exercise, as she, Anna, and Mabel do, and she hardly believes any will find inspiration while trussed up in their best dresses alongside their husbands or beaus. It would not seem womanly, perhaps. It would not seem proper.

People had said the same of Eugen Sandow in the

beginning, William had told her. Muscular strength was the possession of the working man, not the gentleman. But after Sandow opened gymnasiums across America, and thrilled the circus-goers of several countries, and finally took to the boards, those pale, spindly, middle-class men began to look at their reflections differently. Once Sandow had made fools of Sampson and Cyclops at the Westminster Royal Aquarium, it seemed it no longer mattered to the top-hatted of London that muscles were traditionally shaped in the fields – they wanted them, too. Already the fashion has shifted from lissom to brawny. Robust, now, is all the rage.

Well, Kate wondered as she listened to William's story, why couldn't the same be made true for ladies? The question crosses her mind again as she peers out at the frail, willowy women in the audience. Let proper go to hell. She cannot imagine filing in to the seats of a theatre and not wanting to stand up and sing or dance or pose with the act onstage. Where is the pleasure in sitting still and quiet when you might choose instead the simple joy of action? Where is the sense in choosing to be weak, when you might be strong?

Craning around the edge of the red and gold velveteen curtain, she sees rows and rows of burning cigars and smouldering pipes, suspended like fog lamps in the darkness. The mouths clamped around them she cannot see, but she imagines them made heavy by oiled moustaches; the women will not be partaking inside the theatre. Lamplight eases through thick clouds of smoke and catches on the lenses of spectacles, pale pearl necklaces, wedding bands, the rims of drinking glasses. For every puffed pipe, there is a glass of cold porter; for every empty woman's hand, two full man's hands. The pungency of so many different brands of cigar and alcohol intermingling indoors is nauseating. Later tonight, these men and women will take a trace of the theatre home with them, lay it over a chair in a corner of their bedrooms, and sleep alongside the seeping scent of freedom. For isn't that what music hall offers? Freedom? Kate supposes that for some it must be temporary: a merry evening once a month; a date to look forward to. But Kate will not live that way. She will not waste her existence in anticipation of a few stolen hours here, a brief opportunity for laughter there. She intends to laugh every day, and do whatever pleases her best, and love as loudly as she wants. Music hall will have its rules and traditions, of course – everything does – but they will not be dictates which might cause her to shrink. As her father's were. As the church's are. As a husband's may be. Nobody shrinks in the theatre. Instead, they grow and vivify and bloom into their truest selves. William has told her about the women who dress as men to take to the stage, and the men who dress as women, and those artistes who will not give up the secret of whether they are men or women. What beautiful confusion, Kate thinks. What fearless good fun.

She wonders whether she might make a convincing male impersonator, given her wide shoulders, but, glancing down, she smiles the idea away: her hips are just as ample.

'Ready, Kate?' A whisper at her ear; a hand at her back. She shivers at William's touch.

'Vulcana, you mean,' she replies, without turning to face him.

Onstage, the singer is taking her final curtsies and striding off, then pausing to wave and curtsey again, before taking two or three more elaborate strides. A single flower is thrown at her feet and wilts there: a thirsty lily. The woman bends to retrieve it and brings it to her lips. The audience claps harder.

Kate cannot imagine what they might make of Vulcana, so different is she from this matronly performer with her full cheeks and fuller skirts. Kate is clad in little more than her usual black leotard – though this one is ruched at the neck like a sleeveless shirtwaist and made of silk. It is a gift from William. The white belt at her middle, too, is silk and knotted into a large bow: here is your present, William seems to be saying to the audience; savour her unwrapping. On her feet, Kate wears a pair of sandals, which lace up her legs as far as her calves. Lowering her eyes, she notices that William wears a matching pair.

She suppresses a smirk. 'Are we to be gladiators now?'

She feels him shrug. 'Some nights,' he replies, and, catching the teasing in his voice, she turns towards him. In the shadows to the side of stage, his eyes are wide and dark and glinting with excitement. His curly hair is beginning to bounce free of its pomade. His leotard is black to match her own, with the front cut away to better accentuate the chest expansion pose; beneath it, he wears a white vest. She wonders if he is not brave enough to take to the stage with his chest fully exposed. She wonders if the hair across his pectorals feels rough or smooth.

47

Whether it is bravery or thoughtlessness, she is not sure, but as she ponders the choice, Kate lifts a hand and rests it, gently, absently, in the hollow just below and between his pectoral muscles. Chest, she thinks – forty-four inches. Chest, expanded – forty-seven inches. The skin there is hot. Kate watches her own hand, caught in that hollow, and does not know how to remove it again.

Eventually, William lays his own over it and slowly draws it away.

'We're up,' he says, nodding past her, and it is only then that she remembers where she is.

From this new perspective, the audience is not recognisable even as pairs of glinting spectacles or glowing cigar butts. Beyond the glare of the stage lights, they are unreachable dots of brightness in the dark – as distant and tiny as a galaxy of stars. Kate thinks that perhaps she prefers it this way. It will be easier not to see them the first time. For London is nothing like Pontypool or Abergavenny, and here Kate is not the reverend's daughter or the girl who stopped a galloping horse with her bare hands. Here, nobody tells stories about her. She is the first sentence of a book, and though she is the main character, even she does not know what might happen next. The thought straightens her up: she braces from her middle and elongates her body. First impressions are rare enough to warrant valuing, and Kate will not squander this one. Vulcana, William had said. Vulcana would have star billing. Vulcana would visit every theatre in the country. Vulcana would pass by six-foot-high posters of herself when she walked the streets. Not Kate.

She has not asked him where the name comes from. She has already decided that she likes it, for its ugliness, for the hard cut of its syllables: Vul-ca-na. It is the name of a warrior. It is bigger than Kate Williams. It is strange and grand and different enough to grow in to.

On the other hand, Vulcana might be any woman at all. If Kate wants her, she will have to claim her.

She turns to nod at William. She is ready. William nods in return and, stepping forward, begins the routine they have practised: the chest expansions, the poses, the dumb-bell juggling. William is flawlessly confident. Watching him is like flicking through a book of photographs, so still and definite is each of his stances. Kate mirrors him when she ought to and assists him when she is required. Her performance is acceptable, neat, even impressive, in part, she supposes. But she feels none of it. Excepting the thick tack of smoke on her dry tongue and the sweat between her breasts and across her brow, she is numb. Even when they come together centre stage and William's knuckles accidentally brush her hip, her body does not respond as it ordinarily would. It is as though she has clambered outside of herself and is watching from a distance, such is her horror at the prospect of failing him. Such is her dread at the thought of embarrassing herself.

The show passes like a dream: far too slowly and all at once. They invite a strapping young lad up on stage and ask him to lift a drum filled with sand. The audience laughs when Kate

– Vulcana – succeeds where he has not. She is more able than usual to loosen her body for the pose during which she drapes herself over William's opened hand and he pushes her towards the ceiling. At that, the audience gasps. When they change places, however, and it is Vulcana who opens her hand and William who lowers himself over it, ready to be lifted skyward, the audience falls into a stunned silence.

Kate is convinced then that she can hear their thoughts. *Surely not?* they breathe inside their closed minds. *Surely not this young girl? It is a trick. There is a wire.* Their doubt throbs from them like a fever heat.

But Kate will not listen to it. She knows herself capable of balancing William on her palm and, stretching upwards, thrusting him over her head to hang there like a trophy. He weighs exactly eleven stone and six pounds; she can manage more than twelve. He is five feet and six inches tall. They have repeated this lift a hundred times. She sets her feet wide and, as she settles her breathing, shifts her body into alignment: knees over ankles, hips over knees, shoulders over hips. She makes a stone column of herself and, when she is solidly arranged, William arches backwards and falls into her. She can feel the hard, round bumps of his spine beneath her fingers.

He holds himself in perfect taut stillness as she breathes steadily through the lift, and as he rises above her, and as she halts to let the audience exhale their disbelief, and as she bends her knees to lower him back to the floor. It is over in a moment. A pause follows. William unbalances from her hand with the spring of a gymnast and skips across the stage to turn and bow and flourish a hand at Kate. She is shocked when they erupt: whooping, applauding, whistling. Then William does something they have not rehearsed. He stands tall, he takes a deep breath, and he hollers out into the crowd, 'Vulcana, ladies and gentlemen. The strongest woman to be found in our Great British Isles.'

And he smiles, wide and daft as the proudest of men, as the audience claps and claps.

5.

London, England
1892
RUN

'Kate, stop!'

But she cannot. Since her girlhood, she has run across fields and scrabbled up trees and waded into rivers to swim. And now, after her performance, she cannot think to stay still. It matters little that she does not know her way, or that the night is pitch and starless. She will get to the Thames and let the water guide her. She had pulled off her sandals as she descended the stairs of The Washington, and she rushes barefoot now over the frosted pavements, the ruched neck of her leotard fluttering like a panicked crow, the cold pinching her skin closer to her bones, her toes aching. At her back, William's voice echoes like a memory.

'Kate. Hold on. Where are you going?'

Further down York Road, she slows just enough to spin around, arms held out like wings, and call back to him.

'I'm going to run, William.'

For a moment, she is none of the women Reverend Williams cantillated about from behind the shield of his lectern. She is not Leah, nor Sarah, nor even Deborah. She is

Rhiannon of the Mabinogi. Rhiannon, who was bold enough to appear in the world astride an enormous white horse, dressed in a coat of brocaded gold. Rhiannon, who was brave enough to turn her horse and ride away from a prince. Rhiannon, who could not be caught by the man at her back, however many horses he ran to exhaustion in pursuit of her, though her own mount never broke out of a walk.

'She was a goddess, then,' Kate had said, when William had told her the story, just a couple of days since.

'Perhaps,' William had replied.

'But, how did he reach her?'

'The prince?'

'The prince.'

At this, William had laughed. 'How do you know that he did?'

'You wouldn't be telling me the story if he didn't,' Kate replied. Though she could not appreciate their inference fully, she knew, somehow, that those words would carry weight.

'She stopped,' William replied, suddenly serious again. 'But only after he asked her to. "Wait for me," he said. And she did. "Gladly," Rhiannon said. "I will wait. Though it would have been kinder to your horse if you had asked earlier."'

'All he had to do,' Kate mused, 'was ask.' She caught William's eye and held it until he started to colour.

'Yes,' he replied.

And Kate, too, will stop, she decides as she steps backwards along York Street, waiting for William's response – if he asks her. If he says the right words. If he implores her, as Pwyll did

Rhiannon, to stop and wait 'for the sake of the man she most loves'.

William cups his hands around his mouth to yell back, as though he is shouting into a thunderstorm. 'Where to?'

'Anywhere,' she replies. 'Everywhere. I feel like I'm going to burst!' She doesn't realise it until she utters the words, but it's true. She is a quarrel of chittering sparrows, arguing into flight. No – it's stronger than that. She is an old oak, split open by a sudden fork of lightning. She is undergoing a transformation. Before her performance, she was a girl; after it, she is a goddess. All that applause. The smiles and clinked glasses and hollers of 'More!'. It was all for Vulcana. It had swallowed the orderly sounds of her past. Perhaps, she thinks, it is not only William who can look at her as though she is a gleaming pearl. Perhaps there will be others.

'Be careful,' William calls. 'Don't venture too far.'

At this, Kate laughs. She will not say 'all right'. She will not yield to his instruction, nor reassure him. She did not run away to London to be fathered. She could have stayed in Abergavenny and shrugged through Reverend Williams' sermons if that was what she had wanted. What Kate is seeking, she cannot quite define yet, but it is certainly not parenting.

'Good night, William,' she calls back, and without waiting to gauge his response, she spins about again and resumes her run.

Tracing the route she, Mabel, and Anna had taken to the riverside two days before, she soon smells cold water on the air, and within minutes she is moving alongside the silver-slow Thames, the ghost of Rhiannon's horse beneath her. Where it is not shadowed into blackness by a bridge or a ship, a weak moon lights the river's gentle seaward churn. Otherwise, it would appear as still as it had on Thursday morning. The freeze hadn't lasted long. That same night, warmed by skating policemen and playing children and shouting sailors, the ice had started to break. By Friday morning, the fog had returned to steal like a wraith from bank to bank. The only evidence now of Thursday's frivolity are the little ice-maps which float here and there, like continents caught on the currents of a vast, dark ocean, and the thickness of rime gathered at the place where the balusters meet the water.

Kate hears the low, grumbling voices of the few sailors still aboard their ships as she tears past. She smells the sooty smoke of the fires the homeless hunch over, willing them into life. She sees a lamplighter, going about to check his mantles, his ladder strapped across his back. But there is no one around to disturb her rhythm as she sprints along the water's edge, wincing against the small stones which catch under her soles now and then, pumping her arms and legs as though she is desperate to be anywhere other than here, and grinning her biggest, silliest grin, because there is nothing like this. With her own powerful body, she is making wind: she can feel it combing and loosening her hair. She is making sound, with the tick-tock regularity of her stride. She is making joy – for can't she feel that, surging through her blood and muscles? It makes her want to laugh, but she fights her amusement, because she does not want to stop running. Not until she circles all the way back to her shared room, and rushes panting up the stairs, and throws herself through the door to leap, starfish spread and face down, onto her bed sheets. There, and only there, with no one but Mabel and Anna to witness it, can she allow her elation to come squealing out of her. That is how she feels, isn't it? Elated?

Or rather, that is how she chooses to feel. She must remind herself that everything, from this moment onwards, will be her choice. And now, just now, her choice is to run alongside the river in the company of a spirit horse – a white, glancing beauty which had carried Rhiannon towards her very own decisions – and feel herself entirely unencumbered.

I am to be a strongwoman. Those were the words she had written to her parents, and her belief in them had been whole and immediate. She had never before experienced the swell of pride being entirely definite about anything could send through a person, but the thrill of it had shocked her, and she had wanted more.

I am to be a strongwoman, she begins chanting, in the privacy of her own mind. But the stresses of the syllables do not match her footfall, so she settles instead for *I am, I am, I am*, and, after all, that seems a better fit. Never mind home, or her parents, or other people's expectations. Never mind William – this thought sticks a little, but she perseveres with it. *I am strong*, she insists as she strides on under the brightening moon. Despite her abundances, she moves with the grace and ease of a dancer. *I am bold*. She is, it seems, designed for movement. *I am interesting*. She is a spectacle: a rare, unknowing beauty. Back in his hotel room, William cannot stop thinking about her. *I am enough*.

By the time she turns away from the river to start the run back to her room, her feet are sounding out only one word.

Three even beats.

Vulcana.

6.

London, England
1892
DRURY LANE

The following month, they arrange to see Marie Lloyd in pantomime at the Theatre Royal, Drury Lane. Marie Lloyd – William whispers to Kate as they step along, three paces behind Anna, Mabel, and Seth in the breathy fog of a polar December evening – is to be the new queen of music hall.

'Already, she's toured America,' he says. 'And she is not much older than you.'

As young as that, Kate thinks, wanting to roll her eyes but resisting the urge.

'And the Theatre Royal...' she begins, her words whitening on the air.

'They just call it Drury Lane,' William interrupts, before she can finish her question.

She releases a sigh, but William does not seem to notice. He is taut with excitement; he bounces on his usually flat feet. He thinks to impress the troupe, she supposes, with a surprise introduction to Queen Marie. Or, most of the troupe. Abe had declined to come with them. 'There's a cold beer and a sure bet with my name on them,' he'd drawled when invited, and the others had not coaxed him to change his mind.

'Drury Lane, then,' Kate continues. 'Is it very grand?'

William has been talking about visiting for a fortnight, but the Theatre Royal – *Drury Lane* – is almost five miles distant from The Washington, and they have hardly had a night off. They have one week left of their run, which has already been extended, so popular have they proven with their audiences, and then, William says, they will find a new contract and move on. Kate isn't sure what 'moving on' will entail: how far they will go; whether they'll stay together. But she does not want to enquire and reveal her fears that it might all change. Already she is growing too comfortable on York Street: with The Washington's familiar creaky stage, and the bright room she shares with Anna and Mabel; with the easy time the troupe spends together in the rehearsal room, which they call 'the gym' but which was more likely intended originally as a ballet studio; with the walks she takes around London with Mabel and Anna, their arms linked for the warmth when their laughter doesn't provide it; with the walks she takes, less frequently, with William. She and William are careful to keep those occasions secret, though Kate can't imagine why. All they do is talk. About Kate's family and her hopes for a future apart from their stifling beliefs, about the troupe and whether William can make enough of a success of it to avoid returning to the ironworks.

'I can't spend another morning walking towards those smoking stacks, always rising into black rain clouds. I can't... The coal and the steam and the heat and the noise. I'll do anything to avoid that, Kate. *Anything*. That place made an old man of my father before he turned forty.'

Kate clamped her tongue before she could blurt out that forty seemed a reasonable enough age to be considered old, and waited for William to change the subject – which he did with surprising regularity. She had never heard him talk so long and so willingly at home. In London, words fling off the sweeping brush of his moustache as if impelled by the burliest of men. He speaks of the countries he wants to visit, and the theatres he might have them appear at, and every name he says is a spark of bright new colour across Kate's imaginings. The New Canterbury – and she sees the close, romantic spires of the cathedral city. The Brighton Alhambra – that famous palace fortress, nestled in the Andalusian hills. The Crystal Palace – and into her mind shines a dwelling entirely transparent, but for the glint of its perfectly cut turrets in the sunlight. He mentions countries she recognises: Italy, Germany, Canada, Australia. And countries she doesn't: Luxembourg, Romania, Taiwan. And countries she cannot possibly begin to imagine: Brazil, the Kingdom of Morocco, Norway, Mongolia. William wants to travel the world, he says. I know, Kate thinks; I've always known that about you. But she doesn't want him to stop talking, so she urges him to tell her what each country might be like, though he has seen no more of them than she. And she listens and offers wild ideas of her own. And finally, when they have avoided the subject for an indecent amount of time, William talks about Alice and the children.

It seems to Kate that they are at liberty to say whatever they please during these walks, because it is midnight and no living soul knows where to find them, and the strange empty stillness of London affords their words a magical quality – as though they have been made a temporary element of the night and will be expunged with the dawning of the next day, together with their guilt.

And still Kate cannot say what she wishes to say. *I want you. I do not want to want you.* Because she is certain that he is already aware, and has chosen to ignore the fact.

'The owner is a chap called Augustus Harris,' William is saying now. 'I'm told he's a genius. That he's had live horses galloping around onstage. That he even had a real ship brought in only to smash it to bits in a simulated storm.'

'Sounds excessive to me,' Kate replies, turning away to study the head-hung clomping of a passing cab horse. She cannot pinpoint exactly why she is being so testy with him. Perhaps it is because every surge of happiness she feels is chased by a doubt which threatens to swallow her whole. Or perhaps it is that her frustration at being unable to reach for him, admit her intentions, has found its limit. She suspects something more, however – that perhaps her frustration is turning inward and that, in being unable to obliterate her desire for William, she is beginning to hate the private pocket of herself that she cannot control.

'I'm told it's spectacular,' William says, still failing or refusing to notice her mood. 'That there might be hundreds of people onstage at one time. That... Ah, here we are!'

He pauses to indicate a building just sharpening into view some way down the street. It is a great thrusting square of a building: all straight lines and ninety-degree angles. It is painted white, and seems to shine against the sallow glow and grit of London. Like The Washington, is has a colonnaded entranceway, but the Drury's is prouder and juts out over the pavement to set its four paired columns down right there in the street. On each side of the doorway stands a sentry box, complete with a solemn, uniformed soldier to whom nobody pays much heed. Near the entrance columns, frock-coated gentlemen mill about, nodding their top-hatted heads at one another in a prideful manner, each carefully ignoring the peacocking lady on their arm. This is a display, Kate thinks, as choreographed and practised as her own.

At intervals, cabs whoa to a halt and couples climb out. The drivers sit huddled inside multiple coats and woollen scarves. The horses tongue their frozen bits around in the backs of their mouths, unable to dislodge them, then flick their heads up as they are asked, with a click, to move off again. Kate is troubled by the weight at their backs. She feels a sense of ... perhaps it is shame, or pity, to see the horses burdened so. How much more beautiful they would be, stripped of their leathers and harnesses and allowed to run unencumbered. There is nothing as majestic, she thinks, as a horse in full flight. In a dream she has had since early childhood, Kate finds herself standing on open moorland, listening to the approaching gallop of a vivid ginger mare. She knows what the mare will look like before she appears, because she always looks the same: slender, flighty, gleaming. When she sees Kate, she flicks her ears forwards, but does not stop running and, as she passes, so she drags Kate along with her, or absorbs Kate into her own body somehow, so that it is Kate who is galloping across the moor, her four legs strong and sure, her strides in perfect sympathy with the terrain, so that she herself seems to fly.

She hopes Augustus Harris hasn't brought any horses in for tonight's performance. She could not stand to see them hustled onstage to blink in fright under the burning lights and the gawp-and-cheer stupidity of people.

When she notices the title of the pantomime on the hoarding, however, she is reassured that she will be spared the sight of a live animal turned into a plaything. They are to see *Little Bo-Peep, Little Red Riding Hood and Hop O' My Thumb*. This makes her laugh. She can't imagine they'd risk bringing a wolf in, however ambitious.

At her side, William frowns and his eyes are the eyes of an eagle: hooded and severe. 'What is it?'

'It's quite the title.'

William turns to the hoarding, mouths out the words, smiles. 'Yes. It is something, isn't it?' He lowers his voice, as though murmuring sweet nothings to her. 'None of the strength and simplicity of "Atlas and Vulcana".'

'No,' Kate agrees. 'But then I don't suppose the pantomime ever aimed for strength and simplicity. Shall we go in?' She steps ahead to join Seth, who is lingering just behind Anna and Mabel, excluded by the hurtling speed with which they

63

gossip about passers-by, their heads bent close, their pointing fingers revealing their victims.

'I can feel you being cruel,' Kate whispers from behind them, and both women jump to attention wearing such earnest expressions that laughter erupts from Kate.

Anna slaps at her. 'Kate!'

Mabel wraps an arm around her shoulders and draws her closer. Kate inhales the sweet unidentifiable scent of her perfume and the smoother hint of her cold cream. She loves these two women already, Kate realises. Anna, with her funny, dowdy ways and plump cheeks. Mabel, with her tart humour and her big warm heart. They have been nothing but generous to a lost girl in possession of more pluck than substance.

'Listen here, Miss,' Mabel says. 'Mind your business or join in. Now, see that chap over there, wearing the silk cravat...'

Kate's eyes rove the crowd for the poor man in question, but she does not spot him before they are ushered inside, and she wonders quietly at how much the others see that she does not.

It becomes apparent the moment they step inside Drury Lane that it boasts twice the capacity of The Washington.

'Over two thousand, I believe,' William says, when Kate makes mention of the fact. She can readily believe it. The auditorium is a vast echo chamber. Their footsteps, as they file down the aisles, belong to giants. Their voices, though delivered quite normally, are better suited to bellmen. Where The Washington has opted for cream and ivory décor, Drury

Lane has chosen bolder reds and golds. The floor is carpeted with red velvet. The seat backs are covered with gold fabric to match the ornamentations of the box-balconies, which are set over four lofty storeys. The arched ceiling seems so distant that one would need to sprout wings to reach it.

This, Kate thinks, really is the place to hold a spectacle.

They locate their seats and shuffle into comfort. Kate finds herself – though not by design – sitting next to William, whose knee brushes the folds of her favourite emerald-green skirt. She holds her breath and stares straight ahead, wondering if the contact is intentional. He does not alter his pose as the auditorium fills and the orchestra starts up, and nor does she. His closeness might infuriate and confuse her, but it thrills her in equal measure. She does not want to relinquish it.

Little Bo-Peep, Little Red Riding Hood and Hop O' My Thumb feels, from its opening notes, akin to a hallucination. The production is enormous, featuring costumes so extravagant and vividly coloured that it seems a pandemonium of parrots has taken to the stage and is fluttering madly about it. The storylines, such as they are, belong to fairy tales and nursery rhymes combined, and do nothing but fluster Kate with their speed and constant whirling movement. Personally, she prefers her stories to run in simple straight lines, from one end to the other. Augustus Harris evidently does not. The actors deliver their lines quicker and quicker, pausing only to allow the audience to laugh at the barrage of puns, and the stage grows more and more crowded, until, it seems to Kate, every actor in London is crammed up there, racing about in pursuit of dreams and follies, of snorts and guffaws and horse laughs, of admiration.

It is an intolerably long while before Queen Marie takes to the stage. Kate is sure she will know her when she sees her, though she hasn't the first idea of the construction of her features or the particularities of her figure. A peculiar sense of dread rises in her as she anticipates the woman's appearance. She wants to look at William, to study him as he watches Marie arrive on stage so that she might evaluate his appreciation of this reported queen of music hall. Will he sit forward in his seat? Will his leg move away from Kate's? Will his eyes soften in that way they do when Kate amuses him?

Jealousy, for Kate, is an emotion that arrived with William, like the thundering crush of an incoming wave. She could never have foreseen its physical power, could not have imagined that it might rise within her like flames and make her believe she was burning, or drop onto her like all the weight of the sky and persuade her that she was pinned down as pitifully as a butterfly on an exhibition board.

There is Alice, of course. There is always Alice. But William mentions her as blandly as one might a maiden aunt and Kate cannot think that he feels passionately about his wife. The women of London, though, with their expensive dresses, and their worldliness, and their confidences. She cannot stand the thought of him being drawn to them, with their piled-high hair and breasts to match. What could an innocent Welsh girl of sixteen offer in comparison to such sophistication?

When she can suffer it no longer, she leans in to Mabel, on her other side, and whispers, 'When will she come on, Marie Lloyd?'

From side-on, Kate sees Mabel smirk. 'Why, she's already there.' Mabel points. 'Third from the left, at the back. She'll come forward for a solo piece soon, I'd imagine.'

Though Mabel seems entirely sure, Kate cannot believe that woman to be Marie Lloyd. In place of the svelte, storybook beauty she had envisaged stands a dumpy, ill-proportioned creature, with buck teeth visible even from the audience, and a head too big for her body.

Kate turns wide, unbelieving eyes on Mabel, who raises her ample eyebrows and belly-laughs in response. Her hilarity cannot be heard over the cacophony onstage, which now features a large, upright wolf in slow-motion pursuit of a desperate 'Little Red' through a papier-mâché forest. In the orchestra, the violinists hit a tempo which must surely be threatening to snap their strings.

By the time the wolf is dispatched, Little Red is saved, and the harlequinade takes to the boards, Kate has come to understand the appeal of Marie Lloyd. She is funny. It is as simple as that. She is warm and open and brimming with humour, and Kate can hardly contain her relief. Not, as she'd feared, because she is worried William's head might be turned, but because as the minutes of that madcap pantomime pass, Kate comes to recognise a woman, centre stage, with a body that does not conform to any of the expected ideals.

She, Kate realises, *is just like me.* The realisation brings her a hope she hadn't fully known herself in need of, and her heart soars with it.

Later, in their room, Kate, Anna and Mabel change into their nightdresses and climb into their beds, only to find that they cannot stop talking about Marie Lloyd. They have not yet drawn the curtains and the unattended lamp across the street suffuses the room with the soft guttering light of a dwindling fire. Their hushed voices and cast shadows make them feel like boarding-school girls telling ghost stories, as though the words they share are forbidden.

'I just hadn't expected her to look so ... average,' Kate says.

'Me neither,' Anna chimes. Kate can hear the smile on her face from across the gloomy three yards which separate their beds. 'It was encouraging, wasn't it?' There is always a question with Anna. At twenty-four, Kate considers she really should be more definite in her opinions. But then again, opinions do not suit everyone.

'Yes!' Kate agrees, leaning forward and pushing her hands into the mattress with enthusiasm. 'As if anyone might become anything she wishes, if Marie Lloyd can become the queen of the stage.'

In Mabel's bed, a small movement. Kate squints towards her: she is sitting upright, tucking her hair under her cap, and nodding.

'I'd imagined she'd look more like one of the rangers,' she says, and though Kate can tell by the tone that Mabel is agreeing with them, she hasn't the first idea what a ranger is.

'Rangers?'

'The prowlers, you know,' Mabel answers, but this is no more elucidating. When Kate meets her with silence, she continues. 'They were all along the promenade, Kate. Did you not notice them?'

She'd been distracted as they left Drury Lane, caught up as she was in thoughts of Marie Lloyd and her own prospects and the suspicion she had, as she swept away with Mabel and Anna, that William's attention was at her back: she could sense it, a tingling. But yes, she had noticed them, vaguely: strings of beautiful women arranged along the promenade like jewels around an elegant neck. Kate had perceived them as fleetingly as she might a pretty necklace – she never had found interest in such articles – but now that she thinks about it, what a magnificent sight they had been, those women, each more graceful and alluring than the last in their manner of moving and glancing and waiting. They were not dressed gaudily, as one might suppose they would be, but ... expensively is the most appropriate word Kate can summon. Or tastefully, perhaps. In hindsight, they put her in mind of pedigree cats: the slink and ease of them; the untouchable appeal.

Any man seeking them out would know, without doubt, what they were offering.

Kate flushes – at her ignorance and her innocence.

'The prostitutes,' she says finally. 'I didn't pay them much attention.'

'How could you fail to?' Mabel asks. 'I've hardly seen such beauties. Of course, at Drury Lane you only get the highest class of worker. Same at The Empire. I'm sure you'd find a very different sight in the slums. But there's no denying their grace, the West End ladies. I wonder why they don't take to the stage themselves?'

'Perhaps they make better money where they are,' Anna suggests.

Mabel stops fidgeting with her cap and reaches for her cold cream. 'It wouldn't surprise me. I failed to be surprised at what men will pay for a long while since.'

Kate notices but does not question the note of bitterness in Mabel's voice, which sounds as unpleasantly as a sustained minor chord in the otherwise quiet room. Anna's mattress springs creak under her shifted weight, and Kate realises then – or believes she does – that perhaps Mabel came to the troupe out of necessity rather than choice. It is possible, isn't it, that she had chosen domesticity over adventure, wifehood over performance, motherhood over herself, and that her circumstances had simply changed? Kate cannot conceive of being forced to this life. Cannot understand, indeed, why any woman with fitness and muscular strength enough would not race to it. How, she wonders for the first time, do they number only three? Why didn't Alice want this?

But then, Mabel is almost a decade older than Kate. Perhaps, ten years from now, Kate might feel entirely differently about the theatre. Considering how drastically her life has changed this past month, it is only fair to assume that it might change again and again, and in wilder ways than she can possibly envision.

She will not ask Mabel to divulge her secret. Let her keep what is hers.

In the silence following Mabel's observation, Kate reaches behind her for the letter she has stowed beneath her pillow. It is from her parents – she knows this from the hand and on account of it being delivered to The Washington. No one else would know to write to her there. She has been afraid to open it. Something in Mabel's demeanour, though, as she quietly smooths her cold cream over her cheeks, proud and content and successful despite whatever ugly thing she has fought in her past, and the remnants of elation still coursing through Kate's body at having watched Marie Lloyd promote herself above all those more beautiful women, persuades Kate that now is the right time to peel the paper free of its envelope and face their judgement.

I shan't return home except to visit, if you will have me, she had written. *I am safe with William Roberts' troupe, and assure you that there is nothing shameful in this life.*

What would the Reverend and Mrs Williams make of that?

One paragraph is all they spare in the response, it transpires, when Kate finally persuades her shaking hands to unfold the single piece of paper they have deigned to post. In the failing yellow-flamed light, the script is frail and spidery.

Katherine,

We are pleased that you are well and safe with Mr Roberts and his company. We cannot, however, approve of

the life you have embarked upon, despite your assurances.
You are most welcome at home, from the moment you give
up this silliness and return to your studies and your
Christian duties. Until then, you will find that we, your
loving parents, can only hope to watch over your safety
through the eyes of our Lord.
    Your Father.

Your Father. Where was her mother's name in this? Had Robert even shown Eleanor their daughter's correspondence? Was she as keen to reject Kate's wishes as was her father?

I will never know, Kate thinks, as she refolds the letter and slides it back into the envelope. Because I shall never give this up, not for anything. This life is the only life worth living. With that thought, she rises from bed, steps towards the window, grasps the handle just as she had the first morning she had woken in this happy room, pulls back the pane, thrusts her arm out into the frost-nipped night, and lets the letter go.

7.

London, England
1892
VIGILANCE

On their last night at The Washington, the hunched, grey theatre manager brings news to William that the National Vigilance Association intends to visit. William, in turn, carries this burdensome information into the troupe's final rehearsal. They sit dotted about the room: Kate on the windowsill, pulling her slippers back over her swollen feet; Seth near the storage rack, a thick-knuckled fist wrapped around one of the upright posts; Anna on her backside before the mirror, legs sprawled like a toddler, to stretch; Mabel leaning languorously against that same dull-faced mirror, sipping from a cup of water; Abe on his back in the middle of the training mat, his legs cradled to his chest to coax loose the muscles around his spine.

'What on God's good Earth is the National Vigilance Association?' Abe enquires, his eyes aimed at the ceiling but closed as he groans through his cool-down routine.

Standing in the centre of the room, William looks stiff and pale. Outside, the jackdaws that seem to have become their permanent audience croak and cackle.

'A great many things,' William answers. 'It was set up to aid women forced into unfortunate situations,' he says, rather delicately by his usual standards. 'But it has been expanding its concerns, and quite rapidly I'm told, ever since. A woman by the name of Laura Ormiston Chant, who edits the Association's newspaper, has of late decided to wage war on the music halls.'

'On what grounds?' Seth asks.

'Decency,' William replies.

'Decency!' The word escapes Mabel with an accompanying snort of derision. 'Are they to be the decency police, then, the members of this so-called Association?'

'It would seem so.'

William folds his arms over his chest, as though to shield himself from the troupe's questions, though Kate can't comprehend why he should feel defensive about the matter. Evidently, this Association is entirely outside his control. But then, perhaps that in itself is the problem. William prides himself on his self-control. Perhaps he finds himself embarrassed that here, looming over their closing night, are circumstances he cannot influence.

'But we're not doing anything indecent, are we?' Anna puts in.

'Of course not,' Abe replies.

William is quick to echo him. 'Of course not. But Mrs Chant has her own ideas. Already she has accused Marie Lloyd of crudity, and while I don't think that will trouble her at this stage of her career, we are only just starting out.'

That's it, then. It is the fear of being cut short by a nasty newspaper report which has further drained his already pallid colour. It is the fear of the ironworks. Without their fledgling reputation, the newly named Atlas Troupe will not secure another theatre.

'But what's the meaning of it?' Kate ventures. 'Or rather, the purpose. If this Mrs Chant dislikes the music halls, can't she simply choose not to attend them?'

The question is met with silence as the troupe mulls the problem over. On the street below, a cab horse clomps by, the ground hollow-sounding beneath its hooves. Decency, Kate considers, seems a thin veil for the true intent of Mrs Chant's arguments when every theatre is accompanied by its promenade of prostitutes. If the National Vigilance Association was indeed inaugurated to help unfortunate women, it ought perhaps to concentrate its efforts outside the theatres before blundering in.

'Fear,' William offers. He speaks the word at a near-whisper, as though in saying it he might be admitting to his own. 'It's a matter of position.'

'Whose?' Seth grunts.

'Theirs,' William replies, warming to his conclusion, pushing his shoulders back slightly. His arms drop an inch or two. 'They're afraid of the masses. Look how quickly music hall has grown. It's the working classes who attend – mostly, in any case – and they're frightened, I'd hazard, of its exerting an influence over so many people. Can't have the working classes thinking for themselves. That wouldn't do at all.' He gives a short, angry laugh, which makes his face ugly.

In response, Abe emits a hearty hoot. 'What do they think it will bring about – an uprising led by a chorus of singing showgirls?'

A titter moves around the room, but it's an uneasy one. Every member of the troupe needs the show to be a success. Kate because she no longer has a home to go to. Mabel on account of some unspeakable past. Seth because he is the youngest of five burly farming brothers and there simply wasn't any land left for his strong shoulders to tend. And William – her William – because of the nightmares she has begun to share with him since he confided them to her: the towering stack, smoking the skies grey; the unavoidable, skin-peeling heat.

Abe and Anna's secrets she hasn't fathomed out yet, but she suspects they will soon reveal themselves in offhand comments or telling looks, as the others' have. Kate savours the challenge of discovering them. She has always fancied herself something of an investigator of souls.

'And they have a newspaper for this?' Mabel asks.

William nods. 'The *Vigilance Record*.' The absurdity of such a thing brings a smile even to his stubborn lips.

'Oh!' Abe shrieks, pushing up from his curled position and onto his feet in one fluid roll to snap open an invisible newspaper. He clears his throat and adopts his best English accent, which comes out more French than anything. 'On the third Saturday of December, the year of our Lord 1892, Mrs Laura Snooty-Bloomers did observe an indecency occur at The Washington Theatre. The nature of this indecency caused Mrs Bloomers much offence – so much, in fact, that her eyes did pop clean from her head and have yet to be reinserted. Needless to say, the *Vigilance Record*...' The word 'record' he furls from his tongue like a native Frenchman. '... has pondered the decency even of writing about such wayward behaviour, but we feel it must be known that, in full sight of a willing audience, a troupe of strongpersons did take to the stage of that most indecent of establishments and proceed to lift heavy weights far above their own heads.'

By the time he has finished, he has each of them in tears. Kate wipes her cheeks clean with the back of her hand. Anna grips her stomach and moans over its aching. William finally unfolds his arms and reveals the powerful chest which – and this Kate cannot stop thinking about – contains his heart. For two years now she has longed to lay her head against his chest and listen to its muted beat. She is not sure why, but she knows that it will hold for her a deep and bodily satisfaction. She tenses her jaw against the imagined thrumming of it, and her laughter wanes.

'We'll go on as we usually do, William,' she says softly. She means to reassure him, but she knows it is not her place, particularly before the others, and so the sentiment issues tremulously. She blushes a little.

'Too right we will,' Seth agrees.

'Hear, hear,' Mabel adds, lifting her empty hand to the ceiling in a toast.

'You're certain?' William asks. 'All of you? Even if Mrs Chant finds terrible things to write about you?'

'Certain,' Kate answers, her smile widening now that she has the support of the room.

'Certain,' they echo, one by one.

'All right, then,' William announces. 'So get on with it, and no complaining!'

Onstage, Kate awaits the beginning of their last performance at The Washington with her heart louder in her ears than ever. Her father has been haunting her since the minute she arrived in London, but thus far she has managed to banish his ghost with adrenaline and distractions. When she has caught a glimpse of a tall, sallow man folded into the middle rows and believed it to be him, she has grasped the barbell tighter and lifted it with greater ease than she has in any rehearsal. When she has heard the booming proclamations of a Welsh accent echoing through the noisy streets, she has paced faster, chattered louder. Increasingly, though, when she looks out into the audiences, the only face staring back at her is his: his fixed eyes; his clamped lips. From somewhere deep in her psyche, he wills her, continuously, to fail. And tonight, finally, she fears she will fulfil his expectations.

She squints into the semi-darkness, and sees only his face in replicate, paled above the strangulating white flash of the clerical collar. Row after row of Reverend Williamses, unmoving and unmovable. The sight brings a constriction to her throat which she cannot swallow away. As William arrives beside her and gently touches the back of her hand, she cannot take her eyes from the crowd – so still, so silent – which holds its breath in anticipation of her weakness. In her panic, she reaches for some snippet from her father's sermons with which to comfort herself.

For the Spirit God gave us does not make us timid, but gives us power, love and self-discipline, she tells herself. But she does not find reassurance in the words, as the rest of her family would. Instead, she feels disappointed by the implication that God has given her power, love, and self-discipline, rather than recognising that she is already in possession of those qualities. That they are intrinsic to her. That they are as much a part of what makes her Kate as are her skin, her hair, her eyes.

She sweeps the audience again, and this time, her attention snags on a face so very different from Reverend Williams' that it breaks the illusion. A laugh rises from her stomach.

Mrs Chant is, as promised, in attendance. She sits in the front row – identifiable by the great hooked nose the cartoons have only mildly embellished – and scowls in readiness for an evening of immense disappointment. In fact, she scowls for the duration, her arms crossed defiantly over her chest. She is accompanied by two lemon-faced friends, who mirror her pose, glancing over their shoulders now and then to check that they really do need to persist with this difficult hunch. The absurdity of their presence pulls on a thread of defiance Kate hasn't quite been able to bring taut yet, and she turns to William and beams her brightest smile at him.

This is where she belongs. No sour old Mrs Chant is going to ruin that for her.

She goes at her performance with a new and unrelenting

vigour. The rest of the troupe feeds off it, and the true audience, sensing the energy William, Anna, Seth, Abe, and Mabel bring to their poses, their dead lifts, their trick lifts, gasp and cheer with such zeal that Kate is on the verge of tears as she lowers William to the floor in their final stunt.

Tonight, nothing can stop Kate Williams.

And later, when they spill out of the theatre and out into the frost-and-black night, she can feel that belief in every movement her body makes. She is light on her feet; her eyes are rounder and clearer than before; she is standing taller than ever she has. Kate seems not to walk but to dance along York Road.

'What a beautiful night,' she says, tipping back her head to stare up at the low, dappled moon.

'A night worth celebrating,' Anna suggests.

'A night for getting hideously drunk,' Abe adds.

'A night,' Kate insists, her voice gentler and more serious than the others', 'where anything might happen.' At this, the rest of the troupe hums in agreement and falls silent. Their mismatched steps clip over the pavement. At her back, Kate hears William murmur, 'Anything,' and tries to ignore the shiver it sends from the bottom of her ears, around her neck, and down the length of her spine. Though she knows he has spoken so quietly as not to be heard by the others, to Kate his voice sounded as close as though he had brushed his lips over her ear lobe. Indeed, everything feels heightened to her tonight – as though she can see farther and hear better and smell more readily than usual. There are William's footsteps, unnaturally even in their reliable way, on the ground behind her. There is the harsh tobacco whiff of Abe's cigar, which fights against the weaker but more pleasant rosewater scent Mabel has spritzed at her collarbone. And growing stronger as they proceed down York Road and closer to the water, the muggy stink of the Thames. She can hear the water, too: its ceaseless, rhythmic plashing. She can hear gruff-noted conversations being thrust over the gaps between boats, and doors being shut and bolted against the dark, and, somewhere, a cellist practising their scalic patterns: the glide of resined horsehair across taut strings. On a nearby street, a pony snickers as it trots away, its voice echoing over the quiet, smoke-coughing rooftops. Ahead, Seth begins to whistle a tune Kate does not recognise but which has a happy major inflection.

All this world, she thinks. All this life. She wants to imbibe every detail. She wants to take a photograph of each beautiful moment of her new existence, so that when she is old, she can settle in a shaft of warm sunlight and flick through her dusty past and remember. She wants, most intensely, never to forget. That, she considers, would be a terrible fate – to do so much living only to lose it to the shadows of your mind.

But in this easy moment, as they turn off York Road towards the hotel and begin to slow their pace, not wanting yet to depart each other's company, Kate cannot believe that she will ever be old. What must it be like, to know the sagging of your skin and the dulling of your eyes? To look into a mirror and find there a mass of greying lines? To move so very slowly through the day? It really wouldn't suit her at all.

'Goodnight, then,' Abe says as they reach the steps which lead up to their little hotel. It is nothing more than a house, in truth, partitioned into quarters, but it is comfortable, and cosy, and it has been their very own these past weeks. Kate will mourn the place when they move on. 'I've got no sleep in me yet. I'm off to find myself a good old-fashioned song and supper room.'

'I'll come,' Seth answers. 'I could eat a cow whole.'

'Me too,' Mabel replies. 'Shall we all go?'

Anna nods her agreement. 'I really am starving.'

Only William is uninterested in the developing plan. He yawns, then locks his hands behind his back and stretches long and lazily. 'I'm for my bed,' he says. 'You go and enjoy yourselves. I'll see you at breakfast.'

On any other night, Kate might have accepted his claim and slunk off with the others. But tonight, there is something artificial in his words which she cannot overlook. The way he lingers on the pavement, too, captures her attention. William, who is ordinarily as sharp and decisive as a hunting wolf, has suddenly grown awkward. He's like a shy lad at a dance, looking down at his toes and twisting his mouth and waiting for a girl to notice him. She wonders, momentarily, if he is unwell. Then he glances up and catches her eye, and she understands.

'I'm tired, too,' she intones, and so flat are her words that she is sure the troupe will immediately protest against her lie. She is not tired in the least. In fact, she thinks that perhaps she is growing more fully awake with each passing moment. 'I'll

82

see you at breakfast.' She cringes when she realises that she has repeated William's promise exactly, but the others don't seem to notice. Why should they? It is such a small, accidental thing. As William's claim was. And yet...

Kate and William wait in silence as Seth, Abe, Mabel, and Anna tramp away down the street, already teasing about Abe's drinking problem and Seth being too serious and needing to let go a little. Kate does not listen to them. She would not hear them anyway past the thudding between her temples. Nor can she turn to watch them go, for William holds her still with a look of such apologetic need that she is at once heartbroken and euphoric. She hasn't the first clue what to do to break this particular spell, what the word or action is which might move them inside and up the stairs towards the room reserved for William alone. She is caught in a slant of winter lamplight, but the state seems as definite as though she were trapped before the lens of a microscope, to be studied and conjectured about. What, she wonders, would William write in the report of 'Specimen Kate Williams: Unique'?

Pleasing figure, perhaps. *Strong in the shoulder. Ample ambition, with determination to match. Mischievous eyes. Smart tongue. Kind soul. Wanting heart.*

Does he really know her so well?

'Kate,' he exhales finally. His voice trembles.

'Yes,' Kate replies. Her firmness surprises her. It surprises William too, she supposes, since it is enough to snap them out of their absurd street-side tableau and allow them to step towards each other. They halt, still not touching, though their faces are now mere inches apart. Kate can feel the hot rush of William's quickening breath over her lips, taste the stale warm tang of a coffee he drank earlier.

'Now,' she urges him, and without a word, William lifts a hand and presses a rough palm solidly over the spot where her heart throbs under her skin. Kate knows then that she is both safe and undone. To hell with saving her soul. Eternal damnation is worth the risk for this, just this – the touch of the man she already knows she loves.

Intermission

She'd told him that she wanted to fly. *Wouldn't it be wonderful*, she'd said, *to wing about like a bird?* The best suggestion he'd been able to conjure was to ask if she wanted to take a ride in a hot air balloon. Her good, practical, generous man. He's given her so many of her wishes, but not that one. Not quite. He'd come as close as anyone might reasonably expect – she'd felt, once or twice, that she might actually take flight – but she never has left the earth. They did not soar through the air together. It is, it seems, an experience she was destined to have alone, for she is flying now, gliding, arcing high over the ground. There is pain, deep in her hip and her shoulder and her temple, where the cab hit her and tilted her up onto its bonnet before throwing her off. But she can bear it. She has always been strong. She can be strong again. Strong enough not to close her eyes and wince against the hurt, but to face it. And so she watches. She watches, and all that is in her sight is colour: bright, beautiful streaks of Australian dusk blue and Welsh hills green, of Atlantic Ocean grey, and Paris midnight black, and after-show moonlight white. Glorious, she thinks. And she does close her eyes then, tight, to seal it all in. She does not want to forget any of it. Not a single sparking moment. Because it is hers, all of it, and she will not relinquish what she has battled so hard to make her own.

1900 – 1901
Act Two

8.

Paris, France
1900
EXHIBITS

They appear in the smoke and bustle of the Palace, the Empire, the Grand, the brand new Hippodrome, and, when they have proven their worth, the Theatre Royal Drury Lane – as, Kate points out smugly to William, it does indeed appear on the posters. They pack small travelling cases and ride the steam trains up and down the country, repeating their displays of strength to audiences at the Newcastle Empire, the Brighton Alhambra, the Swansea Empire. As the close of the century approaches, Vulcana appears on hoardings from one coast of Britain to the other, blown up to gigantic proportions and styled like a Grecian goddess: a loose white leotard, designed by William himself, and synched in by an ornate gold belt; a cloak draped over her arms but not her shoulders; a decorated headband keeping her iron-teased brown curls from falling over her face.

'Your face is your greatest asset, Kate,' William had said, as he'd pulled and tweaked, positioning her like a china doll for a window display. Really, she didn't mind. If she'd seen more dolls in windows looking like this as a child, she might have come to know herself better. As it was, Kate had not been able to recognise herself anywhere in her girlhood: not in the domestic concerns of her mother and her friends; not in the cradle-and-bonnet games of her schoolmates; not in the religious application of her brother and sisters.

'Not my chest, then,' she joked, thrusting out her generous bust and causing the cloak to slip.

'Kate!'

'What?'

'Listen to me for once and stay still.'

She had, and she was forced to admit afterwards that the photograph did turn out marvelously. But still, whenever she sees it, she considers she must be some disappointment in the flesh, standing at only a bob over five feet, her hair not expertly curled but smooth and wavy and inclined always to drop over her eyes. She is not the divinity in the photograph. She is not truly Vulcana.

In the gloom of a musty corridor eight years before, William had promised her every success, but she had never entirely believed it would happen. And yet, all too soon, the Atlas Troupe had become the Atlas and Vulcana Troupe. And now, though the official title remains unchanged, when the posters go up only one name appears emblazoned across them. They are invited to travel further: to Ireland and France and Holland. Kate learns how it feels to step onto the sway of a ship and trust it to sail you across squally grey seas.

Somewhere between jobs, they lose Seth to a soft-eyed Scottish lass with respectably long skirts and even longer plaits: the wholesome only daughter, it transpires in an occasion of perfect serendipity, of an ageing sheep farmer.

Eighteen months later, they lose Anna, too – to a sensible-looking chap called Willard Poole, who demonstrates a particular fondness for bowler hats and tricky wordcrosses.

'He adores me!' Anna had protested when Mabel tossed her eyes at her friend's beau.

'He's bland,' Mabel replied.

'And those are the grounds you disapprove on, are they? His blandness? I didn't know you loved me enough to be so ridiculous, Mab.' Anna reached out to tighten Mabel into an embrace; Mabel squirmed away. 'But I'll miss you, too. Very badly indeed.'

How she keeps track of them, Kate cannot imagine, but whenever they arrive at a new theatre, there is always a letter awaiting them from Anna, wishing them luck and filling them in on the newest details of her life: the home she is building with Willard; the friends she makes; the child she births a little over a year after their wedding day – a daughter. Seth writes, too, but his correspondences are different: a sentence or two scrawled across a muddied postcard.

> *Beth and myself well. Lambing session tough. Hills magnificent.*
> *Hope you're all happy.*
> *S.*

Abe, to everyone's surprise, sticks loyally to the Atlas and Vulcana Troupe, seeking attention as relentlessly as a child, except during those minutes he spends on stage, when, perversely, he seems quite content to let William be star of the show. Mabel, too, is intent on remaining with the troupe as it balloons and dwindles and transmutes through its various incarnations, picking up new performers and waving sad goodbyes to them as they marry, injure themselves, grow disenchanted with the cruel schedules, strike out to try and make it as headliners on their own.

William and Kate continue to promote themselves as 'Atlas and Vulcana, Brother and Sister Strongperson Act', but anyone who stays with the troupe long enough knows that the relationship is something entirely different. None finds a need to gossip about it. There is far greater scandal in music hall.

By 1900, William has managed to convince every breathing person in their Great British Isles, and numerous others besides, that Vulcana is *the most beautiful, symmetrical and physically perfect woman on earth and the only known woman of absolutely correct measurements, who is able to demonstrate to modern times the beautiful proportions of the female form divine as depicted by the ancients.*

It is obscene hyperbole, of course, and Kate is embarrassed by it. Though the claim of perfect symmetry does bring her to laughter. Kate, with her uneven legs and her slightly wider left eye and her heavier right breast – all of which William knows better than any. Her argument, should anyone question the marketing material, is that she can in fact never be directly compared to the ancients, and so none can disprove William's claims. She carries that explanation close to the surface for a good spell, as ready to spill it forth as she is to clench her fists at bawdy men or crude audiences, but she does not discover a need to use it. The music hall audiences, it seems, are quite happy to believe themselves presented with a deity, even when the presentation quite baldly reveals a stocky Welsh woman in possession of a sunny face, powerful biceps, and as much divinity as the dirty coal scooped up out of the sleeping earth of her birthplace.

It makes sense then that they should return to France for the Exposition Universelle. Persons of almost every nationality will be gathered in Paris, seeking astonishment and entertainment, and though she is evidently not an example of outstanding architecture or a clever piece of machinery, nonetheless, William intends to make an exhibit of Vulcana.

He had not discussed the matter with Kate before they left London. Rather, he has fussed around their hotel room, half-stuffing clothes into cases so that sleeves and legs dangled over the floor like detached limbs, and mumbling about how, 'The crowds would need entertaining in the night, too. It wouldn't just be for the daytime. They'd have the wonders of the daytime, certainly, but they'd want to let their hair down afterwards. They'd want laughs and shocks as well as beautiful objects.' Kate sat on the bed as he stampeded about, and said nothing. She didn't mind that he hadn't asked her first. In the eight years since their first performance together at the

Washington, William had never set her wrong. Besides, Paris was charming.

She is musing on exactly that as she steps now through the waking streets towards the lido. Paris is charming. They are staying at the Hôtel Régina, just across from the Jardin du Carrousel and the Jardin des Tuileries – a place Kate marvels at, containing pavilions and grand statues, an orangery, boating lakes, acrobatic performances, food and lemonade stands, donkey rides, puppet theatres, toy stalls, musicians. By day, the Jardin des Tuileries is a place of laughter and movement, and Kate loves it. But she loves too to stroll past it at six o'clock in the morning and watch the rows of mulberry trees stir. At this time, when the sun slants silver-rich across the city and makes thin shadows of the park railings and catches in the hanging jewels of the red mulberries – the *morus rubra*; Kate had looked that up, wanting for once to know something William did not – she can think of no more beautiful place to be. The Seine is charming in the evening, certainly, when the dusk light and the gas lamps conspire to make it glimmer. But in the morning, it is here Kate feels she must be, walking along the Rue de Rivoli, past the closed and curtained shop frontages, and the wafting scent of baking cakes and pastries, and the boys delivering chopped wood and newspapers and fresh-bottled milk, towards the lido, where she will disappear into the underwater silence and, for a short while, be only herself.

She wears her thinnest day dress, irritated by the fact that she will have to shrug out of it as soon as she arrives at the lido and drag on her bathing costume, then make the exchange again before she returns to the hotel. It would so much simpler to pull a pair of William's trousers over the short skirt of her costume and strut across the city attired like a strongman: trousers and vest. At the thought, she broadens her stance, sets her legs a little wider, and strides as William would.

'Ha!' The sound escapes her unexpectedly and echoes down the street, disturbing a pair of magpies and sending them fluttering away. Kate clamps her hand over her mouth. She does not want to spoil the quiet. That is why she carries her shoes tucked under her arm, tearing the feet of her stockings with every step.

The sun sits below the rooftops still when she reaches the lido. She slips into the changing booth and struggles free of her dress and appurtenances. She steps into the shorts of her bathing costume, pulls the straps up over her bare shoulders, cups her left breast and then her right to arrange them comfortably beneath the snug material, fluffs out the skirt, then releases herself from the booth. So meagrely dressed, she notices the air playing colder over her skin than she had on the walk over, and she tenses, trying not to shiver though her arms and legs are rising into gooseflesh. She enjoys the uncomfortable prickling sensation: she knows it will pass once she is in the water, and it makes the plunge into the lido all the more challenging. At twenty-four and with thousands of successful shows at her back, Kate could perhaps cease challenging herself so very often, but she isn't certain she wants to. If she is to carry on lifting, if she is to sustain enough ambition to see her through another thousand shows, if she is to keep the money coming in, she must continue to challenge herself in these small, continuous ways. She must. Though she would admit it to no one, least of all William, she is eternally fearful of growing tired.

At the edge of the lido, she curls her toes over the white tiles, lifts her arms over her head, locks her hands together, and dives. She meets the water with the fluidity of a mermaid and ripples below, welcoming the pressure in her ears, the tightness in her lungs. It is cold, but it is temporary. She butterflies beneath the surface for half a length, then emerges into a strong front crawl. She is the first to enter the lido today, and no awkward swimmers cause the water to jostle about. Having swum in rivers and lakes since childhood, Kate should find the going easy. Within ten lengths, however, she feels herself collapsing rather than propelling into her tumble-toss turns. Her breath rags up from the depths of her searing lungs. She begins to lift her face from the water every two strokes rather than every three.

She knows what the problem is. She has suspected it for some weeks. But she does not want to know it yet. She isn't ready. Not again. She pushes herself harder, and by the time she completes her fiftieth length of that bright, white-tiled lido, she is giddy and nauseous. Hooking an arm over the side of the pool, she hangs there a while, breathing the sickness away.

She will walk back beneath the mulberry trees, she decides. She will take her time, pause to pluck a mulberry between her fingers and spill its red dye over her skin, brush her knuckles over the saw-toothed edges of the ghost leaves. She enjoys the crooked spread of those trees, the spooky shape of their leaves. Look, but do not touch, they seem to say – just as she tries to, every night she spends on stage. For they come, with their telling looks and their bunched flowers and their proposals – members of the audience who claim to have fallen in love with her. They cannot have, of course: they do not know her sharp tongue or her hot-air-balloon temper; they would not conceive of her impractical pig-headedness. All they see is a girl dressed up as a goddess. All they want is to strip the disguise away and discover if the truth beneath is equally interesting.

William does not see them off, as she sometimes wishes he would.

'What's the need,' he says, when she challenges him on it. 'You can do a better job of that yourself.'

And, arguably, that is the case. Kate is bolder with her words than William, in public at least. She is certainly surer of her convictions. But she cannot quite decide whether William says what he says in admiration or criticism. She cannot pretend she hasn't noticed the way his jaw locks when their audiences cheer louder for her or chant 'Vul-ca-na, Vul-ca-na' louder than they do 'At-las'.

'It's only because I'm a woman, William,' she'd tried, some years since now, as they'd slipped into the side-of-stage shadows together. 'They expect me to be weaker.' William had only shrugged off her touch – her chalky fingertips to his sweaty forearm – and walked back to the hotel ahead of her. He had not spoken to her again until the following evening.

When she has recovered her composure, Kate hauls herself out of the lido and trudges back to the changing booth. She considers her dress, hanging from the hook where she left it as though there is another person within. It has grown tight: at the bust; at the belly. She closes her eyes and breathes through her panic. Then she pulls the dress down off the hook and drags it on over her sodden bathing costume in readiness for the walk back to the hotel. She is in need of a good breakfast and a few hours rest. She has a show to perform tonight.

9.

Paris, France
1900
HÔTEL RÉGINA

Outside the Hôtel Régina, there stands a gilded bronze statue of *Jeanne d'Arc*. Kate knows it is gilded bronze; she asked the hotel staff the day she arrived, when they came dashing out to retrieve her bags and found her stilled before it in awe.

'Gold?' she asked. 'It is pure gold... *or?*'

The maid shook her head. 'Bronze, mademoiselle.'

But to Kate's eye, and that of the morning, the woman is cast in gold. As she approaches the hotel, Kate anticipates the first glinting evidence of her, sitting proud astride her splendidly grand horse. Kate likes to imagine the horse, too, is female. She hasn't ducked beneath to check the evidence, but it only seems natural to her that so brave a woman as Joan of Arc should be accompanied by an equally brave mare. She knows it by the manner in which the horse lifts her fore-hoof, in synchrony with her mistress's raised arm. The first night they spent here, Kate dreamed that horse and rider leaped free of their plinth and galloped off into the dark. So sure was she that she could hear the four-beat of departing hooves over the paving stones, she had rushed to the window, flung it open, and hung out to wave them away. Finding them stationary still on the street below, their gleam turned from gold to silver by a loose-edged moon, she had gathered herself and the drapes hurriedly back inside and slipped into the warmth of her bedsheets before William could wake and witness her foolishness. There is little she has not shared with him during the past eight years, but these dreams she has, of horses, always running... They will remain hers alone.

She catches sight of the ruffle of Joan's banner, held high in her clenched right fist, and increases her pace. She is suddenly desperate to be back in their hotel room, breathing in the moist sleeping air and settling at the foot of the bed to tell William – who will be sitting up against his pillows to scan the morning papers for reviews of the Atlas and Vulcana Troupe's latest performance – what she has decided.

As she passes the statue, she glances up to look at Joan's face, as she does each time: she is unable to resist the expression, stern but feminine; the lips, slightly pursed in determination; the eyes, locked on something directly ahead of her. The future, Kate thinks. And then she steps across the little courtyard and into the shade of the arched terrace which announces the entranceway of the Hôtel Régina. She ascends two shallow marble steps and, pushing on the gold bar of the revolving wood and glass-panelled door, she rotates inside, her heels clipping over chequered tiles now that she has finally put her shoes back on. The foyer is sun-drenched, owing to the windows which match the arches of the terrace beyond in both scale and design. The ceilings are high and white. From them hang three enormous chandeliers, which, Kate can't help but think, must weigh down the plasterwork so much that one day they will come crashing to the ground. She nods to the neat, silent woman on the reception desk, and proceeds across the room, wincing at the echoing cacophony her ten-and-a-half-stone frame creates.

With one hand to the polished wood banister, she walks slowly up the staircase, fighting the urge to run in case the receptionist is watching her. The shallowness of the stairs, though, makes her want to trip quickly up them. Never in her previous life had she encountered such inefficient stairs. If their task is to get you up, these dainty flights do not offer much in the way of expediency. That, she assumes, is intentional: these are stairs designed for ladies to glide down. She rolls her eyes at the thought, and speeds up.

Everything about the Hôtel Régina is sumptuous. Though the abundant windows splay light into every room, there comes, from every eclipsed corner, the glow of a perfectly positioned lamp. In the creation of each staircase and clock surround and light fitting and window frame, the designer has managed to insert tendrils of wrought-iron curlicues. Beneath Kate's feet, the tiled floor of each landing is laid with rugs so thick that, when walking them in heels, it is difficult to balance. For all she had imagined when she stepped off the train at Paddington in pursuit of William that first morning, she could not have envisaged such extravagance as this. And yet, she has quickly grown accustomed to it. That is not to say she feels entitled to breakfast at the Hôtel Régina or drinks at the Savoy, nor fancy treatment at the Theatre Royal or boat trips along the Seine, but only that she has been able to adjust. She is not frightened of these places, as her mother would be; she is not privately scathing of them, as her father would be. She is only interested, and that, she considers, is a much better way to approach anything in life than carrying preconceptions.

The door to the room she shares with William – number seven, though, for decency's sake, number eight is booked out in her name – is towering and heavy. She grasps the gleaming brass knob, turns it, and pushes against the wood with both hand and shoulder. She does not know the type of wood. Words like 'cherry' and 'rose' enter her mind vaguely, but all she really knows is that it is different from the deep mahogany she is so used to seeing in London and Wales. It is richer, brighter, more optimistic – as Paris seems to be.

She creaks over the floorboards, kicking off her pesky shoes and unbuttoning her dress as she goes. She does indeed find William in bed, propped up on his pillows, his moustache hooked over the rim of a delicate teacup. The sight is preposterous. He is a walrus, holding chinaware in a large, clumsy flipper; the cup is surely soon to break.

'And what are you laughing at?' he enquires, hardly looking up from the newspaper she had known would be open in his lap. He has his knees bent to keep it at a good angle.

'Only the *grandeur* of you,' she teases, finally dropping her dress to the floor and clambering onto the bed. She crawls towards him and, plucking up the newspaper, folds it away and slides it onto the bedside cabinet. He puts the teacup down to receive her, then yelps when he realises that she is wet.

'I'm only damp,' she says, falling on top of him to better soak him with her sodden bathing costume. Her dress had kept it from drying on the walk back. William accepts the trick without further protest and she lifts her face to request a kiss. William knows the tilt of the chin well enough, and answers it with his soft lips and his scratchy moustache. Kate ignores the tickle until he draws away, then sweeps the back of her hand roughly across her upper lip, making it red, as she sinks against him.

'I've been thinking,' she says, 'about the house in Bristol.'

They had happened past it after a late performance at the Prince's Theatre. They weren't looking for a house to buy. In fact, they hadn't even gone inside to view it. But they had climbed the walls, giggling and shushing each other under the disapproving moon, to stroll around the gardens which led down to a tiny silkworm of a stream, and Kate had declared it exactly right.

'I want to buy it.'

William sits up a little straighter and clears his throat. She has been avoiding this conversation for some weeks, worried as she is that it will stir up those feelings he still refuses to admit to: the discomfort he suffers that it is she and not he who brings in the most money; the anger his inability to swallow this discomfort causes. William is not an old-fashioned man, but the urge he has to be his family's provider cannot be quashed by the fact that they are amply provided for by Vulcana's name and reputation. That he has invented and promoted her doesn't seem to be enough. The fact is that Atlas is not so well-received by the audiences, and it gnaws away at him. They both train their eyes on the window.

'But... You're not ready to stop, are you? Not yet? I mean... There are so many places left to visit.'

This is an appeal, she realises. It is he who does not want to stop.

'I don't want to stop.'

He sighs out his relief, partially. He still doesn't understand. 'Then...'

'I want to buy it for Alice,' she says, though in truth she wants to buy it for herself, too. There are days when she would willingly swap places with Alice – trade applause for a bedtime story, fame for a summer spent tending her own garden. 'She'd like it, don't you think? The garden. She loves her flowers. And they get smothered by the coal dust where she is – the flowers *and* the children. Bristol would be better. Wouldn't it?'

As he considers this, there begins a humming deep in his chest. Kate puts her ear to it and listens to its music, trying to decide whether she can make out more sad minor falls or happy major inflections in the notes that make up William Hedley Roberts. It is, after all, the sound of the rest of her life.

'It would be better,' William concedes finally. 'But then...'

'We don't need anywhere else. We'll be touring, or we'll be home with Alice and the children.'

'And when we retire...'

'When we retire!' Kate turns her face to show him her

smile. 'We won't retire for thirty years at least, and we'll have made plenty more money by then.'

'Thirty years,' William laughs. 'I don't intend to be traipsing the stages in my middle sixties, thank you very much.'

'Of course you do. What else is there?'

His response is to sigh again, heavier now. Kate rides the deflation of his chest, concentrating on the lowering notes which sound from within. She remembers the time she had stood before him and thought to peel her skin and muscle away to show him her heart, and she wishes now that she could do the same to him. She wants to reveal how robust it is, that heart of his. How reliable. How stalwart. How intense. How tender. Only then could she begin to explain why he ought to trust it. Reassurance is what William needs from Kate. He is naturally more pessimistic than she, more worrying. That, she has long since concluded, is why they fit together – they have sought out, in each other, what they have found lacking in themselves.

'I think it would be nice to take a short break, wouldn't it, once the house is bought?'

She doesn't deliver the line easily enough, she knows. It sounds sharp. It cuts her lips as she forces it through them.

William seizes on the oddity of the delivery and, clasping her closer, says, 'So, you are then?'

Kate offers him brooding silence and a flicker of eyelash. His face flushes from pale to pink-tinged. He sits up straighter, dragging Kate with him.

'I'd suspected. Just, you know, around your stomach. I'd

thought perhaps, but I didn't want to... You are, aren't you? You're expecting.'

In the corridor outside their door, the brisk click of a porter's heels and the echo of faraway voices trailing his hasty path. Beyond the window, the trill and coo of pigeons perched on the balcony two storeys above and pecking about on the street below. She is expecting – another child she will not be there to mother – but she will not admit to it yet.

'It would be nice to see Nora,' Kate replies, after a considered interval. Because this William cannot possibly disagree with. He must miss the girl, too. 'It's been far too long since we've seen Nora.'

10.

Paris, France
1900
THE EXPOSITION UNIVERSELLE

'Gather in,' William calls, flapping his free hand to indicate that they should shuffle to their collective right. 'I want you all beneath the statue. That's it.'

In Paris, the Atlas and Vulcana Troupe consists of William, Kate, Mabel, Abe, and three young strongpersons-in-training, who, inexplicably, William has taken to calling by their surnames. Having been introduced to the others as such, their given names were never enquired after, and they have quite happily accepted becoming Hatfield, Cummings, and Young. Kate suspects that the passing through the troupe of too many Emmas and Johns, Jacks and Elizabeths, has brought about the change of tack from William, and she approves. Hatfield, Cummings, and Young sound like an illusion of magicians, which might just set them in good stead when, inevitably, the time comes for them to move on.

To Kate's immediate right now stands Hatfield, who has the delicate, fine-boned features of a society lady and the ramrod stance of a ballerina. Her feet, Kate notices with amusement when she glances down, are even turned out into first position. Perhaps Hatfield had lied about coming from a circus background. In truth, perhaps she had had enough of being shrieked at in French and strolled straight out of the stuffy order of a dance studio in her satin slippers to find herself a new position. Kate likes that idea. She would admire Hatfield all the more if it were true. As it is, Kate cannot quite admit to herself that she is a little jealous of Hatfield's careful good looks. Kate knows that men find her attractive – they've made that much clear over the years. And besides, William's is the only opinion that matters on that score. But it is only natural to covet – *Envy!* Kate thinks, though she no longer hears the accusation in her father's sonorous voice – that which we admire in others, and Kate knows that hers is a bolder face than Hatfield's. More of an acquired taste, perhaps. She will not age so well, and she worries what that will mean for her and the stage.

To Hatfield's right, Mabel slumps, grumbling. 'Can't we get on to the fair,' she says. 'We've already waited two days.'

'As soon as the photo is taken,' William replies offhandedly.

Cummings and Young fidget a few yards apart, uncomfortable in their best coats and hats. William had insisted they turn out well for their visit to the Exposition Universelle. *There'll be influential people aplenty there*, he'd warned. *You'll want to put your best foot forward*. Kate had smirked at how grandfatherly he sounded.

'And what is that you're holding anyway?' Mabel continues.

'This?' William rotates the box camera in his palms, as if viewing it for the first time. Kate knows him to be inordinately proud of the purchase. To hear it described so flippantly as 'that' will disappoint him. 'It's my new Brownie,' he explains through a pouting bottom lip. 'It's the very latest from Kodak. Just released this year. You'll see – by 1901 everyone will have one.'

'And you'll have been amongst the first,' Mabel larks. 'A forerunner of fashion. Well, well, William – they'll have you in the shop windows next.'

When he realises he is being mocked, William grimaces at Mabel then orders her to stand in a more ladylike manner so that he can get the bloody photograph taken. This, Mabel enjoys. She likes him best when he most resembles the rough son of an ironworker she trained with through the rain-slewed Abergavenny winters. And so, in truth, does Kate. When he is not charming this theatre manager or that marketing officer, William is hewn from dark clouds and heavy industry and the deep-bellied song of south Wales. His words are hammer blows. His hands are coal shovels. His eyes are the green of the mountains viewed through rainfall. She might not want to go back there yet, but she needs reminding, as she dashes about the world, of what home tastes and smells like. The crow-feathered nights and the dank morning air, the lilt and spit of Welsh spoken over fences and across polished pub tables, the ringing unity of sung hymns bursting through the windows of her father's church, the rasping hush of wind over the hills – all that is contained within William, and she loves him all the more for being built from fragments of their past.

'On the count of three,' William orders, and Kate smiles wide despite the uncomfortable weight of the white lilies pinned into her picture hat. She hopes that he has captured Joan of Arc in all her splendour.

'One.'

Kate should like to hang her image on a wall on some as yet unimaginable day, when she manages to entice herself to choose a place to stop and stay forever. Joan reminds her of Rhiannon, riding her horse towards her very own decision. And Jemima Nicholas, who, when French invaders landed at Abergwaun in 1797, armed herself with a pitchfork and some friends, strode out to meet the troops, and held a sorry group of them captive in a nearby church until the French surrendered. She wonders why Jemima does not have a statue like this, facing out to sea, her pitchfork raised and her skirts salt-billowed.

'Two.'

She steals a backwards glimpse at the statue. Today, particularly, she feels she might require a call-to-arms.

'Three.'

With a click, William releases them from their duties and they start to move towards the promise of the fabled Exposition Universelle.

They have been able to hear rumour of it through the hotel windows. Now that they are walking away from the hotel, that rumour is transforming into promise, for already they can make out the clamour of a great number of people gathered together, and the clanging of bells, and drifting accordion music, and the insistent huff-huff of steam-powered engines, and the disgruntled rattle of railway cars.

The heart of the exposition is a little over two miles distant, at the Champ de Mars, but the still air carries its sounds over the Seine towards them readily, like siren song, and they have only to walk down the Rue de Rivoli and along the Place de la Concorde to reach the entranceway.

'Would you listen to that?' Abe says. He is grinning like a child.

'It's like an enormous orchestra,' Kate says, 'tuning their strings and blowing the spit from their brasses.'

Mabel laughs. 'That's exceedingly unromantic, Kate. How could you possibly manage to be unromantic in *Old Par-ee*?'

'Because I'm not!' Kate protests, shoving at Mabel with her shoulder. 'What I'm saying is... It's the messy beginning of something that will become breathtaking.'

Mabel nods. 'That's better, I suppose.'

'I think it sounds like we're walking towards a factory,' offers Cummings, the larger and more bullish of the two boys.

'Now *that's* unromantic,' Abe answers.

'I don't know,' Young puts in. He stands a head shorter than Cummings, though he is hardly less broad, and evidently quakes in admiration of the lad who is, at most, maybe six months his senior. 'I always thought factories were homely.'

'And what's romantic about home?' Mabel enquires.

They listen to the beat of their mismatched steps for a moment as they consider the question. So different are they in height and build that they cannot possibly fall into sync. They are no herd of interchangeable beasts, this troupe; they are as varied as all the landscapes of the planet. They demand the eye. And so used are they to being gawped at that they do not notice the clutches of passers-by who stop to stare at them as they proceed, stately in their own strange way, through the streets of Paris.

'Belonging there,' Hatfield says finally, her voice as timid as her shifting gaze.

'I don't know that belonging is particularly romantic,' Mabel says, not unkindly, over her shoulder. 'I've never been keen to belong.'

Having travelled with Mabel for close to a decade now, Kate knows this to be untrue. Mabel might not want to belong to a place, but she certainly needs to belong to people. Why else would she have stayed with the troupe so long? She is only testing Hatfield, Cummings, and Young with these statements. She is picking at the threads of them, as she always does when she wishes to become acquainted with strangers, to see what interesting information might snap loose or fall easily free or slowly unravel.

She had played the same game with Kate, during their first months in London.

'And what did you find out?' Kate asked, when Mabel admitted to the investigation. She had flushed at the words, having already secretly shared a bed with William on four separate occasions.

'Not enough,' Mabel replied. 'There's much to you, Katherine.' She narrowed her eyes good-humouredly. 'But it's hidden behind the fog of all that damn ambition.'

Kate wasn't so sure she agreed. She still isn't. All that 'much'

– as Mabel called it – really amounted to was confusion. The truth of Kate Williams was not hidden behind the fog of her ambition. It was lost there. Her ambition, such as it is and was, had never been for fame or wealth or medals – though she seems to have acquired all three along the way – but only to feel like herself.

And she has started to… She *had* started to. Before Nora.

When they reach the Place de la Concorde, they find the streets astir. They are hustled along with a sudden crowd, unable to converse now even if they should want to. But they don't. They are riding a carousel of people towards the Exposition Universelle, and it is exciting, and they are more than happy to be caught on this surge towards all that is novel and unknown. None has any honest inkling of what lies ahead of them, but they are buoyed by the mood of this new century, which is proving itself to be teeming with invention and optimism and opportunity.

William was right to suggest that they dress well. The people of Paris, and indeed of all those other visiting nations, have come in their finest. Women strut about in silks and frills, their skirts and coats shining in bright shades of emerald or peach or lavender. The men wear mostly black, but beneath their suit jackets, their white shirts are starched to perfection, and on their heads, their top hats gleam like wet coal. Children race about in ruched dresses and bonnets or tailored shorts and shone shoes. But none of that brilliance compares to what Kate sees when they pass beneath the enormous punctured-iron-and-ceramic vault of the Porte Monumentale, then through one of the twenty-six – she counts them – ticket booths, and finally enter the fair.

What she arrives at then is a city from a reverie. All along the banks of the Seine stand castles and palaces, domes and spires, turrets and pavilions, and structures that Kate doesn't know how to name. From the topmost point of almost every building, flags wave their colours. On the Seine's calm waters, fishing boats and gondolas and yachts steer around each other, their captains shouting passing greetings or insults. They walk in silence through attractions which only increase in grandeur. They are passed by jugglers and musicians, noisily going about their work. Food vendors waft billows of smoke towards them, leaving the scent of hot meat pies and roasted nuts in their noses. The air flits with vapours and melodies.

'The buildings will all be torn down when the exposition closes,' William says. She had been vaguely aware of him, at her left arm. She does not take her eyes from the exhibits to respond.

'But ... the expense.'

'They're not true buildings,' he explains. 'The frames are iron, covered with plaster or staff.'

'It's such a waste.'

'Perhaps.'

'Most definitely,' she replies. 'I think I'll mourn it a little. The destruction of so much beauty.'

'You do find it beautiful, then?'

She does turn to him then. 'Of course. It's like a great parade of celebration. Look what we can do, they're saying – every exhibitor, every structure, every invention. Even the ugly ones are beautiful in that ... endeavour. Is that the right word? Yes. They're all reaching for something, aren't they? Like people.'

The ends of William's moustache twitch. 'Well, who would have known Mademoiselle Vulcana was full of such wisdom?' He cocks his head in veneration of her.

'Well, who would have known Monsieur Atlas wasn't aware of the fact?' she returns.

William tips forward from the waist to kiss her, but remembers himself within an inch or two and straightens up again. They do not risk it when the other members of the troupe might spot them, though Abe and Mabel must surely be fully aware of the arrangement by now. She sends him a look they have shared so often over the years that he could not possibly mistake it: *later*.

They wander for miles through the fair – a loose party of seven, sometimes splitting into smaller groups to stop longer at the Palace of Electricity and the Water Chateau, or to ride back and forth on the moving sidewalk, or to sit in the false railway cars of the *Transsiberien* and be shunted about while watching the painted landscapes from Peking to Moscow roll past.

It is a day Kate could not possibly have imagined, could not even have invented in her wildest daydreams. They walk beneath the glass ceiling of the Gallery of Machines and watch the dynamos whir. They stroll through the Aquarium and observe strange rainbow-coloured fish, stately sea turtles, and quick grey sharks fin by. They sit in the Palace of Optics and gasp as the Great Paris Exposition Telescope zooms them towards the mottled surface of the moon. Kate holds her breath and laughs, and William watches her hold her breath and laugh, and they barely notice the passing of the hours. At dusk, having shaken off the others, they pay their two francs for a first-class car on the Grande Roue de Chicago, an enormous American Ferris wheel, and Kate clutches William's hand as they are rotated into the sky. From the top, they can view all of Paris: the streets which thread away from the river, straight as stitches along a perfect hem; the vivid green canopies of trees which line them; the lilac glow of the Seine under the sun, which seems to have dropped below them, suspended as they are amongst the clouds.

'You promised to make me a great many things, William,' Kate breathes. 'But I never counted on becoming a bird.'

And yet here she is – almost that very thing. She finds herself to be lighter than air as the wheel cranks through the degrees of its rotation. Her head is fuddled, as though she has drunk too many glasses of wine, though not a drop has passed her lips. She stretches her arms out to her sides, and the breeze licks around them, and she knows she could simply take flight, so hollow and weightless are her limbs, so easy are her thoughts, so empty is her stomach. Riding the Grande Roue de Chicago is like swimming through the sky.

'I don't ever want to go down,' she says.

'Nor I,' William replies.

But as they speak the words, they are already curving into their descent. Their legs are wobbly as they step out of the car and rush to reach the next exhibit before darkness falls, but they run the feeling off, weaving through the crowds and bumping people from their path like a pair of naughty schoolchildren. William had promised her a sea voyage before the day was out, and as she chases him through the crowded chaos of the fair, she cannot believe how he will provide it. He has already offered her the sky. He cannot top that. He truly has shown her everything there is to see now. Everything. She will tell him that, when they return to their hotel room and she is able, at last, to kiss him.

That was it, she will say. *That was everything*.

But of course it is not everything – not without Nora.

She presses her mouth shut in disbelief when they round a corner and stop, panting, before the Maréorama. Somehow, off the water and on to dry land, has been brought a colossal, real-life ship. Or so it seems to Kate, for she can identify the great curving hull and she can see the smoking funnels and she can hear the steam whistles shrieking.

'How?' she laughs.

William only shrugs his shoulders and guides her towards the ladder they must climb to get on deck.

Kate goes ahead, her hands gripping the rope sides of the ladder. 'Where will we go?' she asks over her shoulder.

From below, William replies, 'To the edge of the world, of course.'

And perhaps that's what they've been chasing all this time – their road to the edge of the world. Somewhere without churches and ironworks and duties. Somewhere they might eventually hide away. Somewhere they might be only Kate and William and not Atlas and Vulcana. Not the act. *There's your romance, Mabel*, Kate thinks. *Right deep down inside the truth*.

At sixteen, she'd thought she could be Vulcana forever, but she understands – now and very suddenly – that one day, she will have to give her up. And who will she be then? The question is answered by a churning sensation at her core, and silence. She clambers on deck and tries to pace her unease away, but she cannot. Not entirely. Her heels sound too heavy on the wooden boards and she is unsure of her balance. At her back, William's words blur and she cannot bring them into focus. She pretends she cannot hear him past the boarding of the other passengers and the grinding of the machinery, and they move together towards the prow of the ship. Around the ship are suspended ceiling-height paintings of seascapes, and before it is a large, cylindrical structure, wrapped with painted canvas. Evidently, this will unreel as their voyage progresses, showing them distant shores and cities they will never reach.

'Ladies and gentlemen,' a curt voice bellows. Heads turn towards it and the man it belongs to is able to lower his volume for the remainder of the announcement. He does not relax his body, though, as he stands in the middle of the deck in his seaman's uniform, arms clamped to his sides, and stares into the middle distance. He is concentrating on his part, Kate thinks. He is not a natural showman. 'Welcome aboard. We are to voyage today from Villefranche-sur-Mer to Constantinople. We hope you will enjoy the sights. Please move towards the railings for the best view.'

The passengers do as instructed and move to stand against the railings, to better stare out over a make-believe sea, and without any further warning but for the deafening hiss of the hydraulics, the voyage is underway. A few squeals issue as the ship begins to tip and roll, but they seem to be formed more from delight than terror and no one pays them much heed.

William wraps an arm around Kate's middle and grips the railing in front of her. She looks down at the bulges and bumps of his knuckles, at the river-valleys of his veins, at the white blotches where the bone has ventured too close to the skin, at the wisps of fair hair that rise from his wrist. First the ironworks and then the weightlifting have moulded these hands into strong, rough shapes. They look as though they might belong to a fisherman, who plunges them repeatedly into whipping grey waves to snatch out mackerel or trout. Or to a farrier, whose fingers have been burned and trodden on for decades. They are only ever gentle when touching her. She puts her own hand over his and grips, tight. She feels more unsteady than the inching movement of the ship ought to be rendering her. Despite the whirring wind being fanned around them, she is warm and clammy. Giddiness swoops in like a hungry herring gull and claims her and she lists against the listing of the ship. William catches her falling weight and holds her to him.

'Kate.'

She only hums in response, and closes her eyes, to keep the sickness down.

'Kate?'

Absently, she pats the arm he has wrapped tight around her middle. She should have told him when he asked. She should have said, 'Yes,' and smiled and allowed them to collapse into celebrations. She has denied William something precious with her avoidance. It is not right that she knows for certain that their baby is curled tight inside her while he does not. But she is not ready, yet, for his happiness. She is not ready to pretend they already have a neat solution to being unable to tour from country to country with a child in tow. It does not sit well with her that they left Nora behind. She misses her horribly – so horribly that often she grows sleepless with it and spends her nights loafing around moonlit hotel rooms or walking the midnight streets of unknown cities, seeking some echo of her. William does not notice, so soundly does he sleep. She expects it is different for him. He has left all his children behind: not just Nora, but young Alice, Grace, Reginald, Ernest, and Winifred, too. He is practised in this. But she is not, and it does not suit her, and Alice can only look after so many children, surely. Kate will have to go back home. She wants to...

Not back, she insists, her eyes twitching behind her closed lids. *Don't think 'back', just think 'home'.* But she cannot summon one word without the other. Back home. Back home. Because going home would be to go backwards, wouldn't it, away from all this wonder and all the marvels that might follow? And towards Nora. Her sweet cherry girl. Her plump little songstress, who sung before she could speak. Her moody, dancing daughter, who swings from joy to fury as readily as her mother.

'Kate!' It is a man's voice, louder than before, and her eyes spring open but she cannot think where she is, swaying and bumping about like this. There is whistling in her ears, and hissing, and pumping. The world is shuddering and smoking. She needs to get home, to Nora. She grips the railings she finds under her palms tighter, lifts a foot to the bottom rung, and heaves herself up. But there is a weight at her back, anchoring her, and she cannot rise off the tilting wooden planks. She tries again, straining with all her might. The anchor remains steady.

'Kate! Stop! What are you doing?'

And, despite her confusion, Kate answers the question automatically, as honestly as she can.

'I'm going home.'

11.

Paris, France
1900
THE OLYMPIA

The Olympia, number 28 Boulevard des Capucines, sits neatly and unobtrusively among its neighbours, wearing the same pale Lutetian limestone and enjoying the shade of the same row of plane trees which obscure the windows and doorways of thousands of similar tall, narrow buildings up and down the endless street. For that, Kate much prefers it to Drury Lane, which is too showy, and the Hippodrome, which is too dazzling. The Olympia draws people to its canopied entrance doors with its quiet class. Above the doors, the letters O L Y M P I A are arranged in a delicate arc; at night, they are lit with soft yellow bulbs. Quaint, Kate thinks – that's the best word to describe the Olympia. She would like to perform here for a year straight.

She would swim at the lido every morning, and eat pastries in bed at the Hôtel Régina – *Gluttony, surely!* – while William scoured the newspapers for reviews, and sit on the banks of the Seine with Mabel and drink coffee, and explore the strange and magical avenues of the Exposition Universelle, and, come dusk, she would stroll over to the Olympia and take to the stage and soak up the applause of an appreciative French audience.

Life could be just as she'd imagined it could be when she woke, on that first bright morning in London, to the sound of Mabel and Anna chattering happily over breakfast tea.

But she has denied herself all that with her carelessness. Within a year, she will have delivered her second child and travelled to Wales to dump her into Alice's waiting arms. Good, patient, uncomplaining Alice: Kate does not deserve her; William certainly does not.

She swallows the thought and pushes her face into a smile as William prepares his Brownie and positions her before her poster, which has her hovering above the pavement at eight or nine feet high, clad in her Grecian outfit. Her likeness takes up the entire side of the boxed ticket booth. William wishes to photograph her in duplicate. He really is enamoured of that camera. He had excused the cost of purchasing it by explaining that if he could take her promotion shots, they wouldn't need to pay a photographer, and Kate had only nodded. She hadn't asked or wanted to know how much he paid for it.

She waits dutifully for the click, then turns into the building. They have already agreed between themselves that tonight she will lift Hatfield above her head for the finale rather than William. Hatfield's eight-stone-nine will feel comfortable by comparison to William's eleven-stone-six. They have blamed the change on Kate jarring her back on the Maréorama the day before, and, while the rest of the troupe might doubt the explanation – Mabel had lifted an eyebrow quizzically at Kate, knowing her to be more robust than that – they will no doubt accept it and forget it soon enough. Kate and William, though, are worried about that strange fainting episode: William because he knows that she didn't have this sort of trouble with Nora; Kate because she feels certain it had nothing to do with the pregnancy, but cannot imagine what else might have caused it.

'Ready, girl?' Abe asks as they mill about backstage, dusting their hands and wrapping their wrists. Kate sends him a wink. She understands, now, that the address is an affectionate one, but she will never forget the irritation it had caused her when she really was a girl. How the rest of the troupe had tolerated her, she can't suppose. All that pretension and insisting – as if she knew anything.

'Always,' she tells Abe. He returns her wink and wanders away to find a drink.

'You're certain?' comes a quiet voice from behind her. Mabel. 'I could go on in your place, if you needed.'

Kate spins around to face her friend, showing her a gentle smile. 'I'm on all the posters,' Kate says, knowing that Mabel will understand this as a burden rather than a boast.

Mabel pats her on the shoulder and nods. 'Well, if things get desperate.'

'Yes.'

This 'yes', Kate knows, Mabel will understand to mean 'thank you', but, to her mortification, she finds she cannot utter the actual words without summoning tears. Kate loves performing. It is her greatest talent. Her joy. Her purpose, in so many ways. But just sometimes – when she is under the weather or the schedule is too full or she needs to breathe in the smell of Nora's skin – she contemplates what it might mean, to stop. She finds herself wishing she had good reason to. Or rather, a reason she could admit to.

Whether William has noticed it, she is not sure, but she has seen what the touring life does to its more popular names. She had not been able to forget for weeks afterwards how sad Marie Lloyd looked the last time they'd seen her in London. And poor Dan Leno – for all his success, the only way to describe him is haunted. In recent years, a darkness has so engulfed his eyes that Kate suspects he will never again glimpse light. If music hall kills Dan, he will be neither its first victim nor its last.

With a final squeeze of Kate's shoulder, Mabel disappears to find her slippers, and Kate is left alone behind the curtain. She inches closer to it and inhales its weighty, beaten-dust smell. They have changed the routine for the Olympia, so that William goes downstage and teases the audience with a short – though none the less dramatic for its brevity – narrative about Vulcana, the strongest woman in the world, who can carry cab horses on her back, who can outshine any man willing to try his luck in a weightlifting contest, and who still manages – heaven forfend – to retain her womanly charms. Kate huffs or titters to hear it, depending on her mood. The strongest woman in the world. Really, how did that come about? She is strong, yes, but only in so much as she can lift heavy items above her head, which really has only very limited application. Does that make her stronger than those women who live at the snowy tips of Norway or Finland and do constant battle with the clawing grey wind for survival? Certainly not. Stronger than those women who were forced to hide their babies in the fields they worked? No. It is an embarrassing claim, though she understands the making of it. Vulcana is the world's strongest woman in the same way that a café might claim to make the world's best cup of tea. She is a sales pitch, a slogan, a shared delusion.

The Paris audiences have been no less receptive for it.

William concludes his story with a flourish. Taking her cue, Kate grabs the weight bar at her feet and, hoisting it into a snatch, thrusts it directly skyward. And that, when the curtains draw back, is where they find their Vulcana, standing sure-footed and proud, the bar held up on extended arms and the downlighting arranged to fall over every curve and flick of muscle in her arms and shoulders and chest. She is a sculpture of warrior womanhood. She maintains the pose, biceps and trapezius burning, until the lights blink out and she is able to shuffle into her next demonstration. Moving towards the middle of the stage, she lowers herself to the floor, flips onto her back, straightens her arms and legs into the legs of a sturdy table, and waits for William to lie across her flattened palms and soles. When the lights go back up, he will be lying there in repose, looking easy about it though he knows that the pressure blares pain through the bent joints of Kate's wrists and ankles and does his best to keep his mass evenly distributed.

At each reveal, the audience whoops and claps. Their collective sound is richer than that of a British crowd: it gurgles up from low in the throat. Kate has learned, over the years, that the sounds shift with the geography and that it is not a reflection on their performance. In London, the audiences are made to sound colder by more clapping and less cheering. In Scotland, they clap slower but more heartily and their voice is deeper. In Wales, they chorus their appreciation and hardly bother with the clapping.

She flinches to notice, though, that here William's tricks do not bring about the same enthusiasm as her own. Each time he makes a lift or shapes a pose, the response is notably more muted. She glances across to check his face and, finding his eyes cold with panic, feels a crushing sensation clutch her heart. Poor William.

The Lord Almighty has a day in store for all the proud and lofty, for all that is exalted (and they will be humbled). She can't help but recall her father's recital from the pulpit. Isaiah 2:12. Or perhaps it is Isaiah 23:9.

They progress through the usual routine: chest expansions; lifts; challenges to the audience. They close, as arranged, with Kate suspending Hatfield over one extended arm. And by eleven o'clock they are stepping out of the theatre and back towards the hotel.

'Drinks?' Abe suggests as they pass through the Hôtel Régina's revolving door and into the moonlit foyer. Murmuring in agreement, they cross towards the bar, their clumsy shadows spoiling the immaculate silver-light arches which decorate the floor. As they go, Kate is pitched by a sudden impression of unbelonging. She rights herself as they choose a table and settle around it, gathering additional chairs from neighbouring tables.

Abe, Cummings, and Young order brandies – the fools. Hatfield opts for a glass of red wine: better. And William, Kate, and Mabel – who learned long ago not to excite themselves further after a show – take a pot of tea. In 1892 and '93, into '94 even, they had often drunk themselves raucous after successful appearances. But the repetition of the act, and the travel from place to place, and the sheer volume of alcohol they imbibed as a result left them tired and miserable. Only Abe had kept up the habit – though it was a habit well-ingrained before he ever met William. Hatfield, Cummings, and Young will realise their mistake soon enough.

William is quiet as the others gabble about the highs and lows of the evening, as is their habit.

'They loved Kate's lift, didn't they?' Cummings offers.

Mabel grins. 'They always love Kate's lift.'

'I was a bit nervous,' Hatfield admits, smiling. 'But once I was up, it was brilliant.'

Ordinarily, William leads the after-show discussion, like a schoolmaster congratulating and educating his students, but Kate knows he is feeling dispensable tonight. Under the table, she grasps his hand and holds tight. His flesh is cold beneath hers. She runs a finger over a crack in his middle knuckle, where the talcumed skin has grown sore. When he looks at her, she is shocked to discover a well of tears glinting along his lower lids. She releases his hand and, retrieving the teapot, begins to pour.

'We should take a boat ride tomorrow,' she says. She and William have already taken a trip privately, which took them gliding past the Eiffel Tower in misty, mid-morning rain. But she would like to do it again, in better weather, and besides, it gives her something to say to change the subject.

'I'd love that,' Hatfield replies dreamily. 'I think I'm in love with Paris.'

'No doubt you'll fall in love with the next city we visit. And the one after that, too,' Mabel says, kindly. 'It's what keeps you going past the exhaustion.'

'No.' Hatfield sits back and sips her wine, her eyelids heavy. 'I think this is the place for me.'

'It's the first place you've ever been,' Young jokes.

'And what of it?'

'Well, give the rest of the world a chance.'

'Here, here,' Abe puts in, raising his glass. They all chink – teacups rattling against tumblers. 'Though you can probably avoid America. I never much rated it.'

'Is that why you came to Britain?' Hatfield asks, big-eyed now with wanting to uncover the mysteries of this loud, complicated man.

Abe shrugs. 'It seems as good a reason as any,' he says.

Hatfield will not be dissuaded so easily. 'But is it *the* reason?' she prods.

In the silence that chases her question, Kate is surprised to realise that she doesn't have the first clue how or why Abe came to be in Britain. She doesn't really know anything of substance about Abe, even now, after all this time. Perhaps he was a criminal, in another life. Or perhaps he wronged a lover and was chased out of town by her tribe of enormous brothers. Or perhaps he ran away from debtors; he does like to gamble.

'It's not important,' Abe answers.

And no, Kate supposes that it's not, in truth. Abe might sneak off on his naughty jaunts come midnight, but he has never brought trouble to the troupe; he's never missed a performance; he's never upset any of the other troupe members in a lasting, serious way.

'What is important,' he continues, 'is that we were lucky enough that circumstance conspired to bring us all here, together.'

'Here, here,' Mabel interjects, inclining her head in Abe's direction.

'And that we're admired across half the globe.'

'Hear, hear!' Cummings joins in.

'And that our Vulcana is the talk of this grand and beautiful city.'

At this, Kate colours in frustration. She brings her teacup to her mouth, to hide her blush behind. She had wanted to divert the conversation, not set herself more firmly at the centre of it.

'You're right about one thing, Abraham,' she replies. 'We are fortunate to be here, at the start of an entirely new century. It feels promising, doesn't it? It feels like anything at all could be ahead of us. Perhaps we should drink to beginnings.'

She raises her teacup again and is met with a refrain of, 'Beginnings.' Better.

'All right,' Mabel says, clunking down her cup and, thankfully, taking Kate's lead. 'One hope for the new century. Young, you first.' She shoots him with a pointed index finger, and he flinches as though he truly has been hit. 'Go.'

'Oh, urm... All right... Just one... I suppose, I would like to travel to India.'

'India!' Mabel's face scrunches inward at the idea. 'Too hot. Right.' She slams a flattened hand against the table, making the drinks jump inside their glasses. 'Cummings.' She is moving clockwise around the table, Kate notes. That will give her some time to think, but not much.

'I...' Cummings frowns as he searches for something impressive but impersonal to say. He gives up. 'I want to headline my own show.'

'Good,' Mabel announces. 'Ambitious. Hatfield.'

'Easy,' Hatfield grins. 'I'm going to marry.'

Mabel's hand is already raised in anticipation of the next slam, the indicator that the next person should answer, but at Hatfield's response, it stops, suspended, and refuses to drop downwards.

'No!' Mabel glares at Hatfield, who, slumped back in her chair, does not seem to notice. 'I'm not having that. *I'm going to marry* is no sort of intention at all. Pick something better.'

'Really?' Hatfield enquires, straightening up a little.

'Really,' Kate replies.

'I see.' Hatfield pouts her perfect strawberry lips as she

ponders the instruction. 'Well, then, I suppose if I'm not to marry...'

'Always better not to,' Abe chimes.

'Then I would like... I mean I would hope...'

'You can say it,' Abe urges. 'Your secrets are safe here. I won't remember them come morning.'

'It's not so much a secret, really,' Hatfield explains, 'as something I've just never said aloud before. It always seemed too big an idea.'

'No such thing,' Mabel insists.

'It is my intention, then, to save enough money to open a school for girls.'

'*That's* more like it!'

Hatfield places her wine glass down and reinhabits her ballerina's poise; she is warming to her confession. 'Perhaps even here in Paris,' she concludes.

'Good girl,' Mabel roars, then slams her hand down again against the polished wood of the small, round table. Kate wonders if her hand might go straight through, should she keep punishing the same spot. 'Abe.'

'To win a million at a game of twenty-one, of course.'

Mabel tosses her eyes, but does not push him for a better answer.

Slam goes her hand. 'Kate.'

To run like the horses in my dreams, Kate's mind insists. She rifles her every thought and memory for other, less secret words, but all else is a whisper by comparison. *To run like the horses. To run like the horses.* It is as if a piano tuner has lifted the lid on the instrument of her brain, and now that she can see the strings, she understands that the internal chant which sounds, as metrically insistent as a gallop, has always been there. She has simply never allowed herself to listen to it before.

'To visit ten places I've never seen before,' she garbles. She catches Abe's eye and is surprised at how dejected he looks. He shrugs and shows her a sad smile, which Kate returns.

'William!' Mabel roars. She is growing more excited with each hand-slam.

William is ready with his answer, though he delivers it with a slow consideration which is completely at odds with the game Mabel has started.

'I am going to work hard enough to ensure I leave more than a name behind for my children,' he says. And Kate's stomach withers and churns, because she knows that those are the truest words any one of them has spoken. She will tell him properly about the baby tonight. She must. She might even tell him about the horses.

William endures the silence around the table for two seconds, possibly three, and then he stands up, whips up Abe's brandy, tosses it back, gasps, and in his best showman's voice says, 'And of course I'm going to make damn sure the Atlas Vulcana Troupe is the best the world has ever known!'

The others burst into applause and cheering.

'You know, it sounds better without the "and,"' Mabel shouts over the noise they are making, just the seven of them, which is fit to wake the hotel's every guest.

'It does?' William replies. 'The Atlas Vulcana Troupe it is, then.' He brandishes Abe's almost empty tumbler, and Kate watches the last dribble of honey-rich liquid swirl around its thickened glass bottom, waiting for it to slop out onto the floor. 'To us.'

'To us,' they echo. As they do, so William's hold on the tumbler slips, and it somersaults downwards, glinting sharply, until it crashes against the cream and brown chequered tiles and shatters.

12.

Paris, France
1900
REFLECTIONS

Later, Kate stands at their hotel-room window and watches the moon drape its eerie light over the distant point of the Eiffel Tower, the street after street of stacked-up houses, the slow-roving river, the unmoving trees, the cleanly swept pavements, the shining statue of Joan of Arc and her wonderful horse. At her back, William snores gently, his arms and legs thrown out among their tangled bedsheets. A valise lies open on the woven rug in front of the hearth, spilling out a disorganised mix of dirty shirts and laundered dresses. On the table beside the fire, five stained teacups sit on saucers flecked with pastry crumbs, unwashed since they breakfasted there this morning. The newspaper has been folded and slotted between two cups. Kate doesn't mind the mess very much when it is contained in a hotel room. A house of her own she would feel differently about, she is sure, but a hotel room is only a passing place; it is closer to a tram stop than a home.

Outside, a lonely horse and cab plods the empty street. Kate pushes the window open a touch and listens to the melancholy clip-clop of its passage. The sound is haunting, amplified as it is against the hushed murmurings of the rest of the sleeping city. She watches it jounce up the Rue des Pyramides towards Rue Saint-Honoré until it vanishes from sight. Then she envisages it shedding its leathers and flying through Paris's boulevards, its velocity and its black coat rendering it invisible in the darkness, the only evidence of its presence the four-beat of its hooves and the silver plumes of its breath.

One of William's snores chokes into a snort and wakes him. She hears him patting the mattress in search of her, then groaning as he sits up, but Kate doesn't turn around. She quite likes the idea that he might see her framed in the window as she is, her nightdress shifting on occasional gusts of air and her hair loose down her back, the moonlight making a spectre of her. She holds her breath and waits for him to speak.

'What are you looking at?' he asks, his voice still tacky with sleep.

'Nothing really.'

'Then come back to bed.'

'No,' she replies. 'It's too beautiful.'

'The nothing?'

'The nothing. Come and see.'

He groans again as he swings his feet to the floor and rises, and Kate wonders if he is getting old. At thirty-six, he might well be. She can't know what it feels like, to have lived twelve whole years longer than she has. Beneath his muscle, his bones could be starting to thin and become brittle; she sees little streams of white dust, falling secretly away.

At the window, he wraps his warm body around her, and the white dust stops falling. William is strong. He will be strong still when she is an old woman and has no desire to lift anything above her head but her plump, wriggling grandchildren.

'I'm sorry I was miserable tonight,' he says, and his voice is a low vibration which moves through his chest and into the back of her ribcage: his very own musical instrument. She presses herself against it.

'You weren't miserable for long.'

'Too long.'

'You are allowed, William. Everyone is.'

This is not the way he sees the world, and she knows it, but the knowledge has never prevented her from offering a different perspective.

He shakes his head, brushing his chin across her shoulder.

'No. It's not fair on you, or the troupe. Nobody was in the wrong.'

'Then what is it?' she murmurs. Naturally, she knows what it is. It is his doubt. It is always his doubt. But she also knows that he won't admit to it unless she invites him to. 'You can tell me.'

His chest expands against her as he heaves in a great deep breath, then slumps away as he releases it. His lungs are an accordion.

'I'm scared, Kate.'

'Of what?'

'Becoming ... redundant.'

She grips his forearms, which are crossed over her stomach. Once, she would have sucked her stomach in at his touch, but they are beyond such diffidence now. She is glad to be beyond it. It reassures her that, whether she is a strongwoman or a dowdy housewife, William will still want to hold her, and she is surprised that she needs that reassurance, but then, why wouldn't she, given that Alice... Oh, how easily Alice might have been she, and she might have been Alice.

Kate is not sure which of them has the better part of their husband.

'You, William, are entirely ... *dundant*.' He laughs quietly into her hairline, making the darker hairs which grow there dance. 'And I won't have you thinking otherwise. There's no time. Don't we have a globe to conquer?'

'We do.'

'Well, then.'

Outside, a bat flitters past the building in a blur of soaring joy.

'How is it you manage to make everything sound so simple?' he asks.

Kate shrugs. 'I don't want anything to be complicated.'

'I didn't realise it was a decision.'

They look out together as another cab glides into view. The horse, this time, is a dapple grey – a perfect reflection of the moon it labours under. Kate wonders if the animal is granted a day off a week. If so, it is more than she gets.

'Sometimes it is,' she answers. 'Sometimes it isn't. But when it is...'

'Yes. I see,' William says. But she's not sure that he does. Not truly. It's about how we respond, she wants to explain. There is so much we can't control, but we can always control our responses, steer ourselves one way or another, improve ourselves in order to improve our situations. It's an understanding she has only lately come to. It's the understanding which made her utter the words she is pretending she cannot remember saying, and which William is refusing to mention.

'I'm going home,' she had said, and a huge, screaming part of her had meant it.

'Let's spend a month here,' she says. 'If the Olympia will have us. And then work our way home. We can fit a few more London shows in, on the way.'

'And then what?'

'I want to be close to Alice's,' Kate replies. 'When the time comes...' She gets no further. William slides his hands down to cup her belly and smiles and smiles. She can see his reflection, ghosted in the window, and she cannot bring herself to smile back.

13.

Abergavenny, Wales
1901
NORA

On a windless early-March day, Kate and William sneak down the lane behind a row of dark terraced cottages towards number seventeen – the home William and Alice shared as newly-weds. As they go, their ankles rick on the loose stones, and they gasp and shush each other, then laugh before shushing each other again. They hold their forefingers up to their lips, like children out to steal milk bottles or hanging apples. They look ridiculous, crouched like stage-criminals so that their heads do not show over the topmost bricks of the walls which mark the ends of long, narrow gardens, hung with flapping white sheets, and grey trousers, and shirts which reach for the clouds. Now and then, they pass coal sheds tall enough to allow them to stand up straight and ease their lower backs, and they pause there for a second or two before bending back into their game. They have come to surprise Nora.

They have come to surprise the other children, too, of course. But with Young Alice and Grace out working now as a kitchen maid and a maid-of-all-work respectively, and Reginald and Ernest already being very grown-up boys of ten and eight, they don't anticipate much of a reception from anyone except Nora and Winifred, both aged four.

They had written ahead to Alice, but had not given her an exact date.

'I don't want to disappoint the girls if we're away longer,' Kate had argued, and William, as was becoming an increasing habit, had acquiesced.

They reach the green wooden gate of number seventeen and William puts a careful finger to the latch. He presses it down ever so gently, but he cannot silence the clunk of its release. They halt, still enthralled by the idea of rushing up the garden towards a window full of shocked faces, but as they do, they hear the high-pitched squeals of two little girls, approaching at full tilt. They have been discovered. William pushes the gate so that it swings slowly open and, as it does, so it reveals all the colour and energy of the world, bundled into two small soft bodies, and hurled, smiling and giggling, down the garden towards them. Instinctively, William and Kate drop onto their haunches and open their arms, and the girls hit them with a thunk: Winifred wrapping her arms around Kate's neck and squeezing tight, and Nora latching her head between her daddy's chin and collarbone and pinning herself to his chest. Just as her mother so often does, Kate thinks.

They are a jumble of words and smiles then, the four of them.

'How did you know we were coming?'

'Look how big you are!'

'We saw you. We were waiting.'

'You're all round and fat.'

'Aren't you surprised we're here?'

Alice follows more sedately down the lawn, running a tea towel over wet hands and grinning wide at the unfolding chaos. Alice, Kate knows, will bring order to the day: she is the quiet safety the children retreat to when they have been exhausted by William and Kate's noise and hurly-burly. Even her manner of walking is calming, so measured are her footsteps, so still is she from the hips up. She is wearing a simple brown dress and a pinafore, twice-knotted around her waist. Likely, she has been cooking. It seems to Kate that she has never yet arrived at this warm, simple house but to find Alice cooking. The sugary smell of a fresh fruit crumble from the oven. The steam rising off a seasoned chicken waiting on a countertop to be carved and plated. Alice keeps a spotless house and beautifully turned-out children, and she manages it all without loosening a strand of the hair she wears always in a neat bun. Now, she tucks the tea towel into the string of her pinafore and lifts her chin to call, 'Well, finally.' Her voice is a cast feather. Outwardly, Alice has the solid build of a woman who might have grown up wrangling sheep with older brothers – her hips and shoulders are wide and sturdy – but everything that comes from within her is as tender and delicate as the curled inside of a rose petal. She is forty-three years old. Greys thread through her straight auburn hair.

'What do you mean?' William calls back, standing.

'We saw you from the top of the lane,' she replies, laugher

142

lilting her words. She lifts a hand and mimes two legs walking with her first and second fingers. 'We've been waiting that long. You're not so much of a surprise as you like to think, Bill.'

The contraction hits Kate full in the stomach, as it always does. She wants to lurch over the impact and vomit, but she holds tight to herself and does not allow it: none of this would ever work if any of them acted like hysterics. And Alice, she forces herself to remember, had him first. He was Alice's Bill long before he was Kate's William.

'All that fuss,' he says, pointing back up the lane, 'and you were watching us all along.'

Winifred nods gleefully. 'You looked silly.'

'I bet we did.' William scoops her up and settles her on his forearm, then indicates that Nora should climb aboard the other arm. He strides off up the garden – his garden – with the two girls balanced like the weights at each end of a barbell. He greets Alice with a kiss on the cheek, then wanders into the house, leaving the two women alone.

Kate stands beside the coal shed, the gate still unlatched behind her, as though she might yet be planning an escape. She watches Alice's approach and finds herself devoid of a single sensible reaction. She might be gawping; it is hard to tell. She feels as though a steam engine is rolling towards her, not a mild and steady housewife of five feet and no inches. They spend so long apart from Alice that, for Kate, each visit feels initially like stepping into the life of a stranger. Or crashing, rather. It settles, she tells herself. It always settles. But at first it is difficult, and especially so today.

'How long, then?' Alice asks, nodding at the precise but proud dome of Kate's stomach as she reaches the bottom of the garden. She is wearing the pregnancy tidily, as she did the first – she insists to any who will listen that this is because she remains active for as long as the baby will allow – and you could hardly tell that she has only seven or eight weeks to go. She had been onstage up until last week, albeit bearing lighter weights.

'I think May,' Kate replies, as hesitantly as a schoolchild answering a mathematics problem. 'Late May.'

'A May baby. She'll be a strong one, then, you watch.'

'Strong?' Kate asks.

'Everything comes back to life in May. The flowers, the animals. So it must be the best time to be born, don't you think?'

Kate hasn't thought about it at all, but she is inclined to agree. Alice, having birthed five healthy children and raised them so effortlessly, must be right.

'I suppose so... What makes you say "she"?'

Alice shrugs. 'Does it feel like a girl?'

'I don't know.'

Kate stares down at the unknowable mound beneath her dress. If she were a good mother, she would know these things. She would say, *Yes, I seem to be carrying high like last time*. Or, *Yes, May really is the perfect time*. But these kinds of sentiments can't seem to find a way to her tongue, and she supposes that can only mean that she is a bad mother to Nora and that, consequently, she will be a bad mother to this new baby, too.

She cannot imagine how she might be a good one, given that she appears only briefly and unexpectedly, then disappears for intervals of months. When she returns, Nora is so much changed that Kate does not know her.

Already she has lost her plumpness, her toddling walk. She moves now with a litheness and grace that is incongruous with her age.

Tonight, Alice will light candles in the front room and Nora and Winifred will spin around in the guttering light and claim that they are dancing a waltz. Their ponytailed hair will sway from side to side, and their cheeks will fill with laughter, and they will seem to float with the bliss of it. But they will not move like twins. Winifred will be freer, flowing instinctively with the song they have begged Alice to sing – an old Welsh song which Kate knows the sounds but not the meaning of, and which Alice delivers in a surprisingly accomplished rasping alto. Nora – a musician too, but, it would seem, a gymnast first – is more decisive about her footing, the shapes she makes across the floor, the positioning of her arms. Despite their twinned upbringing, each girl is her own person. Good on both of you, Kate will think. You keep on being yourselves.

'So are you coming inside, then?' Alice asks now. 'Or am I going to have to bolt that gate?'

Instinctively, Kate turns to consider the open gate: her escape route. She does not need it.

'Oh,' she laughs. 'No. Of course not.'

Alice smiles again and it is not the same smile she showed

William: it is slower, truer. This smile, Kate realises, is just for her. A gift. And she catches it and clutches it to her breast, because anything this woman gives her she wants to treasure.

As they walk, side by side, up the garden, Kate dares to slip her arm through the loop of Alice's and take hold of the other woman's hand.

'She's very happy, isn't she?' she enquires, nodding towards the house as though Nora needs any sort of indication.

Alice nods. 'I think she is, yes.'

'I know she is,' Kate replies. 'Thank you.' They are the smallest words she has ever spoken.

14.

Abergavenny, Wales
1901
MONA

Kate glares up at the ceiling as though, if she thinks hard enough about it, she might persuade it to open up and reveal the heavens to her. Air – that's what she wants now. The chill midnight air. For there is none in here and she cannot breathe. If she turns her head to the left, she can glimpse, between the partly drawn curtains, a thin column of bruised purple-blue sky shot through with an arrow of silvered light. But it is not enough. She wants the roof to be torn off the house, the slates scattered and smashed, the joists and rafters bared, so that she might throw back her head and suck all that is outside into her dry, crumpled lungs. The clouds would moisten them. Right now, if only she could be rid of that roof, she would swallow the moon whole. There is enough space within her, for she is already as round as it is possible to be. The moon would fit into the gap the baby will leave, and then she could float up, up, away from all the decisions she will have to make next. Away from the guilt of delivering another baby who, her father would insist, is destined for damnation. *'Behold, I was brought forth in iniquity, and in sin my mother conceived me. And in sin my mother conceived me.'* Psalm 51:5 stalks her here on Earth. But wouldn't it be nice, she thinks, to watch her babies grow from high above, where she might admire them but do them no harm. She would make a better guardian angel than she does a mother. And that is fortunate, really, because the pain and her inability to breathe are going to kill her soon.

'Kate?' A soft voice threads through the heavy air towards her. It takes a long while, meandering as it must. 'Kate. Can you push again?'

'I can't breathe,' she manages to croak. Her eyes close with the effort. She feels tears leak from their corners and run down towards her jaw, growing cold as they go. Her hair is already wet.

'You can, I promise.' And then, to someone else, 'Go and open the window, far as it will go.'

Kate hears a shuffling as a shadow moves across the room – *thump, thump, thump* – pulls the curtains back across their pole – *csh, csh* – then pushes the windowpane wide. Outside, there is the rush of moving air – like a billowing sheet, whomping in her ears. An owl *hoo-hoo*s then *cree*s away. Her every sense is sharpened, but the fact does not bring the world into relief; rather, it is blunted. So overwhelming is the creaking of hinges in a window frame, or the tilt of a passing owl's feather, or the warm reassurance of a voice, that she can concentrate on nothing but the pain – which is alien and wrong because she cannot run or swim it off, as she usually would. She cannot move. She cannot flee the throbbing waves

148

which thunder towards the shore of her body and crash over it, depositing their shingle agony. That's it, then. She is drowning. That is why she cannot breathe. She does not need to draw the sky down over her; she needs to rise towards it. She clamps her mouth shut and braces her body and kicks, envisaging the moment when she will break the surface of the water and gasp into herself again. Because this is not the Kate she knows, pinned down by a hurt which is buried deeper within her even than her heart. She has never been held down by anything. She kicks again, but her legs cannot move freely. They are wrapped tight.

'Kate, don't kick.' That voice again – so patient and even. As dependable as a cliff face. 'You'll hurt yourself.'

I cannot hurt more than I am now, Kate thinks.

'You can do this. You've done it before.'

Kate begs to differ. This is not a state any body could endure twice over. She has never done this before. At any rate, she can't remember it. But then, her body is playing tricks on her tonight. Float up, it tells her. Plunge down. Kick. Lie still. Open your eyes. Close them. Clench your fists. Release them. She can do nothing right. She must be confusing her mind's intentions, because every thought is chased by a new and opposite one, and each seems just as vital as the last or the next.

Save me, she wants to cry, but she knows that would sound feeble. She has never asked for rescue yet and she won't ask for it now. Listen to that other voice, she urges herself. The one that isn't yours. Follow its instructions. It wants to help.

'Kate, listen,' the voice says, just as gentle. 'It'll soon be time to push again. Are you ready?'

Kate nods. The movement draws more tears from her screwed shut eyes.

'All right. Good girl. Now, after three...'

She heaves in a deep breath and her lungs ache.

'One...'

Kate bunches the sheets up in her fists and throws her head forward and pushes with all her might. The effort brings about a laugh. Her own? She doesn't think so. The voice floats towards her again.

'Always so contrary,' it muses.

Yes, Kate thinks. Always contrary. It's the only way she knows how to exist in this big, noisy world. Contrariness is the armour she wears when she strides into battle – against the troupe, against the audiences, against the training she sat through on hard wooden pews, against the public and their backward ideas about femininity and strength and what it is supposed to mean to be a woman. She likes, when she moves, to recognise her body as an engine of power. She doesn't care a jot if that means she doesn't fit into tiny stays or tight dresses. She would rather have a solid front crawl under her hands than jewels. The last two weeks of her pregnancy have rendered her rotund and useless, and she can hardly think how it would feel to be so weak in normal circumstances. She could not tolerate it.

Outside, the owl shrieks again – *cree* – and Kate wonders, not for the first time and not for the last, how it would be to fly. She lifts her arms and is sure she feels the filaments of feather poking through the skin. She need not swallow the moon if she can grow wings. And yes, she is sure they are breaking through the undersides of her arms now, lengthening, ruffling in the wind the opened window is letting in. If she could just reach the window, she could climb up on the sill, and leap through, and soar away into the dark. What a relief that would be, to feel the air beneath her and the sky above her and to be released from all this ... expectation.

'You're nearly there, Kate,' the voice insists.

Yes, Kate wants to say. I am. I am ready to take flight. She throws out her arms, and hurls her body forwards, and her back feels suddenly damp as she lifts right off the bedsheets, and she opens her eyes to scream and scream through this transformation she is aware of but cannot pinpoint. Whether drowning or soaring into flight, she is on the verge of something momentous, and the world knows it and is building to a crescendo. Alice's voice is clear as a church bell now. 'Well done, Kate,' it chimes. 'You're doing brilliantly.' In the window, the curtains *flap-flap* noisily against the frame. In the corner of the room, someone scuffs their socked feet over the floor in an ebb and flow rhythm: *hish, hush, hish, hush*. On the street outside, two cats bawl over their territory, wailing from octave to octave like deranged sopranos. A door clatters open and *thunk*s shut. A baby keens through another open window. Someone sets three milk bottles down on their doorstep with a *chink, chink, chink*. A low voice murmurs wooing words against the ear of a lover; their footsteps canter over the pavement as they sneak towards the castle, where everyone in Abergavenny knows lovers go to hide. And Kate has opened her mouth to scream it all into silence, but, she realises slowly, no sound is escaping her. She is gaping like a stranded fish, but she is making no noise. She is clenched and strained and unable to move through time as once she did. And then, finally, with a loud wet *thwop*, the baby delivers and Kate sinks away into darkness.

And in the darkness, are the horses.

15.

Abergavenny, Wales
1901
THE RIVER USK

The weather warms of a sudden, and on the first Saturday of the summer, all of Abergavenny pulls their bathing costumes on under their clothes, packs a picnic basket and blanket, and goes down to the River Usk to settle on its banks and eat and swim and play. Grace and Young Alice are released from their duties – 'Only given that your father is home to visit, mind' – and walk home at dawn to join the others. Young Alice brings an apple cake and clips Ernest around the ear when he asks her if she stole it.

'Ow!' he cries, rubbing at his blushing ear. Then, turning on her, from between clenched teeth, 'That really hurt. Mammy must have called you after Alice of Abergavenny!'

It is another story William has told her, and Kate tries not to laugh at the comparison between the sylphlike Young Alice and the fearsome Alice of Abergavenny, who, it was said, lost her lover in the twelfth-century Battle of Baginbun Head and, in bloody revenge, took an axe to seventy prisoners the Normans were holding and single-handedly hurled their mutilated corpses over a cliff edge.

Not quite comparable, then, to the theft of an apple cake and a slap.

'I did not steal it,' Alice says evenly, raising an eyebrow in response to her little brother's anger. 'I made it. Cook said I could 'cause the apples were past their best.' She places it proudly on the kitchen counter and peels the tea towel off with all the care of a magician revealing her finest trick. The others 'ooh' and 'aah' on cue, and she smiles, satisfied. She rewraps it carefully before the Robertses set off towards town.

It is impossible to walk through Abergavenny without passing a church or chapel. There is the Baptist Chapel on Market Street, the second Baptist Chapel on Frogmore Street, the Presbyterian Chapel also on Frogmore Street, the Congregational Chapel on Castle Street, which is neighboured by the Wesleyan Chapel, Holy Trinity Church on Baker Street, and the Primitive Methodist on Victoria Street. There are, perhaps, more pews in Abergavenny than there are backsides to fill them. Especially on a day like this, when all anyone wants to do is step from the dark interiors of their homes or workplaces and out into light.

The Robertses step along Lion Street, avoiding the churches, then cut down past the market building towards the river. Today, the market is quiet. Market day is always a Tuesday, when the stalls are stocked with fresh fish, meat, butter, eggs; on Fridays a fruit and vegetable mart spills over with red apples, soil-spotted potatoes, pink rhubarbs, shining strawberries, fat cabbages, podded peas. Yesterday, Alice came and filled a basket, arranging the different-coloured items into a bright bouquet, which is hooked now over Reginald's aching arm. He had wanted to show his father how strong he is and insisted on carrying the entire picnic by himself. Were he a different kind of boy, he might say something like, 'Do you think I'll make the troupe one day, Father?' But Reginald only waits silently for William to notice his efforts and make the declaration unprompted. He is not rewarded as they traipse through the busy town.

On mild days, Abergavenny defies its smallness with its bustle. The Corn Exchange and the adjoining Town Hall see suited men shaking hands over trade deals or the agreement of dates for orchestral shows or the next cattle market. Queues form outside the banks and the post office, the haberdashery and the barber's. On the edges of town, the bang-and-grind operations of the corn mills and lime works and maltings and engine works echo against the quiet hills. Further out still, the iron foundries clang and smoke. And over it all, the four-dialled Town Hall clock tick-tocks, tick-tocks, reminding every passing person that nothing changes. *No-thing, chan-ges*.

'I don't want anything to eat,' Ernest announces as they walk. 'I only want to go swimming.'

'We'll have to see what the water's like,' Alice replies.

'Will we, Dad?' Ernest asks, lifting his head to William.

Listening from two steps behind, Kate wants to clip his head, just as Young Alice did earlier, for that deferral; her breath catches as she resists the temptation. Say it, she urges William silently. Tell him.

'Yes,' William answers. 'Like your mother says.'

155

And Kate exhales. Good. It has become apparent over the last few weeks that she had not been entirely sure what kind of father William is. Sometimes, she considers, he is too lenient. Other times, he is distant. But when he stops dreaming and planning and engages with his children – setting them on his knee to read before bed, or teaching them weightlifting tricks in the garden – he is fair but fun. Warm and patient. With them, he remembers not to lose his temper. Kate wonders whether he remembers not to lose it with Alice, too.

The riverside is already crowded when they arrive, so they stroll along the bank to a bend where the water runs faster and deeper. Kate inhales the slightly sulphurous stink of the water, caused, she supposes by its flow over ancient layers of mud and rotted reeds. It smells of her childhood. Often as a girl she had crept down here and plunged into the water, returning home with dripping hair to disapproving looks from her mother. Not that it was the boyish activities Kate insisted on pursuing that she disliked – as long as they were kept private, of course – so much as the ruination of the dresses Kate tore and stretched and muddied beyond saving. Kate smiles to herself at the memory. Her parents' attitude towards her choice of career has unstiffened as her fame has grown and she has brought no trouble to their doorstep – which, incidentally, she has been invited to cross without the attendant threat of a lecture on her 'silliness' in recent years. It is not only 'through the eyes of our Lord' that they watch over their daughter now. Indeed, they even have newspaper clippings of her reviews and interviews folded into a kitchen drawer cleared especially for the purpose. But then she has said nothing to them of Nora and Mona, her matching dark-eyed girls, and so they have no grounds to think themselves so very badly disgraced.

Disgrace: Kate can hardly think of such a word being spoken in the same sentence as the names of her gleaming little pearls. But people are so often wrong about so many things, and she knows how the talk would go. In Abergavenny, Kate is a colleague of William's and the children are Alice's. In London or Paris or Edinburgh, Kate is William's sister and there are no children. It is as simple and complicated as that. And so it must remain – she understands.

Unless.

Unless she could look forward to a time when she would turn her back on the stage. The lights, she thinks, grow dimmer with every month she spends apart from her children.

In the weeks since Mona's birth, she has been working up the courage to ask Alice about the *unless* that, more and more, she cannot keep from her mind. But whether bustling around the kitchen late at night or pegging out the washing with the sunrise, Alice is never still, and Kate has not brought herself to interrupt the business of her life with such a hideous indulgence as a conversation about her feelings. That Alice can even stand to look at her – this woman who has stolen her husband's heart and flaunted his babies in her very own home – is too much. And yet, Kate can think of no one else to ask in the absence of Mabel. It is not a conversation she can have with William.

As Alice and Kate flap the blanket flat and set out the picnic, William takes Grace, Young Alice, Reginald, and Ernest to paddle in the river. Winifred and Nora play nearby, engrossed in an intricate skipping game and one another. Their brand-new Mona, Kate sets down on the blanket under an umbrella, where she smiles and grabs at shadows with tiny creased hands.

Kate had never suspected she could find delight in observing shade falling across a baby's skin. But then, she had never expected that damn *unless* would skulk into her mind either.

The two women sit, one either side of Mona, and begin to unwrap the fruits, breads, and cheeses from the basket near their feet. Kate takes a deep in-breath, and, finding herself still too cowardly to speak, sighs it away.

'Well,' Alice says, her hands and eyes occupied with the food, 'that was a telling sigh. What's wrong?'

Kate opens her mouth to deny that anything is wrong, then closes it again with a small laugh. She must be truly translucent. Alice seems able to see her thoughts as easily as though they were one of those creatures Kate had watched in the aquarium at the Exposition Universelle. Though they would not prove as interesting as a sea turtle or a shark. Kate is a simple goldfish in a tank.

'Am I so obvious?' she asks, lifting a red apple and turning it in her hand to watch the sunlight shine on the peel.

Alice is too considerate to answer such a question directly. 'I think perhaps that you can't hide your honesty, and I'm glad of it. I don't think I could have liked you otherwise.'

Kate's neck grows hot. She hadn't imagined for a minute that Alice would ever come to like her. Tolerate, perhaps, but never like. Then again, she hadn't imagined she would like Alice, either, and undeniably she does: Alice is serene and tender and she doesn't give a damn what anyone else's opinion of her amounts to. It is that Kate admires about her most – the quietness of her confidence. Given the fair hair and light eyes the Roberts children sport, it is apparent to anyone who might care to stick their nose in that Nora and now Mona, with their big brown eyes and brunette curls, are not of the same parentage. Alice has never yet complained of meddlesome talk or unpleasant looks in the town. That's not to say, though, that she has not endured them. Kate studies her face as she leans over the picnic basket and carefully retrieves Young Alice's apple cake. Her delicate nose and mouth are framed by cheeks made wide not by jowls but by a firm, just-washed-in-cold-water look, which they owe to a natural rosy colour. Her eyes have a kindly downward bent, accentuated by the fan of lines at their corners, which do not age her but only give the impression that she is always on the verge of laughter. And perhaps she is. Perhaps she finds all of this entirely ridiculous. Or perhaps she feels she must laugh to hide the misery of her situation. Kate's stomach plunges at the thought that it might be the latter, but she cannot ask whether or not Alice is happy. She cannot bring herself to listen for the answer, knowing how instrumental she has been in shaping it. And she suspects that Alice would not offer a true insight in any case. This woman – this brave, beautiful woman – must surely have more locked up inside her than Kate could ever guess at. How else would she cope with having her wandering husband and his lover under her roof? Stoicism is the lifeblood of Mrs Alice Roberts.

Kate keeps her eyes on the rotating apple. 'I saw a house,' she begins. 'In Bristol. I told...' No. She does not want to mention William's name in this. 'I thought you would like it. There'd be plenty of space for the children and there's a wonderful garden, which I thought you might like to plant, given how much you enjoy your flowers. There's a little stream at the bottom, too, and...'

She trails off, not knowing how to say, 'I would like to buy it for you,' without sounding so tremendously pontifical that Alice would no longer be able to deny the urge to slap her raw.

'And I thought, if we ... owned it, that I might be able to be there more, to spend more time with the children and... I don't know. Do you think it's an awful idea?'

Alice takes a moment to contemplate the proposal. 'I don't,' she begins, and Kate presses her lips shut as she waits to discover what will follow the 'but' she can already hear on the air. 'I think it's a wonderful idea.' She really has been badly treated here, then. She wouldn't want to leave her home otherwise. Not Alice. 'But that's not the question you're having such difficulty posing, is it?'

'No,' Kate concedes. 'Only part of it. You're right.'

'Comes with age,' Alice jokes, and they share a quiet smile.

'All right. I just... Do you think it's wrong that I leave her? Them?' The words leave Kate's lips in too fast a jumble and Alice is forced to spend a moment untangling them.

'You don't want to go back on tour,' she says. It is not a question.

'No,' Kate replies. 'Yes. I don't know. I do, but I don't want to be without them either. And I thought, in Bristol...'

'It would be easier to come and go, see more of them.'

'Yes. And that I might only do shows in London, maybe, but then...'

Alice reaches out and cups her hand over the apple Kate is spinning and spinning.

'So what would be the problem with that?'

Kate glances towards the river's edge, where William sits now with his trouser legs rolled up and paddles his feet. Reginald sits beside him, demonstrating his manly disinterest in splashing about, while Grace, Young Alice, and Ernest stampede over the stones and reeds to flick water at each other and shriek. The water arches over them in parasols of silvered light. Already, they are submerged to their waists. Their clothes are wet-darkened. Their squeals blend into the choir of all the other children up and down the river, whose shouts and hoots are accompanied by the laughter of siblings and parents and friends. How could Kate not want more of this?

'William... Well, Atlas – he's not so... I'm earning all the money,' Kate admits.

'Oh,' Alice replies. 'I see.'

They fall into silence, Kate and Alice, Alice and Kate,

together with the knowledge, finally communicated and understood, that it is they alone who must maintain the fine balance of this strange, wonderful life of theirs. On the river, William and the children play happily.

The roar for help sounds so impossibly close and desperate that Kate, stirring from her catnap, thinks it part of a nightmare she has already mostly forgotten. She shoots up into a sitting position, knocking Mona's umbrella so that it rocks on its canopy and causing the skin between her legs to pinch. She is still sore there. She has teased William, in passing whispers, that he is not to touch her for a year. As she squints into the glare of sunlight, the cry comes again.

'Help!'

The word is odd, exclaimed in actual terror. Inadequate. Particularly when issued in a child's voice. She leaps up off the picnic blanket and begins to race towards the riverbank before her sight has readjusted to the brightness. Electric spots of pink and blue swim around her eyes. Alice and the children have formed a crowd at the water's edge. William, she notices, is already in motion. He sprints along the bank.

'Hold on,' he bellows.

All the squeals and laughter of before have stopped. There is only the repeated call for help – a boy's voice, shivering with fear – and William's response. And beyond that, the birdsong, which is louder now in the comparative stillness of a day struck by sudden disaster.

Reaching the others, Kate looks in the direction which has

them all transfixed and sees, further along, in a reedy bend in the river, two boys tangled and flailing. At that point, the bank is a sheer drop of perhaps six feet. The one boy is shouting, as rhythmically as a clock: 'Help, help.' The other is slumped over his arm, dropping lower and lower into the water as the first boy's strength fails. His other arm is hooked through a root which bows out of the bank. He is maybe ten years old. His friend is just conscious, but fading.

'Look after Mona,' Kate says, grabbing Grace's shoulder and pointing back towards the blanket where her daughter lies. Grace nods and spins around to retrieve the baby, switching from child to woman as quickly as she had switched the other way that morning.

William has almost reached the spot where the boys struggle now. He flings himself to the ground and onto his stomach and, angling his hips to hang his torso over the river, reaches down for the first boy.

'Grab on,' he instructs. 'I'll pull you up.'

William cannot reach unless the boy climbs up a little and lifts his arm, but the boy is shaking his head. No. He does not trust this stranger to haul him to safety. Why should he? He doesn't know how strong William is. He doesn't know that his body weight is only a tiny percentage of what William lifts for training, let alone a performance. William is only a reddening face and a blond walrus moustache, looming over him, and the boy is frightened.

'He's strong,' Kate calls as she catches up to William. 'Let him lift you.'

'I can't,' the boy stutters. 'I can't let go.'

But as he speaks the words, his grip on his friend loosens and the second boy is dragged abruptly downriver. He slips apart limply, like an old jumper cast into the flow. He must finally have lost consciousness. The first boy lets out a howl, but Kate cuts it short before he descends into mindless panic.

'Stop!' she shouts. The boy's eyes roll loosely towards her. 'Now listen. Keep holding on tight. I'll get your friend and then I'll come back for you. Do you understand?'

The boy nods.

'William.' Kate snaps her attention round to where he lies on the grass. 'Follow me along the bank.' She is already unlacing her shoes.

'Kate, you–'

'Along the bank, William,' she insists, before he can launch a real protest. Then, slinging her shoes aside, she sits down on the grass, shuffles on her backside to the edge of the drop, and pushes herself off. The water, against her sun-warmed skin, is glacial. She gasps as she begins to wade down the river, the water rushing around her waist and her skirt ballooning around her. Between her legs, at the place where Mona tore free, she feels a sharp new pressure, and she thinks that perhaps her healing flesh has ripped again. For now, though, the cold is numbing it somewhat and she is able to sweep down the river after the floating boy. He is a dark shape on the surface: a lost picnic blanket, wrapping around and around itself as it travels further from her. He is sinking lower. Realising that she will not catch up to him wading like this, Kate ducks her shoulders below and assumes a clumsy front crawl. In her soaked clothes, it is heavy and difficult, but with the surge of the water behind her, she manages to slop after the child. She grabs for his ankle. Misses. Grasps his icy toes and holds tight. He is bleeding from his temple, she notices: the blood sticks in his sandy hair. He must have dived in and struck a stone on the shallow bed. With her other hand, she takes his ankle and begins to haul him in towards her like a fisherman's netted catch. It is awkward, with cold and shaking hands, but eventually she draws him against her chest and, clutching him there, kicks for the bank, where William awaits her, arms outstretched.

A swarm of people, led by Alice and the children, has followed him, but they stand back at a respectable distance. They know better than to interfere with a rescue.

Though William is on his stomach again, the drop is just too far for him to reach the boy and pluck him up. Kate can see that. She cradles the boy and, positioning him carefully, props one hand between his shoulders and the other against his backside. Then, on the count of one, two... she drops her head, raises her arms, and lifts him vertically over her head with a clench-jawed grunt.

William snatches him from her and sets him down on the grass.

'Alice!' he says, though Alice is already leaning over the lad, checking his breathing, tipping him onto his side.

'The other boy,' Kate orders, and she and William take off back up the river, he running, she swimming.

When they reach the first boy, he is shuddering under the burden of his own sobs.

'My brother?' he asks, his face blotched and swollen and desperate.

'He's fine,' Kate says, her breath heaving. 'Do you want to go and see him?'

The boy nods sadly.

'All right. Then I'm going to crouch down a bit, and I want you to put your feet onto my shoulders so that I can push you up to William. Do you see William?' She points, and the boy nods, faster this time. Now that he has been told his brother is well, his body is submitting to the cold. Kate has seen something similar in the theatres: the adrenaline leaving the body; the shutdown. 'William is a famous strongman. He's going to keep you safe. Now, feet on my shoulders, and I'll push you up to him. Can you help me with that?'

Another nod.

'Then let's try it.'

It is easier with this boy, though he is the larger. He clambers onto her shoulders, as instructed, with his wet, slapping feet. She loops her hands around his ankles to steady him, and, counting them into synchronicity, they thrust up, up, until they are both standing as tall as they can and William is able to scoop the boy apart.

As his weight is lifted free, Kate eases back down into the water. She is bleeding, she is sure, from between her legs, and she does not want to scrabble up and flop onto the grass in full view of all those people fussing around the two boys.

Especially not if her skirts are stained. Instead, chest pumping, she shoves her way twenty feet or so further up the river, to a place where the bank has been shaped by generations of feet into a rough set of steps, and there, she climbs up out of the water.

Alice is waiting for her, the picnic blanket held open for Kate to step into. As she does, Alice wraps it tightly about her and speaks into her ear.

'That was much too soon after the baby,' she says. 'Are you quite well?'

'Yes.' Kate nods. 'A little sore, but well enough. Just, a rest...'

Alice hums her agreement as she rubs Kate's back and upper arms to warm her again. 'Yes. From all things perhaps.'

'Perhaps,' Kate replies.

'Let's go home so you can change, then. Come on. The boys' parents will be with them soon. They'll be fine.'

Kate allows herself to be led apart from the crowd, the picnic blanket still drawn around her like a shawl. As they go, she feels a tugging at the red and tan striped wool and, thinking it caught on some scrubby grass, turns to pull it loose. The girl clinging to the end blenches, as though expecting to be hit, before remembering herself and standing taller. She is dainty, pigtailed, pigeon-toed. She has brilliant ginger hair and an unfortunate frown line between her eyes which makes her look angry. She fidgets the blanket between her fingers as Kate and Alice stare down at her, but does not let it go.

'You're her, aren't you?' she whispers.

'Who?' Kate asks, since it is Kate the child is staring at.

'Vulcana! I know you are. You're the strongwoman.'

Kate exchanges a glance with Alice. 'Oh!' she whispers back, crouching down to bring herself level with the girl, who is maybe six or seven years of age. 'That's right. I am. But listen, can we keep that between ourselves for now? I'd like it to be our secret.'

The girl nods and grins a wide gummy grin, evidently pleased to be sharing a confidence, and Kate feels bad for thinking any part of her appearance unfortunate. She's a lovely, sunny little thing, really. She is proud looking. Kate would like to tell her so, but she can't think how to phrase it.

'Our secret,' says the girl, hooking her finger and holding it aloft so that Kate can loop hers through it in a pact. Kate obliges and the two shake.

'Thank you,' Kate says. 'I appreciate that. You see, it's my day off from being a strongwoman today.'

The girl frowns again, adamant that Kate is mistaken. 'It can't be. You got those boys out of the river, I saw you, and that took strength.'

Kate meets the claim with amused silence. Outsmarted by a child. The girl continues, undeterred.

'Can you tell me another secret?' She is looking down at her own grubbied shoes now. She pulls the wool of the blanket tight then releases it, so that it makes a soft clapping sound, like that of a bird's wing when it passes in flight.

'If I know it,' Kate promises.

'Can you tell me how to be brave like you?' The girl's voice catches, and Kate wonders what she can possibly have seen in her short life which might cause her to pose such a question. She cannot ask. It is not her place. She drops onto her knees and puts her palms gently around the girl's upper arms; the girl stiffens. 'Please?' the girl says, without raising her eyes. The sun shines from behind her lowered head, lighting her hair to gold, and Kate wishes she could see herself. How perfectly luminous she is.

'Look up,' Kate says. The girl complies. '*That's* how.'

The frown line deepens into a cleft. 'What's how?'

'That's how to be brave,' Kate explains. 'By always holding your head up high, and by always sticking to what you believe.'

'And that's it?' The cleft smooths away.

'That's it,' Kate confirms. As the girl takes off skipping, Kate wonders when she lost sight of that simple truth, and how she might find her way back to it.

16.

Abergavenny, Wales
1901
MEASUREMENTS

Kate is standing, arms held straight out to her sides, in a room as close and hot as a glasshouse. She is balanced on a stout wooden stool, like a poodle at the circus. Her arms ache. She clamps her eyes and mouth shut as, with the drop, stretch, pull, and pinch of a measuring tape, she is reduced to her dimensions.

'Height,' the mousy man fretting around her calls out. He has a shiny bald pate she had wanted to laugh at as she stepped up, as instructed, onto the stool. Ever the show-woman, she had managed to round her smirk into a look of friendly innocence when he eyed her accusingly. 'Five feet and three ... no, *four* inches.'

In the corner, a pencil scratches across a sheet of paper.

The tape is looped about her cranium. 'Head.'

The man's voice echoes in the small, bare space, and Kate waits for the dread moment when he will move his hands around her waist and draw the measuring tape tight. The nooks and dark angles of her, only William is permitted to touch. She is tactile enough, in appropriate circumstances, but she cannot tolerate the enforced intimacy of this procedure. This jittery, sweating man will want to measure her wrists, her hips, her thighs. She can already feel his touch spidering over her skin and she shudders at the expectation of it.

'Head is … twenty-one inches.'

Twenty-one inches of what? If a phrenologist were to run his hands over her skull, would he discover a bump above her ear indicating a destructive nature? Or a particular contour revealing a propensity for aggression? Is she made up of ideality or conscientiousness or some uglier traits? She wouldn't really like to know. She has always felt certain that her character must be shaped by her experiences and her decisions, by her own will, not some accident of design.

'Wrists,' the man barks finally.

Kate lowers her arms and studies the hands which protrude from her five-and-three-quarter-inch wrists. Dusted still – from the photos she had postured for, with the weights drawn up in a curl – they appear to be caught in a slant of broken sunlight, the ruddy skin illuminated in map-like patches. The palms are square. The fingers a little too stubby perhaps, and blunt-tipped, for the nails have been clipped as short as practicality. She would like to sport the slim piano fingers she sees on the dancers in the theatres, but it cannot be. Her hands are her tools, not her ornamentation. They are not to be adorned with glinting rings, nor the nails shone with lavender oil. She does not know how many inches her palms measure, but she knows how many pounds they can lift and how many more pounds they can earn. She knows that when they grip the bar, they are steely and unyielding. She knows how often they yearn to reach for William's chest, and how they sometimes flinch with the memory of setting hymn books out along the pews in her father's chapel, and how it feels when she slots a little finger into the baby's mouth and lets her suckle. These hands, she wants to say, have cradled life.

But the measurer has moved on. Her extremities are of no import to him.

Kate remembers a time when she had her palms read in Brighton. The woman had called herself a chiromancer, and spoken in all sorts of terms Kate did not understand, explaining about Kate having fire hands, the Mercury line and the Girdle of Venus, tridents and stars and something called the Luna mount and the plain of Mars. Kate, too excitable to stay still and pay attention, had taken little from it. She had, however, listened for the terms she knew: the heart line, the head line, and the life line. What she noticed was that each of these three lines on her right hand was deeper and longer than those on her left. Did that mean that her odds were split? That she might live a long life full of love, but that she might equally live a short life devoid of it? It was the only explanation she could envisage, so she did not ask the chiromancer to confirm or deny it. There are things she does not want to know.

'Waist,' cries the little man. In the corner, the pencil scribbles out the five letters. 'Twenty-five inches.'

'Thighs,' he announces, and Kate cringes. Is it really necessary? But she knows that it is, at least in the eyes of the journalists. This is not the first time she has been measured up, so that her particulars can be printed alongside a magazine interview where her words account for one quarter of the copy and some man's description of her claims the other three. She doubts it will be the last. 'Twenty-five inches.'

'Ankles,' says the man. 'Seven and three-quarter inches.' And Kate imagines what it would be like to write her own magazine article. She would preach the same message, of course: that girls should take vigorous exercise as often as boys; that brisk movement is as beneficial for the mind and spirit as it is for the heart and lungs. She cannot understand why any sensible person would assume otherwise. But there would be no concentration on the apparently startling fact that Kate looks just like a woman – a fascination, it seems, amongst the male journalists. And in place of the list of measured inches, she would write:

Head – packed full of dreams

Wrists – strong enough to allow me to climb trees

Waist – expanded to grow a beautiful daughter

Thighs – powerful enough to propel me through water

Ankles – sturdy enough to support a full-grown man, or to hold up while kicking would-be attackers.

Those are the facts girls and women need to know. The numbers she thinks bald and reductive, and besides, they might change as readily as an opinion. Kate need only eat a large dinner to ruin those carefully recorded figures.

'I shan't stand for this,' she says finally. Stepping down from her stool, she strides across to the little desk in the corner, whips up the paper, and, through the measurer's spluttered protestations, proceeds to tear it into tiny squares and toss them over her shoulder.

It is as she makes that throwing motion, flicking her arm backwards, that Kate gasps into waking. She is in the box room at the back of Alice's cottage. The room is thick with darkness, except for a finger of moonlight, visible through the open curtains, which points down the garden towards the coal shed. Kate sits up. The dream was entirely real, right up to the point where she protested and tore up the paper – that part she had only wished.

She rises from bed, pulls the blankets neatly back up to meet the pillow, straightens her nightgown, and drags on a pair of William's socks in order to go down to the kitchen and fetch a drink. Her tongue is bloated and dry. She wonders if those little boys have managed to drop into sleep tonight after their ordeal in the river or whether their nightmares are taunting them.

Across the landing and down the stairs, she holds her breath against the giveaway creaks of the floorboards. She is not sure why she wants to be alone, only that she does. She rounds the bottom of the staircase and, down the hallway, spots a shimmy of light moving around the kitchen. She stops, one foot placed in front of the other, as if she is about to start a race. Waits. The candle bobs towards the mounting hiss and whistle of a nearly-boiled kettle. Kate hears the candle being thunked down onto the counter. She spins on her heels, meaning to creep back up the stairs, but of course the traitorous floorboards betray her and as she pauses so does the movement in the kitchen.

The throbbing beat of a heart, and then, 'Kate?'

'Yes,' she replies. 'Yes, I...' She rotates again and pads down the hallway to the kitchen door, where she lingers, neither in nor out of the room.

'Tea?' asks the figure, which is a hunched pillar of blackness, made near-invisible by the pinpoint light of the candle.

'If you're making,' Kate replies.

'Couldn't sleep either?'

'Not well.'

'That was quite a day.' Alice lifts the kettle and tips it over two waiting teacups. The gurgle of water leaving the spout and hitting the china is loud. Steam wrings the oxygen from the air.

'It's not just that,' Kate ventures.

'I know. I've been thinking about what you said.'

'About Bristol?'

'About Bristol, yes.' Alice shuffles over to the table and sets down the cups. She indicates them with a jut of her head, and finally Kate steps into the room. It's like the garden gate again; she cannot seem to move freely over the boundaries of Mrs Roberts' house. She scrapes out a chair opposite Alice and seats herself, the two women moving in mirror image as they settle themselves, lift their cup, sip, exhale. 'And,' Alice continues, 'about the money.'

'I shouldn't have mentioned it.'

'Why ever not?' Alice replies. 'It's nothing to be embarrassed about.'

'No, but...'

'William would be?'

Kate holds her cup against her bottom lip and nods over it. A sudden gush of fresh blood escapes from between her legs and soaks into the rag she has stuffed into her knickers. She fidgets against the wet heat.

'Well, more fool him,' Alice snips. 'He's always been too prideful.'

At this, Kate cannot help but laugh. '*Yes.*'

Alice smiles in return. 'Nothing changes,' she muses. 'But here's what I've been thinking: things *can* change, for *you*. You're in control here, Kate. You can decide what you want to happen next. You can go back to London or Holland or Spain or wherever it is you're planning to go, and you can do your shows, and you can come back and visit the girls as often as the schedule allows. Or you can buy the house in Bristol, and stay in it, and send William off to perform his own shows with the troupe. Or ... well, there are a hundred different ways you could shape this, Kate. But it has to be you. You have to make a choice.'

Kate takes another slow sip of her tea and listens to the shifting and moaning of the house. Downstairs, the windows are all closed, and the thick stone walls silence the birds and the foxes fleeting by outside. The grey town smokes on, unobserved. For Kate and Alice, there is only the wood of the floorboards and the joists, resting and clicking, and the breaths of the sleeping bodies upstairs: William, Grace, Young Alice, Reginald, Ernest, Winifred, Nora, Mona. Her babies, Kate thinks, closing her eyes. Her lullaby girls. How can she leave them again? And yet, how can they become a family of ten, all screaming and dancing and laughing and eating and fussing and crying under a single roof? Neither scenario seems possible.

Life in the theatres has taught her that a thousand circumstances and scenarios she could not have witnessed through the obscured windows of her father's church are, in a hundred different towns and cities, already a reality. But to share a husband with another woman, openly, is inconceivable. Shame prickles around the base of her skull, and she shudders: logically, she is certain she ought not to be ashamed of these incredible people, and yet, she cannot help but see herself perched on a damp wooden pew, a small girl again, entirely alone in the church, waiting for the sensation in her gut to resolve itself into some variety of being who has come to drag her into eternal darkness.

'But I don't know what the choices are,' Kate admits. She is careful to keep the lilt of a whine from her voice.

'Do you want to hear what I think?' Alice asks. Even now, in the privacy of some small time after midnight, she is being too generous. It cannot have been the same for Alice and William as it is for Kate and William, Kate concludes. The passion must have been missing. For had it been present, Alice would clamber over the table now, while she has her chance, and claw Kate's eyes clean out of her head. She would not be able to do otherwise. It is what Kate would do, were the situation reversed. She would become a perfect banshee.

'Yes,' Kate says. 'Tell me.'

Alice fixes Kate with a long look. 'You're not going to like it,' she warns, but Kate urges her on with a shrug which says, *Still, I must hear it*. 'All right,' Alice continues. 'Seems to me you only have two choices.'

Two. How can there only be two? Kate cannot stand the duality of just a pair. Stay or leave. Him or her. This or that. They are ghastly oversimplifications. Even in William's marriage, there are not two but three.

Kate waits for Alice to reach her conclusion, and when she does, she speaks the exact words Kate had hoped she wouldn't.

'Motherhood,' she says, 'or stardom.'

17.

London, England
1901
PLANS

The night they go to see Marie Lloyd at the Hammersmith Palace of Varieties, it rains and rains. Kate and William listen to it hammering against the roof of their hansom cab as they jangle through the streets, watch it flicking in arcs off the cab's two enormous wheels. The driver and his bay gelding were soaked through when they collected 'Miss Vulcana and Mr Atlas' from the foyer of their hotel – the driver's top hat and the horse's rump shone with it – and Kate had slipped two shillings into her skirt pocket to tip him with later. She intends to drop them onto the seat when she gets out and only motion to the driver from the pavement. She does not want him to fuss about the amount and feel he cannot accept it. After all, whose job is harder than his? Winter has hit London suddenly and purposefully, as though bearing a grudge. Night after night, water roars down drainpipes to rush along the kerbs. By day, jackdaws and pigeons stumble through rough skies. The wind whistles and shrieks. And this man and his horse must stand out in it, waiting on people, and she does not envy them the chore.

'I fancy driving a hansom cab one day,' Kate says, staring out through the side window.

'Whatever for?' William asks.

Kate shrugs. 'Just to see what it's like. I want to see what everything is like.'

Isn't that the truth? Alice had helped her understand it. They had talked for hours, and what they had come gradually to realise, as they sipped tea in the kitchen dark that night, was that neither one of them wanted to be the other.

'I'm a home bird,' Alice had said. 'I don't want anything more than my garden and my own bed and the children's laughter. Maybe a good cup of tea. But you're different, Kate. You're ambitious.'

Alice was right. Kate wants all sorts of things besides those on Alice's modest list. Much as she misses her children – and she does, in such a way that she carries a permanent pain in her abdomen now which she refuses to mention to William since she knows it has no physical cause – she is so excited by their newest plans that she has barely slept all week. Instead, she has watched London go about its inky rage through the hotel-room window, and wondered whether she should join in.

'What do you want to see most?' William asks as they slow to round a corner.

He has always enjoyed playing this game with her: drawing forth all her fancies and wild hopes so that he can set himself the challenge of seeing her fulfilling them. And while she doesn't entirely understand it, Kate is not an opponent in the game but a team mate. Didn't she vow that she would convince this man to show her the world? She sees no reason to cease convincing him now. The first point on her list, which she did not offer to Alice in a fair exchange, has surely always been 'William'.

'The earth from far above,' she replies. 'Farther even than when we rode the Ferris wheel.' It's not an answer she has thought about particularly. She only wants to test him, as she still seems to feel she must. Early on, she had begged him to divorce Alice so that they could be together freely and, when he had flatly refused, she had squalled and broken like a thunderstorm, demanding impossibilities in place of the one possibility he had denied her. As the years have turned, that protest has grown quieter. And now, here it is: a throwaway sentence muttered against the rattle of a bouncing hansom cab.

'As in, from a hot air balloon?' William asks.

'Perhaps.' She does not miss that angry girl who fumed for what she wanted. She does not miss her because she has not gone. It is only that Kate has started to tame her, in order to put her to better use. 'Wouldn't it be wonderful, to wing about like a bird?'

'I'm not so sure,' William replies. 'I'd sooner be on solid ground, I think.'

'And where's the adventure in that?' Kate asks, turning away from the window view and shifting closer to William to rest her head on his shoulder.

William takes up her hand and, bringing it to his mouth,

gives it one of his scratchy kisses. 'We've had plenty of adventure, haven't we?'

Kate smiles. 'We have. And there will always be another.'

'Is that so?'

She feels the words rumbling through William's body, but the tone is unfamiliar, and she cannot tell if he is being wishful or faltering. She lifts her head to check his expression and finds him in profile, a small smile tweaking his lips and his eyes fixed emptily on the falling rain.

The horse trots onto King Street, and rather than listen to his hollow steps, Kate says, 'Do you think she'll seem changed, Marie?'

'She's only been away a few months,' William replies.

'Yes. But still.'

Though they have made a habit of seeing Marie Lloyd whenever she and they are in London since that first performance at Drury Lane, tonight their intention is to ask her for information. The other side of the world is a long way to go without the first inkling of what they'll encounter when they get there.

As they proceed down King Street, they see a line of figures, black hatted and coated, huddled along the pavements in pairs or threes. They hear the driver slowing his horse with a kindly, 'Whoa.' William half stands to push the trapdoor in the roof up and speak to him.

'What is it?' he asks, squinting against the weather.

Kate hears the driver's response as though from a distance. His voice is low and sooty. 'It's been the same all week, sir.

Turning people away every night. Everyone wants to see Marie Lloyd since she's back.'

'I see,' says William. 'Thank you.'

The man grumbles in response, though not bad-naturedly. He is, Kate can tell, a man of few words. She remembers to slip the shillings from her pocket as they slow to a halt outside the theatre.

They duck out of the cab – William followed by Kate – and scurry towards the front of the line, William opening an umbrella as they go. They do not need to join the queue. So long as they write ahead, Marie leaves instructions at the ticket booth to let them through. Sometimes, too, the staff recognise Vulcana or Atlas in spite of their ordinary dress and wave them inside. Tonight, however, they are compelled to stand in the rain as a young usher wearing a look of mild panic lifts bouquets of white roses from the entrance doors and carries them away by the armful.

'Sorry,' they hear him mutter as he rushes past the ticket booth. 'I can't clear them quick enough.'

William smirks and bumps his shoulder against Kate's. 'They're certainly glad to have her home.' There is a glint in his eye then that makes her truly believe for the first time that they will do it. That they will sail to the other side of the world and see what it has to offer them.

She jostles him back. 'Do you think she'll do "Feminine Moods and Tenses"?' she says, biting at her lip to hide her amusement. William is irritated by that song and they both know it.

'I shouldn't doubt it,' William replies.

'Good.' She loops her arm through his and leans closer. 'Then I promise you a kiss for every time she winks during the rendition. Will that ease the pain?'

William stands a tad straighter. 'It might go some way towards it.'

'Two then,' Kate replies. 'But that's my best offer.'

'Then I'll take it,' he laughs, as the usher returns, perspiring, to gather another pile of flowers.

'Sorry, sir, miss,' he says, inclining his head as though to royalty. 'Do you have your tickets?'

'They're at the booth,' William replies.

'Yes, of course. Step through, then, please.'

To Kate's undisguised delight, Marie does in fact perform 'Feminine Moods and Tenses' later that evening. Kate counts five winks, though William swears to seven, and possibly eight. They tease over this as they wait in the foyer for Marie. They know well enough that she always leaves through the front of the theatre, to better interact with her audiences, and when she does, they are going to invite her out for drinks. They have already picked out a venue a little way up King Street, anticipating a long night of laughs and scandal.

On this occasion, however, Marie does not pause to greet them, as usually she would. Upwards of half an hour after the show closes, she sweeps through the foyer, pursued by two harried-looking theatre workers. Her hair is loosed at the back and needs re-pinning. Her eyes are black.

'Marie?' Kate says as she passes. She does not call out, only breathes her friend's name, for close to, Marie looks shocking indeed. Her skin is grey and pinched. Her lips are cracked. Her dress seems ill-fitted as she strides towards the front doors, though Kate knows full well that Marie makes her own dresses and so it cannot be the wrong size. It is as though someone has collected up all the elements of Marie Lloyd but failed to arrange them into a convincing whole. What could possibly have caused Marie to come apart like that, Kate does not want to suppose. She only knows that it must be something terrible.

William takes half a step forward, as though Marie has collapsed and he is preparing to catch her. And it is then that Marie, who remains steady if tentative on her feet, sees them.

'Oh, dears!' she cries, and her voice is a muted version of itself. 'I didn't see you there. Listen, I'm rushing. Can you meet me tomorrow night? The Savoy?'

Kate is about to nod: yes, of course. But Marie is looking straight through her, as though she cannot remember who she is, and before Kate can entice herself to do anything at all, Marie turns away and is gone.

Momentarily, Kate and William are dumbstruck. They watch Marie, suddenly so bedraggled as to appear recently mugged, hasten out of the theatre and into the street.

'What do you think it is?' Kate asks.

Already, she is listing invented possibilities: the National Vigilance Association have finally had their way and she is to be forced offstage; she has just received news of a bereavement; her husband has betrayed her again; she cannot find another engagement to follow this – though that is least likely of all, given the crowds she has attracted. Kate trawls through every explanation she can summon before she allows herself to consider the first one that entered her mind. The life has got her, she thinks. The schedules, the travel, the crowds, the demand, the ugly newspaper articles, the uninvited attention, the criticism, the hecklers, the applauses that just don't come, the endless expectation. Since arriving in London that frosty winter, Kate has seen music hall take some of its best.

But, please, she thinks as she and William step out into the cold to find a cab home. *Please don't let it have Marie.*

18.

London, England
1901
THE SAVOY

She arrives late, wearing a gargantuan picture hat piled with crimson roses and a bright ivory dress which, when she walks across the dining room of the Savoy, swishes to reveal pleats in the skirts lined with red silk. Kate has the unpleasant impression that she is watching a person split open to reveal their secret flesh over and again with each of Marie's steps. The dress is clever: a statement. Marie will have considered its optical effect well enough. She pauses mid-room – her neck and limbs extended as though she is the subject of a photograph – and glances about, seeking her friends. When she spots Kate and William, already seated, she breaks into a smile and relaxes a little. Marie is never beautiful, but she knows how to train all eyes on her, and her clicking sashay between the cotton-clothed tables does exactly that. Before she even approaches Kate and William's table, she brings silence down on the chatter and clink of the Savoy's restaurant.

'How does she do that?' Kate whispers to William.

'The same way you do, I expect,' William whispers back.

They are seated near the raised platform in the centre of the room, around which is arranged a large iron birdcage, painted cream, and upon which is positioned a black grand piano, polished to a gloss. The pianist is the only person in the room now who is not looking at Marie – and not, Kate suspects, because he needs to look at the keys, but because his job is not worth the indiscretion. His duty is to remain in the background. His songs are chosen as carefully as his black dress coat and shone shoes – for their lack of individuality.

'Dears!' Marie says, expansive, when she finally reaches them. She has not rushed. Whatever happened last night, it seems she is returned to herself. She pauses while a waiter hurries over to pull out her chair, then flounces down on to it. The dress rustles. 'So sorry I'm late.' She lifts the flute of champagne they have ordered for her and tosses it away with one gulp. Some of the roses in her hat, Kate notices, are beginning to curl and brown at their petal edges. 'You know how it is.'

Kate smiles. She does not know what the 'it' is referring to, nor does she want to. She only wants Marie to be her old self, and make them laugh, and tell them all about her escapades in Australia. Marie always has a tale to spin. Sometimes, Kate wonders if perhaps half of what she says is true. But it doesn't really matter. Marie is a storyteller; it is why people love her.

Kate and William ply her with two more glasses of champagne and a plate of briny oysters before they ask about Harry Rickards and his recently rebuilt Tivoli Theatre.

'Well,' Marie replies, her glass rim tilted against her top teeth, as though she is shy. 'He pays as much as they say he does, so don't let him diddle you there. You want to go yourselves, I assume?'

William is quick to answer before Kate does; he already suspects she has doubts. 'Perhaps. If it's worth the trip.'

'I'd say so. Some of the audiences were a little dry, you know. A little stiff. But in general, I'd say they understand British sensibilities. Unlike the pesky Americans.' At this, she tosses her eyes.

Kate laughs. 'You'll never forgive the Americans, will you?'

'I will not,' Marie huffs.

'We shan't bother to visit them, then.'

'I shouldn't think it worth the trouble,' Marie says, her eyes sparkling. 'In any case, now that we've damned a continent, tell me more about this story I read, featuring the famous swimming strongwoman who threw two drowning boys from a bursting river.'

'That's just him and his slick marketing,' Kate says, thrusting a thumb in William's direction. 'Nothing more. I merely lifted them out.'

Marie laughs, then tips back another oyster, drops the shell, and pinches her fingers around the tablecloth to clean them. 'Then they were really drowning?'

'Yes.'

'And you did jump in and pluck them out?'

'Well ... yes.'

'Then you're a hero!' she declares, lifting her champagne flute for a toast. 'You can't blame William's advertising for that.'

If only it were so simple, Kate thinks. She is used by now to Marie's wilful oversimplifications. They are headliners, after all, she and Kate – and headlines, by definition, must be short, snappy, and simple. 'Strongwoman Saves the Day' serves their purposes much more readily than would the truth: that she, a new mother, plunged into a river in a stupor because she saw a child in danger and she had begun to understand... She can hardly frame the thought for herself, let alone present it eloquently to another, but she thinks it is something like grief. She has begun to understand grief. It had been the same when Nora was born. Kate had found herself overwhelmed by a distinct sense of loss, not for herself but for her daughter, who was burbling and smiling and reaching out for the world without the first notion of how much it could hurt her. It was intolerable, that void between what Nora knew and what she would come to know. The first weeks Kate had wasted setting Nora down to better do battle with her tears. But as weeks shrank into months, she learned instead simply to rise from bed when everyone else was sleeping and, hidden in the silent folds of the night, lift her daughter from her cot in the dark, when she could cry freely over all that forecasted loss she could not explain. The feeling had flooded back when Mona was born. And so, when she had woken on the riverside and heard the bleat of a frightened child, of course she had rushed toward it. That was instinct, not heroism.

'I just don't want...' she begins. Marie slurps away another oyster. William pokes at the remains of his pâté with his fork. 'I want to make sure I recognise myself in her, that's all.'

'In who?' Marie asks.

'Vulcana.'

'Oh, dear! But you *are* Vulcana. She doesn't need to be every aspect of you to be worthwhile. She is the part of you that belongs onstage – it's really as straightforward as that. You're not conning anyone, Kate. You don't owe the audience every ounce of yourself. Quite the opposite, in fact. Give the bastards just enough, and let them yearn for the rest.'

'I couldn't have put it better, Marie,' William says. Naturally William agrees, Kate thinks. After all, how much of William does she truly have, beyond Atlas?

Marie cocks her head. 'No, I don't imagine you could. Now, flag a waiter for some more of these oysters, won't you. I've got a story to tell you about dear old Harry, and it's rather a long one.'

'The story, or dear old Harry?' Kate enquires, batting her eyelashes in a mockery of innocence. She needs to keep things light, to fend off the thoughts which are darkening around her more and more. Kate or Vulcana? The theatre or the children?

Marie flings a napkin at her. 'Those eyes!' she shrieks. 'My darling, you could sink ships with a glance.'

Kate laughs, made easy again. 'What a thing to say!'

'It's nothing but the truth,' Marie insists. She grabs a menu and uses it as a shield with which to exclude William from what she says next. He can hear her, of course, but he takes his cue and concentrates on the pianist, tapping his foot to his legato three-four to prove his attention. 'There's someone looking out through those eyes, Kate Roberts, who is wiser than the ages, and don't you forget it. You might just be the most powerful woman I've ever met, if you set your attention to it. The most beautiful, too, but never mind that. Power is the thing.' Kate opens her mouth to protest, but Marie cuts her short with a look. 'You'll know it one day. Remember me when you do. Do you promise?'

'I promise,' Kate replies, unnerved by the blank intensity of Marie's stare and the way her irises seem to have turned the same pitch black as her pupils. She means it.

'Ah, wonderful!' Marie cries when a waiter appears beside her, hands locked at the small of his back. He offers his service with nothing more intrusive than a bob of his head. 'Some more of those fine oysters, please,' she says. She is turned back to herself again, as abruptly as a feather might switch on the wind. Her eyes are dancing, and her back is straight, and her voice is the chime of a perfectly balanced striking clock. Really, Kate thinks. How does she do that? 'And three bottles of champagne,' she continues, dropping her fingertips lightly onto the waiter's forearm. 'We're celebrating.'

'In advance,' Kate adds, because already it seems set in stone that Marie will put a word in with 'Dear Old Harry', and that Kate and William will go to Australia, and that is certainly worth celebrating.

'To you,' Marie says, raising her empty glass.

'No,' William interjects. 'To all of us.'

Marie gives a small smile. 'All right then. To us.' But Kate knows that the toast is empty. Behind that shine Marie wears like a cloak, she has nothing left to give.

Kate removes her shoes as they walk back from the Savoy. The pavement is frozen and burns the soles of her feet, but she doesn't mind it. Better that than the spiteful pinch of too-tight heels: she has run and boxed barefoot for so many years that her feet are tougher than most women's; most men's, too. The walk is a short one, during which Kate and William link arms but do not talk. They are ruminating on the evening, and the changes in their friend, and what might lie ahead both for her and for them. She had gone on to mention that the National Vigilance Association was still gunning for her, but Marie had always brushed them off before, and Kate wonders whether the rumours about Percy Courtenay aren't true after all.

'What do you think it is with her?' she asks, as they step past the jeweller's where sometimes Kate pauses to gawp at diamond-studded bracelets and gold lockets and ponder why she does not covet them as other women do.

'I couldn't guess,' William replies. 'They do say, though, don't they, that Percy...'

'Yes. I'd assumed it was just rumour.'

'The rumour started somewhere, I suppose.'

To be beaten, by your own husband. Percy is a man about town, true; everyone knows that. But to strike her. Kate couldn't conceive of it. No man has ever raised a hand to her. And she's been lucky in that, perhaps, given how foolishly she had chased off after William and thrown herself on the mercy of an unknown city filled with unknown people. Anything could have befallen her that night. She sees that now.

She leans closer to William. 'I'm so very fortunate to have you,' she says.

William pretends at a tickle in his throat and makes a scene of coughing it away. Strange, that he is so uncomfortable with honest words when with his touch he might as well be spouting love poetry. Kate has learned about everything he feels for her through his hands, which, despite their red and roughened appearance, are not clumsy but careful, responsive, articulate. The absent-minded play of his fingertips down the curl of her ear is better, she thinks, than muttered sentiments. So too the way he reaches over her in his sleep to tuck the bedsheets tighter about her body. And the press of his coarse knuckles against her upper arm or her cheek to check whether she is warm enough. These things are preferable to common declarations because they are uniquely hers. A million women have heard the words, 'I love you,' repeated in passion or desperation. None other, except perhaps one, has been wrapped into sleep and held tight there by William Roberts.

Back in the fire-warmed privacy of their hotel room, Kate undresses for bed and William sits by the window to inspect his Brownie. She watches him a while as he turns it about, frowns at it, considers it from a new angle.

'How is it that you only get that out when we're touring?' she asks finally.

'What do you mean?'

'You didn't use it once in Abergavenny.'

William turns his furrowed brow on her. 'Of course I did,' he says, surprise evident in the pitch of his voice. 'I took a hundred photos, when we were all at the river, and in the garden, and when you were baking with Grace and Alice. You just don't notice it when we're home.'

Kate laughs. 'Is that true?'

William shakes his head, amused. 'You're different when we're there,' he says. 'Rapt, with the children.'

'Hmm.' Kate goes to the wardrobe to hunt out her nightdress. Since they have a new run starting tomorrow in the West End, they will stay in this room long enough to warrant the organisation of their clothing, but Kate cannot turn her attention to the task. 'I'm sure,' she calls over her shoulder as she rifles about, 'they make for very flattering viewing then. Me, asleep with my mouth open. Me, scrunching my face up as I race with Ernest. Really, William.'

'First,' William answers, 'you are never more lovely than when you don't know the camera is there. And secondly, I am more than happy to take another shot of you now, while you are fully aware of it.' He pauses, and then, quieter, 'Pose for me, Kate.'

'Oh, all right.' She finally locates the nightdress and steps back across the room, clutching it before her. She lays it on the bed, in order to straighten it up and slip it over her head.

But, 'No,' William says. 'Just you. No distractions.'

'Nude?' Kate asks, and excitement trills through her at the question. It will be the perfect prelude to their lovemaking.

William nods.

'Is there enough light?'

'Here.' William indicates a spot on the rug, where a silver

beam of moonlight slants in through the window. 'With the lamps, too, it'll work.'

Kate nods and moves towards him, loosening the waist of her silk knickers and working them slowly down over her hips. When her feet find the rug, she drops them and steps out, leaving the frilled legs sprawled on the floor. And all the while she makes certain not to break eye contact with William. She does not want him exploring her yet. She wants this game to last for hours. He has seen her body a thousand times, but to stand naked before him and be examined through a camera lens feels different – more rousing. The room is not chill; there are still embers glowing in the grate. But stripped completely, and newly aware of it, Kate feels gooseflesh rise on her arms and legs. Her nipples tighten and lift, and she resists the urge to touch them. All the hairs on her body stand erect, except that between her legs, which is too thick and downy to respond. She is shocked to find her breaths coming quicker.

'William,' she murmurs, whenever his eyes threaten to flicker down over her chest, her stomach, her hips, her thighs. He obeys her calls and trains his eyes on hers, and she wonders then what he sees looking out at him. Is it the strength Marie described? Or uncertainty? Vigour, longing, zest? She thinks perhaps her eyes are so bright because they brim with a confusion of too many emotions, and she wants to show them each to William, separately and in turn, so that he might appreciate how full she is. How unbearably full. How desperately, gloriously full.

'William.'

There is no swelling yet, but she already knows that she is pregnant again.

'Look at me.'

And he does. He looks and looks, with such intensity in his seashore eyes that Kate finds herself softening. A tremor starts up, somewhere at her middle – the first jutterings of a storm – and she embraces it. She wants to tremble and crash under his gaze. She wants to rear and fall like squally waves thrown about by a gale. It is all right, sometimes, to let him be the stronger.

'Kate,' he says, and what she sees in him is pride, and lust, and the desire to really take control of her, just for a short hour or two. It is a request he would never make verbally. She doubts that any two people have ever studied each other as deeply as have she and William, but here, standing in the pearl-glow light of a midnight moon and just watching each other, they have discovered something more than observation. It is as though they are communicating telepathically.

'Raise your arms up above your head,' he says. Or thinks. Kate can no longer tell. But she raises her arms as he wants her to, for the composition of the photograph, and then she wrenches her eyes from his to look up, through the closed window, at the blank-eyed expression of the moon, and ask it what might happen next.

Intermission

Words scatter around her like stars.

'Missus? Can you hear me?'

'Are you hurt?'

'Can you move, missus?'

She considers these questions for some time before she decides how to answer. She wants to ensure, as always, that her response is just the right blend of off-hand humour and gratitude. She may no longer have a stage, but she remains a performer. Keeping her eyes firmly shut, she wiggles her toes, flexes her ankles, tenses her thighs. She taps her fingers against the hard surface she finds them resting on, rolls her wrists, tightens and releases her biceps. She thinks she does. She feels herself run through the movements. A deep flaming ache licks through her every joint and muscle, the back of her head throbs, but all seems to be in general working order.

And yet, the questions continue. The voices, like instruments in an orchestra.

'Can you speak, missus?'

'Nod if you can hear me.'

A blaring trombone. A whistling flute.

'She can't hear us.'

'I don't think she's breathing.'

A tremoring violin string. The boom of the timpani.

Perhaps she ought to break into song. Perhaps that would enable them to understand her. It always served Marie well enough. But she does not know the tune.

She parts her lips, which feel newly heavy. I'm just fine, she will say. And once she has sat up and waved all these voices apart, she will prove it, and be allowed to carry on in peace. It is only then that she notices that the drone of the traffic has stopped entirely. Surely she cannot have stopped all the London's traffic? Not this little incident, from which she will soon stand and walk away?

'I'm just fine,' she says, but no one seems to hear her despite the thudding silence surrounding those insistent scattered words.

'Is an ambulance coming?'

'I think it's too late.'

'She's not moving.'

'Is she breathing now?'

Yes, she thinks. Yes, for goodness sake. Clearly, I am breathing. Watch my chest rising and falling. Put your ears to my mouth and listen to my exhalations. It seems she will have to sit up and show them. She would rather rest a while, but she never has been one to disappoint. She makes to open her eyes... She tries... She cannot lift her lids. Indeed, she cannot press her palms to the ground and push herself upwards. She cannot drag words up her throat and propel them out of her mouth. She is paralysed. At least, the outside of her is. Her shell is. But her interior self is louder than ever. Fear tunnels, quick and cold, through the core of her. Her soul starts up a scream. *I am here. I can hear you. I am scared. Please help me.* But the words are able only to ricochet around the dark inside of her. Everything she is or ever has been is entirely within her reach, and she has no means of presenting it to the world, and the knowledge is terrifying.

There has only ever been one answer to terror, as far as she is concerned, and that is to move: to run, to leap, to plunge, to box, to kick. She needs to do all those things as hands clasp her legs and shoulders, and as some unknown item is slipped beneath her body, and as she feels herself lifted off the ground. Her nerves shriek, but they fail to relate any message at all to her limbs. God – how to fight without one's body? She knows that she cannot, but neither can she silence her own voice within her mind, and so she must listen to it as she is carried away by invisible hands.

Stop, she cries. *Please*, she cries. *No*, she cries and cries and cries, because she knows where they will take her now.

And nobody hears her.

1903 – 1904
Act Three

19.

London, England
1903
EMBARKATION

In the dock, the steamship sulks. It is larger than any Kate has yet travelled on: a colossus, with a broad riveted steel hull and two shining funnels rising between its twinned foremast and mizzenmasts. The hull is painted a glossy charcoal black, with a red stripe around the bottom, where the hull is submerged by the water. The weather deck is white. The funnels buff-coloured.

'I'm told she can reach up to sixteen-and-a-half knots an hour,' William says. His voice is high, excited: a child smiling over a new toy-set.

Waiting on the dockside, Kate feels she hardly wants to look at the ship, which hisses and groans like a tethered sea creature as it awaits its cargo.

They've had to wait such a long while to take this trip, and with every passing day, it seems, William has grown more enamoured of it. And Kate more doubtful.

'She weighs over six thousand tons.'

'Is that so?' Kate says.

The ship seems to her to have a glower about it, as though

it has a beating heart within, and that heart is being consumed by some private fury. Kate has a vision of it being captured from the depths in an enormous net and dragged to the surface, the water rolling off its funnels and decks as it meets the air for the first time. It is like a whale, or a giant octopus, or some equally fantastic creature, reduced to servitude. She does not admit the thought to William – she is positive he would laugh at her – but there is something living about this ship. She knows it. It is proud and menacing and sad.

'Did you know she was built by the Barrow Ship Building Company? For the Pacific Steam Navigation Company?'

'I did not,' Kate answers. Her tone is not dismissive or cruel, but measured. It does not arouse worry in William; he is too distracted.

'She's one of the Orient Line.'

How he knows these things is beyond Kate. But William's interest in the world is one of the qualities she most admires in him, and she wishes to continue to admire it, so she does not ask.

'Oh.'

She turns her eyes on something – anything – else. There is much to see beside the ship, despite her stature. Along the dockside, vast red-bricked granaries await their wares. Merchant ships lower their gangplanks to allow sailors to manoeuvre great crates full of fruits, vegetables, tobacco, and meats down to waiting carts. Horses drag the loaded carts away, their hooves silenced by the hollers of sailors and dockers and granary workers. A wiry brown and white dog trails his master through the hulking shadows the ships cast, tail erect and nose high, letting out an occasional solitary bark. Above, herring gulls wheel and scream, swooping down now and then towards some glint or scrap they have mistaken for glimmering fish scales, their mirrored grey shapes flitting over the ground in perfect parallel. Steam garlands around and between all this motion, thick and purely white. Bells clank, and the water laps, and unseen loads thud like punctuation through the ceaseless noise. And Kate takes a deep in-breath and savours the salt on her lips, the smoke in her nose, the first stirrings of an October wind through her hair.

She is ready. She has to be. She has left half her heart behind before, and she can do it again. Just one more time – if everything goes to plan.

She has on her winter coat, and she is pleasantly warm inside the thick fir-green wool. She reaches for William's hand and finds his skin reassuringly rough against her palm. They are embarking on a new adventure, just as some part of her had wanted, and it is right to be excited – however frightening the *Oroya* might look, however far it might carry her from her babies. They have secured a twenty-one-week tour with Harry Rickards, moving from the west coast of Australia to the east. He is paying them hundreds for each engagement. Even Queen Marie could not have asked for more.

Still, it is not surprising that a stream of worry has bored down through Kate's stomach and opened up there the beginnings of a well. It really is such a long time to leave the children, and home, and she's never yet found a ship she could travel easily on. Even the exhibition ship at the Exposition Universelle had thrown her badly off-kilter, and that with no coal to power it and no seas beneath. But she decides that she will settle once the anchor has been thrown – the expression is her own, and likely makes no sense at all in nautical terms – and their voyage has commenced. It is her decision to make, after all. She can control her responses as readily as she can perform a slow lift.

It is how she has convinced herself to look forward to this trip. Over and again, lying awake in the midnight dark, she has led herself to the same conclusion: she will give everything she has to ensure they take Australia by storm; they'll know more fame and earn more money than ever they have before; and then she will find a way to reframe Atlas as the star of the show – it is what William wants, after all, deep down – and she will retire quietly to Bristol and her children and her heart will be whole.

Everything rests on Australia. If she can make this tour big enough, it will be her last.

She tilts her chin up determinedly as they deposit their luggage, produce their tickets, and step onto the gangplank to go aboard. She finds the wood slippery underfoot and stifles a gasp as her heel slides back and bangs into the nearest cleat. She makes the mistake of looking down. Below, churning grey water slaps at the *Oroya*'s hull, making small, pathetic sounds – like the wing-crack of a trapped bird – and immediately her nausea rises.

Evidently, she cannot control all her responses. It had taken her years, hadn't it, to stop springing awake at half-past-five every Sunday morning, her arms already lifting in anticipation of having her nightdress tugged off, suffering a tepid flannel bath, and then having her best dress dragged on. They would sleepwalk to the church before dawn, Reverend Robert Williams leading his wife Eleanor, then Kate, Margaret, Young Eleanor, and little William behind him as though they were a trail of obedient ponies, to set about their private prayers before the early congregation arrived at seven. On the coldest of those mornings, Margaret had cried, but Kate had not.

She takes another deep salt breath and steps more carefully up the next cleat. Lift your head, she tells herself. Don't be weak. She straightens her back and tilts up her chin once more, and she sees, over the funnels of the ship, deep purple and pewter clouds gathering. Rain is on the way. Well, good. Kate lived long enough in Wales to be familiar with every variety of rain: the mizzle, which settles on your hair and eyelashes like a dusting of diamonds; the driving diagonals, which plaster your clothes to your skin; the torrential bursts, which bounce off the ground to dart back up as quickly as they fall. Whatever she and William are about to sail into, she will recognise it, and the recognition will put her mind at ease.

'Do you think they'll like us,' she says over her shoulder, 'in Australia?'

William is at her back, where she always positions him when she wishes to ask a question to which she only wants to hear the most optimistic response. He had still been talking about the ship, and the three thousand tonnes of Welsh coal waiting aboard to power them all the way to Australia, when she interrupted him. His breath is hot on her neck. Her hand is cold where it had been pressed against his but is now freed.

'Certainly,' he answers. 'How could they do otherwise?'

But his voice is not as steady as it could be, and they say no more as they climb onto the ship. Kate keeps her eyes on the drifting clouds. How rapidly they come in, she thinks. How quickly they change.

20.

London, England
1903
THE *OROYA*

Those ladies and gentlemen already aboard are taking turns about the promenade deck. Kate watches them strolling easily along – arms locked, canes clicking, skirts rustling – and feels that familiar queasiness rising through her. Though the ship has not left the harbour yet, it seems to jolt and list beneath her feet. Here and there, wicker chairs are set out; young girls and old gents sit in them, staring wistfully out to sea. At the bottom of the railings, great lengths of rope loop through gold hooks as thick as a man's neck and rise towards the tops of four enormous masts. The ropes creak against the tension. Kate closes her eyes and sees cello strings held under violent vibratos, the pinnacle of a dramatic scene.

'Shall we play a game?' she asks William as they wander along the deck, William squinting down at their tickets, then up at the signs above each doorway, trying to locate the way to their cabin.

'Mm?'

'A game,' Kate repeats. 'To amuse ourselves.'

'If you like,' William replies.

Kate brightens. 'All right.' She sidles closer and rests her hand on his wrist. He pats it absently with his free hand as he continues to inspect the tickets. Kate breathes away a flash of annoyance: why can't he simply memorise the numbers and fold the papers back into his pocket? She doesn't want to comment and cause an argument. 'I,' she says, 'am going to make one lap of the deck, and choose a man, and by tomorrow, you will have to have engaged him in an arm wrestle.'

William smirks. 'That is a cruel game, Miss Vulcana,' he says, letting his tongue linger over the name the newspapers like best.

'How so?'

'You will choose the largest man,' William replies, 'and then laugh at me if I don't win.'

'But you shall win.' She's counting on that much.

'You're certain of that, are you?'

'Of course,' Kate protests. 'I wouldn't have chosen any man but the strongest as my own.'

'All right, then,' William concedes. 'What's the prize?'

Kate glances up at the leadening sky and hums as she pretends to think this through. Just below the clouds, birds twist and scatter like fire ashes. 'A night with a world-famous strongwoman.'

'And if he wins?'

'The same.'

'Oh,' William replies, lifting his eyebrows comically high and causing his forehead to wrinkle like an un-pressed sheet. 'Then I should choose carefully if I were you.'

'I've already declared you the winner,' Kate retorts.

'Ah, yes,' says William. 'But if you select a giant of a man, and he happens to be an ugly brute, I might just lose on purpose.'

At this Kate laughs, loud and unashamedly. As she always does. As she wishes other women felt able to. She has no patience for polite titters behind raised hands. When a person is truly inclined to laughter, they should have no thought for the exposure of their teeth and tongues.

'William Roberts,' she says. 'You wouldn't dare.' And snatching the tickets from his hand, she stuffs them into the pocket of her coat, and strides off in the direction – she thinks – of their cabin. She would rather walk the corridors a hundred times to find it than stand about staring at her boots. In her stillness is the nagging doubt that, despite her best-laid plans, she should not be making this trip. That it will prove too far.

That night, they dine in the first-class saloon. It is a grand affair, positioned between the creaking main and foremasts on the main deck, and occupying the whole width of the ship. Knowing this, they have dressed for dinner: William in a fine black suit and Kate in a deep emerald dress, since green is her favourite colour and reminds her of home. For some unknown reason, however, she is still surprised when she enters the room to find table after table lined with ladies in expensive gowns and men in black dicky bows and waistcoats. It seems incongruous, aboard a ship, to be so elaborately attired. And yet, it goes some way to putting her at ease, as does the unmistakable chink of cutlery against chinaware and the chorused, 'Yes, sirs,' of the waiters.

The saloon itself is as well-dressed as its patrons. The walls, panelled in rosewood and satinwood, sport on two sides intricately carved coats of arms, and on the opposite two sides mounted stags' heads: Kate is careful not to look into their glazed eyes; she imagines glimpsing the terror of their last moments. The high arched ceiling is dotted with globes of glass, and she recalls reading on the handbill William had been waving about that the *Oroya* promised electric lighting throughout. If she had anticipated the same being garish, she would have been wrong, for the saloon is as classy as many a fancy restaurant she has eaten at in London or Paris. And really, why shouldn't it be? The fact that it is steaming across rough sea will be of little consequence once everyone grows accustomed to the swaying.

'Miss Roberts,' says a waiter who appears before them, inclining his head. 'Mr Roberts. Can I show you to your seats?'

They follow the young man and the aroma of roasted garlic towards the furthest corner of the saloon, where they are offered a table draped in an impossibly clean white cloth. At its centre is positioned a potted plant, from which delicate lilac flowers droop. Kate does not know their species, though Alice would. When the waiter moves off to fetch them their drinks, Kate plucks one of the buds free and lays it on top of her napkin. She will press it inside a book, so that she might ask Alice what its name is when they return.

'Do you see your man, then?' William asks. He has his back to the room, while Kate faces into it.

Kate scans the other diners. 'I do,' she says. It had, in the end, required three laps of the promenade deck to identify anyone who might challenge William for strength. The figure she finally alighted upon is perhaps twenty-five years old and possesses the broad chest and low belly of a countryman. With his thick brown beard and ruddy cheeks, she can just see him astride an enormous stallion, poised to shoot a buzzard or a red kite or some other feathered majesty from the skies. Later, he might well feel a pang of humiliation that a man of inferior height and superior age has capably bested him. But it is only the harmless sport of distraction, and Kate thinks nothing of encouraging it. After all – she will tell William, should he question her intent – what else will they turn to but games when they are trapped together for weeks on a ship which must sail all the way to Gibraltar, Naples, Port Said, Ismailia, Suez, Colombo, and Albany, before it reaches Adelaide? Kate wonders idly if she might start up a ladies' boxing club each morning before breakfast. That would be something. Tomorrow, she'll enquire about a room.

It takes them no time at all to ingratiate themselves with the party of ten positioned at the largest table, set in the middle of the crowded saloon, which contains William's unsuspecting target. William – as determined as a child when confronted with a challenge – orders a drink in addition to his own, then goes over to ask whether it is in fact one of theirs, wrongly delivered to his table. He uses their pause to start up a conversation, and before the desserts are brought out, Kate and William have been coaxed – begged, really – to pull up their seats. William is regaling the group with tales of losing their luggage in Holland, and the wonders of the Paris Exposition Universelle, of the performing polar bears and the two-hundred-foot-deep water tank at the London Hippodrome, of a rough crossing they took once to Ireland – which Kate determinedly does not listen to – and the folklore of Wales.

They have discovered that the man he is to begin a competition of strength with is called Gordon. He has a burred Scots accent and an easy manner – not an Australian, as Kate had hoped. The picture Kate had invented, of Gordon trussed up in his hunting gear, has been replaced with one of him chopping wood in his shirtsleeves on a bright winter's morning outside a modest forest lodge.

She may have chosen badly.

But she knows William to be as good as the contest, and besides, she knows that he will not give it up now whatever she says. It really is best to say nothing.

'Another drink?' asks the man at the head of the table, who is trim and upright in his early sixties, and whose name is Leslie Rothcoe. Kate thinks that perhaps he is a lord or an earl of somewhere or other. It's written in his demeanour: wealth; privilege.

'Or a wager?' William suggests.

'Interesting,' replies the older man. 'What will we bet on – a pod of passing dolphins?'

'Not a race at all,' William counters. 'But a test of power.'

The table falls quiet as they wait on William's next words. It was clever of him, to tell all those stories. He has taught them that listening to his voice will lead to certain reward: a laugh, a nod of admiration, a tear, a gasp of disbelief.

'I will challenge Gordon to an arm wrestle. We can all put in a shilling, and if I win, I take the pot. If Gordon wins, he takes the pot *and* he has my permission to invite my sister on a date.' Kate kicks him under the table; the connection between the toe of her shoe and his shin thrums satisfyingly. '*Invite*, mind you,' William adds quickly. 'It is she who must decide whether or not to give her consent if you win your prize.'

Gordon weighs William up, just as those mounted stags might once have weighed each other up in life, and, as predicted, considers that his antlers are the bigger. It is apparent in William's posture alone that he won't make a weak opponent, but at half a foot shorter than Gordon and a good deal narrower, any man would be forgiven for imagining him the poor bet.

'Right,' Gordon says. 'Let's shake on it. And order a couple of brandies to start us off.'

They slug back the brandies as though they are dying of thirst, while the others go about clearing the tabletop of plates and glasses, flowers and candle holders. The din and clatter of the saloon has calmed now. The diners on adjacent tables have noticed that some merriment is in progress and put down their cutlery to watch; their neighbours have followed suit. The waiters have retired to the walls instead of bustling around, and stand there like sentries. If this were third class, Kate thinks, they would have joined in or called it off by now. But this is first class, and where money rules anything goes. If William and Gordon were to strip off their shirts and, taking up their steak knives, begin to grapple on the table, she does not think these boys in their matching suits and smiles would so much as flinch. Across the room, a white-haired old gent sporting impressive mutton chops leans back in his chair and lights a cigar. The bitter tobacco bite of it is on Kate's tongue in an instant. The air thickens with smoke as he puffs and puffs. And as the room fidgets and waits, Kate hears the sea for the first time since they left their cabin for dinner: it sloshes heavily against the ship's hull, shouldering the vessel into a tilt, which the *Oroya* rolls with for two seconds, three, before she recovers. Kate's stomach lurches, and she sweeps up the nearest drink and throws it back. Port – thick and sharp. She does not look about to discover who the glass belongs to.

'Who will adjudicate?' asks a woman on another table, who purrs like a cat when she speaks and has a languorous attitude to match. 'One man might cheat if they are not closely watched.'

Volunteers are pulled from other parties to crouch beside the table, watching William and Gordon's hands and elbows carefully as they prepare. It is decided that the elbow must rest three inches from the table edge, to ensure no advantage to one or the other, and that the free hand must be placed flat on the tabletop and remain unmoving throughout. A twitch of a forefinger, the lift of a thumb, and disqualification looms.

A crowd has formed around William and Gordon by the time they are ready to start. Drinks are hastily swallowed as people light cigarettes or bet amongst themselves. This, Kate considers, is going better than expected.

'The big chap,' someone grunts. 'Two shillings.'

'Four on the other,' someone else replies. 'I wouldn't be so daft as to tip my hat against a Welshman.'

Kate settles in her chair with a snuffle of laughter. Nor would I, she thinks. That man has more determination than any I've ever met; he'll see his arm broken before he allows himself to be beaten. Naturally, her opinion of William has shifted over the past eleven years. On occasion, he has a temper like a distress flare. On others, he permits himself to be bested by his eagerness or his pride. He frustrates her as much as any husband must frustrate his wife. But he is as tenacious as a dog with its jaw clamped around a fresh bone, and the fact stirs in her the same trill of need as does the way his chest hair curls above the top button of his shirt.

She will take him back to their cabin aroused by his victory – that is her trick – and entice him to the kind of desperate lovemaking they manage when they do not need to share rooms with the troupe, and when they are not sleeping under Alice's roof, and when they have no fear of their brother and sister disguise being thwarted. As she watches him clamp hands with Gordon and, on the count of three, begin steadily to force the larger man's knuckles towards the table, she feels her breasts harden under her dress and a throb start up between her legs. Later, she will open the cabin porthole and sit astride him, the cold salt air licking her skin, and move in a way she cannot imagine being possible with anyone other than William. She cannot share him in that. There have been no more children for Alice since Winifred.

The crowded diners cheer as Gordon's hand nears the table. Gordon grits his teeth, pushes harder and William's arm is forced slowly back towards the perpendicular. William clenches out a smile, then redoubles his efforts. Both men are growing red in the cheek, but neither risks breaking the rules of engagement. They strain and grunt and the cheers mount. William knows this is too good an audience to lose. No matter that they are not paying. No matter that he is not Atlas now but simply William Roberts, ironworker, Abergavenny. She has seen the way his shoulders fall when he fails to garner as much applause as she at the theatre; she has welled up at the sadness that dulls his eyes when chants of 'Vulcana, Vulcana' start up, and he moves offstage to let her perform the encore alone. She should not have started this game, but now that she has, she needs him to win it. She always did. If he is to go ashore at Adelaide with a reputation she can build upon, these are the games she must play. William is more than worthy of them. She leans forward in her chair, far enough to catch his attention, and shows him one deliberate nod. *You are in control. See it out.*

Some of those who have laid bets are thumping the tables with balled fists now. The ship shifts and a tumbler left too close to the edge somersaults to the floor, where it spatters its contents and rolls away without smashing. A woman's laughter rises over the grumbling and guffawing of the men like a new melody line.

Come on, William. You've got more than this.

Gordon lowers his head in an attempt to add weight to his trembling arm. Spittle sprays from his lips and blotches the tablecloth.

That's it, Kate urges. *He's moved. He's weakened while he's moving.*

But William knows this. The fact is a regurgitation of William's training. His eyes tighten as he casts Kate a look she cannot decipher. Then he clamps his mouth shut, grinds his jaw a little to the left, and, with one last thrust, slams Gordon's hand against the table. Knuckle bone on wood. Thunk.

Those who have bet on William erupt, banging their fists harder and tossing empty glasses into the air before catching them and holding them aloft like trophies. The groan from those who have bet against him is only just audible beneath the celebrations.

William shoves back his chair and stands, offering a rough handshake to Gordon. Still seated, Gordon accepts. He is chuckling, easy and gracious in defeat. This contest means nothing to him. But, though he tries to hide it, Kate can see that William is fired up – his eyes flame; his chest pumps – and it pains her like a sudden cramp. Poor William, that he should need to prove himself that much. She had not appreciated the depth of his self-doubt. She should never have manipulated him into this display of... What? Manhood? Shame burns through her. Has she truly grown so desperate to bring all this to a close that she is willing to risk hurting William? Perhaps she has.

She reaches out to grasp his hand, and holds on tight.

William and Kate burst out through the saloon doors and onto the empty deck, keen to return to their cabin. The cold air smacks into them so violently that, for a moment, Kate thinks a sail has loosed itself and swooped down to sweep them overboard. She gasps, then laughs at herself. Never is she less brave than when she is at sea. William throws his arm about her waist and draws her to him, and she enjoys letting him. Tonight, she has shocked herself into feeling the best of her love for him; perhaps she had been in danger of forgetting it.

After their audience had settled down, William and Gordon had embraced across the table and shared another drink, and the laughter in the saloon has barely ceased since. William had been at his expansive best: performer, storyteller, strongman. And now he and Kate are drunk and on a high, and the tip-and-lean rhythm of the *Oroya* persuades them that they are on the wildest of adventures. The dark, too, is strange enough to feel exciting. Dense clouds skim the tops of the masts, rendering the sky starless, but the moon has fallen down to rest on the black pencil-line of the horizon. Its solemn face is made up of all the iridescent shades of pigeon feathers.

'Look at that,' she says. 'I didn't know the moon had so many colours.'

'The moon is white.'

Kate settles her elbows on the railings and William echoes her with his left arm; the other remains curled around her. She tips her head back so that it rests against his shoulder. Sea spray salts them, damping their coats and their faces.

'You can do better than that.'

'You always seem to think so.'

'I know so,' Kate insists. 'Now try.'

William sighs, squinting. 'All right. Well, there's grey, I suppose.'

'Which shade of grey?'

'Charcoal,' he answers. 'And ... slate. Flint, maybe.'

'What other colours?'

She listens to the reverberation of his heart around his drum-like chest as he thinks.

'Purple.'

'Be more specific,' Kate urges.

'The same as those flowers Alice likes... Irises. Is that what they're called?' Kate nods. 'And there's a hint of green, too. Peridot.' He pauses, then emits a sound which is somewhere between a bark and a hum.

'See,' Kate says. 'I knew you could see it.'

'You allowed me to see it.' He presses a kiss into her hair.

'Is that why you love me?' she teases.

'It is. That, and a hundred other reasons.'

Kate smiles into the moonlit darkness. He must be drunk to make such an admission. They stand and breathe a while against the slap and shush of the sea and the creaking of the ropes, the snapping sound the masts make as they brace against the wind, the huff-puffing of the funnels and the mechanical bellow which rises from the ship's belly, drowning out the desperate bawling of the sheep and bullocks trapped below. The night smells of cold and coal smoke. She wonders whether the rest of the troupe believed William's claim that he could not secure them passage on this ship. Instead, he had booked them tickets for a ship leaving in two weeks' time, and he and Kate had revelled secretly in the idea of forty days spent only together. They have grown somewhat distant of late, always being surrounded by the troupe or Alice and the children. It is often the case for Atlas and Vulcana, the brother and sister act, that they have to close down their hearts for a week here, a month there. They have become used to it. The trick is to make sure to plan the way back to each other.

'Name them,' she says finally.

'What?'

'The other hundred reasons why you love me.'

William drops his head into the crook of her neck and nudges at her with his nose. 'Don't make me,' he pleads quietly.

'It would distract me,' Kate counters.

'From what?'

'The seasickness,' she says. Daft, though, really – that she will only offer him the obvious glinting snowcap of her troubles. Most of the time, she suspects, people cannot be convinced to be honest even with themselves. Kate knows that she is not. But still, there remains a gulf between what she admits to William and what she admits to her own nagging mind. When she says *the seasickness* what she means is *the length of this journey; the distance it will put between me and my children; that one day you might tire of the charade we have to act out and only want Alice; that I will grow old and weak and we will lose everything; that without Atlas and Vulcana, I might have no place in the world.*

She shuffles against him. 'Go on, William. Please.'

'All right, all right.' He takes a long inhalation. 'I love that you're never scared,' he says.

And Kate laughs, surprised that, for all he knows her, he should begin with a statement which is so wholly wrong. The black weight of the sea echoes the laugh back at her, and it is something like comfort, to know that she has been heard.

21.

R.M.S. *Oroya*
1903
SHIP GAMES

The guilt Kate feels at having set William up in the arm-wrestling match gnaws steadily at her, but, determined as she is to ensure that they disembark at Adelaide followed by a loyal and spirited crowd, she cannot give up her scheme, so she enquires about a room for her boxing class, thinking to build one success upon another.

She is granted the use of a smoking room between six and eight o'clock each morning, provided she moves the furniture against the walls before she begins and replaces it afterwards. This the man she negotiates with seems to imagine a hardship, but Kate is not in any way averse to shifting around a few tables and chairs, and she is pleased to accept the offer. She speaks of her intentions to any woman who will listen, in the dining saloon and in the music saloon and on the promenade deck. She promises to teach them how best to defend themselves should the unfortunate happen, and the way to practise jabs and hooks to improve their strength and posture, and privately she is envisaging a roomful of women who will spread their stance wide beneath their skirts, raise their fists, and drop their shoulders in relief for the very first time. Laughter will echo around her smoking room, she thinks, loud enough to quiet the sad bellows of the cattle she cannot stop thinking about now that she knows they stand below deck, stumbling against their tethers in the dark, waiting for death.

'Come,' she says, smiling. 'You'll surprise yourself with how much you're capable of.' Some of the women smile back and nod, and some ask questions, and Kate turns away satisfied that she has enticed them to do something, just one small thing, for themselves.

Three days later, on the tick of six o'clock sharp, she stands in the middle of the empty smoking room and waits. At the windows, the blushed peach glow of dawn. At the door, not a soul. By quarter past six, she is pacing the floorboards, her heels echoing eerily in place of all that dreamt-up laughter. After another five minutes have passed, she props the door open, hoping that the women are only too anxious to push through it and step inside. After ten minutes more, she gives up and sets about moving the tables and chairs back to their original positions.

'No one came,' she tells William when she returns to their cabin. 'Not one person.'

'They will,' he mutters. He is curled beneath their bedsheets, caught part-way between sleep and waking. His voice is muffled against the cotton. She can smell the stale warmth of his body on the entombed air of the cabin, feel his wet breath spreading into every nook of the space, which is finely decorated but suffocating all the same. Kate slumps down on the sofa, kicks off her shoes, and puts her heels up on the foldaway table. William lies only her leg length further away: a fidgeting cotton mound, contained by the stumpy metal railings which edge the bed.

'To keep you from falling out during inclement weather,' William had said, when they had first entered the cabin and Kate had run a fingertip over the curls of those railings.

'It would need to be more than inclement,' she'd replied, 'to toss me from my bed.'

Unable to settle on the sofa, Kate stands and moves to the compactum to wash her face in one of the two sinks the cabin steward fills with hot water every morning.

'Did you sleep while the steward was here?' she asks.

A grumble. *No.* 'I got back in. You should, too.' There follows a spell of writhing and huffing while William tries to find the end of the sheet and throw it off. Kate smirks into the compactum mirror, then catches the lopsided appearance of her face in reflection, and stops. She is a distortion: her left cheek and jaw droop away from her eye; her nose is twisted. Is this really what she looks like? She sees photographs of herself, of course, but they are always artfully lit and carefully framed. They might not be offering an accurate picture. And it unnerves her to think that she might not truly know the face the rest of the world sees. How unfortunate it would be, to recognise the interior of yourself so thoroughly but not be able to match it to the exterior.

'Why do you think it is they didn't come?' she continues

as she soaps her hands, watching the white liquid bubble and froth. 'What are they scared of?' Then, quieter. 'Do you think it's me?'

'They're scared,' William says, finally extricating himself from the blanket and pushing himself up to sit against the wall, 'of being different. Of having a single thought that isn't shared with the woman in the next cabin.'

Kate glances at the swell of his chest through the mirror, thinks about running her hands through the light-brown hair there, then looks back down into the sink. She isn't in the mood to be drawn back into bed. She wants to be outside, with the wind cold in her face and the pinprick spit of the ocean on her skin. She wants to squint into the light and hold her hat on lest it blow away. She wants to breathe in all that wild and mighty motion. The sight of the sea with nothing beyond it overwhelms her in a way she has never experienced before, and she does not want the feeling to stop.

'Why would that frighten anyone?'

William yawns, loud and long, enjoying the stretch of it. 'It frightens nearly everyone, I'd imagine.'

'I don't believe it could. Are they scared of being strong, too, do you think?'

'I'd wager they are.'

She turns and leans against the enamel. 'Nonsense. Why?'

William shrugs. An idle smile has captured half of his face. 'Because it doesn't fit with their idea of things, I suppose,' he replies. 'People like to be told what to think, Kate. It gives them an excuse not to do it for themselves. And they've been

229

told for so long that women ought to be weaker than men that it'll take a good deal longer than one steamship journey to persuade them otherwise. You're making a start, though – that's what's important.'

Kate pauses in consideration of this. 'I don't like to be told what to think,' she says.

'And well I know it. But you're not like most people.'

'Good!' She goes back to the sofa and leans over it to open the porthole. A shock of air shoves in. 'I wouldn't want to be so ready to believe any daft thing I was told.'

'You'd certainly be less than you are for it.'

Kate laughs. She knows, because she learned to speak William's private language years ago, that this is code for 'I love you'.

'I love you, too,' she says quietly. They are the only words she cannot bring herself to pronounce loudly. 'Now get dressed. I want to go out on deck and show all those moping women how to be strong and active and interesting.'

'And how will you do that?'

Kate grabs a hat, any hat, and thrusts it onto her head. 'I haven't decided yet,' she says, and lifting a pair of William's crumpled trousers off the back of the sofa, she throws them to him.

They wander the promenade deck all morning, calling out greetings to the other passengers, grinning when the *Oroya* leans and they lose their footing, wiping the sea spray from their faces before going back to the railings to be dampened over again.

Kate's stomach roils now and then, but she talks over it, wondering at the little cannon which points out to sea, ready to fire a distress signal, and the thunderclap noise the swell and suck of the sails make. She stares into the scoop of the stored lifeboats and thinks it a miracle that anyone should survive open water sitting on a few nailed-together planks of wood. Surely the waves would overcome the tiny vessels within minutes? She swallows that thought and concentrates instead on the lifeboat drill taking place before them: the shouted order to 'Go to the boat stations'; the thud-thud of smartly suited sailors finding their positions. There is reassurance in such calm order.

At eleven, it is announced that games will soon be commencing between the rear masts, and Kate turns to beam at William. 'See,' she says, squeezing his upper arm. 'I knew I'd get my chance.' And rushes off to join the passengers crowding along the railings.

First, there is pillow fighting on the spar. Two men remove their shoes and climb astride a horizontal mast, letting their legs dangle down to each side. Beneath them are laid cushions and blankets, to soften the fall should one of them tip or be knocked from the beam. When they are in position, they are handed a pillow, with which they whack and whump each other until the feathers burst free and soar around the deck, sticking to ropes and hats and lips.

Next comes the men's potato race.

'I'm plumping for the one on the far left,' Kate tells William as a group of ten men line up, clamp spoons between their teeth, balance their potatoes carefully on top, and – after a rather dramatised call of 'Ready. Set. Go!' – take off wobbling towards the finishing ribbon.

'I'll go with the far right, then,' William replies.

All but two of the men lose their potatoes, which the other passengers take to chasing around the deck, shrieking and bumping heads as they bend to reach for the rolling articles, and roaring with laughter. Neither Kate's nor William's bet crosses the finish.

'Next,' a member of the ship's crew calls, 'the men's jockey race. Gentlemen, if you would like to select a partner.'

Kate turns to William. 'The *men's* jockey race,' she says. 'The men's pillow fighting. The men's potato race. Really?'

She does not give William a chance to respond before she is jumping up onto a nearby bench. 'Don't you think,' she shouts over the heads of the other passengers, 'that it would be more sensible to carry a lady on your backs? They might offer a lighter load, after all.' The gentlemen readying themselves for the race pause, then, realising that she is right, begin glancing around for their wives, their daughters. Kate raises her voice further. 'Shouldn't the men's *and women's* jockey race be the next competition?'

This is met with a cheer – something easily enough brought about, Kate thinks, with a dash of confidence and the right tone of voice. Soon, ten ladies are hitched up onto the backs of ten men and the horses and riders go trundling up and down the deck. The addition of the women seems to cause a new surge of competitiveness and within minutes heats are being organised and the trundling mounts to a full gallop.

Hats and shoes are lost. Horses trip and send their riders sprawling. William and Kate win their heat and, while preparing for their next race, make the swap Kate has silently intended since she climbed up onto the bench and declared the rules of the game changed. She hunkers down slightly, spreads her hands out behind her, and waits for William to hoist himself up. Then she straightens up and stares directly ahead at the finishing ribbon, a barely contained grin trembling about her lips, as the mouths of the horses and riders to either side of her fall open.

'Eyes forward,' she warns eventually, 'or you'll miss your start.'

She gives a nod to the crew member who stands braced, his makeshift flag held aloft, to send them on their way.

'Ready,' he calls. 'Set. Go!' And they are off, tilting and swerving with the motion of the ship. Kate wishes she had on her leotard and tights rather than this cumbersome skirt, but she has done enough running in unsuitable attire to soon find her stride. She charges along the deck, aware of two horses who are threatening to overtake her. She hears one grunting, and pushes harder until the sound begins to fade. The other horse stays with her. The rider on his back is squealing – perhaps in fear of the speed or perhaps in terror at her newly elevated height. Either way, she is not assisting her horse as William is, tucked low and tight against Kate's back and gripping her so that she does not have to support him. It is to the competitor's detriment. Though he is tall and leggy, he is staggering about and being forced to take a longer path than Kate; he is slowing to adjust the lady on his back; he is puffing like an old pig.

233

They break the finishing ribbon together and collapse into the waiting crowd of passengers. When William slips off her back, Kate remains upright, smiling and shaking hands offered to her with such energy that she might just have won an Olympic medal. Her competitor, however, rolls on the deck, wheezing and purpling at the cheek.

'Good lord, miss,' he manages to gasp. 'You might have warned me you were a runner.'

'But I'm not,' Kate laughs.

The man frowns up at her. 'What are you then?'

Kate waits a moment before she answers, to let her new audience settle. Then she straightens up and shows them her fullest smile.

'I'm a strongwoman.'

After that performance, she considers her boxing class will be fully subscribed come the morning. As she and William step towards the dining saloon, stomachs tightening in anticipation of a well-earned lunch, she decides that she will rise early and ready the smoking room again, just in case.

'I'm sure it will make a difference,' she tells William.

But she never does discover whether she is right. If anyone arrives at the smoking-room door the following day, and knocks at it, or even plucks up the bravery to open it and step through, they do not find Kate inside. Because that night, held in the sea-swayed black cradle of a dreamless sleep, Kate falls gravely ill.

22.

R.M.S. *Oroya*
1903
ARTHUR

Arthur is sick. She knows it as surely as she knows her own name. He should be a picture, laid on the soft white blanket which has been knitted especially for him – no hand-me-downs for little Arthur, there not having been a boy for such a while – but his face is bruised with screaming and his gums hang with slaver and his eyes, usually as clear and green as his father's, are only tight black stitches, leaking a tides-worth of tears.

'Arthur,' she coos. 'Arthur. It's all right. Mam is here.'

But Arthur cannot seem to hear her. He screams and screams. He is starving, she realises. He needs her milk. How could he be expected to thrive without her milk, being as little as he is? She pulls at the neck of her nightdress, meaning to expose her breast and hook her nipple into his waiting mouth, but the ruched cotton only tightens, noose-like, and begins to choke her. She coughs, but cannot seem to open her throat. It is clogged by something heavy and bitter-tasting.

'It's all right, Arthur,' she says again, and the words are a gargle, unintelligible. 'I won't be long.'

She drags at the nightdress, hears the light pop of cotton snapping, but still she cannot remove it, and Arthur cries and cries, and his tears form waterfalls and slosh over the sides of the bed, and Kate looks down to find her feet submerged. She lifts one foot, watches as its distorted form returns to normality, then lowers it and sees it made short and pale as a flatfish once more. Arthur's tears rise to surge around her ankles, and then her calves, and she feels herself pulled away from the bed. She makes a lunge, meaning to scoop the little boy up and press him to her chest, but the bed bobs away from her, its wooden legs lifted on the rising water, and tips backwards, and she screams, because he is going to slip off the back and drown. Her precious, green-eyed boy. He is going to drown in his own tears, because he was too small, far too small, and she shouldn't have left him to grow without her milk and her arms and her scent. She makes another grab for the bed and manages to clamp her fingers around the edge of the blanket. This, she hauls towards her, arm over arm, like a fisherman. She will bring him in, then – a prize catch. But his stout body is a rock in the middle of the blanket, and it is growing heavier somehow, and Kate can hardly shift the blanket now, but she keeps on dragging and heaving until, with a sudden slackening, the blanket falls away from the bed and settles, rippling, on the surface of the water. It is entirely empty of Arthur. As she is.

She recoils from the blanket as, under the weight of the tears her little boy is crying for her, it begins to sink away. Over her nightdress, she grasps at her breasts and squeezes, wondering why they are not full and hard with milk. It should not have dried up so soon. Arthur will need it.

'Mam is here,' she tries again. But the words jam in her throat. 'Arthur. I'm here.'

And with this claim, finally, she jolts up, rolls onto her side, and vomits all over the cabin floor. She is not there.

The seasickness continues for days. William sits beside her, clutching her hand and murmuring promises she cannot understand. He props her up and pours water between her lips. Kate chokes up what she does not dribble down her neck. He cuts dry, pale meat into microscopic cubes and coaxes her to chew it, but the action of grinding her teeth backwards and forwards only causes her to gag. Her olive skin fades to a chalky grey; her eyes grow glassy. After four days of being unable to swallow water, she is still vomiting and her lips are cracked and bloodied. When she attempts to talk, more skin tears off and she tries to lick at the cuts, but her tongue is too dry. After six days, her eyes are slow and black and her face is sunken around them, as though the skin is glued directly to the bone. All the flesh of her is disappearing. After eight days, she vomits repeatedly in her sleep and William lies wrapped around her, angling her head so that she will not choke. There is no food left to bring up, but her stomach convulses and her throat contracts and she ejects a frothy mixture of spittle and blood.

At intervals, she gasps awake and seizes William, though he cannot imagine where she finds the strength.

'Turn the ship around,' she begs.

William brushes damp strings of hair away from her face. 'Hush.'

'Arthur is sick,' she explains. 'You have to turn the ship around. We need to go back to him.'

'No,' Williams whispers. 'No. You can't turn a steamship around just like that. Arthur is fine. Well. He's a strapping young man. It's you who is sick.'

It's you who is sick. The sentence plays around Kate's mind with all the boom and resonance of a brass band. It writhes and slinks and blares. It skitters and heartbeats. She does not think it can be true.

'I've never been weak,' she insists. And William shushes her and settles her back against her pillow and she closes her eyes and the children are there. Nora – spinning, arms stretched wide, in the middle of the garden behind the Abergavenny house, her skirt whirling around her knees to make a spinning top of her, and her dark hair gleaming under the watching moon. Mona – perched, buckled shoes and lace-topped socks swinging, on the piano stool in the hallway and pressing an exploratory finger to one ivory note at a time. Arthur – grinning gummily up from his cot and extending a soft, starred hand out for his rattle, then chuckling at the smooth wooden touch of it. Her heart shatters at the thought of Arthur, reaching up out of his cot and finding no one smiling down at him, and she grabs at her chest, as though she might be able to press it back together if she only clenches her fist tight enough. But the sensation only worsens the harder she tries; this is not a problem she can solve with determination and strength. It is not that she loves Arthur more than she loves the girls, but rather that she thinks him more in need of her. From the first, when he had been blanket-wrapped and lowered into her arms, he had been more docile, more hushed, than had Nora or Mona. Where they had wriggled and whinged, Arthur had only stared up at his mother, cow-eyed, and opened his mouth to a tiny yawn. She had known then that he would break her.

The ship's solitary doctor visits 'Miss Roberts' daily, ducking through the cabin door with his leather bag held out in front of him like a shield, then straightening and pushing his glasses up his nose with a crooked knuckle. Sometimes, Kate is conscious and partly alert for these visits. Other times, she does not even know he has been. Today, on the eleventh day of her complaint, she is awake and sitting up in bed, but she hasn't the power to move. William has washed her and positioned her here like a china doll, and she had no option but to let him. Her muscles have melted to nothing. Her eyes linger in one spot far too long. Even her thoughts are slow. This seems to have persuaded William that she cannot hear him, but quite the opposite is true. Her hearing is amplified. Every word William speaks is a shout which echoes around the lonely cove of her illness.

'It can't just be seasickness,' he says. 'She isn't improving. There must be something else...'

The doctor gives a sniff, thinking perhaps the pause will give more weight to his response. 'Has she always suffered during your travels?'

'Not like this... She's dying, isn't she?'

'She's badly dehydrated,' the doctor replies. 'But there's nothing to stop her from making a full recovery. You've told me she is strong...'

'Even the strongest people are made weak on occasion,' William mutters, his hand bothering his brow.

The doctor claps his shoulder with a big, steady paw. 'She's not well, Mr Roberts. But she might be well enough again, given time. Get as much water into her as you're able and be patient. I saw her carting you along the deck in that daft race.' He smiles kindly. 'Easy as anything. I can't say I've ever witnessed a woman do the like. I've every faith she'll start her fight soon.'

But Kate does not want to fight. She wants to sit with Arthur draped heavy across her lap and rock him into sleep. She wants to hold a skipping rope for Nora and laugh when she tangles up in it. She wants to throw a ball to Mona and cheer at the delight on the little girl's face when finally she catches it cleanly. Contrary to the doctor's wishes, Kate, who has always known how to fight, thinks she ought now to set about learning to be gentle.

Psalm 46 is jammed in her mind. *God is our refuge and strength,* recites her father, *an ever-present help in trouble. Therefore we will not fear, though the earth give way and the mountains fall into the heart of the sea, though its waters roar and foam and the mountains quake with their surging.*

Soon, they will all fall into the heart of the sea, Kate thinks as the ship jolts and dips beneath her. Perhaps it is time to start listening to Reverend Williams. Perhaps it is God, after all, who will provide her with strength now.

Arthur is out on the hurricane deck. Kate wakes with the knowledge already on her tongue. 'Arthur,' she says. William, slumped into unintended sleep on the sofa, does not move except to fall from side to side as the ship leans and drops. Outside, the waves have turned violent. The porthole offers her only a round black glimpse of empty sky, distorted by the slap of driving rain. Arthur will already have caught a chill. She glances around the cabin and, seeing her coat thrown over the travelling case, pulls it on directly over her nightdress. The cold material shocks against her clammy skin like electricity. She buttons it quickly and looks around for a pair of boots. William's slippers catch her attention first – she pokes fun at him for bringing slippers when they tour, but she is glad of them now – and, pushing them on, she staggers for the door.

The lights in the passageways flicker against the mounting storm, and Kate runs a palm along the wall to steady herself. Her vision is unreliable in any case, so giddied is she by rising from bed for the first time in nearly a fortnight, and she is less troubled by the intermittent darkness than she is by the lurching of the ship. How enormous she had seemed to her the day they came aboard. How much more gigantic the waves must be to toss her around so. Kate hardly wants to think on such magnitude; it makes her feel too small by comparison.

She shoves the thought aside and steps quicker, along the corridor, up the steps, past the music saloon, and finally out onto the hurricane deck, where she is promptly thrown to the boards.

Kate sprawls across the swilling deck, her hair plastered over her eyes, her mouth gaping and spluttering. The axe-drop of rain has winded her and she cannot breathe. Angry gusts pin her down as another wave, dark-arched and white-headed, rears over the railings, crashes onto the deck, and washes away.

'Arthur!' she cries. 'Hold on.'

She knows by instinct where she will find him. Between the second mast and the stored lifeboats, there is a thick coil of rope, deep enough to hide a man inside. Before she fell ill, Kate had sat on it while William took photos of her with some of the white-whiskered crew. Her son, she is certain, with his brimming curiosity, would have scaled the mountain of rope in order to climb inside the nearest lifeboat and take a closer look. That's where he'll be, held small and safe inside the lifeboat. But he is not much more than a year old, and he might so easily have slipped in. All that black sea, which can conceal creatures as big as whales and wreck ships without a splinter of evidence, would make nothing of a bright-eyed little boy. He would be swallowed whole. And then, so would she.

Kate scrambles up onto her hands and knees and begins crawling the endless length of the *Oroya*. Her progress is slow, hampered as she is by the rhythmic crashing of the waves, and the weight of the water, and William's oversized slippers, and her slopping wool coat. She stops to kick off the slippers. She unbuttons the coat and casts that off, too. It is easier then to move forwards, to edge nearer to her handsome, so-ready-to-smile Arthur. Art, she thinks. Perhaps she will call him Art for short from now on, because he is surely a masterpiece. Those exquisite soft curls at the nape of his neck. The deep plummet of his Cupid's bow. The shadowed dents on the backs of his hands which will eventually fill with knuckle bone. If they protrude like his father's, she will teach him to box and he will become a prizefighter. If they do not, she might steer him towards ball sports. Rugby. Or tennis, should he grow tall and long-limbed. Or perhaps he will be a scholar rather than a sportsman. He might study the law, or medicine, or engineering. He will be more introspective than his sisters. Nora is already a showgirl. Mona, though quieter, has an ear for music which will bring her to the theatres. But Arthur... It is as though Kate knows more and less of him than she does the girls. As though, somehow, he contains more possibilities. And one of those possibilities remains disaster.

She cannot fathom how she had forgotten he was aboard ship. She cannot think how she might have lost him. He should never have been out of her sight.

Kate is shaking with cold by the time she sights that thick coil of rope. Her hands, spread like starfish on the deck before her, are mottled grey and blue and purple. She cannot feel her feet. Heaving herself up onto her knees, she grasps the rope as best she can and hauls her slick, lumpen body over its scratchy surface. The rope fibres pick at her skin through the wetted cotton of her nightdress; her pale parts redden and smart.

Overhead, another silver-wedged blade of rain descends, ready to separate Kate from her child with a single chop. She moves faster.

And beside her, suddenly, there comes a woman. Or the impression of one. She is a collection of shifting white lines, arcs of light perhaps, drawn together to take the form of a warrior, striding along the deck, her long plaited hair sailing behind her, her right hand bunched around the hilt of a sword and her left hand carrying a rounded shield. The wind pulls at her, distorting her edges, but she is not deterred. She is strong. Indomitable. Her eyes are set in anger and her chin is high and her shoulders are pitched forward. She is, Kate knows by some instinct, moving towards her son. She is Gwenllian ferch Gruffydd, come down through the trees with her two boys to lead the attack on the Norman stronghold at Castell Cydweli, and she is both terrifying and beautiful.

Kate knows she is only a spectre, a flicker of a story she knows about a woman who was brave enough to find her way into history, cast out by her desperate mind, but she is bolstered by her presence all the same. Gwenllian: terrifying and beautiful. A singular woman, then, really is able to be both. Fierce and gentle. Proud and reticent. Strong and feminine. And isn't that the paradox the newspapers cannot reconcile – that Kate is both strong and feminine. Time and again they exclaim that she appears 'womanly despite her strength', that she is 'not what one might expect of a female athlete', that in her everyday clothes she might be 'entirely normal'. Well, she is entirely normal. She is a woman, with all

244

the attendant fears and loves and doubts one might expect, and she loves William with a passion she had never expected, and she loves her children with a force she had not known existed. And oh, to be a mother is to be strong. How is it that the newspapers don't know that? How is it that they do not recognise that there is no greater strength than that required to expose your children to the world? To be strong is the measure of womanhood.

She can hardly believe that she had thought, however briefly, to look to God now. She reaches into her mind for her father's voice, for those words he took such comfort from, so that she might examine them anew, but her search is met with silence. His voice is gone. It has been replaced by her own.

When eventually Kate drags herself to the top of the coiled rope pile, she is bleeding from both knees, one foot, and the right side of her torso. Her nightdress has torn open to reveal her gashed ribcage. Two shaky red railway tracks mark the deck behind her. She twists about so that she can dangle over the gunwale and reach into the lifeboat, but when she peers inside, there is only darkness. She wills a flash of lightning to appear and illuminate the vessel, but none does. The sky is an inverted fen, a smoky sump, and she wonders at light ever having managed to penetrate it. Dawn seems to her a make-believe as she leans further over the gunwale and attempts to find detail in the gloom. The lifeboat plays tricks on her then. In place of the bench, she sees a child's back, hunched protectively over his own arms and legs. Where a lifebuoy has been discarded in the footings, she sees the curve of a skull.

Arthur.

She brings her feet up underneath her, meaning to clamber down into the boat and clutch him to her, rub warmth into him, bring him back to life. But in rushing the movement, she giddies herself again, and she is compelled to close her eyes. As soon as she does, the blank place behind her lids makes its claim on her, drawing her into darkness. Seasickness, the doctor said. But Kate knows that it is more than that. She is not only seasick, she is heartsick.

It is the last thought she has before she drops into a faint.

Beneath her limp body, the heavy rope slips a little. Above, the gleaming pitch underside of the next thundering wave rises.

The *Oroya*'s route to Australia is set and she will stop for nothing.

23.

Perth, Australia
1903
OPENINGS

Somehow, they find the fortitude to ensure that their opening night for Harry Rickards at the Perth Royal Theatre, on November 19th, 1903, is a roaring success. Outside, dusk falls like a drunk: slowly and then all at once. Inside, the billed Atlas and Vulcana juggle the fifty-pound barbells, tossing them back and forth to each other to cheers from the invisible audience. They slow press increasing weights, announcing each augmentation as though they might not be good for the challenge: 'One hundred and seventy-five pounds!' 'Two hundred pounds!' Vulcana tucks herself onto a pedestal and turns and tenses to best display the lines of her musculature under the stage lights. Atlas pivots a one-hundred-and-eighty-pound barbell with his feet.

The only difference – and it is a change the audience will be completely unaware of – is that tonight Vulcana is taller and broader and older than ever she has been. To her irritation, she is forced to skip the big finale. They will save her lifting William one-handed into the air for Sydney or Melbourne. She is not ready yet, and William knows it.

Perhaps she never will be. Mabel never has been as strong as Kate.

Afterwards, in their hotel room, William paces about pretending to tidy away their clothes and cries silently at the effort the evening has cost Kate – to give up her place onstage so that the show might go on; to train with Mabel beforehand, both to remind Mabel of the poses and to test how her own body dealt with them; to walk back from the theatre to the hotel. On her return, she had collapsed into bed, her face shining with cold, tacky sweat. And there she still lies, shivering, as William hangs his head, avoids her eye. He does not know how to help her. He cannot stand seeing her so vulnerable. He fears, as much as she does, that she has given everything she had to give.

But isn't this what women do? she wants to ask him. *Isn't this what women are* expected *to do? To keep on and on, regardless of exhaustion or fear or distress. To bear their pain quietly. It is only what men have asked for centuries.*

As she watches William push the back of his hand across his jaw and sniff away his tears, she wonders whether he will suggest breaking their engagement with Harry. But nothing follows except his shallow stuttered breaths as he attempts to calm himself, and she cannot find the energy to articulate her thoughts, so she wraps her arms around her middle, curls onto her side in the lonely bed, and descends into an empty sleep.

'Tomorrow,' she says. William watches her closed eyes as

she speaks into her dreams; his tears well and fall again. 'I'll be well enough to go on tomorrow.'

At breakfast some mornings later, William flutters the *West Australian* at her like a magician holding a newly revealed dove aloft to spread its wings. Kate winces against its flapping. William, oblivious, snaps the newspaper in half and takes a sip of his tea.

'Listen to this,' he says. She concentrates hard on his voice amongst the rattle of spoons against teacups, the hiss and gurgle of boiled water being poured. The breakfast room is a fug of ground coffee beans and sizzled meat, of twenty-degree air and chit-chat. '"There is only one woman in Perth being talked about just now, and she is Vulcana, the lady muscular wonder performing at the Royal."' His voice rises slightly higher than usual, squeezed thin with excitement.

He grins and reaches across the table to press his thumb to the fleshy place between her thumb and her forefinger. It is how they have always held hands: loose enough to be able to extricate themselves in a hurry; close enough for Kate to feel William's pulse throbbing against her own skin. She watches the steam from their teacups rise between them like a smokescreen, and tries not to wince at a simple touch. Every inch of her hurts.

'Isn't that wonderful?'

'I suppose it is,' Kate replies. She is foggy still, after her seasickness, after forcing herself onstage these last nights. Where, ordinarily, William would appear sharper in her sights than anyone else, today everyone and everything inside the breakfast room is a touch out of focus: like buildings viewed across a street blurred by rain. The stolen scents of other people's breakfasts cause a resurgence of her biliousness, and she tries to close her nose and mouth against it without making a fuss.

William massages her hand with his thumb. His skin snags against hers, but she enjoys the pressure. The sharp points of pain it causes keep her closer to consciousness. She thinks about the action of swallowing as though she must offer herself instruction in it: the pooling of saliva on her tongue; the tightening at the back of her throat; the rippling downward convulsion. She is too hot.

'It is,' William insists. 'It goes on. "And she is worth raving about."' He looks up from the newspaper to flash his eyes at her. She softens a little. It's nice that he is pleased. William never ceases to be proud of his... That old automatic process makes her want to think 'wife', though she will never be truly that. The role is already taken. She is, and ever will be, simply 'his Kate'. He reads on. '"In repose, Vulcana is as beautifully round-limbed and proportioned as any woman ever made." See,' he says. 'Didn't I always tell you?' He clears his throat and continues. '"But once her muscles are asked to come into play, they stand out all over like the knots on the back of a sturgeon."'

'A *sturgeon*?' The oddity of the comparison brings her back to herself. She snorts a little but manages to keep the spittle from escaping her lips. True, her weight is returning day on day, but she is not the woman she was and her muscles remain leaner and tighter than they had been.

'A sturgeon,' William confirms, biting down on a laugh.

'All that, and they've compared me to a fish! What a denouement.'

'Well, it is a muscular fish,' William offers.

A vision enters her mind, of herself as some novel species of mermaid, which, rather than retaining the beautiful parts of a woman and a colourful shiny-scaled tail, is made up instead of a gawping grey fish head and the brawny human body of, say, a coal miner. The result is hideous, and she descends into laughter as she attempts to communicate the invented monster to William.

'Does the transition to human form happen at the waist or the shoulders?' William asks.

'At the shoulders,' Kate decides, since that would make for the most disproportionate composition.

'And would the creature speak from the fish mouth or be mute?'

'Mute, I think. Since it would have no human throat to shape the words.'

William nods in agreement. 'You're quite right. It would swim, though, even without a tail.'

'It would.' Tears of amusement course down Kate's face now. 'Though not well. It would not be very streamlined.'

'No. Rather too weighty in the head department, I should say. If the head is of giant dimensions, that is. I'm imagining the fish neck to begin at shoulder-width.' He holds up his arms to demonstrate, and Kate weakens further. She lays her hands on the tablecloth and drops her face into the crook of her elbow. She makes an 'ooh' sound as she exhales, trying to slow down her breathing so that the ache in her stomach lessens. There might be people staring at her; there might not. Kate doesn't much care. She and William haven't laughed like this in weeks.

'Shoulder-width,' she agrees. 'Yes. *Ooh*. It might even be feasible that the human body has some fins. Growing out from the forearms, perhaps. What do you think?'

'Why not,' William smiles. 'The creature is ours to design, is it not?'

'It is. Though I wonder at why we haven't made it beautiful in that case.'

'Well. Firstly, because it was the sturgeon who began it, and the sturgeon, for all its qualities, can hardly be considered a beautiful fish. And secondly...' He pincers a slice of apple off his plate, bites half of it away, then speaks past the chunk. 'Because we are not so predictable as all that.'

'We certainly are not,' Kate agrees. The thought comes to her again, that she will never be his wife. It is a thought which insists, at intervals, upon being heard. It tempts her to speculate about what life might have been, if William had married Kate instead of Alice, and they had stayed in Abergavenny, and raised their children under the cloud of the ironworks. She would have had her babies at her skirts, if it had happened that way. People would pass her in the street and call out '*Bore da*, Mrs Williams', and she would smile and smile to be addressed so. How easily their lives might have taken that path.

But they would not have been truly happy. William would have greyed into misery and returned home from his shift each night unable even to play with the children. And Kate... Would Kate have been as content as Alice is? She suspects not. She can hardly bear to acknowledge the fact, even to herself, but it is possible that, however much she longs for the world to recognise that they belong to one another, the reality of having William and nothing more would not have been enough. She needed all of this. Or, she needed it at first at least.

She plucks the other half of the apple slice from between his fingers and pops it into her mouth. In response, William rises a few inches out of his chair, leans across the table, and kisses her quickly. The impact is a tad too rough and smarts her lips, but she hardly minds. William's affections have never come particularly smoothly.

When he lowers himself back into his chair again, his face is suddenly serious.

'We can tell Harry we can't do it, you know. It wouldn't be the end of the world.'

Kate feels her body slacken for the first time since they boarded the *Oroya*. Her shoulders fall away from her ears. She slumps slightly, from the spine. Some unnameable part of her, deep inside her ribcage, opens up again.

There it is – William's unspoken, 'I love you.' It is exactly what she needed to hear. It persuades her, on the instant, not to tell William that she isn't sure she can carry on; that her strength is not returning as it ought and that she is teetering constantly on the brink of something unknown and frightening; that this Kate hasn't the power to make Australia their biggest tour yet and that her grand plans are doomed to failure. It persuades her, too, not to tell him that some splinter of Arthur's spirit – his milk-cry, his soap scent, his laughter – has been haunting her ever since they stepped off the *Oroya*. It persuades her, for a moment, to forget the lives unlived.

24.

Melbourne, Australia
1903
A FIASCO

They sell out nightly at the Perth Royal Theatre, and sit late
over brandy and cigars with Harry Rickards to plot a route
across the country. It is decided that as they travel from west
to east along the coast, they will stop in Adelaide, Melbourne,
Sydney, and Brisbane to charm a succession of new and
hungry audiences. Australians, Harry explains, adore British
music hall, and given their experiences in Perth, Kate and
William would be fools to doubt the claim.

The troupe now is made up of Mabel, Abe, Hatfield, Young
– Cummings having struck out on his own in London, though
Kate hasn't heard how he has fared – and a new addition
called Jem. Kate does not know and has not asked what 'Jem'
might be short for, but she has decided that she likes the lad.
He is energetic and cheeky and a little too much trouble, and
she admires that in a person. Nobody ever changed anything
without proving themselves to be a little too much trouble.

Jem claims to be eighteen years of age – but then again, so
does Kate when the Australian newspapers ask. On the other
side of the world, perhaps fifteen-year-old Jem and twenty-

seven-year-old Kate can be any age they choose – within reason, of course; Kate is already pushing it – and they enjoy being eighteen. It has allowed Jem, Kate suspects, to escape an orphanage childhood. It allows Kate to pretend, as she must, for her sanity, that she is not a wanderlusting mother of three who has relinquished her children to another woman's care.

It impresses the journalists, too, when they believe her barely free of her adolescence. They write gushing articles about her. *The Argus* calls her 'a marvel' and claims her exhibition worthy of disturbing 'long-established views concerning the "weakness" of the opposite sex'. She certainly hopes that might be the case. In the black, windswept heart of that night when she had crawled along the sliding deck of the *Oroya*, she had understood what she wanted to leave behind her when she was vanished into the sea, and it was only a belief, for her children. It is harder to express, now that she is safe and well again, but she has thought it over and the gist of it is this: 'You can be just as strong as you choose to be, all by yourself'.

It is an idea she has been stumbling towards for years. But now she has it in her grasp. And she wants to communicate it to as many people as possible, in case, just in case, it is the exact truth they need to hear.

The troupe wins over Adelaide and rides the railways to Melbourne, where they arrive in mid-December. Against the rattle and wheeze of the train, Kate considers that she learns two things about this strange new country they have disembarked in: firstly, that it is bigger than she ever could have envisaged; and secondly, that it is almost entirely empty. The train window shows her boundless grass plains, and white beaches which reach further than can her eye, and a glimmering sea which ruffles into nothingness. All about is made flat, a mere drawn line, by a sky so big it leaves Kate breathless. Until they arrive at the cities.

Melbourne shoots up out of the Australian earth like an automaton, all glint and angle and metal-on-metal noise. It is built on a square-grid system, to allow squealing cable trams to run easily up and down its countless straight streets: streets which are crammed with workshops and warehouses, banks and dress shops, grand hotels and merchant buildings, cafés and coffee palaces. And all of them rising, storey after storey. Melbourne bustles as surely as does London, and surprises Kate with its sophistication, its speed. Laneways hidden within blocks conceal terraced houses. Fine town houses line those blocks like uniformed soldiers, looking out over tree canopies and rooftops. Whopping great mansions stopper the street corners and invite you to turn onto another. Melbourne leads you through its maze by convincing you that you are not lost, and amongst the shoppers and the coaches and the cable trams, there are such birds. Thousands of birds. Birds the like of which Kate has never seen, with wings like paint splashes and eyes like jewels.

On the afternoon they arrive, she and Hatfield stop off at a bookshop and buy a compendium so that they might identify them. They are immediately fascinated and, while the others take their luggage to their respective rooms and wash and gulp back glass after glass of cold water, Kate and Hatfield settle on a bench beneath a particularly dense tree canopy and take turns at pointing out the passing creatures, then scouring the pages for their names.

'A crimson finch,' Hatfield announces, some minutes after a tiny red bead of a beast darts past them and they have riffled the book's pages. They startle at the intensity of the cobalt and aquamarine feathers of... 'A blue-breasted fairywren.' They wonder at the vibrancy of the ruby-and-emerald-coloured king parrot and the sun-and-sky shades of the pale-headed rosella.

'We're so dull, aren't we?' Kate says. 'We ought to be more like birds, and go about flaunting our colours.'

Hatfield smiles. 'Perhaps we would, if we had any.'

'But we do!' Kate insists. 'We're just so terribly good at hiding them. Look...'

She flicks a hand to indicate the passers-by, all of whom have been made invisible, until now, by the birds. Kate and Hatfield consider them together momentarily: their white, fawn, or grey clothing; their everyday skirts and shoes and shirts. None wears anything vibrant or unusual. None sets himself apart from his neighbour, as the birds do, with plumes of brighter colour or daring displays. They blend each into each into each: men, women, and... Kate rises abruptly from the bench at the sight of a child some way down the street. A young child. A boy. He is of an age where he finds himself just capable of tiptoeing the pavement, so long as he is held by the hand. He has his back to Kate as he trips along, but she is certain she recognises the sturdy little body, the weight of the head, the soft inward dip of the hair at the nape of his neck. He looks down as he goes, making a game of stepping only on the ladder of tree-trunk shadows which stripe the pavement and avoiding the sunlit slats between.

'Arthur,' she breathes. She knows it is him, though she cannot imagine who might be holding his hand. She can only spare a glimpse for the adult figure: a man, in shirtsleeves, fair head bent over her son. She does not want to look away from Arthur for a second longer, for fear that he will disappear again.

'What?' Hatfield asks, rising to look in the direction Kate's eyes are fixed. 'Who is it?'

Kate cannot answer. She is immobilised by horror. She is torn between racing down the street, scooping the little boy up, and rushing away with him, and going off in search of a policeman to report the man – shirtsleeves, fair hair, tall, slim – who has kidnapped her child. Her little Art. How could she have forgotten that he was here with them? How could she have misplaced him, again? Arthur – who is being taken away from her, just as easily as that, and there seems nothing she can do to stop it. The connection between her mind and her body has come loose. She cannot move. She cannot breathe. Arthur, Arthur, Arthur. If she could only call out to him... If she could only impel herself in his direction... If she only knew what best to do.

'My...' Kate begins, but before she utters the word, she catches sight of Hatfield's confused expression – her bunched eyebrows, her parted lips – and she stops. She is brought rushing back to herself. She listens to her own galloping breath and she concentrates on slowing it down, down, to an even pace. Arthur. Her boy. Her heart. Her son.

Of course he is not here. He is half a world away. Safe.

When she looks again at the child, he is fairer and slighter than Arthur. In actuality, he bears no resemblance at all to Arthur Roberts.

'Nothing,' she says. 'I just thought I saw somebody I knew. It was ... nothing.'

She lowers herself slowly back onto the bench. Hatfield follows suit. And there they remain, exclaiming at the beauty which happens so accidentally before them, flipping the pages of their new compendium, smiling when they discover the bird they are seeking to identify, until the light flattens and the street lamps flicker on and they rise to stretch.

When eventually they retire to the room they will share tonight, they find Mabel already soundly asleep, and creep inside like picklocks, undressing with shushes and giggles. It is only when she lowers herself into her bed that Kate recognises she is bone tired.

'Goodnight, Hattie,' she murmurs. And even before she hears Hatfield's reply, she is drowsing away.

That night, Kate dreams of kestrels and black kites, spiralling on the air. She dreams she can feel the wind skimming through her own stretched feathers. She dreams that the earth is a soft black veld, which sparks here and there as though littered with dropped stars, hastening past beneath her as she flies higher and higher. When she wakes, she wonders how long ago the horses abandoned her dreams, and how she could possibly have failed to notice them go.

They open at the Opera House the following evening and almost immediately they hear news of a German strongman called Herr Pagel having put out a challenge to Atlas. Herr Pagel – or the 'Lion Lifter' as he is otherwise known – is performing with the Wirth Circus and is purportedly a titan. Six-and-a-half-feet tall, broad as a bear, angry as a god, the Lion Lifter has made it known across the city that he will be bested by no man for strength.

Here, then, is her chance. If Atlas can best Herr Pagel in front of a big enough crowd, his name will bound across Australia before them on a chorus of disbelief. People will talk of a man so unfeasibly strong that he can not only lift lions but wrestle them into submission, a man made so heavy by his musculature that he must have an entire train carriage to himself on account of how his bulk causes the wheels to grind against the tracks. If she handles this right, she can make Atlas a myth. And then she will be able to go home.

'Don't engage with him, William,' Kate warns. She needs time to plot this all out, to arrange the right competition and the most enthused audience. This is her best, perhaps her only, chance to capture Australia's imagination. She knows, though, that William is not at his strongest. As her star has risen, so he has stood further aside, trained less, failed to challenge his own records. To beat Herr Pagel, he will really need to apply himself. 'Not yet,' she says.

William pacifies her with a small nod: he won't.

But she knows what he is about and her heart burns with it when, later that week, he stands onstage and puts out a challenge of his own: To 'any man in Melbourne' who can lift Atlas's own weight as he does, 'with one hand', he will gift fifty Great British pounds.

The audience cheers. 'Come along! Fifty pounds!' William bellows, lifted by the crowd's excitement. 'Any man!'

Naturally, this 'any man' – who they all know to be a very specific man indeed – hears of the invitation and appears the very next evening to take it up. Kate sees nothing of him until it is too late. She waits, as usual, for lovely old Mr Winton to finish his funny turn with his ventriloquial dolls. She watches from the wings as Mabel and Hatfield draw 'oohs' from the audience with their weightlifting feats. She stretches, steps onstage, executes her first tableau, then retires again to the wings while the biograph is set up. During this demonstration, it is her habit to stretch again and more thoroughly, in readiness for her big finish, when she will lift Atlas above her head. The operator turns the handle and the biograph cranks into life. It is a vista of the Thames Harry has chosen to display to his Australian audience, and as the river begins to roll softly across the screen, accompanied by a pleasingly sweet melody from the orchestral stalls, so a large, brutish figure clambers up onstage and menaces before it. The operator, ignorant of the interruption, continues to urge the Thames along its course, but for the audience the view now consists almost entirely of an enormous man held in silhouette.

In her waiting place, Kate withers. The man now onstage truly is as broad as a bear. He can be none other than Herr Pagel.

'Get down,' someone bawls.

'Don't you know we can't see?'

But Pagel is not to be deterred.

'Ladies and gentlemen,' he roars. 'I am here about the challenge that was made yesterday evening. I am come to claim Atlas' fifty pounds.'

There follows a moment's silence before the audience decide that yes, this is something they want to see. They send up a cheer and Kate feels it as gooseflesh down her neck. She looks around for William, meaning to grasp his arm and dissuade him from taking the stage. But she does not see him until he strides on, from the opposite direction, and meets Pagel at the footlights. The two men stand toe to toe. A gasp from the audience. Despite his fire and his spunk, William is dwarfed by his opponent. He is a child, standing before his father to endure a telling off. Both are cast in long, angled shadows. The orchestra has stopped playing; only the reverberation of released strings sounds around the theatre now. Finally, the biograph operator stops turning the handle and the picture of the Thames shutters off. The lights go up.

'You have not put down your own fifty pounds insurance,' William says, loud enough for the audience to hear.

Pagel growls. 'There is no need of it.'

'That's as might be, but that was the deal.'

Mr Winton, lingering in the wings, calls out, 'Perhaps you

ought to both put up fifty pounds now, and make it a like-for-like competition.' But William will not hear of it.

He turns to the audience. 'Mr Pagel can lift any weight he should like, but I'll not lift with him. Not tonight. He was to put down his fifty pounds insurance in advance, and he has failed to do so.'

Kate feels herself pale: William has not filled his weight with sand, she realises. He has lifted it empty. He'll be revealed as a fraud if he goes head-to-head with this giant German and cannot raise the weight he claimed earlier to have no trouble with.

Hoots and boos issue from the crowd.

'What about last night?' they call. 'Any man, you said.'

'Not tonight,' William blusters. His ears are burning red now: crimson finches, Kate thinks. The colour spreads in blotches down his neck. 'Mr Pagel has insulted me from all parts of the town and seeks only to do so again by appearing without the required sum. Just last night, my name was mentioned scurrilously in his establishment and in the press.'

Kate does not know if this is true. If it is, William has kept it from her. But why didn't he just prepare? Why didn't he fill the weight?

'No!' cries the audience.

'Yes!' William persists. He is spluttering now. 'And I am now in the doctor's hands for rheumatism.' If he had hoped this would elicit sympathy from the audience, he has gauged them badly wrong. Laughter erupts in the aisles. Kate's eyelids flutter against it. William shouts louder over the chaos. 'So I will lift no more tonight. But let Mr Pagel lift my bar. It can be brought out on the instant.'

Why hadn't he filled it with sand earlier? Kate wonders again. All this embarrassment could be stopped if he had simply filled it and could lift it again. Certainly, the German would be fit for the challenge. His forearms are bunched with muscle; his upper arms are as wide as tram wheels. William, for all his bravado, could not equal him. But he could lift that weight. He should be able to. Kate has seen him do it a thousand times before.

'Should I have it brought out?' he asks the audience, but they will not be drawn back to the man they had so recently whooped for. They want a head-to-head, a battle of brawn, the Welshman versus the German. They are wild with frustration now. They bray and bark like animals. Some are out of their seats, shaking their fists. Others cup their hands round their mouths to amplify their screamed demands. The noise is tremendous. Kate can feel it in her stomach – a tremor. Beneath her feet, the stage boards seem to quake. She steps out to stand alongside William. Pagel is trying to make himself heard. His mouth is moving, but no words can be discerned over the audience, who are closing in on the stage now. The orchestral stalls have been deserted. One man hops over the divide and into the stalls, knocking a standing double bass to the ground with a hollow, reverberating thud.

'Enough,' Kate says, more to herself than to anyone else.

Pagel's mouth is still pumping, and William is moving closer, ostensibly to listen to the larger man's complaints, but he cannot seem to stop talking himself. Kate catches snippets. 'What is it? Twenty stone to eleven. And I'm expected to dance like a monkey on a chain. Well, no, sir. How dare you come parading into my theatre without warning...'

Without warning, Kate thinks. Quite. Warning which would have allowed you to set him up. She glances about herself, for something which might constitute a weapon should the audience finally breach the stage and begin a brawl. She sees only Mr Winton, shuffling towards her as fast as his arthritic legs will allow. He looks naked without his puppets. She turns to meet him and claps her hands around his shoulders. She does not want him involved in this ... fiasco is the only term she can attribute it.

'The police have arrived,' he says into her ear. 'I've seen them from the window. They have instructions to clear the stage and the auditorium if order can't be maintained. Come away now, miss. Come away.'

And, to her surprise, for she has always been more than willing to lend her weight to the ending of a dispute, she does. She takes a deep breath, tilts up her chin, and steps offstage after Mr Winton with all the grace she can manage. Because, in turning to speak to Mr Winton, she has spotted him again. Her little lad. Arthur. Someone has propped him in a seat on the front row and he sits there now, his tiny leather shoes flapping just over the edge of the seat cushion, his chubby hands slapping at the fabric, and cries into the ruckus. He is overwhelmed by the noise. He does not understand that he is surrounded by so many dangers, but he senses it. He might be knocked from the seat by the rush of policemen into the auditorium. He might be trampled by the rioting audience. Pagel might abduct him and threaten to hold him hostage unless William competes. How he keeps managing to slip away from her, Kate cannot say, but it seems that always in Australia Arthur is at one remove. Sometimes, he is altogether invisible. But she sees him now, and he is close by, and she can go to him.

As she passes the confused and frightened biograph operator, she signals to him to begin turning his handle again. The lights are promptly brought down and the audience, soothed by the returned sight of the shimmering Thames, gradually abates. Herr Pagel and Atlas stand onstage a while longer, positioned nose to nose and returned to silhouettes now by the footlights, until finally, the deflated victims of an increasingly uninterested audience, they are obliged to turn and walk away.

Reaching Arthur's seat, Kate finds it abandoned. Like my children, she thinks. Like my heart.

'You should have told me you were going to set that up,' Kate hisses into William's ear as they ride the tram back to the hotel. 'I could have...' *Made sure it went to plan*, she thinks, but she does not finish the sentence. The clunking movement of the vehicle pushes them towards each other to bump shoulders before the impact repels them again. In, bump, out. In, bump, out. Like two magnets, Kate and William.

The rest of the troupe are chattering about Herr Pagel and how mad he is.

'Everyone knows you don't stomp all over another performer's stage,' Jem declares. 'If he wanted to take up the challenge, he should have done it properly, by appointment...' Jem's eyes are trained out through the darkened windowpane, and he does not notice Mabel and Abe share a smile at his expense. *Just a boy*, their eyes say. *Everyone knows, indeed.*

'Do you think it would have come to fisticuffs, had the police not been called?' Hatfield wonders.

'I wouldn't have liked to have taken him on,' Young says. 'Did you see the size of him?'

'Big as a bear,' Abe agrees.

Young nods. 'And just as grizzly.'

'I thought he was quite attractive,' Mabel puts in.

'You did not!'

'I certainly did. I like a man with a rough edge.'

Jem's eyes pop open. 'He was so rough he didn't have any edges.'

Through the laughter that follows, Kate waits for William to spill a response into her ear, but none is forthcoming. He is apparently newly fascinated by his hands, which he knits and unknits in his lap: the protruding knuckles slot into each other like pipework into its elbows. She angles a glare at him. She is angry. Of course she is angry. For a fleet moment, she had thought him in real danger and been truly frightened. But since that moment passed, all she has been able to think of is their big chance at greatness. Wasted. And for what? Pride? Even now, she is not convinced about how much of that ridiculous scene William had intended. Impatient, again, he had obviously wanted to lure Herr Pagel into a contest too soon – why else make that stupid announcement? – but he surely hadn't meant to humiliate himself so? Under the doctor for rheumatism? She's heard nothing of it. An off-the-cuff lie, then, to cover his lack of preparedness when Pagel came without the warning William had expected. To cover the fact that his weight was unfilled. But how long has he been performing with empty weights, and why? Oh, she'll tempt the facts out of him in the end. But for now, she only wants to be alone with him, so that she can fume more effectively.

'I think I'll get off at the next stop and walk the rest of the way,' she says.

When she does, Mabel follows her, but William does not.

25.

Melbourne, Australia
1903
THE NEWSPAPERS

'Tell me,' the journalist says, 'if before all this physical culture you were a weakling?'

Kate eyes the man meditatively. He is a weaselly little chap, perhaps five feet in height, with small round glasses pushed too far up his nose and too-eager a head. Every time he speaks, he bobs towards her, pencil poised, as if braced to physically catch the words she might speak in response. Kate feels for him. He has the jittery disposition of one desperate to please.

She does not particularly enjoy interviewing with the newspapers. They always seem more interested in her childhood than her adult self, and she's never entirely sure she has kept the story straight: William as her significantly older brother; their invented father encouraging the pursuit of athleticism; the poor excuses for William being so fair in appearance and she so dark. They had not had a chance to invent a solid backstory before they had gained a name for themselves and were being asked for one, and this bundled-up narrative has accumulated inchmeal over the years as the questions have been posed. Still, Kate does not feel confident delivering it. And besides, her objective in agreeing to the interviews is not to talk about herself, as such, but about her purpose as she now understands it. That belief she had so wanted to communicate to her children the night she was very nearly swept off the *Oroya* is not, in fact, just for her children, but for all the women who might be ready to hear it.

And in Australia, it seems, there are plenty more women listening than in Wales, England, Spain, and France combined. Every night this week, the Opera House auditorium has been packed with women. Perhaps, she thinks now, she will ask William about including a caption on her posters. Those words – *You can be just as strong as you choose to be* – directly beneath her name. That would be something.

'What did you say your name was?'

He had given the name of the newspaper – *The Herald*, was it? Or *The Courier* perhaps? – but had not offered his own. Sad, Kate thinks, to deem yourself of such scant import.

'My name?' he replies. 'Oh. Yes. Sandy.'

He does not divulge whether this is his given name or his surname, and Kate does not enquire further.

'No, Sandy,' she says. 'I never was a weakling. I was quite strong from the start. In fact, I remember being only eleven years of age and lifting heavy logs above my head. Do you know, not long after, I even stopped a runaway horse with just my hands and a determined attitude. But that's the better part of it – a determined attitude. It is my belief that you can achieve just about anything you wish if you are in possession of such a thing.'

'And what else do you wish to achieve, Miss Vulcana?' the man, Sandy, continues. 'That is to say, you have hundreds of medals attesting to your strength. Is your determined attitude still intact now you've achieved what you set out to achieve?'

This is a better question, though the assumption as to her intent is entirely incorrect. Kate smiles at Sandy. How old is he? At first glance, she had thought him in his middle-forties, but she sees now that he has no wrinkle lines and barely a whisker of facial hair. His eyes, though, are deep with the knowledge of something or other, and wide with kindness. He might be anywhere between twenty and fifty. She has already decided to offer him the most truthful answers she can muster.

'Quite intact,' Kate replies. 'Perhaps more so than ever. You see, my purpose is not to win medals, but to impress upon other women the importance of physical culture, and to encourage them to take it up. Swimming, skipping, training with dumb-bells. Whatever it might be.'

She looks about her dressing room for a more profound way to conclude the point, which seems so straightforward and ordinary now that she has come to understand it. The room is small, functional, containing two chairs, a narrow table, and a large mirror – which she presently faces away from. On the table behind Sandy, or Mr Sandy, are the lengths of cotton she wraps tight around her wrists to perform, unwound into curls, her hairbrush, an opened tin of talcum, and a stout china teapot. A lone lamp, positioned near the door, illuminates the room. And so much the better, Kate thinks, for she would not want a better view of the smoke stains on the walls or the holes the mice have gnawed through the skirting boards. For all the care taken of the foyer, the auditorium, the stage, this closet space has been neglected. She wonders if that is because it is allocated as a ladies' dressing room.

'Women,' she says, picking the thread of her thought back up and pulling it taut, 'must disabuse their minds of the idea that to develop the limbs spoils their beauty. There is no occasion for a woman to have muscles unduly obtrusive, but there is every reason why they should be sound and strong.'

Their bodies *and* their minds, she thinks. She cannot imagine why anyone would see fit to separate the two.

'You've heard the ditty going about, I imagine,' Sandy says. His smile flickers. His eyes dart from Kate's face to his notebook and back again.

She clears her throat as though she is about to begin a grand recital, and sits up straighter in her chair. The wood is hard under her backside, but she shan't hold the position for long.

'O Great Vulcana!' she begins. 'Let me pray
You will not teach our wives the way
To bring their muscles into play
Like cords and ropes entangled!
For if you should, it seems to me,
When we've been out upon the spree
On reaching home at midnight we
May find ourselves half-strangled!'

She settles back in the chair again, suffocating a laugh. She has Sandy spellbound. It is an expertise she has been perfecting for some years – this way of drawing people near enough to her

273

to ensure the shows are successful, but being able, too, to ease apart from them – and she feels she might finally have the balance of it. It is as Marie told her once: 'You don't owe the audience every ounce of yourself.' Vulcana dishes herself out now in measured portions: it is the only way to keep herself from feeling constantly clamoured for, as she had at the start. Sometimes, she wonders if Marie does the same. Surely William must, if he really has consulted a doctor without telling her.

'Very good, miss,' Sandy says.

'Isn't it,' Kate replies, feeling her way towards a joke. 'The rhymes are strong and the rhythm flawless, don't you think?'

They share a smile. 'I should say.'

Kate allows a pause to hang in the stale air of the windowless room. She is about to shift the direction of the interview. She is keen now to make her points and retire to bed. Tomorrow they are to board the train to Sydney.

'Am I correct in thinking,' she begins, 'that the women of this country have been granted the right to vote?' She knows she is correct in this. The Commonwealth Franchise Act of 1902 had granted them that parity with men. She had discussed it with William on the ship over.

'That's correct,' Sandy confirms, licking the nib of his pencil and letting it hover a finger-length above his notebook.

'And don't you think,' she continues, 'that a woman whose mind is as robust as any man's should ensure that her body follows suit?'

Sandy's eyes narrow slightly. He is catching up. 'You're referring to your opinions on the subject of corsets, Miss

274

Vulcana,' he says, curving his pencil through the air in a plain 'I've got it' motion. He is pleased, and she is happy to have made him so.

'You've heard them?'

'I have.'

'And do you concur with them?'

'Oh, I...' Sandy stutters. He uncrosses his legs and, turning them about the opposite way, crosses them again.

Kate laughs. 'Don't worry,' she says. 'There are greater matters for a gentleman journalist to consider, I'm sure.'

The man exhales heavily.

'But my feeling is this... If a woman is laced up tight, she cannot take in those deep breaths; the wearing of stays restricts the expansion of the body, and does harm. What I say is, it is an advantage to leave them off sometimes, and thus teach the spine to support itself, allowing, at the same time, the other muscles to rely upon their inherent strength. You see, all I am suggesting is that women be free to celebrate their natural form. I do not think that can be considered disagreeable. Do you?'

Sandy capitulates, as she had known he would. 'Oh, not at all, miss.'

'Wonderful.' Kate shows him her widest smile, then brings her hands down with a slap on her knees, and makes to stand. 'Now, Sandy, I hope you can excuse my rushing off. I have a train to catch in the early morning, you understand, as we are expected in Sydney.'

'Oh, of course. Of course.' Sandy flusters around, as though he is gathering his belongings to leave, though he came with only his notebook and pencil and his hat. Kate plucks his hat up off the back of his chair, where he had hung it, and offers it to him.

'A pleasure,' she says.

Sandy flips his hat on, nods, and sees himself to the door. He is in the doorway, framed by the darkness of the corridor, when he stops.

'One last thing I intended to ask, Miss Vulcana, if you don't mind.'

His pencil is gripped between his thumb and forefinger but pointed at the ceiling. His notebook is stuffed into his trouser pocket. Whatever her response to this final question, he does not mean to write it down. Perhaps he believes he will not need to. She inclines her head mutely to invite him to continue.

'Would you say it has cost you anything? Fame?'

Her cheeks pale slightly and she turns to slide her chair back under the table, as though tidying this messy little box is suddenly imperative. She needs the time. She cannot say, 'Certainly, Mr Sandy: my parents, my siblings, my very own children.' She cannot say, 'In many ways, everything.' She bites those revelations back.

'I'm certain either that it must have or that it will,' she says instead. 'But I'm more certain that a life without regret would be a life nowhere near full enough for me.'

Before Sandy has the chance to speak again, she lifts one of her cotton wraps off the table and begins winding it around her flattened hand. Head bowed, she listens for the thunk of the latch before she breathes out.

26.

South Coast, Australia
1903
LADY'S OWN

When it transpires that the troupe are, on the trip from Melbourne to Sydney, to be tasked with transporting enormous crates containing Harry Rickards' theatre equipment safely along with them, and are consequently to make the journey by boat, Kate refuses. She will not step foot on another boat until she boards the one set for home. She cannot. The idea alone turns her green. It is therefore agreed that she will make the journey by steam train and, to negate the risks of travelling alone, that Mabel and Hatfield will go with her. They will, they assure William, Abe, Young, and Jem, reserve their seats in the Lady's Own, where they will be perfectly safe.

Still, the men insist on waving them off at the station the day after Kate's newspaper interview. They stand on the platform like a clutch of lost schoolboys – forlorn and mismatched – and from inside the train, the women secretly laugh at them.

'Would you look at them?' Mabel says. 'Standing there like they've lost a pound and found...'

'A penny,' Hatfield offers.

'I was going to say a lump of coal,' Mabel replies.

The morning is bright hot, and Kate supposes the men can see nothing in the train windows but their own reflections. They wave for a minute more and then, gathering themselves, file away down the platform. Kate, Mabel, and Hatfield find the Lady's Own compartment – just as they promised – and the moment they are inside, push open the windows despite the trail of black smut which will inevitably blow through when the train moves off. It is too stuffy to do anything other.

'I've always wanted to travel alone, you know,' Hatfield says as she shoves her valise into the rack above her seat. Her ticket drops from a side pocket and swoops to the floor. She bends to pluck it up, then slips it into her jacket. She is, as ever, neat and delicate in a navy blue and white striped shirtwaist and a lighter blue skirt. The white jacket is thin and designed to be fashionable, not warm. To her hat is pinned a sprig of blue delphinium. Or at least it looks like delphinium. Kate has no idea whether that particular flower grows in Australia, or even at this time of year, but she remembers Alice mentioning the name once when Kate said that she liked them: delphinium; it had sounded like the language of dreams.

'Where to?' Kate asks. Hatfield's ticket is still visible inside her jacket; perhaps she wouldn't be so good at travelling alone.

'Nowhere particular,' Hatfield answers. 'It was more the act I'd imagined than the destination. I'd see myself on a train...' She pauses and raises her hand as if in wonder and smiles. 'Or on a ship. I'd see myself in transit.' Having finished fussing

278

with her valise and gloves, she removes her jacket to take her seat. The ticket escapes again and drifts towards Kate, who catches it and hands it back. 'Perhaps,' Hatfield continues, 'I didn't foresee a specific place because I never really thought it would happen. And I know I'm not exactly alone now, but this, with the two of you, is close enough. Perfect, in fact. I feel like we're on a real adventure.'

'Oh, Hattie,' says Mabel.

Nobody remembers exactly when they had taken to calling her Hattie, but Kate considers again, as she watches the balletic young sprite across from her straighten her sleeves, that it suits her an awful lot better than her true name. Who would christen such a pretty girl Maude?

'What?' Hatfield asks.

'Nothing,' Mabel says. 'You're just a sweetheart. I'm sorry I ribbed you before, when you said you wanted to marry. You should marry. You'd make the most beautiful bride.'

A tiny crease appears above Hatfield's nose. 'When did you rib me?'

'When you said you wanted to marry.'

'When did I say I wanted to marry?'

'That night... Actually, which night? When was that, Kate?'

'In Paris. After the Exposition Universelle.'

Mabel clicks her fingers. 'Yes.'

'I don't remember.'

'You were rather drunk,' Kate puts in.

'Was I?' Hatfield takes a moment to consider this, as

279

though she is troubling out a story she has been told about someone else. 'Well, I've changed my mind.'

'You have?'

'I most certainly have. You,' she points at Mabel, 'are not married. And you,' she points at Kate, 'are not married. And you are two of the finest women I know. I am perfectly happy to remain just as I am. Me.'

Mabel laughs and raises her empty hand in a mock toast. 'Congratulations,' she cries. 'You have reached true spinsterhood. We shall have to be buried alongside each other, us three, and commission identical headstones.'

'That,' Kate says, 'is morbid. Being a spinster is just fine.'

'More than fine,' Hatfield insists. 'Hattie Hatfield can do as she wishes, and go where she pleases, and think what she likes. And would I be able to do any of those things if I were Mrs Somebody or Other? I very much doubt it. I'll stick with my own company, thank you kindly.'

'But don't you miss *it*?' Mabel asks. She has pulled a cigarette from somewhere on her person and twirls it absent-mindedly between her fingertips. Kate snatches it from her and throws it out through the window. Mabel opens her mouth to object, but desists at Kate's raised eyebrows.

'Miss what?'

'Sex.'

'Mabel!'

'Well?'

Hatfield's face flares as intensely as if a flame has been struck under her chin. She sweeps her head to left and right, to check that no one has heard. None of the other passengers has yet boarded; the compartment is empty.

'I can't say... That is... I wouldn't...'

'Hattie?' Mabel ducks down to look into Hatfield's lowered eyes. 'You have...'

'No,' Hatfield interrupts before Mabel can say the word a second time. 'No, I can't say I have.'

'But... Never?'

'Never.'

'Well, well...' Mabel slumps back in her seat, exhaling heavily. 'I hardly know what to say to that revelation. No, I do. What I will say is this. Listen carefully, Hattie. Marry or don't marry, I don't care a damn which, but do not let yourself miss out on what you are owed as a woman.'

The phrasing draws Hatfield out of her embarrassment and entices her to laugh. 'Owed, you say?'

'Absolutely.' Mabel nods seriously. 'Owed. Consider all we must put up with as women.' Four passengers rustle into the compartment and go about the business of settling themselves. Mabel drops her voice, but not by much. 'We are second to them in politics.' She props her elbows on the table and uses one hand to count off the fingers on the other. 'Property. Platform. God, even if you're the first-born child of royalty and you suffer the misfortune of being a girl, you have to wait for some younger brother to die before you're made queen. They work better jobs. They demand better wages. They take no part in the care of children, then claim them without question when there is a divorce.' Mabel has run short of fingers and begun the rotation again at her thumb. 'They take ownership of their wives by replacing their names with their own. They are better respected in almost every part of society. They're stronger – usually.' She pauses to take a breath. 'The least they can do, Hattie, is ensure that you get your pleasure.'

At the pained expression on Mabel's face, Kate and Hatfield erupt into noisy hysterics. After a spell, Mabel joins in. The women who have just entered the compartment flutter in fright, like a shooed flock of pigeons, then relax again.

'And when did you last "get your pleasure"?' Kate stutters past her tears.

'I have an agreement,' Mabel says, straightening up in her seat as though she is offended, though Kate knows she is not. Mabel is too practical to take offence at anything so trivial as the spoken word.

'An agreement?' Kate can hardly believe it. All these years, she has thought Mabel chaste, though now that she reflects on the idea it seems ridiculous. Twelve years they have been touring together. Mabel has met a thousand men who might have offered her their affections. And Kate has always thought her beautiful in her own aloof way: so straight-backed, so tall, so blessed with that thick auburn hair. She had only thought her damaged in some way – too badly hurt by some unknown past to contemplate dabbling in romance again. And perhaps a little masculine. Perhaps inclined, as certain masculine women are, more readily towards other women. 'With who?'

'Well, not with Jem, Kate.'

'Abe!' In her realisation, Kate is close to a shriek. She raises her hand in apology to the two elderly women now entering the Lady's Own. They clutch their bags to their chests and smile meekly in response to her wave. *Be bolder*, she wants to tell them. *There is nothing to be frightened of here.* But she does not know how it feels to be grey-haired and hunched over and near seventy years of age. Perhaps a life so long bends you into that shape, however hard you fight it.

'Yes, Abe.'

'But he's a fake American!'

'Good lord. He is not a fake American. You honestly hadn't noticed?'

No, Kate thinks. She had not. She had been far too busy hoping that no one noticed the way she looked at William to even become suspicious of the way Mabel might look at Abe.

'Do you love him?'

'No,' Mabel replies. 'Of course not. I like him well enough. He's funny and he ... handles me with care.'

'It's just...?' Kate will not say the word 'sex' now that the compartment is populated.

Mabel nods. 'And very enjoyable it is, too. Now, Hattie...' Through this, Hatfield has sat stunned and amused, her smile caught halfway between rising and falling. 'What do you make to our Mr Young?'

'No!' The horror that crosses her face causes them to descend back into laughter. 'No, not Young. But maybe... Maybe I'll keep my eyes better open.'

On the platform, a whistle sounds, followed by the slamming of doors. They are about to depart Melbourne, and it will be for the last time, Kate thinks. She knows she will never come back here. She takes one last look out through the window, hoping to catch sight of one of those wildly colourful birds she has so admired – and there, perched atop the station clock as though just for her, is a little flat-headed, blue-winged kookaburra. It is so far out of its habitat that she doubts her eyes for a moment. She leans closer to the window, squints. She has studied that compendium well enough these past weeks. It is definitely a kookaburra. Its wingtips glint like cut aquamarine as it shuffles its feathers, twitches its head.

Lost, she thinks. Or perhaps resting on its way to a completely new somewhere. Or perhaps on its way home.

She watches it until they depart the station and all behind them vanishes under the pluming smoke from the steam engine. In a blink, the city is gone. Like an illusion. As if it was never there at all.

By turns, they nap to the chuntering of the train wheels over the tracks, dusty sunlight slanting in through the windows to warm their faces and light the little hairs across their cheeks, around their lips. When they do not nap or talk, they read. Kate has with her a battered copy of *Alice's Adventures in Wonderland*, which she is reading at the behest of Young Alice, who had pressed it earnestly into her hand the last time they had visited the Bristol house. She had declared it a perfect adventure story, and Kate had wondered how much more adventure she could possibly need, but she is reading it all the same, and when she gets home, she intends to read it to the children. Already she can see them all huddled into blankets near the settee in the front room, eyes shining at the thought of a cat who could disappear at will and a mad tea party attended by a March hare. She will have Arthur bundled in her lap, and the girls, thinking themselves too grown up for cwtches, will sit cross-legged in front of her, and they will gasp and giggle together, the three of them, to the hushed rhythms of their mother's voice painting pictures in the shadows cast by the firelight. It is a hope she is so desperate to fulfil that she feels it as a tingling in her hands, a burning at her throat. She wants Mabel and Hatfield to start talking again, so that she can think of something other.

Though she feels selfish doing it, she is about to shake Mabel's shoulder and rouse her, when she is startled from her intention by a thump and then a clattering: the compartment door, being thrown open and bouncing back off the wall. The door is not caught by the man who steps through it and continues to swing, trembling, between frame and wall. Kate wonders at how the glass panes have not shattered. Opposite her, Hatfield has flinched immediately awake. At her side, Mabel follows more slowly.

'Hello, ladies,' the man calls down the compartment. He is standing like a cowboy about to engage in a shoot-out, his legs braced wide, his arms held apart from his body like brackets. He is making himself big. Though he need not aid his physicality in that respect: he is already quite big enough. He is tall – perhaps six feet and another two or three inches – and broad. His neck is wide and somehow equine. He wears a thick beard which reaches the collar of a chequered blue and green shirt. On his thighs, forearms, and cheeks, streaks of black filth. 'I've come to see if you needed any company.'

The statement is met by silence. The train bumps and wheezes.

'This is a Lady's Own,' Kate offers eventually – long after it has become apparent that no one else is going to brave speaking.

The man's head snaps immediately towards her. The tendons in his neck twist. He is strong: a digger. 'So it is,' he replies, giving a hollow laugh.

'Then you should not be in here,' Kate continues. Even. Calm. This is not her first experience of dealing with an obnoxious man.

'Are you an American?' the digger asks, rocking towards her now on his bandy legs. The stink of spirits drifts ahead of him. 'Have you *bought* this train?'

He expects, she supposes, that at this she will drop her head, sit a little lower in her seat, be quiet. Kate sighs, and stands.

'I am not and I have not. But I have paid for my seat in this compartment, as has every other lady here, and if you were a gentleman, you would go out.'

The digger fishes around in his shirt pocket for something and, retrieving a cigarette, flips it between his lips. Next, he feels around in his trousers until he finds a matchbox. Extracting a single match, he rasps it into flame and, holding it up to his face, lights his cigarette.

'I will do nothing of the kind,' he says. He makes a show of looking just over Kate's shoulder. It is an attempt to make her feel small, of course. Kate puffs her chest: chest, expanded – thirty-nine inches. 'You might call the guard, miss, or anyone else you like, but not one of them will be able to put me out.'

He drops with a thud onto a nearby seat and throws his grotty boots up on the seat opposite, then proceeds to take a long drag of his cigarette. It is apparent from his repose, his slovenly manner, the way he cocks his head when he speaks, that he thinks himself desperately attractive. Perhaps anyone might, under the influence of so much alcohol, but Kate considers the misconception fairly embedded in this one – sober or drunk. His attitude, however, is too ugly to be disguised by a pleasing exterior. She makes certain not to look at any of the other women in the compartment. She does not want them or him to think that she is seeking their support.

'I don't require the guard to put you out,' she says. 'I shall do it myself.'

The digger throws his head back and laughs, the sound big and absurd and accompanied by a dirty cloud of tobacco smoke. Kate glimpses the ridged roof of his mouth. It is too pink and clean to belong to such a man. She wants to stab something sharp into it and feel it wedge in against the resistance. How dare he barrel in here looking solely to frighten someone?

He lifts a fat-knuckled hand to his mouth, takes another wet-lipped drag on his cigarette, then grinds the burning end out on the table. He leans further back, as though he might close his eyes to sleep. And that is when Kate marches the few steps it takes to reach him, grasps his shirt collar, and propels him forwards into the aisle. Caught by surprise, and knocked off balance, the digger tips clumsily onto his knees; his kneecaps thud painfully down. Taking her advantage while it is on offer, Kate wraps her other hand around his belt and shoves him, at a crawl, towards the exterior door. She closes her nose to the rise of his sweat.

'Kate!' she hears Hatfield cry.

'It's all right,' Kate huffs. 'We're slowing.'

The digger is beginning to struggle now. He kicks out and catches her ankle bone. It smarts, but Kate does not retaliate. She is concentrating all her efforts on containing the man, who is brawny and drunkenly without care. He thrashes his head. He swings a fist around and cracks her on the cheekbone. She grits her teeth and shoves him more roughly. Finally, at the door, she snatches her hand swiftly away from his belt, slams the door handle down, pushes her shoulder into the frame to steady herself against the sudden wind and the jerking of the carriage, and pitches the digger bodily out of the train. It is she, after all, who might be Alice of Abergavenny. Or perhaps just Kate of Abergavenny, avenging not her lover's death but that of her hope. For she is stuck with this now, isn't she? Touring from place to place, showing her strength, giving interviews, missing her children. It will go on forever. She will never be allowed to stop. Unless...

The digger lands, with a thump and a roar, on the trackside. Kate shuts the door and steps back into the compartment only to find the other passengers pinned to the windows, all of them talking simultaneously.

'Is he hurt?'

'Did you kill him?'

'Nicely done, Kate.'

'I can't see him. Can you?'

'No. He's disappeared.'

'Under the train?'

'What a sort!'

'Well done, miss.'

'I really did think he was going to hurt someone.'

'Me too.'

Kate wanders back to her seat while the others go on searching for the interloper. She brushes the back of her hand over her cheekbone, then turns her hand over and presses down experimentally with her fingertips, waiting for the jolt of pain. It scatters backwards along the side of her face and into her hairline, as she had expected. The swelling is already coming up. By tomorrow, she will be sporting a mottled blue and purple bump. She'll get Hatfield to do her make-up before she goes onstage at the Tivoli.

Shortly, there sounds a whistle – much the same as the one which saw them away from the station, but more frantic somehow – and the train wheels screech in an unpleasant F sharp as the brakes are locked on. The soothing chug-chug-chug of the engine ceases and, eventually, they shudder to a noisy stop. The windows, still open, betray the voices of the guard as he leaps off and goes in search of the man and the passengers who call to him from above: a nasal baritone answered by a flittering soprano; a mellow alto; a gruff bass.

'Suicide.'

'Must have been.'

'Do you see him?'

'Nothing?'

For ten minutes or so, the guard and some of the more enthusiastic passengers search for the digger, but they find no trace of him. The only evidence of his existence is the scuffed patch of tufted ground where he landed and disturbed the sandy soil. He is soon declared 'escaped', and the guard orders all heads back inside the train, then begins his duty of moving along the carriages, checking the door handles. His whistle is already held between his teeth.

Mabel slumps down opposite Kate. They share a smile.

'You know William is going to cause a riot with this?'

Kate rolls her eyes but does not drop her smile. 'I know.'

'You'll have every headline in Australia before long. Britain, too. Mademoiselle Vulcana – Protector of the People!'

'Oh, Mabel. Don't.'

A frown rumples her forehead. 'Where did the "mademoiselle" come from anyway?'

'I haven't the first idea.'

Mabel lets out an amused snort. 'Oh. Well, I'm sure it won't stick in London... Are you all right?' She nods at Kate's swollen cheek, which is settling into a steady throb.

'I'm always all right,' Kate replies.

'No,' Mabel counters. 'You're not. Not always. So here's what we'll do. I'll pretend I didn't just ask you that question, and then tomorrow, when you've had a chance to really think about it, I'll ask you again. And I want you to tell me the truth, Kate. The honest truth, please. Will you promise?'

With a grunt and a huff, the train begins to move forwards again, and Kate tilts her head to look out of the window. She finds no ghost of herself in the glass. Onwards, then, she thinks. As ever.

27.

Sydney, Australia
1904
THE TIVOLI

Outside the Tivoli, there is propped a life-sized hoarding of Vulcana. No, it is greater than life-sized. It is perhaps seven feet high; far taller than she. On it is the old photograph of Vulcana in her Grecian goddess garb, all easy youth and gusto. Kate is sure her eyes do not shine like that anymore.

'It's mortifying,' she says to William. It is late, near midnight, and they are standing outside the theatre in the muggy heat, William in his shirtsleeves and Kate in her thinnest cotton dress. They have spent the evening depositing the rest of the troupe in their hotel rooms, unpacking theirs and Harry's luggage, and rushing to order the last meals the hotel kitchen was willing to serve.

'It's beautiful,' William replies. 'Like you.' He touches again the bump on her cheek where the digger struck her. She looks up past the tenderness on his face – she cannot bear it – and into the sky. It is lilac-coloured and perfectly flat. Darkness has still not fully descended. 'I'm sorry I wasn't there, Kate.'

He has been saying the same thing since the men and women of the Atlas-Vulcana Troupe met at the hotel. Kate can only think that she didn't need him there, though naturally she does not say as much. He has not yet admitted anything to her of the unfilled weights, and she doesn't want to entice him to that conversation now. She is too tired.

'It wasn't anything at all, really. He was just a sad drunk. I handled him.'

'I know it,' William answers, slipping his hand down her cheek and around the back of her neck to draw her to him for a kiss. He tastes of fruit – the pineapples and cherries he'd picked from the plate at the centre of their dinner table – but the taste is not sweet.

She turns again to the theatre. It is their first sighting of the Tivoli: newly built, Harry has informed them, on account of a devastating fire in '99. Kate considers it is one of the more beautiful venues they have been booked to appear at. Arches of twisted iron protrude onto the pavement from the ground floor, each hung with its own round lamp. The second and third storeys are built around three columns – a central column, adorned with the word 'Rickards', and one to each end of the building, carrying the words 'Tivoli' and 'Theatre'. At the second storey, set into the columns to either end, stand two robed women. Kate does not know who – if anyone – they are supposed to represent, but they remind her of the statue of Joan of Arc positioned outside the Hôtel Régina and, for some reason she can't quite verbalise, she finds it comforting. So, too, the symmetry of the structure. The Tivoli Theatre is both delicate and confident.

The only aspect of the frontage which troubles her is that,

read from left to right, the columns say, 'Tivoli Rickards Theatre'. This, she considers untidy.

'It ought to be cold,' Kate says.

'What?'

'It's January. Winter. Doesn't it feel strange to you, that it's so hot?'

William shrugs. 'It's summer here.'

'Yes, but ... I don't know... It makes me feel out of kilter, I suppose.' She is picturing how wonderful the Tivoli would look on a frosted midnight: the string of lamps throwing streaks of gold over a snowy street; the women's carved stone robes glinting under a sharp-rimmed moon; the warm indoor lights glowing like beacons in the heavy dark.

'Australia hasn't been kind to you.'

The pitching ship, the storm, the rearing sea – they flash across her mind like images from a nightmare or a frightening storybook. She pushes them down into the pit of her stomach, which roils at the intrusion. No, she thinks. It is me who has been ill and you who we are somehow looking after.

'Parts of it have,' she replies. She is thinking, quite purposefully, of the birds, of the way they pull her lips into a smile whenever they swoop overhead. She feels herself lifted by them, lightened, as though one day she might simply take flight and soar away with a passing flock. What a life that would be – to exist so far above all the noise created by people.

She had felt that way in Paris, too. She can hardly believe it is less than four years since they were at the Exposition Universelle. When did she grow so heavy?

'Will you be ready to go on tomorrow?'

'Why ever not?'

'Your...' William indicates his own cheekbone with a swept forefinger.

Kate waves the concern away. 'Nothing,' she says. A bruised cheekbone really is the least of it.

'Did anything ever hurt you, Kate Williams?'

The 'Williams' hits her like a slap. *That did*, she wants to say. For such a long while now she has been Kate Roberts – a name which has been assumed for her, given that she is supposed to be William's sister, and which she has accepted as readily as a new bride.

She gives a little laugh. 'Not a single thing,' she replies, when what she ought to do is offer William a list. The unalterable fact that he chose to make another woman his wife before they ever met; the distance which so often lies between her and her children; her inability to make such a simple claim as, 'This is my daughter' or 'This is my son' when they are introduced to strangers or acquaintances; the lack of certainty which comes with the adventure and excitement she has craved; those rare occasions when William misunderstands her.

This, she knows deep down, is not one of those occasions. What William is doing now is not misunderstanding her but offering her the opportunity to spill out all the horrible feelings in her soul. She is not in the mood to take him up on it. Not now, when they have a whole new city to explore. Australia might not have been kind to Kate so far, but it has not entirely dislodged her faith in a fresh adventure. Despite the sucking melancholia she has been attempting to drag herself free of since they disembarked from the *Oroya*, she has not yet been beaten. She might have been denied a good opportunity to make William famous across a continent, but Kate has never mourned an opportunity before. She has only ever sought out another. Very well, then, she thinks. She will trouble out a new scheme to take herself home. After all, she cannot give up. What would her children think of her, if it was not apparent she did everything she could to return to them?

William runs his hand down the inside of her arm and locks his fingers into hers. The line he has traced over her skin tickles. Nothing, it seems, can alter her physical need for this man. She is as excited by his touch now as she was that first night, when he pressed his palm over her heart on the pavement outside their York Street hotel.

She turns into him and, lifting his hand, presses it to her breast, as he had more than a decade before.

'I keep thinking I see Arthur,' she admits. 'Walking down the street, sitting in the auditoriums. Our son is haunting me, William.'

He pulls her to his chest and cradles her head. 'That's the cost of love, isn't it?'

'I don't think so. It's not the same as thinking about him or remembering him. It's more that I see him, or his likeness, and I get this jolt.' She clutches her chest to demonstrate where she experiences the cold sensation. 'Of fear, or horror. I think, for a moment, that I've forgotten him – left him on the *Oroya*, or

on the train to Melbourne, or in a hotel foyer somewhere –
and that he is entirely lost.'

'Yes. Love,' William nods his head. 'There is nothing more
frightening than being in love.'

'Really?' Kate isn't sure she would agree. She is not afraid
of her love for William. She might be breathless with it, or
made stupid by it, or even angry at it sometimes, but she does
not believe she has ever feared it.

'Really,' William insists.

Kate does not contradict him. Love must be different for
everyone, she supposes.

'I think he'd like it here,' she says instead. 'Arthur. All the
colours and the sunshine and the birds.'

'We'll bring them with us one day,' William replies, and
Kate tightens her arms around him, and wishes that were true.
Two lives – that's what she had thought, all those years ago, in
London. William was building two separate lives for himself.
One with Alice; another with his troupe. She had not
imagined that she would need to be part of both of them.

The next night, Harry Rickards waits for them in the
backstage curtain-dust, holding a tray of fluted champagne
glasses and wearing an enormous grin. Cheers and applause
are still ricocheting around the auditorium. The floorboards
bounce under stomped feet. Vulcana has already been on for
two encores and cannot face another: the heat; the
expectation. The Tivoli audience is perhaps the most
adoring they have yet met in Australia. The newspaper

interviews and the magazine pieces William set up seem to have paid off.

'They're a crowd, aren't they?' Harry shouts over the din.

At sixty, Harry is squat and silver at the temples and nothing like Kate had initially expected. Though he is short of stature, his is a bold body. His stance is military-straight. His eyes are at once dark and brilliant. In appearance, he is far more Italian than English, but there is no mistaking his London accent.

'They're feral!' Kate replies, laughing. It has been a good night. Hatfield and Mabel's weight-juggling went down a storm. William lifting Kate over his head one-armed had them in a frenzy. And when Kate laid on her back and performed presses with her hands and feet, first with Hatfield balanced across them and then William, they exploded in admiration.

'They know quality when they see it,' Harry replies, lifting a champagne flute off the tray and handing it to Kate before offering the same to William. 'Drink those,' he orders them. 'Then get changed. I've got something to show you.'

'Something we need to get dressed for,' Kate quips. 'Harry, you do disappoint me.'

Harry laughs and flashes a look at William. 'Do you know a single man who could keep this one in line?'

'I do not,' William concedes, pressing his smile away under his moustache. It is true, he does not. 'I wonder if such a man ever existed? He would be a saint.'

'A saint!' Harry helps himself to a glass and tosses back the champagne. 'He would need to be a god, I think.'

The sentence is spoken in jest – in adulation, even – but Kate finds herself wincing against it all the same. Saints. Goddesses. Angels. Heroines. She's heard herself described variously as each of them in the years since she first took to the stage, but all the words provide is a means of forgetting that what she truly is is a woman. She smiles and leans forwards to kiss Harry's smooth-shaven cheek. He means well. But, oh, how she wants to scream: *I am a woman, and only a woman, and that is enough.*

They throw on their everyday clothes and follow Harry up staircase after staircase until they climb a small, ladder-like structure and emerge onto the Tivoli's roof.

The night is dry and close. A warm wind ripples along Castlereagh Street and weaves through Kate's hair but hasn't the impetus to lift it away from her clammy skin. She gathers her hair up in her hands, rolls it into a chignon, holds it there a while to let the air find her neck, then drops it again. Lingering on the wind are the scents of woodsmoke and hot tar.

'There's nothing up here, Harry,' William says.

'Nonsense,' Harry replies. 'There's a whole city up here. Look. Come over to the edge.'

He walks them to the stone parapet which fronts the roof. It stops just above waist height, and they are comfortably able to look over it at the sprawl of Sydney. Sand- and grey-stone buildings rise out of groves of silky oaks, six, seven, eight storeys high, their roofs pointed with spires or turrets. Chimneys blow their smoke towards a misty moon. The last trams are crossing the city, ringing their bells and clanking along their tracks. Soon, Sydney will hush. But not yet. Birds prattle and trill invisibly from their roosting branches. In London, they would have quieted hours since, but in the sky over Sydney, a pencil-slash of sapphire light keeps them awake. In the topmost floors of the hotels, lamps in the windows glow like fireflies, but most everything else is in darkness. Footsteps slough over the pavement below them. Somewhere, someone is whistling a melancholy tune. Kate traces a path towards the harbour, where the roofs are lower and longer. Oblong-shaped warehouses skulk in the shadows the rest of the city casts. And what beautiful shadows they are. Wherever Kate settles her gaze, it is met with perfect grey outlines: a row of chimneys, the domed top of some sort of observatory, the thin stem of a gas lamp, a bicycle abandoned up against a wall. They cross and double over each other. The moon brightens and Sydney becomes a painting made up of silvered shapes: triangles, diamonds, sickles, circles, rectangles, beams. It is a glorious view, but Kate does not feel about it the way she did about the sight of Paris from the window of her room at the Hôtel Régina. Australia holds no romance for her. Or perhaps she has lost the willingness to be wooed.

'See the new street lamps?' Harry asks, pointing, though it would be impossible for Kate and William to follow the direction of his fingertip. 'There'll be an electricity supply come July. This city is going to light up.'

'And that's what you wanted to show us?' William's voice is low and even. He knows where this is going, Kate thinks,

300

just as well as she does. But she will not help Harry towards the offer he will make next. 'The street lamps? The promise of electricity?'

Harry turns his back on the streets below and, leaning against the parapet, fixes his regard on Kate and William. They are Atlas and Vulcana to him – the brother and sister strongperson act. They are not travellers. Parents. Lovers. They are a transaction. His eyes flare with excitement.

'I want you to stay another year,' he says, and Kate feels something deep inside her plummet.

28.

Sydney, Australia
1904
STORMS

Two or three hours before dawn, she wakes and takes to the streets, as she once had in Paris and Edinburgh, Cardiff and Nice, when she could not rest. She cannot rest in Sydney, either, it seems, and she wonders in fact if she can name a solitary place in the whole world where she has looked forward to retiring to bed. That, she thinks, is a sign of being at peace. A hundred times, as she had perked and budded into adolescence, she had watched her parents glance at the clock and sigh in relief to find that it was time to go to bed. She had pitied them. What a waste, she had thought, to anticipate sleep. She knows now that what they were awaiting was comfort.

Though the hotel Harry has reserved for the troupe overlooks Sydney's own Hyde Park, she does not wish tonight to walk there and be reminded of that girl, just sixteen years old, who had wandered through London's Hyde Park in search of William, believing him in possession of all life's answers. Instead, she turns the opposite way, towards Kent Street. She will go to Darling Harbour, on Cockle Bay, and watch the fishermen and the warehouse workers leak out of the shadows with the day's first light. They will begin as blank grey shapes and, as the morning plumps out, so they will brighten into dips and lines of colour and become their fullest selves. She adores that time of the day, when nothing is quite yet what it might be. She has seen enough dawns spill over enough cities to know that they don't alter so very much, one to the next, but also that they are each entirely different. They are all singular breaths of discovery.

She turns right onto Kent Street and thereafter left onto Market Street, which she follows until she sees Pyrmont Bridge come into view.

Kate and William had walked over to Darling Harbour just a few afternoons ago, in the throbbing Sydney heat, and near expired amongst the crowds. The sun was not interrupted by cloud and they had never felt heat like it. They had stopped to buy iced lemonades and sat rolling the place name around their mouths with the bitterness of the drinks. *Darling Harbour, Cockle Bay*, they said, time and again, enjoying its rounded sounds and taking turns at pretending to be Marie Lloyd – the only person they knew who threw the term darling around in casual conversation. *I'm going to Darling Harbour, darling.* Neither one of them could come close to a good impersonation.

Kate stops just short of stepping onto the bridge and looks down the line of huge square warehouses to her right-hand side. There is no movement yet from their wide double doors. It is too early. Only the insomniacs and the stars are awake.

She tips her head back to consider the clear expanse of sky above her. It is still cloudless, as it has been every day and night since their arrival in Sydney. Despite the hour, it is not a thick, syrupy black, but a crisp admiral blue. The stars are so incredibly small and distant that Kate can hardly tell which are really glinting and which are only tricks played by her searching eyes. Real or imagined, they are company, at least. As she takes a pace onto the bridge, she casts a quick look at the boats and ships anchored along the harbour. A retch gathers itself in her stomach, ready to surge up her throat. She closes her eyes and wills it away.

By day, Pyrmont Bridge is clustered with men and woman walking in matching pairs along its pavements, with blinkered horses who smack their lips at one another as they go, with passenger coaches and traps carrying sacked vegetables or grain from one side of the city to the other, with the drivers who steer them wearing soft hats which Kate considers look like inverted flowerpots. It is a clattering place, full of hollers and smiles, greetings and frowns. Boys sit on mounded potato sacks, legs swinging. Smaller boys scurry between trotting hooves, trying to scoop up the mess the horses leave behind. It might be a busy marketplace, so crammed is it, were it not for the constant back and forth of its traffic, both over, beneath, and through the bridge – a swing bridge, Kate has learned, operated by electricity, the middle section of which rotates to allow a clear way for ships with masts and funnels too tall to pass beneath. It is, she is told, an innovation.

She has no desire to look down into the water, to think of

those ships powering away into the south Pacific Ocean. She can smell it well enough: tangy brine and, chasing after that muscular scent, the strange clinging cold which can rise only from unknown depths. She cannot fathom how anyone would feel comfortable sailing over a sea they could never reach the bed of alive. She cannot suppose how she is going to get home.

She thinks again of the hot-air balloon and wishes she could be carried all the way back to Wales in one of those swinging wicker baskets.

She walks down the middle of the bridge, fascinated by how different it feels at night, when it is empty. She had not realised previously how wide it was. Or how long. Or that the metal balusters are criss-crosses decorated with four-pointed blooms, and that they offer a feeling of safety. Or that there is a visible split between the bridge sections, edged by a black metallic arc, which she must step over to continue to the other side. She hesitates – because she can hear the lap of the water beneath and it entices her momentarily to giddiness – then walks on.

Her time on stage has given her a heightened awareness of the way she moves, and she deliberates now on the degree at which her foot makes contact with the ground, the flex of her ankle, the softening of her knee and forward jut of her hip. These smallest details are important. She has to get them right, always, if she is to impress her audience. It is not enough to lift weights most men would crumple under and bunch her muscles. She has to do more than the men might. She has to execute every movement, every pose, beautifully.

How had William phrased it in the advertising copy?

Vulcana, he claimed, possessed all the *beautiful proportions of the female form divine*. The female form divine. What a standard to have to live up to.

She relaxes into her looser natural gait. There is no one here to see her now.

Or rather, there is, but she has not noticed yet that he is following her.

When he calls her name a breath later, she leaps momentarily out of her skin. Snapping around, she adjusts her feet for a wider stance and brings her fists up before her face. She is ready to fight. She always has been. The man before her ducks backwards slightly.

'Christ. Don't hurt me, will you?' he says, raising his hands.

And, once they have found each other's eye in the dark, they break into laughter.

'That depends,' Kate replies, stepping closer to slip a hand around his back and draw him in for a kiss. What she would give to be able to do that on a crowded street, in daylight. 'What are you about?'

'I came to join you.'

'Why?'

'Why not?'

Kate shrugs. 'No reason why not, I suppose.' Though she's not sure she wants to let him into this private ritual. There is so little left of her which goes unseen that to share her night-time wanderings feels akin to peeling off layers of skin and flesh and revealing to him the bones of her. And there are some things, she has learned, which ought to remain secret, even from one's love.

She locks her hand into his and they stroll to the other side of the harbour in silence, listening to the night sounds of the city: an unseen animal rummaging in a stack of discarded crates at the harbour's edge; the bark of an owl. Four jetties of varying lengths stretch out over deeper water. William chooses the longest and tugs Kate to the end of it. They sit down and let their legs dangle past the wooden slats like children. Were Nora here now, she would be crouched over the jetty's edge, pulling faces at herself in reflection. She would persuade Mona to join in, though Mona would not lean over so far.

'Do you miss the children?' Kate says. Had she thought about the question first, she would not have uttered it. But she is caught up in her vision of Nora and Mona playing on the jetty, and haunted by all those mistaken sightings of Arthur: at the train station as they pulled away from it; disappearing away down a crowded Melbourne street; sitting amongst the audience at the theatre.

William cocks his head at her, frowns. 'Of course I do. How can you ask me that?'

She twists around to face him. 'You never talk about them.'

At this, his eyes darken; the shining green irises dull.

'How could I bear to,' he answers, 'when I can't say that they're ours? How could I tell everyone how proud I am of them, when I can't tell anyone how much I love their mother? A hundred times a day I start to say, "Our Nora is strong, just like her mam", or "Our boy will be more like me, I think". But

I catch the words, because we're building them a life, aren't we? A different life from the one we were offered. A life not lived in the shadow of the ironworks at the end of the road. God, yes, I miss them, Kate.'

In the pause that follows, she shuffles around to look over to the far side of the harbour. This is the narrowest point of the harbour and she can see clearly the bows and the jibs and the masts of the moored yachts; a ginger cat, perched on the edge of a barrel, licking a forepaw; three large black and white wading birds – larger, indeed, than the cat – who strut along, plunging their long, hooked beaks into boxes and sacks in search of food. Their black heads and scythe-like beaks lend them the look of reapers.

'And what about this?' Kate asks. 'Would you miss this?'

William sighs. He understands that she is telling him they have to choose. That it has gone on too long.

'This. Yes. It's a dream, this. Every second of it.'

'Even the bad seconds?'

'Even the bad ones,' William agrees.

Of a sudden, the wind is picking up, and Kate tucks her hair behind her ear only for it to whip immediately free again. She had not bothered to pin it up to walk alone at the witching hour. She gathers it in her palms and rolls it around and around itself, then pushes the tightened coil into the neck of her dress.

'The weather's changing,' she says. Already, the water is ruffling. The smaller boats rock from side to side, sails snapping.

'Look at the clouds.' Kate and William tip their heads up to watch low, crow-feather clouds scud in off the sea. They move fast and smooth, as though painted on a carousel. They are followed, almost immediately, by angry forks of lightning, which crackle and flash like fireworks. Patches of the city light up and are plunged back into darkness as the storm approaches the harbour. The wading birds take flight, croaking in disgruntlement as they pitch across the water, their long, fanned wings thrown out, their feathers quivering frantically. Their ungainly beaks spear the clouds as they rise into them.

'What on earth...?' William begins.

'White ibis.' Kate has seen them on the brink of the city, scrounging for scraps. She has looked them up in her compendium.

'They're ghoulish,' William says, and she understands his reaction. Their ghostly white feathers, their scaly black legs, their bald heads. There is something of the vulture about them. Something other-worldly. They look powerful and menacing and Kate thinks they are exquisite.

Their gravelly croaks are still echoing in their wake when the rain hits. It does not start out at a spit and build to a deluge, but seems to fall all at once. Heavily. It is like standing beneath a tank of water and having it tipped directly over your head. Kate and William find themselves instantly soaked and begin to run, but they soon realise that they cannot outrun this and, clothes already sagged, they slip into the alleyway between two warehouses and press into each other, watching the lightning shoot and scatter across the rectangle of sky visible between the warehouse roofs. The noise is thunderous. A flag torn from the top of a ship's mast whips by.

'We can't live in a dream,' Kate shouts. She feels braver, now that she can scarcely be heard, about saying what she means. Besides, he has surely felt that everything has been wrong since they came to Australia: Kate, always fit and strong, being so ill; the kerfuffle with Herr Pagel; the incident with the digger on the train. 'It's like a wild story, William. The ships and the seas and the theatres and the posters. It's something we ought to be reading about. It's not real. It can't last forever.'

This, she realises, is how she feels about London. It is as though the whole city is at play. The raucous performances, the flamboyant prostitutes, the folly the newspapers report on, the money they get paid to stand onstage and tense their muscles, the blank-eyed elephants they drag into the Hippodrome to perform stunts, the ruins it makes of men who just want to be loved. Parading around that great, queer playground is not life; it is a game. And look at what it does to its players. Look at what it has done to poor Dan Leno. 'The saddest eyes in the whole world' – that's what Marie Lloyd said about him. And that is all the damned newspapers wanted to write about him last year. Nothing of his generous soul. Nothing of his charitable works. Nothing of the people he had made laugh until they ached. Only that offhand comment Marie made: 'If we hadn't laughed at Danny, we would have cried ourselves sick'. His one true talent, reduced to a snippet. No wonder the man has lost his mind.

Kate wonders now if Marie was talking more about herself than she was Dan when she gave that interview. Kate couldn't hit on it before, but she can pinpoint it suddenly, what has changed about Marie over the years. It's her eyes. Her eyes have grown sad. Perhaps music hall is finally killing her, too.

'It's real to us,' William shouts back at her through a barricade of rain.

'Is it? Tell me what's real about us being brother and sister.'

'It's easier, Kate.'

'Is that so?' The rain rushes down her face, slick and cold. 'I don't think it's easier. We should have been married years ago. I should be able to kiss you in the street and sleep in your bed every night. We should be able to share our children with the world. You've never even told me that you love me.'

'I have.' William's expression opens in protest and, under the flare of the lightning, his irises are greener than ever. If Kate never saw this man's face again, she knows that she would die with its every detail imprinted behind her lids. He belongs to her, and that, perhaps, is why she is so angry. 'I did, just this evening.'

'No!' she wails. 'You didn't say "I love you". You can't.'

'This is stupid, Kate.'

He makes to grasp her elbow, but she bats him away.

'Say "I love you",' she insists.

'No!'

'Why?'

'Because it isn't enough!' he roars. His face is suddenly close to hers. She can feel the warmth of his breath against the cold of the storm. 'They're just words. Words I've said to my parents. Words I've said to Alice. They're not for you, Kate. You're more than that. You're...' He glances around, as though searching for an explanation in the howling wind, and she

311

notices that he is sobbing. 'This. This is how I feel when we're together. How I've always felt… Just like this.'

'Battered?' Kate asks.

'Yes. Yes – battered. Damn!' He pounds a fist into the wall above her head.

Kate gulps in a deep breath. 'But–'

'No.' He holds up a finger to shush her. It is pale and trembling. On the harbour, they hear the crack of wood splitting: a mast, maybe, being broken in two. 'Don't you dare turn that into something bad. It's not bad. It's … overwhelming. You overwhelm me, Kate, and I feel like I'm just … holding on, trying not to get washed away, and I keep making it bigger, making all of it bigger, because none of it is big enough to show you how I feel. Christ!' He lowers his clenched fist, spreads it flat, and wipes it over his face. 'Jesus fucking Christ, Kate. You know this. Surely you know all this?'

Kate shakes her head slowly. She doesn't know any of this. William grabs her shoulders and holds on tight. He is panting. His beautiful chest rises and falls like a wave, and she wants to touch it – her favourite part of him – but she doesn't. Gusts dart down the alleyway and pull at his hair, his shirt collar. Her own hair is tangled over her lips, her eyes. Her dress hangs sodden from her as she shakes and shakes.

'Say "I love you",' she says again, quieter this time.

'No,' William insists. 'I won't. Because I don't just love you. I am you.' It makes sense, she supposes. The way they look at each other sometimes, their hideous words. We're never more cruel to anyone than we are to ourselves. 'That's how it feels,

Kate – as if, without you, I'd disappear. Do you understand? Without you, I amount to nothing. I am… I *am* you.'

Though it is she who has begged for his words, she does not let him go any further. Bringing up her hands, she thrusts them into his chest and drives him back against the other warehouse wall. She feels the thudding impact of his head against the brickwork, but she does not pause to check if he is hurt. Her mouth is already on his and they are desperate for each other. She fumbles to unbutton his trousers and William stands tall to let her, then, when they are dropped, he snatches up her skirts, wraps his hands around her thighs, and lifts her up to clamp her legs about his hips. Turning, he presses her to the brick wall and it scrapes at her shoulder blades and the bared tops of her buttocks as he pushes into her, but she does not feel the blood rising to the thinner skin there. She has her palms wrapped around William's neck and she tilts back her head and stares up into the quick obsidian chaos of the storm as he lowers his forehead to her collarbone and thrusts as far inside her as he can.

'William,' she says. 'William. Look at me.'

He does as she asks. His softened expression makes him appear younger than his years. Vulnerable. He can no longer lift the weights. Her William, she understands then – her bold, clever William – is a man terrified of himself. Indeed, it might be that that is all they both are – two terrified people blundering around the globe in search of vindication.

She holds him tighter.

'I am you, too. And I don't want to do it anymore.'

313

29.

Bristol, England
1904
THE BRISTOL HOUSE

She fidgets on the doorstep, listening to the echo of the brass door knocker along the hallway, and waiting, breath held, for a response. It is late June and certainly not cold, but she finds herself shivering. In anticipation? Perhaps. The house is substantial, and she can hear no movement within yet. She tiptoes up to press her face to the fan of stained glass. A polished sideboard displays a jar of freshly picked white and blue violas and a stack of books; a sand-coloured runner stretches long over the patterned ochre, jade, and olive tiles; sunlight leans across the place where the hallway becomes the kitchen. Silence. Come on, she thinks. Quick. Before I swallow the words.

The front door is of panelled mahogany. Its deep red shade appears richer still by comparison to the ivy which crawls around the door frame and towards the upstairs windows in irregular patches. She tips back to look up the front of the house. White casement windows; palest cream render; two sturdy chimneys. It is the house, the life, she would have built for herself, given the chance. It has been so long it feels as though she is seeing it for the first time.

She grips the knocker between thumb and forefinger, lifts it, and gives two more knocks. It is in the shape of a horse's head, protruding out from halfway down the neck. A beautiful thing. She wonders if one of the girls chose it ... if horses thunder through their dreams as they used to hers.

She steps back from the door and paces down the path which wraps around the house, then back up it again. The gravel crunches under her boots, dusting the leather. Sweat collects in the dimples at the small of her back. June. Almost a year since she last set eyes on her children. They will be different children now.

She rushes back to the doorstep when she hears footfalls, steady, along the hallway. The clack of a lock turning. The clunk of a bolt. It takes an interminable amount of time for the shining front door to be drawn back and for the woman drawing it back to break into a smile. She opens her mouth, pushes the tip of her tongue against her lower teeth to make a hard 'K'.

'I was wrong,' Kate blurts, before Alice can utter a word.

Alice sighs into her smile. 'All right,' she says, stepping aside to open the door wide. 'But never mind that now. The children will be so happy you're here.'

30.

Bristol, England
1904
GROWTH

On the top floor of the Bristol house, Kate sighs into an enormous white boat bath, tossing her hair over the back so that it hangs down to brush the floorboards. The rose-scented water laps just an inch below the lip, threatening to spill out whenever she moves, and Kate closes her mouth tight and dips her chin below the surface, but not her whole head, as she wants to. Steam has transformed the bathroom into an opium den. An open window drops a beam of sunlight in to warm her feet, which stick out of the water. With it, comes the children's laughter. The day is hot and still and they are playing in the stream at the bottom of the garden which had first persuaded Kate they should buy the house. Alice and William – Mr and Mrs Roberts – watch from the outside table. Earlier, Alice and Kate had set it with a freshly baked loaf, a plate of cheeses, a mound of grapes, strawberries, and raspberries, a pitcher of apple juice. Now and then, Alice calls out that the games have become too boisterous and urges the girls to 'be gentle'. Nora and Mona do not often see fit to play gently, and Kate smiles at the sounds of them wrestling in the shallow water. She knows that neither one of them will let herself be brought to tears.

A butterfly flusters in through the window, wings busy, and lands on the edge of the sink. A painted lady. Kate, Mona, and Winifred had spent a contented wedge of yesterday afternoon wandering around the garden finding them. Winifred, somehow, had known all the names. Red admiral. Small tortoiseshell. Common blue. And Kate was glad of the lesson – a welcome distraction.

They are all pretending – Kate, William, Alice. They do not know how they will afford to keep the house if Kate will not go abroad again.

She looks down the length of her body, searching for signs. Her chest and shoulders are as well developed as ever. Her breasts, where they crest the water, are familiarly firm. The nipples dark and neat. She catches the right between her thumb and forefinger and twists lightly: tender. Her lower stomach sags a little – the result of three heavy pregnancies – but the skin has stayed close enough to the flesh that, with a petticoat on, the sagging is not visible. Her thighs appear softer than she would like, but powerful enough. Her calves are sturdy and taut. Her feet more delicate than perhaps any other part of her.

They will swell, she knows, with the passing of the months. What else will a fourth pregnancy do to her body? It seems to Kate that immediately she births each baby, so she forgets the particular agonies of carrying them: the firing along every threaded nerve in her back; the skin of her hands tightening close to bursting; the sleeplessness.

317

The earliest stirrings had struck her on the ship home: the fatigue; the tetchiness. She wondered then whether it had been that night at Darling Harbour, but it was impossible to say. Afterwards, she and William had conspired to make love every night for a week or more, until finally she had grown sore and put him off. Well, here is her reward for so much reckless pleasure. William had marvelled that she did not fall sick again once they were sailing open seas, but Kate suspects that perhaps her fretting had kept the illness at bay. She had known immediately that it would be different this time.

Different how? She soaps her arms as she attempts to reach out and grasp hold of the idea. Different because Arthur is still a peach-headed baby? Or because her body isn't ready yet after her illness? Or because she has been having ideas of retirement? It is getting harder and harder, this life. In three years, she will have had a baby, toured Australia, and had another baby. That is not a schedule anyone can reasonably be expected to keep. She is twenty-eight years old and she feels herself nearer fifty. Later, she will check her hair in the mirror for strands of grey.

'Nora,' Alice calls. From here, her voice is small but clear. Her tone is always mild. 'Kindly don't drown your sister, will you?'

Kate can't help but laugh.

When Alice speaks again, she has moved closer to the window. Her words climb the ivy and float inside. 'And I can hear you laughing up there,' she says, pretending at severity though laughter lifts her own voice, too. 'Come down and see what they're doing. Come on. They're a pair of hooligans.'

Good, Kate thinks. I could not ask for anything more.

'Two minutes,' she calls.

She finishes washing, fills a jug and pours it over her head, then stands and wraps herself into the waiting towel. If she and William were in some hotel or other now, she would parade around nude until she gained his attention. She would let her hair dry against the pillow while they made love. But the Bristol house belongs to Alice, in spirit if not in deed, and she would not dare step across the landing to the bedroom she occupies alone here unclothed. She partially dries herself and pulls on the white blouse and mulberry-coloured skirt she had hung on the back of the bathroom door. She twists her hair into a thick plait and lets it drip down her spine. Then, barefoot, she skips down the stairs to join her family.

In the garden, Kate finds Nora and Mona sitting at the table wrapped in towels, their legs swinging in the space beneath their chairs and the ends of their hair straggly with stream water. They pluck grapes and strawberries from small plates Alice has put in front of them, avoiding the bitter tang of the raspberries.

'I don't like rapserries,' Mona announces.

'*Ras*-berries,' Nora corrects. Nora is seven and knows everything.

'*Rap*-serries.'

'No!' Nora's face darkens and Kate understands that she is about to lose her patience. Kate, too, warns the world with her face before she tips over into a temper. But she does not want her daughter to storm on so beautiful a day and draw clouds over everyone else's moods. The Bristol house has been such a happy place this past week that Kate has not felt herself torn apart by the question of whether or not she must return to the stage. She is calmed by the easy energy under this roof, the unhurried comings and goings, the chatter that steals under doors and up the staircase. Here, Kate sits alongside Alice while she reads, and helps her carry plates through to the kitchen, and towels the children as Alice lifts them from their baths. Vulcana ceases to exist.

'Raspberries or rapserries,' Kate sings as she approaches the table. 'I don't mind what you call them so long as I can eat them all!'

The girls are instantly reunited by a simultaneous, 'Urrrgh!'

Kate and Alice share a smile. 'William?' Kate asks. She cannot bring herself to call him Bill, even when she is speaking to his wife.

'Keeping Ernest from cutting his hands off.'

For most of the afternoon, Ernest has been engaged in building a bird table: an idea William put into his head without a thought for the attendant use of numerous sharp tools. At eleven, Ernest is both too reckless and completely unwilling to accept help.

'Any screams?'

'None yet.'

Kate takes the chair across from Alice and, tucking her feet up under her skirt, watches the girls counting out the last of the grapes to make sure they have even numbers. Across the lawn, Winifred lies belly-down on a picnic blanket and sketches in a small leather-bound book she carries about for the purpose. She is, for a seven-year-old, quite the artist. Her sketching is the reason she knows the names of the butterflies, Kate realises; she has copied their likenesses from the pages of a guide. Reginald has been in the kitchen washing and chopping dinner vegetables since before Kate went upstairs to bathe. He is thirteen: almost as tall as his father now, and as desperate as ever to gain his approval quietly. He has been nothing but industrious since Kate and William's return – helping to prepare the dinners, carrying wood in for the fires and stoking them, hanging bedsheets out to dry one early morning after Mona soiled them, climbing up a ladder to hack back those tendrils of ivy threatening to grow in through the windows. And yet, it is Ernest who commands his father's attention. He is the bolder, after all, and William cannot help but admire boldness.

'I suppose Arthur will need waking if he's going to sleep tonight,' Alice says. 'Do you want me to go?'

'I'll go,' Kate says, without looking at Alice. It must upset Alice, that the children get excited when Kate returns, that they squeal towards her at the gate or the door and away from the woman who raises them year round. And yet, if it does, Alice is careful never to show it. 'I suppose Arthur will need waking,' she says, when what she means is, 'I wake Arthur every day at this time and you don't know it.' Kate is not here.

She had sailed all the way back from Australia telling herself that, from here on, she would be. The decision had seemed easier with each passing wave. She would simply do in London what she had intended to do in Australia and install William as the star of the show. It would be tougher with a British audience, who were far more familiar with their act, but not impossible. Not... Everything had shifted with William's admission.

'I'll go and get him now.' She does not mean immediately, and Alice knows it. It is only their way of speaking. The sounds and patterns that have followed them out of Wales. 'I could sit here forever, you know.'

'You could not,' Alice laughs. 'You don't know how to keep still.'

'No,' Kate agrees. 'Perhaps I should learn.'

'Why? There's no need for you to change. You do very well just as you are.'

'Professionally.'

Not knowing how to respond, Alice reaches over and pats the back of Kate's hand. She is right, Kate supposes. It wouldn't do to pretend to be something other than what she is naturally predisposed to be. But she might be more than one thing or the other, mightn't she? She might grow and change and strengthen, just like the baby she is carrying. She might be more. And what of Alice? Is she everything that she could be? A thought which returns to trouble Kate at increasing intervals is that Alice does all she does because she is scared. Scared that to fight would be to surrender her husband entirely. Scared that to complain would mean the loss of her children. Scared that without this strange, misshapen family, she would be left entirely alone: forty-six and tired, with nowhere to go. Have they trapped Alice here, in this big house, occupied more and more by children who are not hers? Young Alice and Grace have never even lived here. They visit, of course, when their work allows, but... Kate is too mortified to broach the subject – in case she is right. It is easier, after all, to pretend. They have, each of them, been pretending at so much for such a long while.

Kate looks down towards the stream. Nora and Mona, having eaten the sweetest of the fruits, shrug away their towels and go off to disturb Winifred. Kate hears Nora entreating her sister – she would not think of her in any more complicated terms – to come and swing a skipping rope with her.

'I didn't know what I had here,' she confides quietly.

Alice purses her lips slightly: the reverse of a smile. 'Home is something you have to grow into.'

'I'm twenty-eight,' Kate says. 'I should have done my growing years ago.'

'Nonsense. We each do it in our own time and in our own way.'

Which, Kate thinks, is precisely what a great mother would say. Perhaps, then, her location is not what prevents her from being a proper mother to Nora, Mona, and Arthur. Perhaps she just does not have the same instinct for it as Alice does. Kate cannot summon, on the instant, reassurances which sound so convincing you might believe you've been hearing them your whole life. She cannot heal twisted ankles or nettle

323

stings with smiles. She cannot weigh up the needs of eight such different personalities and find ways to entertain them all at once.

Alice is the woman for the job. But where does that leave Kate? She is not mother. She is not wife. More likely it is she who will end up with nowhere to go.

To prevent her thoughts from trundling any further down that particular path, Kate idles inside to fetch Arthur. The even thud of Reginald chopping potatoes reverberates along the hallway, and she pads towards the staircase quietly so as not to disturb him. She does not want him to emerge from the kitchen until William is back in the garden, where he might appear to be sharing his affections equally amongst his children. Upstairs, she reaches into Arthur's cot, slips one hand beneath the curve of his head and the other under his backside, and scoops him up. He is not yet two, but he is sturdy and cumbersome. He could easily walk himself from the bottom of the stairs out into the garden, but she does not want him to wake yet. She knows him better when he is asleep, and she can believe he is the boy she saw in Perth and Melbourne and Sydney. The boy she crawled across a storm-tossed deck to reach in the dark. Asleep, he is her little Art. But awake, troubling her out with his shifting frown and his huge green eyes, he exposes her as a fraud. She hardly knows him.

She sits with Alice at the table in the garden until the light falls lengthways, printing imitations of the trees across the lawn, where they shift and dance. All the bustle and racket of the bunched-up city stills, gives way to birdsong and the distant creak of ships' masts down in the harbour. Even from here, they can see the gulls: loose white threads blown about a silky sky. Everything is soft this evening: the gulls' cries; the patter of water spilt from a watering can over the flowers; their voices. William and the children come and go. Reginald had declared this morning that tonight the children would cook dinner for their mothers. William has been supervising this effort since it came time for the stove to be heated.

'Do you think he set it up?' Alice asks.

Kate has been recounting, in sporadic whispers, the story of Herr Pagel. It is a tactical choice, beginning with this story, but Kate is attempting to put the idea of tactics to the back of her mind. Planning the conversation in advance feels underhanded, but she does not intend cruelty. Indeed, it is the opposite. She is seeking to lessen the blow. She needs Alice to understand why she might have to leave her with a fourth child to care for and disappear again.

'I don't know. I thought so, but then, why would he...?'

'If he couldn't lift the weight.'

'Exactly.'

'Unless he didn't realise he couldn't lift the weight until afterwards. After he'd made the challenge.'

'That was my thought,' Kate says. She is pleased that Alice has taken the conversation in the direction she had intended. 'But I knew he wouldn't tell me if I asked. He didn't say anything until we were on the ship back, and...'

'And it was exactly what you were expecting,' Alice concludes with a small smile.

Kate laughs. Of course Alice can predict William's behaviour, his funny ways. She has known him so much longer than has Kate.

'Not this time.' She glances behind her, to make certain he is not walking across the garden towards them. 'He said he couldn't lift the weight. Just like that. That he'd been draining the sand out of the heavier weights for weeks.'

Alice leans closer. 'But why?'

'I have no idea.'

'Has he been ill?'

'Not such that I've known about it. Apart, perhaps, from when I was ill myself and too insensible to witness it, he has been entirely himself. Or so it seemed to me.'

Alice swats away a persistent fly, then runs her hand around her jaw in contemplation. 'But he's only thirty-nine.'

'You don't think he should be losing strength yet?'

'I definitely do not. He might not seem it compared to others in the theatre, but he's still young, Kate. He surely shouldn't be growing weak. Although...'

'What?'

'His father was not a strong man. He died young. Worn out by the work, the family always said.' Alice wags a finger over her shoulder, in the direction where they would find the ironworks, were they still in Abergavenny.

'But that's not to say William should follow,' Kate tries. The words, though, sound as weak as William's imagined father. She has seen how craftily music hall strips people of their strength. Look at Dan Leno. Not far past forty and already the theatre has spat him out a senile old man. It's the unfeasible schedule, the glare of the lights, the crushing pressure, the ridiculous highs and their proximity to the crashing lows, the addiction to admiration, the fear that every show might be the last. Perhaps William simply is not built to withstand all that. From the night on Darling Harbour to the day they sighted home soil, she had been convincing herself that, when they were back in Britain, she would send William out on his own; that she would stay in Bristol with Alice and the rest of the troupe could continue without her; that maybe Hatfield could become the new Vulcana, and that, given time, Vulcana might become a role that was held and performed and then passed on to a waiting protégé. That way, Vulcana would never have to grow old and weak. She could live forever. Kate should like that.

A clatter echoes inside the house, followed by a yell. A serving spoon, perhaps, or the lid from a pan. Dropped. The women wait for one child or another to come screaming out in search of help, but none appears. There is no crisis for them to attend; they must see this conversation through.

'He says he's just tired,' Kate continues. 'That once he's rested a while, he'll be back to himself.'

'And what do you think?' Alice asks.

It is rare for Kate to pause to think about anything for very long, but at this question, she does. She stops. She flicks through different answers as one might a pack of cards and tries to establish which feels like the best explanation for what she suspects about William. Only then, in endeavouring to fit it to words for Alice, does his problem slot into focus. It is as though she has been striving to see something impossibly far off and has just now peered into the eyepiece of a telescope. William has not become the man he set out to be. That's it. Atlas isn't as well-loved as Vulcana, and William is surprised to find himself feeling jealous, and he is questioning his purpose all over again. It is not his strength he has lost but his confidence.

Kate, then, will help him find it again. And when that is done, she might well be able to bring him back to full strength. That's it. That is her way forward. She should never have doubted that her plans were the right ones, however many obstacles remained stubbornly in her way, because ... perhaps all life is simply the facing of one impossible obstacle after another. Perhaps to think otherwise was only the innocence of youth. Perhaps the acceptance of not knowing is, after all, to truly know yourself.

'Alice,' she says, standing abruptly. 'I bloody love you. You do know that, don't you?' Before Alice has a chance to answer, Kate plants a kiss roughly on her cheek. 'Come on. Let's go and save this dinner before one of them burns down the house.'

They look back towards the house, all shadows and ghosts in the falling dusk light. The back door is open wide. From the kitchen, the muted gold glow of the lamps and the muddled chatter of the children.

'I think it's best we do,' Alice replies.

Kate slips her arm into Alice's and, skirts shushing over the grass, laughter caught in their cheeks, the two women step across the lawn together.

Intermission

Cold as a sudden sluice of sleet. Cold as a closed tomb. Cold as the deck of a ship storm-tossed across the Atlantic Ocean. Cold as the black-bottomed depths of the sea. Cold as winter winds furious across Welsh mountainsides, or a tiled floor beneath the warmed skin of a bare foot, or ice cracked from the surface of a lake. Cold as nightmares jinking down a spine, or the realisation of deep-buried fears. Cold as betrayal. This. This place. Where she has been laid out and forgotten.

For years and minutes and lifetimes she lies – on porcelain, she thinks; cold porcelain – listening to all the horses who have graced her dreams galloping past the walls of the morgue she has found herself abandoned in. Listening to the birds of her imaginings as they dart and skim over the roof, trailing their screeches and yawps behind them. There is nothing else to listen to here. No visitors. No music. No life. Nothing but what is outside, beyond her reach. They think she is dead.

It grows dark and it brightens again. Though the room is windowless, a slat of light shows beneath the door. She can sense rather than see it, for she cannot turn her head. She knows only what can be discerned through the shutters of her closed eyelids. Her skull throbs with the effort of having tried and tried again to lift her fingertips, to twitch her toes. She is concentrating now on her lips. If she can only persuade them to part...

There comes a snick, a light scrape, a swoop of air. The slow one-two of leisurely footsteps. Something metal is lifted, adjusted, set back down. The wet rasp of inhalation and exhalation heavies. Footsteps close in. The breathing grows louder. The undertaker has come to perform his autopsy, finally. He is going to slice her open and lift out her organs. She is going to be hacked up. This dangerous world has been too good to a girl who ran off to London and managed to get exactly where she intended to go without harassment, without getting lost and falling in with the wrong kind of women, without encountering anything of the poverty and disease she saw and ignored when she should have done more. And now she will have her comeuppance. She will die in this morgue, because they think she is already dead, and there is nothing she can do to show them that she is not. She is still here.

No. She kicks her feet: nothing. *Stop.* She tenses her stomach and attempts to flip, like a stranded sea creature: nothing. Perhaps, if she can just blow, she might cause her hair to flutter, and then he will know that she is alive. That she's still here. *Out,* she thinks, willing her breath up her throat and *out.* But she cannot summon the force. Her heart clenches tight and bursts loose so violently that it must surely be perceptible at her breast – if he looks. But she cannot rely on his looking, this man who is invisible to her. Who owes nothing to her. Who believes her to be already dead. Her killer.

Please, please, please, please, please, she thinks, and every muscle in her body screams, and every tendon seems ready to snap, but nothing responds. She cannot even grunt or shiver as the faceless man draws the sheet off her – she hears it slip away – and contemplates where to begin his gruesome work.

Please, please. She can hear her own sobs, echoing inside her mind, though she knows that her face is not contorting, that her chest is not heaving. She is not truly crying. And yet, a tear beads at the corner of her right eye and rolls on its own weight until finally it drops and spills down her cheek.

Only then does the man at her side speak. It is hardly more than a whisper, but she hears him well enough, given that he leans so close over her that they are almost touching and breathes the words against her skin.

'Jesus Christ,' he says. 'You're alive.'

1910
Act Four

31.

London, England
1910
MISSING

London, when she returns to it, is grotesque. The National Vigilance Association sends its most buttoned-up members to hound the more famous acts. The theatres put on increasingly obscene performances: more grandeur, hideous expense. The performers find their wages being cut and cut again as the theatre owners splurge on herds of dancing horses, on boats that sail through the auditoriums and into giant water tanks, on ceilings which can be retracted or illuminated and through which gymnasts leap and tumble. Spectacle is held in higher esteem than talent these days, it seems to Kate, and in 1907, she joins the picket line at the Music Hall Artistes Strike and campaigns, vociferously, for a living wage for all.

Fortunately, she and William have no pressing financial worries. Vulcana is still in high demand. She has been declared the World's Strongest Woman in some book or other – Kate has not looked at it – and she is able to command a good price. One more night, she tells herself, as William traipses her round all the usual haunts. One more week. One more month.

And soon, music hall seduces her all over again, and she cannot think of giving it up – not even for Young William.

The part of her which belongs to Vulcana revels in the busy schedule, the applause, the fancy dinners, the posters dotted around the city which shout her name. The part of her which belongs to Kate throws herself into her work with the Music Hall Ladies' Guild and tells herself that she is doing good here. That all four children are better off with Alice. That she is yet to make the changes she set out to make. That she is not finished.

Kate and William are in London so frequently now that they take a house in Fulham. It is not so grand as the Bristol house, but it is light and spacious and Kate feels herself the mistress of her own home for the very first time. She revels in deciding where to position this piece of furniture, on which wall to hang that photograph. William's box camera has been upgraded year on year – this one, apparently, is the Kodak Number 2 Brownie, with leatherette cover – and they have hundreds of photographs: of Kate; of the troupe; of statues and bridges and skylines in the various countries they have visited; of Alice and the children. Her favourite, taken in the garden of the Bristol house, hangs over the fireplace. In it, she smiles straight into the lens, flanked by Nora and Mona. The girls wear matching dresses and plaits, and hold up a string of conkers they have threaded. Kate has her arms thrown over their shoulders. Every time she looks at it, she remembers standing for the camera and believing that Nora and Mona were staring straight at their father, as she was, but in truth it is only Nora who imitates her mother's pose. Mona glances shyly away to the left. It fascinates Kate that she could not have seen that detail, had William not snapped the image at that precise moment, and she stops to study it each time she passes through the house.

Today, however, she does not. Today is different.

This February morning, she blusters in to find William installed at the kitchen table, sipping from his coffee cup. She has been out early, walking. Her skin is taut and red from the cold. Her nose and fingers are numb. Her thinking is sharpened by the frost. Kate invariably feels more alive when the temperatures are cruelly low.

'Would you look at this?' she says, too loud, as she strides into the room. She is flapping a newspaper at him, but allowing him no opportunity to actually see it. She does not want him to take it from her and calmly peruse the orderly lines of type. She is too incensed. The world is too messy to be so neatly set down. It cannot be trusted.

'What is it?' William obliges. He puts down the paper he had been reading when she slammed through the front door and looks at her over the top rim of his glasses. He only wears the glasses when they are at home. On stage, he claims, they would make him look ridiculous. Secretly, Kate likes the way they frame those familiar bright green eyes, but she does not tell him as much: he would claim she was only flattering him, as always he does when she mentions how handsome he is or when she presses her face to the dip of his chest just to feel the brush of his hair over her skin and listen to his heart thrum.

337

'He's only taken out an advertisement.'

'Who?'

'Crippen!'

'No.' William rises from his chair, indicating that Kate should lay the paper out on the table for them both to view – he is always so calm, so contained of late – but Kate cannot stop pacing, and waving the paper, and rambling. The crackled pages accompany her words; her footfalls are a thumping drumbeat.

'A bloody advertisement, William. Appealing for her to come home. How can she come home? He's done away with her, I'm telling you.'

'Kate...'

'There is no way that woman has just disappeared,' Kate replies, flashing a warning glance at William. He meets it with silence, as she wishes him to. 'God knows she's desperate for the stage, and that she's always chasing after some man or other, but it's all part of the game. She wouldn't run off to America with a single one of them. She doesn't love them. That's not what they're for. And–'

'When did you last see her?'

'A few weeks ago. I'm not sure. But that letter he sent to the guild, William; it wasn't even in her hand. She's the treasurer! We see her handwriting. And that wasn't it. Moreover, Elmore was spelled with two "l"s!'

More and more since Belle's disappearance, Kate has been thinking of the strike. It had started at the Holborn Empire and dragged on for two full weeks. To their credit, some of the

338

best-known came out to stand amongst their poorer colleagues: Gus Elen, Joe Elvin, Marie Lloyd. Marie made as much of a show of picketing on a pavement as she did of appearing under the lights at Drury Lane and soon she took to warming the January gatherings with a song or two. Everyone joined in – Kate, knowing herself to have an atrocious singing voice, rather quietly – but it was Marie all eyes stayed on. Tiny Marie with her trademark enormous hat and skirts, her breath clouding on the icy air, became the image of that strike. But Belle Elmore was there every hour of every day. People made fun of her, as they so often do: plump as a pigeon; the Belle of no one's ball; talentless 'Cora Crippen'. Unfortunate, that her married name, in its alliterative CC, allowed people another means of mocking poor Belle. Kate closed her ears to it. Yes, Belle was a little too hungry for stardom, and her singing voice was not especially strong, and she did not help her own cause by fussing about like a peacock – all flounce and feather and brazen-faced ambition. But Kate attributed all that to Belle's wretched need to impress. What nobody else cared to notice was that Belle worked endlessly for the music-hall charities, and that she was committed to that strike. Never was anyone out before Belle and never did anyone retire after her. She was tenacious, and she bore the mockery of others bravely, and that was why she and Kate became friends.

'Do you think you ought to go to the police?' William asks.

He has resumed his seat and has his coffee cup poised before his mouth. Kate finally stops thundering around the kitchen and looks at him properly. It is not yet fully light outside. The morning is grey, promising only flat skies and dank air, and though he sits near the window William is thrown into shadow. Despite being unable to see the flecked gold-green of his eyes, Kate can tell that his eyebrows are raised, that his face is mildly arranged. He does not think she is being ridiculous, then.

'Do you think I could?'

'I don't see why not,' William replies. He sips his coffee, the ends of his moustache curling over the white china cup. 'She has, undeniably, vanished.' *Sip*. 'Crippen doesn't seem overly troubled to have a missing wife.' *Sip*. 'It surely wouldn't do any harm to voice your concerns.'

Kate slaps the folded newspaper down on the table. 'They'll laugh me out.'

'Why would they?'

'Because I'm a woman.' She is thirty-three years of age, she earns the money which pays for this house and another besides, and still she is shocked by the refusal of men to take her seriously. The way they defer to William in conversation prickles like gooseflesh all over her head. The shift in their eyes when they call her 'young lady', as though it is a compliment, makes her stomach churn. God, even now, after all these years, her father will not accept the love and honesty which fills this life she has made for herself. It is not the right shape. She is not the right shape.

'Evidence is evidence,' William says, quite reasonably. Whatever his faults, he would never condescend to call Hatfield 'young lady'. 'Should it matter who hands it to them?'

'No,' Kate replies, finally deflating and stepping behind William to wrap her arms around his chest and rest her chin on his shoulder. 'No, it shouldn't.' She knows it will. 'But I'm not even sure I can call it evidence, to say that the handwriting on the letter is not hers.'

'I'm sure you can, if you provide other documents which demonstrate it.'

'You're probably right. You're usually right.'

She feels William's chest pump out a laugh. 'You don't believe that.'

'No... Well, sometimes I do.' She presses a kiss to his whiskery cheek. He is in need of a shave. 'There is the dinner on the twentieth,' she continues. 'Perhaps I'll wait to see him there. He'll have to come, won't he?'

'I expect he will,' William replies. Already his eyes are drifting back to his own reading. Understandably, he is not expecting anything very dramatic to happen at a benevolent fund dinner of the Music Hall Guild. Neither, in truth, is Kate. It seems, however, that Dr Crippen cannot help but court controversy, for the scene he so quietly causes just two weeks later is soon the talk of London.

32.

London, England
1910
THE DINNER

On the occasion, Kate finds she can muster little enthusiasm for the Music Hall Guild Benevolent Fund Dinner. February, flat and grey, has stretched on interminably. Outside the Fulham house, barely formed raindrops catch in the lamplight and hang there, suspended, as though stopped in time. Kate knows that within moments of shutting the front door and stepping onto the pavement, her curled and tucked hair will be reduced to kinks and frizz. She stands before the mirror in the front room and fusses with the strands which surround her face. She doesn't truly care about her hair, of course, but in her eternal indecision about what she is and where she belongs, she is being transformed into this person: a person who buries her discontent inside trivialities.

'Then don't go,' William says. 'We won't go.' He is smart in a crisp white shirt and black suit. His skin is still tight and warm from the bath. Kate, watching him dress from their bed, had twice told him there was a crease in the back of his shirt, causing him to remove and inspect it, and once claimed an iron burn in the seat of his trousers. He had thrown his bow tie at her when he'd realised she was only stalling their being ready. Kate had caught it and slipped it round her own bare neck with a grin.

'I have to go,' she replies.

'Because of Crippen?'

'Because I'm the vice-president. And, yes, because of Crippen.'

They take a cab to the Criterion Restaurant in Piccadilly – a little late, admittedly – and, on entering the second floor, find a good crowd already in attendance. A gramophone scratches out tunes, but it is in vain against the burble of voices and the chiming of glasses. This crowd don't need music beyond the cadences of their own conversation. Kate had shrugged off her coat at the door and is still fidgeting with her dress. Her shoes and stockings are spotted with rainwater and she feels badly put together, though she doesn't look it. The feeling is symptomatic only of her grouchy mood. William stands beside her. She can feel the weight of him there and wants to hold his hand, but so accustomed is she to suppressing these urges that her own hand does not even flinch in response to it.

'Here we go then,' she says quietly, sighing and straightening up at once.

'Your smile is faltering,' William whispers.

'Let it,' Kate replies, though William's tease has already transformed it from false to genuine.

Side by side, Kate and William make to weave a path

through the chattering guests – just one or two are yet seated at the large circular tables – but they are, as usual, impeded at every turn.

'Miss Roberts! How glorious you look.'

'Dear William. Will you grace the Lane this season?'

'When will we see you again at the Savoy, Kate? We've missed you of late.'

And on and on it goes. Kate and William smile and clink glasses and touch arms and nod, and it is all a blur. The room is a carousel of black suit jackets and white shirt collars, of ruched skirts and red lips, of cigarette smoke and sloshed wine glasses, of draped white tablecloths and floral centrepieces, of jewels glinting off clavicles and ear lobes, of polite laughter and words shared behind fanned hands, of footsteps and footsteps and footsteps. Kate searches the room for Dr Crippen, her friend's strangely silent husband, until she is giddy with it.

'Kate, darling.' Lips meet Kate's cheek with an exaggerated smack, followed by a heavy waft of orange blossom and tobacco: Marie. Despite the popularity now of the more slim-line dress, Marie is as flounced and frilled as ever, and Kate loves her for it. Marie Lloyd will change for no one. In the last five years, she has divorced Percy Courtenay, married and then separated from Alec Hurley, and is now, rumour has it, about to set up house with a jockey by the name of Bernard Dillon, who is all of twenty-one years of age. There has been gossip at Albion House, where the Ladies' Guild have their office. There has been gossip on every street corner in London, in fact, but Kate has not asked Marie for the truth of any one of her supposed affairs. Love affairs, she should like to remind all those tattling mouths, are not always sordid matters to be giggled over or gasped at. After all, her love affair with William has lasted longer than almost any marriage she hears of amongst the music hall gangs. He is the only man she has ever known; the only man she ever will know.

'Marie,' Kate says, and returns the kiss.

Close to, Marie wears the ink of all that vicious newsprint as dark shadows, beneath her eyes, around her lips. She has just turned forty – she is only six years older than Kate – and she is fading and lined and appears to Kate like a poorly developed photograph of the woman she once was and still ought to be. All her bright lines have been smudged.

'Have you seen him yet?' Kate enquires.

In Room 63 of Albion House, New Oxford Street, Kate, Marie and a few of the other guild ladies – Lil Hawthorne, Margaret Smythe, Melinda May, Clara Martinetti, Bessie Brown – had vowed to keep a close eye on Dr Hawley Crippen tonight. They had pored over that ridiculous letter together, and agreed that Belle would never have taken off to America without a moment's planning or a hint to her closest friends. It had to be her husband's doing. Hawley, with his staring eyes and his lingering way, had never held any real affection for his wife.

'Not yet,' Marie confirms. 'I shouldn't be surprised if he doesn't show.'

But soon enough, he does.

William has been whisked away by some acquaintance or other, and Kate has taken a seat alongside Bessie. Amongst the numerous ladies of the music hall guild, Kate likes Bessie perhaps best of all. Tall and thin as a cello string, Bessie has painfully straight blonde hair and a delicate face – all bones and skin and next to no flesh at all. She is around twenty-five years of age and thinks nothing of herself whatsoever. That is to say, she is entirely without pretension. She has no aspirations to fame, she is not chasing after a moneyed bachelor, and she causes no arguments or jealousy amongst the other women – which cannot be said of all their members. Bessie simply loves to sing and longs to help. The work of organising this benevolent fund dinner had therefore fallen mostly to her, and she has done a splendid job.

Kate takes a look around, meaning to find something specific to compliment Bessie on. The menus are elegantly done. The centrepieces just enough. Halfway between the high ceilings and the tables, lights have been suspended at some length so that the atmosphere is soft and flattering. She turns in her chair, and it is then that she spots him. Dr Crippen. Pausing near the doorway to remove the furs from the shoulders of a slight young woman in his company. Certainly not Belle, who, for some time now, has grown plumper by the week.

'Bess,' she hisses, reaching backwards to grasp Bessie's hand in her own. She finds it chill, the skin frail. She fears she might snap a bone if she squeezes too excitedly.

'Ouch. What?'

'He's here. Look.' She nods towards the door and Bessie's head appears at her shoulder to get a better view.

'So he is,' Bessie breathes slowly. 'Would you warrant that? Who's the girl?'

Kate has not yet begun to study the girl. Her attentions are fixed on Dr Hawley Crippen: his enormous Hungarian moustache; the thin comb-over he has made of his remaining hair; his small, wire-rimmed glasses; his large, bulging eyes. His suit is neat enough, but the man himself cannot seem to appear neat within it. There is something slovenly about him. He is the kind of man she wants to smack between the shoulder blades with a metre stick and instruct to 'stand up straight'. All the more so considering he stands at only five foot four – her own diminutive height.

Kate and Bessie stare, open-mouthed, as Dr Crippen's young companion spins around, furs removed, and clasps his hand. There is something shy in her deportment, but she seems to know she has every speck of Dr Crippen's interest, for she casts him fluttering looks and, when they are returned, poses under them as though the man's spectacles are in fact the lens of a camera. It could not be clearer that the two are lovers.

'He's brought a woman,' Kate says, as though perhaps in saying it she might begin to make it believable. It has been less than a month since Belle vanished. 'Where's Melinda?'

Kate feels Bessie glancing around for her, though she herself cannot take her eyes from Crippen. 'Two tables over.'

'Come on. Melinda will know who she is.'

Still clutching Bessie's cold hand, Kate drags her up and towards Melinda's table. They bump against a chair as they go, causing the legs to screech across the polished floor, but the sound is lost to the room. Reaching Melinda, they crouch beside her and she swivels around in her chair with a whip of her shining black hair.

'What on earth...'

'Look,' Kate urges her. 'By the door.'

Dr Crippen and his companion are stepping further into the restaurant now, searching a table with two empty places. They are unashamedly hand in hand.

'Who *is* she?'

Melinda scans the guests until she spots her targets. She squints. She thrusts her head forward, stretching out her neck, and squints again. Then her face opens into shock.

'That's his bloody *typist*!' she gasps. She turns a furrowed brow on Kate and Bessie. 'He's brought his typist?' The three women look from one to the other in silence. Kate can feel her heart gaining pace. 'He's brought his typist,' Melinda says again, and this time, the words are entirely altered.

Kate's nerves jangle through the starters, she is unable to touch the main course, and by the time dessert is served, she is clammy and cannot concentrate well enough to conduct a basic conversation. She apologises. She excuses herself. She manages snatched exchanges with Bessie and Melinda, Marie and Lil, Clara and Bessie. And each of the women does her best to ensure the success of the evening, but they have lost all ability to charm. To be sharing dinner with a murderer. It is almost too ridiculous to comprehend. And yet, it has to be so: Kate has seen what the typist – a Miss Ethel Le Neve – is wearing on her breast. The proof is unmistakeable.

She absents herself at the first opportunity, but given the protracted nature of these events, it is near midnight before she can rush William down the stairs of the Criterion and out onto Piccadilly. The evening cold seizes her chest and she coughs once, twice: pale bursts, which fade amongst the new illuminated advertising hoardings of Piccadilly Circus. She stops and puts a palm to one of the two tall iron lamps supporting the building's canopy. William stops alongside her and waits. He hasn't the first clue what is going on, but he knows enough of her to understand that it is serious, and that he must not push for an explanation. Instead, he buttons his coat, slow and methodical. Order, she thinks. He is offering you order. Watch his hands. Compose yourself.

'He's in there,' she says, pointing up at the huge fan window above them. Running around the curve of the window are the words 'The Criterion Spiers & Pond' in cast-iron lettering half the height of a person. It will look grand in the newspapers, Kate thinks, when Hawley is discovered. 'In there, as though nothing has happened, but I know that it has.' She jabs an erect forefinger into her own chest. 'I know. I saw it. He's killed her, William. He's killed Belle. And now he's in there and that young girl and, well, what if he means to kill her next?'

She begins pacing, as she had in their kitchen when she first saw his notice in the paper: *Will Belle Elmore communicate with H.H.C. or authorities at once. Serious trouble through your absence.*

'What did you see?' William asks. He does not step towards her or attempt to still her. If he does, they both know she will lose her temper.

'She's wearing her brooch, William. The girl he's brought. She's wearing Belle's brooch. It's pinned to her bodice, bold as you like. God, what should I do?' She presses her hands to her face, firmly. When she lowers them again, the lamps pick out clear white blotches on her skin.

'Go to the police,' William answers quietly. 'I think you must.'

'But...' She so desperately wants to hold William now. To be held by him. His proximity – the thud of his heart against her chest; the particular, slightly metallic scent of his skin – is often all she requires to set everything straight again. At the least, the solidity of him will convince her that she is making the right choice. But she cannot press herself to him until they are home and safely hidden behind drawn curtains. She has to bear her deductions alone. 'What if I'm wrong?'

'You're not wrong, Kate. You wouldn't feel so strongly if there was a chance you were wrong.'

She emits a sound, somewhere between a snort and a hum, and drops her arms to her sides. The fabric of her dress rustles. She is, she realises, panting. She concentrates on calming her breathing.

'Kate,' William says. He takes one careful step closer: a man approaching a lioness. His pupils are black beads. His lashes have stolen the shine from the lamps. 'Do you doubt it?'

Her head twitches, almost imperceptibly. She wants to shake it from side to side, but she cannot quite commit to the movement.

'Do you doubt what you saw?' William pushes.

Don't make me, she thinks. Don't force me to a decision. She doesn't want to reach this conclusion alone – not without William – because she knows, she knows that she will not be believed. She might be royalty on the music hall stage. She might be known across half the world as a woman so strong she can lift men above her head one-handed. But they will not listen to her thoughts. They have never listened to her thoughts. For more than a decade now she has been talking to the papers, the magazines, anyone who will listen, about the benefits of exercise for a woman's body *and* mind. She has been promoting physical exertion as a means of developing a healthy mental attitude. And still, they print her measurements.

William is close enough now to touch her hand and, without scanning the street to check if anyone is watching, he takes it tenderly in his own. He risks that.

'Do you doubt yourself?' he says.

And Kate's answer is immediate. 'No.'

33.

London, England
1910
NEW SCOTLAND YARD

Shortly before dawn, Kate stands on the Victoria Embankment, the grey Thames water slopping at her back, a light wind pulling at her hair, and stares up at the two tall buildings before her. She is trying to decide which she is supposed to enter by. The pair are linked by an arched stone bridge, and though they are mirrors of one another – built of matching bands of red brick and white stone, and resembling in pattern, Kate thinks, a mint humbug – they do not share an entranceway. Over the roof tiles, the first trace of morning marks a cold, pale line. Curved turrets flank each building, which – Kate counts them – are stacked five storeys high. There are two more rows of windows in the roof-space. The design, she suspects, is predicated on the desire to keep members of the public from feeling themselves welcome to just wander in. The New Scotland Yard is grand and imposing and shuttered-looking, and it makes her feel small.

But she has never tolerated belittlement before now, and she does not mean to begin today. She takes a deep breath, straightens her hat, and steps towards the nearest door. She will rattle at them all in turn until she brings someone running. It is not yet quite seven o'clock – the lamps along the embankment are still aglow – but she has seen the odd splay of light through the windows, the flitting shadow of a figure across a room, so she knows that there is at least one person within.

Stepping away from the river and into the deeper gloom cast by the building, she grasps the brass knocker and hammers it insistently against the paintwork. In the endless dark hours since she left the Music Hall Guild Benevolent Fund Dinner, she has only grown more convinced of what she must report to the police. Dr Hawley Crippen, she will tell them, of 39 Hilldrop Crescent, has killed his wife, Mrs Cora Crippen, more commonly known as Belle Elmore, and disposed of the body. There is no other explanation. And they won't want to hear it, all these uniformed men with their waxed moustaches and their shone boots and their important files folded under their arms, but she will make them listen. She must.

Eventually, a door is swung open, and Kate almost falls through with the abruptness of it. She rights herself quickly. Though she had done so just prior to the dinner, she had bathed again in the small hours, wanting to arrange her hair in a flatter fashion, and then put on her most business-like dress – charcoal with a fine white pinstripe – with the intention of presenting to whichever police inspector she managed to lure to the case a woman altogether serious and sensible. And not at all attractive to the opposite sex. It is no good looking like a doll, she has discovered, if you want to be truly listened to.

The man before her is, it transpires, little more than a boy. A clerk, perhaps. Or a junior police officer new to the Metropolitan Police. He has a mass of tight brown curls, which he has tried to slick down but which strain against the persuasion of the comb and will, by the end of the day, no doubt have sprung loose. His eyes are round and that unsettling shade of blue which is too vivid to seem entirely natural. His demeanour is clipped but kind as he leans towards her – the faint scent of bergamot – and says, 'Miss? Are you hurt?'

'I am not.'

'Oh, good.' He taps the place where his heart beats. 'You just about frightened the life out of me, banging like that. I would've thought you were being chased down.' He mimes being chased down by bunching his fists and swinging them, as though he is running. 'What can I do for you?'

'I need to report a murder,' she replies.

'A murder?'

'Yes, indeed.'

The boy exhales loud and long. 'Well, I imagine you'll be needing the chief inspector for that, miss. But he's not here just now. Why don't you come in and give me the details? We can wait for him together.'

Kate follows the boy – 'Constable Fouracre, miss' – through a series of dim hallways and up two flights of stairs before they reach a heavy internal door. Constable Fouracre pushes it open and, hand splayed across the wood, motions for her to step inside. For a moment, she is chilled by the ludicrous idea that he will lock her inside and that she will never be seen again; that she, like Belle, will simply disappear. She ignores the feeling and steps through.

The room is small and square. A desk is positioned in front of the window, with one chair set behind it and two before. On the desk, cardboard files have been built into towers. In the wall to her left is another door.

'Is this the inspector's office?' Kate asks, though she knows it is not. It is not grand enough. She is only inviting Constable Fouracre to confirm the whereabouts of the room she is seeking.

'Oh, no, miss,' the boy replies, pointing to the door in the wall. As she suspected. 'But listen, let me take down some details so that we have a straight story for Inspector Dew when he arrives.' Constable Fouracre moves around the desk, opens a drawer, retrieves a pen and, to test that it has some ink, scribbles in the corner of a notepad which is already lying open.

'Shall we start with your name, miss?' he says, looking up and indicating, with a nod of his head, that she should take a seat.

'Kate Roberts,' she replies, obliging. 'Miss.'

'And the victim's name?'

'Belle... I should say, Mrs Cora Crippen.'

'Very good.' Noting that Kate has now settled, Constable Fouracre lowers himself into his own seat and flashes her a smile. His teeth are pleasantly white; he does not smoke. 'Go ahead, miss. Tell me everything you know.'

She spends perhaps half an hour in the telling of it, interrupted now and then by Constable Fouracre's keenness – which is, she suspects, fed more by his passion for impressing the mysterious inspector than by his desire to bring the killer of a poor murdered woman to justice. She begins to like him less for it, and wonders where the chief inspector is and why such a man allows his subordinates to reach the offices before him. Does he walk to work, stopping along the way to be served breakfast? Does he sit in his bed reading the papers and drinking coffee, with nothing to stir him but his sense of duty? Does he *like* women? The question of his admiration, or lack thereof, for the opposite sex is going to prove important here, she suspects.

'So the lady has already been reported missing?' The young constable's frown has been growing steadily deeper, so that now it appears less a line and more a ravine. She wonders, if she were to snatch the pen he has made a baton of and is now twirling across his knuckles, and slot it between his eyebrows, whether it would stay put.

'I believe it to be the case,' Kate answers, 'but I could not say for certain. Your records, perhaps, can do a better job there.'

'Certainly, miss.' Constable Fouracre keeps his eyes on his notepad and nods, like a suitably chastened little boy. And it is at that moment that the Chief Inspector announces his entrance. Kate had not heard footsteps along the corridor – a wonder in this big, echoey building – and ponders whether the man has been standing at the door, listening. Constable Fouracre leaps into action, jolting out of his seat and seemingly having to stop himself from snapping his hand into a salute.

'Detective Chief Inspector Dew,' he gabbles. 'This is Miss Kate Roberts. She would like to have a quiet word, sir. She's...'

'Miss ... Vulcana,' the detective says. He points a blunt finger at her. 'I recognise you from your posters.' He reaches out to shake her hand and Kate rises to meet him. 'To what do we owe the pleasure?'

'An unpleasant business, I'm afraid, Inspector,' Kate replies, making sure to hold his eye. He is a large man, aged somewhere between forty and fifty, with a straight nose and a square head. He wears a tight, bristly moustache – very neat – and is beginning to bald on top. What remains of his hair is cropped short, to lessen the contrast. His shirt is startlingly white and when he moves, he gives off an agreeable mixture of strong soap and gentle cologne. He is a man whose arms a woman might feel safe in. At least, physically. Kate has yet to determine his character, of course, but she likes the look of Detective Chief Inspector Dew. He has promise.

'Then you'd best come through,' he says.

He shows her into his office. She finds it almost exactly as she had expected. The furniture is heavy and dark. The desk is positioned facing the door, so that he can greet whatever comes through it from a place of safety – his back to the wall. Or perhaps to demonstrate that a man such as he does not waste an ounce of time looking out at the moody flow of the Thames. He is far too important a figure to be caught glancing through the window in contemplation or repose.

As he steps around the desk – is he a little stiff at the hip? – and settles himself, Kate lingers near the doorway, making a show of considering the photographs hung on the wall which faces the window: a few hunting scenes; a dramatic seascape; some police officers in uniform. Impossible to know whether the officers who stare solemnly out at her are relatives or predecessors or both, but she does not wish to ask.

'Would you like to close the door, Miss Roberts?'

She wouldn't particularly. Inspector Dew has left a Persian fumigating ribbon burning overnight to mask the scent of his cigars, and she fears the combination of stale tobacco and the sickly rose otto, musk, orris, and myrrh of the ribbon might become quite overwhelming. Still, this is a private matter, and so she eases the door into its latch before she takes her seat.

'Murder is a word my ear is particularly attuned to, Miss Roberts,' he says. So, he had been listening. 'Would you care to elaborate?'

Sitting consciously upright and neat across the vast leather inlay of the inspector's desk, she begins again, interrupted only occasionally by Inspector Dew's gruff requests for clarification. The sudden vanishing. The letter. The handwriting. The disinclination of Belle Elmore ever to do anything quietly. Dr Crippen's shifty behaviour. The changing story. Dr Crippen's blatant affair with his typist, a Miss Ethel Le Neve. And, finally...

'Only last night, Inspector, mere weeks after he himself informed us of his wife's death in California, he attended a benevolent fund dinner of the Music Hall Guild with Miss Le

Neve on his arm. That might seem a matter of impropriety alone, I know. But then, I doubt that music hall could claim the highest standards of propriety, if we're speaking honestly, and still their appearance caused a scandal. Miss Le Neve, you see, was wearing items of Mrs Crippen's jewellery. Bold as you like. With my own eyes, Inspector, I saw pinned to her bodice a brooch which I would swear in a court of law belonged to my friend.'

'You have a good description of it?' Inspector Dew asks.

'It has the shape of a peacock, sir, and is inlaid with sapphire and emerald. It is quite distinctive. There must surely be records of Belle's ownership of it, don't you think? And what kind of woman would wear her chaperone's recently disappeared wife's jewellery to a function of that lady's own guild? Indeed, what grieving husband would allow her?'

'That is an apposite question, Miss Roberts.'

Kate does not possess the vanity to blush at the inspector's approval. It is not what she came here for. She wants simply for him to believe her and interview Dr Crippen on the matter. She is sure, then, that the story will crumble entirely.

'Enough to warrant your paying Dr Crippen a visit?'

Inspector Dew props his elbows on the desk to mull this over. He grows eerily still, but for the twitching of his moustache. Kate is put in mind of a weathervane, trembling in a strengthening wind. It is not an incoming storm which heavies the air now, however, but the inspector's gusting instincts.

'I should say so,' he says slowly.

They go through the necessary paperwork to make Kate's report formal, and, as daylight finally feathers over the city, soft and white, Inspector Dew stands, shakes Kate's hand, and escorts her to the door. Scotland Yard, by now, has filled with every manner of person: clerks and constables, inspectors and chief inspectors, accusers and accused. Constable Fouracre is to be found on the ground level, booking in a short line of questionably accommodating women. Kate offers them a nod: you cannot begrudge a prostitute her living; no woman would choose to rent herself out if she had available to her a better option. She hopes the law will not be too tough on them, though she is not convinced that the women will be treated fairly, given the satisfied smirks the two police constables now flanking young Mr Fouracre are already wearing.

'Gentlemen,' Kate says, in a small attempt to remind them of how they should behave.

At the desk, two other police constables look askance at her. The men are of roughly the same height – perhaps five feet and ten inches – and one is naturally broad while the other works hard to make himself so. Kate can discern this much without seeing the men stripped of their clothes. Her strongwoman training, her time in gymnasiums across the country, has taught her to understand the make-up of a body. The naturally broad chap is perhaps ten years the senior of the other, but they are both quite blatant in their appreciation of the women recently brought into their care. Constable Fouracre, to his credit, does not join in with their muttered remarks.

'Inspector Dew, sir,' the older constable says, standing up

from where he had been leaning on the desk when he notices his superior's presence.

'Hamilton,' Inspector Dew replies curtly, and Kate wants to smile at him for that – for letting the man know, without more than the utterance of his name, that his behaviour has been noted and disapproved of – but naturally she does not. She arrived here certain that she would not be taken seriously, but she believes, as she steps towards the door she had entered by, that Inspector Dew has listened to her; that he is a genuine sort; that he cares about his job. She is starting to believe that all this time spent asking people to listen to her, demanding that they do, has led her here – to the fight for justice for a wronged and voiceless woman. If she can win this fight, it will have all been for something ... won't it.

'Who's that lady, sir?' Hamilton asks. His voice is at her back, but it is loud without intention and carries beautifully in the tiled entrance hall. 'I'm sure I recognise her.'

'As well you might,' Inspector Dew replies. 'The lady is Miss Vulcana, a famous music hall artiste.'

Kate cringes. One strike against Inspector Dew. Not, of course, because she is ashamed of being a music hall artiste. Far from it. She is proud of what she represents when she is on stage. She is more determined than ever in the message she wishes to convey to women up and down the country. But to name her a 'music hall artiste' rather than 'a lady concerned for her friend' or 'a lady who has brought in some important information' demonstrates something of Inspector Dew's feelings on the matter. While his interest might have been piqued, this is not yet a murder case to his mind. Kate will have to find alternative means of persuading him of it.

'Why is she here, sir?' Hamilton pushes. He is after a scandal, perhaps. Well, Kate thinks, I have just handed your detective chief inspector one, should he wish to squint down his nose at it.

'She is worried about a missing friend,' Inspector Dew replies. Better. 'Now, get this place cleared, will you. It's not even past breakfast and already I'm being confronted with a backlog.'

Inspector Dew strides away. From the doorway, Kate hears his perfectly even footsteps retreating along the corridor he had accompanied her down. He had come out only to see her away; he had not been in need of anything from this part of the building. He might just be a good man after all. At least, she hopes he is.

Rather than do as his superior has instructed, Hamilton drops his elbow back down on the desk and resumes muttering to his colleague. She does not catch all of it. She is not supposed to. But she hears three words, loud as a candlestick dropped on a chapel floor: 'Another hysterical woman.'

All these years, she thinks, of touring and speaking and training and sacrifice, and in so many ways, she remains powerless. A mere three words are all that is required, in this particular space, to silence her.

Without a glance backwards, she pulls open the door and walks out into the blank white page of the morning, her back straight and her chin high. Hysterical she will not prove herself. But correct she most certainly will.

34.

London, England
1910
TEA AND CORSETS

Perhaps three weeks before the Music Hall Guild Benevolent Fund Dinner, Kate had been on the lower floor of the Criterion for a meeting she had mentioned nothing of to William. Just one week after her visit to New Scotland Yard, at around nine o'clock on the blustery first day of March, she once again takes the charcoal dress with the white pinstripe from her wardrobe and buttons herself into it. Today will be her third time attending these meetings at the Criterion, and she does not mean to draw attention to herself. It would not do to be recognised and have the newspapers make mention of her sympathies when next she is being plastered over the front pages for some story of heroism or daring. It would, she suspects, discourage certain people – men, particularly – from attending her performances, and that would not help either her own cause or that of the women meeting for afternoon tea later today.

In truth, she considers they are in possession of two separate causes, but that they might overlap one another quite significantly. They must, if either is to reach its fullest potential.

She brushes the static from the dress with her palms and

sets about gathering her hair into a neat chignon. She needs no mirror for this, and as she tucks and pins, tucks and pins, she wanders about the bedroom she shares with William. The view from the window this morning shows her only shadows and ghosts, printed onto the roof of the house across the street by a flimsy square of pale sunlight: the bend and flick of branches tossed in the wind; the too-quick flit of a bird, two, overhead and then gone.

She pushes the last pin into the bulk of her hair and goes to her bedside table to retrieve the letter from Alice. The two women write each other a long letter once a week: Kate telling Alice of the various shenanigans of the London theatres, and Alice detailing funny moments with the children and what she calls the 'tedious day to days'. Kate does not find them tedious at all. She reads Alice's letters as avidly as though they are works of great literature. This, the latest, informs her that Arthur, nearing eight years of age now and still quiet and contemplative, has lately started teaching himself to play the harmonica: *though only when he is alone, of course, behind closed doors, for fear that the girls will taunt him. The instrument is not Bill's, I think, but perhaps left behind by the previous owners of the house.*

Nora she declares *as tempestuous as ever. She believes herself in love with the neighbour's lad, presently, but luckily for us – in the long run, I hasten to add, for the heartache is making her most unpleasant currently – he is seventeen and will not look at her.* This, Kate laughs at. At thirteen, Nora is only two years younger than Kate was when she first met William.

She scans the lines of Alice's heavy, slanting hand for Mona's name, and pores over the section dedicated to her second daughter. *In her heart, I believe her as much Nora's shadow as she ever was, but with Nora so distracted, Mona and Winnie spend much time sitting toe to toe in the window seat, passing books back and forth. It makes me fancy them great scholars, though I suspect they are greater romantics than anything.*

Initially, Alice had been reluctant to put details of this kind down on paper and post them to Kate. To take the fragments of a household and describe them, she said, might lead to wrong impressions, might even lead Kate and William to worry. But Kate had begged, and Alice had capitulated, and the letters have proven to bring such joy to the Fulham house. They contain all the wild soars and dips of childhood, the desperate ebbs and flows of mood and favour. To have that much intensity recorded is precious in a way Kate can't quite describe. She has never once worried about any of it.

She turns the page and scans down to the place where she knows she will find her fourth child's name. She has read the letter that many times that she practically knows it by rote, but she enjoys going over and over the words, savouring them in the slow, deliberate way one might savour unwrapping a chocolate truffle. It is through these words that she gets to know her children.

As to Young William, Kate reads. Already she is smirking. The phrasing says it all. The boy is but five-and-a-half years old and already he is a handful. *It seems he fancies the percussion, for he has developed an unbreakable habit of emptying the cupboards of all their pots and pans, turning them upside down on the kitchen floor, and battering them until none of us can hear ourselves think.*

Kate folds the letter carefully and slips it into the drawer which contains her stockings. It will be a month yet before she has enough consecutive nights off to travel down to Bristol and see her babies. She has been counting the days. Particularly given that Alice has not been well. *Something and nothing, perhaps,* she had written. *I have every certainty that it will pass.* But Alice would not have mentioned it were she truly on the road to recovery, and Kate can only conclude that her help is required. She is happy to offer it, but always it seems there is some obstacle: the money, William's intermittent crises of strength or belief, Belle's disappearance.

'Soon enough,' she tells the room, and her sigh is almost as loud as her words.

After Young William's birth, she had sworn there would be no more. No more curled up new-borns to thrust into Alice's arms. No more tearful goodbyes as they were waved off at the train station by yet another unknown child. No more cries to call her from her sleep. She had sworn it to herself, something like a prayer, and surprisingly she has avoided a fifth pregnancy in the years since. She cannot say how, exactly, since she and William make love almost as often as they ever did, and, for a time, the children had followed in such quick succession. She had thought – dramatically enough – that they might kill her in those three years when she delivered Arthur, toured Australia, and travelled home just in time to deliver William.

366

But since – not even so much as a scare. Her mother, she thinks, would put that down to God's grace. Kate has decided to ascribe it to her age. Somehow – and really, she cannot say how this happened without her noticing and putting a stop to it – she has reached her middle-thirties. A strange and precarious time, she considers, when it becomes apparent that what lies ahead of you might be all the world and might be nothing very much at all.

Which is perhaps why she has become so taken with the meetings at the Criterion. Or rather, with the woman who leads them. Christabel Pankhurst is a few years younger than Kate and she has not only seen the inside of a prison cell, so staunch is she in her belief that women should be given equal voting rights to men, she has also been installed as the organising secretary of the WSPU – the Women's Social and Political Union is no small body, Kate has learned – *and* obtained a law degree to boot. Not that Kate would like to see the inside of a prison cell, mind you, but the fact does demonstrate a certain strength of conviction that anyone would be proud to possess. And to have a law degree. Kate has, on occasion, thought herself impossibly grand: travelling the famous theatres of the Continent; dining at expensive restaurants with lords and ladies; seeing photographs of herself erected all across cities on the other side of the world. She believes absolutely that she has something important to say to women – about power and selfhood. But she has had no thought for the politics of any of it. No one has ever enabled her to have such thoughts. 'Votes for women', however, is surely synonymous with 'votes for power', and so if she is to continue seeking an audience for this message, which she does not yet know exactly how to name, then she must surely understand the politics of it. In three short months, this pursuit has become her duty.

'William,' she calls as she descends the stairs.

'Hmm.'

She follows the sound and finds him sitting behind a newspaper in his favourite wing chair. He will be reading the reviews of all the shows across London last night. It is his morning ritual. The chair cushion has started to take the shape of his buttocks.

'I'm going out,' she says, swinging around the door frame and part way into the front room.

'Anywhere nice?'

'Just to tea.'

'Tea? With who?'

'A few of the guild ladies,' Kate replies. She wonders if he knows what her lies sound like. She does not think she can ever have told enough of them to allow him to recognise the tone. She has never had any reason to be dishonest with William. Indeed, she does not think she has any reason now, but instinct is telling her to keep this to herself. Just for now. Just until she can trouble out her feelings about it all.

She secures her hat and steps outside, deciding that she will walk some of the four miles to Piccadilly and thereafter hail a cab. She might take the underground, but Kate habitually finds a reason not to disappear into the rattle-and-dark tunnels below the city. It is suffocating down there. In Abergavenny, the skies were always bigger than the earth; in London, it seems to her the other way about. And Kate, as ever, wishes to be outside – with the wind roughing her cheeks, and the cold nipping her skin, and the endless sky shifting from ash grey to starling's egg blue above her, so that she might throw all her mad thoughts and ideas at it and let them be blown away.

The tables in the Criterion's lower floor restaurant have been arranged in a loose semi-circle around a small podium. Kate chooses a seat towards the back of the curve. Thus far, the meetings have consisted of a light lunch and the opportunity to mingle followed by a short speech from Miss Pankhurst, and she does not wish to be too near the front. All that blaze and gusto! She will keep some rows of women positioned between herself and Christabel Pankhurst – like a shield.

She is a tad early, and the restaurant is yet to fill, though Kate is certain it soon will. She glances around to see if Mabel has arrived. A hundred times she must have changed her mind before she plucked up the courage to ask Mabel along. Why it had made her so nervous she cannot say, even now, but she knows that the fluttering in her stomach won't settle until Mabel is stepping out of the Criterion fired up with passion and purpose. Then, perhaps, she will feel vindicated in her fascination with Miss Pankhurst's words.

She is still scanning the backs of around thirty heads when Mabel appears at her side.

'And what are you looking so twitchy about?' she grins.

'Nothing,' Kate replies.

'All right,' Mabel returns, removing her coat and rearranging the front of her dress. 'Then why are you so much in need of my approval?'

Kate frowns at her old friend. 'How do you know that?'

'You're entirely transparent.'

'Only to those who have watched me grow up,' Kate counters.

'Perhaps.' Mabel raises one eyebrow. 'Nearly twenty years is a long time. I should think I know *everything* about you by now.'

Kate suspects that Mabel is probably right. They have never spoken directly about Kate and William's relationship, but Mabel – the only original member of the troupe still performing with them – must know. She must have known for the longest time. What a friend she has been to them both, keeping it under her hat. London society is certainly not rural Wales – it has loosened its stays in so many respects over the past two decades – but still no one would accept an unmarried woman permanently occupying the bed of a married man more than ten years her senior. They certainly would not look favourably on the four beautiful results of their union, and Kate will not inflict such speculation upon her children.

'I think you likely do,' Kate admits. 'But I cannot say the same of you.'

'Can't you?'

Kate shakes her head. She knows that Mabel rents a small flat in Pimlico – she has visited – and that it is stylishly kept, with white walls and cream muslin curtains and a huge leather couch which all but swallows you into its cushions. The shelves are stacked with books and on the walls hang framed photographs of their travels in Wales, Scotland, France, Spain, Australia, Gibraltar. It is one of the quietest homes Kate has ever entered.

'Do you miss Abe?' she asks.

'Abe?'

It has been two or three years now since Abe left the troupe, citing a sister at home in America – the accent wasn't false, then – who needed to be cared for following a stroke. They had asked whether there was anyone else who might take up this duty on his behalf, but Abe had waved their questions away, and in the end they had realised that his sister's illness was also a means of his retiring without revealing that he was simply too exhausted to go on. Kate had never managed to pinpoint his exact age, but he had to be somewhere in his fifties. They had surprised him on the dockside the morning he boarded the steamer for New York, waving banners and flailing their arms and whistling and shouting until every passenger on deck was laughing at them. Every passenger except Abe, who stood with his hand clamped over his heart and cried.

'Yes, Abe.'

'We write often.'

Kate nudges Mabel with her shoulder. 'That's not an answer.'

'Then, yes. I do miss him. I miss him just as badly as I would

miss you or William, if I was so far away from either of you.'
By Mabel's standards, this is a revelation, and she is careful not
to meet Kate's eye as she delivers it.

'So you didn't...'

'What?'

'Fall in love with him?'

'Good God, no,' Mabel laughs. 'I don't do falling in love.
Not like that.'

'Why?' It is the question Kate has wanted to ask since her
first visit to London, and it drops from her mouth
accidentally, too small and too quiet in comparison to the
weight of the answer which must belong to it.

'I was always too...' She pauses and glances about, using the
arrival of more women – their chatter and umbrella shaking
and kissed greetings – to straighten her thoughts into
sentences. 'My mother... She didn't have an easy time of things,
with my father. He was less a husband, really, than a
businessman. A conman. He ... only showed up when he
wanted to take...'

'You were scared,' Kate says, at a whisper.

Mabel twists her lips in an impression of a smile. 'I suppose
I was.'

'But...' Kate cannot reconcile her love for William with the
idea of a choice. She was not able to decide, when she
discovered he was married, that she simply would not need
him anymore. It had claimed her, love. There was no way out.
'It's not optional,' she says.

'Oh, my sweet Kate,' Mabel replies. 'You'd be surprised.'

They eat sandwiches cut into tiny columns and pastries and little buns coated in a sticky glaze which Kate does not know the name of. They pour each other tea and sip from china cups patterned with roses and daffodils. And they discuss, as prompted, the argument that as taxpayers women should necessarily be allowed to vote.

'She's right,' says the woman to Mabel's right between dainty bites of her cheese cracker. 'It is fundamental to the sustenance of the British constitution. It's written there, in black and white, that taxation and representation are to go *hand in hand*.' She emphasises the last three words by bobbing the cracker up and down.

'Ought we to argue then simply not to pay the tax?' answers another woman, of perhaps forty-five, with the delicate hands of a pianist and the voice of a fishwife. 'That would soon have them standing to attention, wouldn't it?'

Mumbled assent follows.

'Happen they'd agree to it, and then we'd have no leg to stand on.'

'But the loss of income…?' offers a stout, younger woman, nervously.

'They'd tax something else to make up the shortfall, no doubt.'

'We'd have nothing without the tax,' says the first woman as she reaches out in contemplation of another cracker, then changes her mind and diverts her attention back to her companions. 'Think about it. We pay our taxes; our taxes pass into the hands of Parliament; Parliament convenes and decides how best to spend those taxes. And there's not one woman present to add her voice to the discussion of employment, health care, education.'

'It can't be right.'

'Certainly not.'

Through this exchange, Kate and Mabel remain quiet. They are here, for the moment, to listen and learn, not to contradict or question. But Kate feels Mabel leaning further forward in her seat, sees her head turning to watch the next woman who speaks as the discussion ricochets around the table. She, too, is enthralled.

Finally, when they are so bloated with tea that they fear their bladders will fail, Christabel Pankhurst stands and glides towards the podium. She is impossibly elegant in her high-necked white shirtwaist and caramel-coloured skirt. Her curly, chestnut hair is rolled tidily up. She moves like a swan – slow and stately – and, reaching the podium, stops there a while in silence, looking out at the crowd of women and allowing them to look at her. It is powerful. A demonstration of her control. The room is rapt.

'Ladies,' she begins, opening her hands. Kate is put momentarily in mind of her father, sermonising from his pulpit, but she shakes the memory away – she can do so easily now. 'I have listened with interest to your conversations this afternoon. I have heard each of your voices.' Her accent contains all the distortions of the upper classes: 'ah' in place of 'a'; 'ee' instead of 'i'. *I hahve leestened weeth eenterest.* The corners of Mabel's mouth tweak in response, but she stifles her laughter successfully, and soon she is taken enough with Christabel's speech to forget the particularities of her voice. Christabel's features are soft and neat, her cheeks wide and smooth. Her every movement is balletic and decisive. The clink of spoons against saucers stops; the glug of tea poured from spouts stops; the susurration of napkins spread open and smoothed flat stops. Christabel talks and the room listens.

The rhetoric is well-practised – that much is apparent – but the practised quality does not lessen its impact. Never before has Kate sat in such concentrated contemplation of her position as a woman. Never before has she asked herself whether her actions are born of instinct or learned response. Never before has she considered whether, in fact, all of her values and ideals have been installed by a society shaped and controlled by men. She is a free woman, of course she is, but how much of the soul Kate deems to be her very own has been influenced by the structures and ideology of a male society? Gosh, hadn't her father's beliefs persuaded her, for such a long while, that everything she had come to love and admire was wrong, sinful.

She will write to Alice about it, she decides. Then, when she goes home, they will wait until the house is asleep and sit to discuss it over tea at the kitchen table, as is their habit. During these midnight chats, Kate is often surprised to find that she and Alice agree on so many issues, given how different their lives are. But then, Kate supposes, perhaps their lives are growing closer together with each passing year. She will be interested to know how Alice – a wife of two decades, a dedicated mother, a silent saint – will respond to the idea of suffrage.

'Remember the dignity of your womanhood,' Christabel says. Her volume is rising slightly now, but she is far from shouting. She is projecting, and that is enough to call these women to arms. They sit erect in their seats, as though fighting the urge to rush forward and touch the magnetic figure at the helm of their ship. Beyond Christabel's voice, there is only the thud of their hearts.

'Do not appeal. Do not beg. Do not grovel.'

Never, Kate thinks. She does not intend to. Not ever.

'Take courage,' Christabel Pankhurst says, and as she does, she seems to grow in stature. She becomes one of those carved stone women, mounted on a plinth, holding up a flag or a scroll. She is Joan of Arc, gilded in bronze and sitting tall astride her proud mare, her fist clenched and raised in determination.

'Join hands. Stand beside us,' Christabel urges. 'Fight with us!'

And the ground floor restaurant of the Criterion erupts.

'So...?' Kate ventures, as she and Mabel step out onto Piccadilly and look around for a cab. Mabel is still buttoning her coat. Down the street, a hawker hollers at passers-by about the exemplary quality of his fresh bread. Closer to, a cab driver with a fare already aboard yells his dark bay horse into a trot as two suited men stride past in blaring conversation, their briefcases swinging, their shone leather shoes pounding the pavement. A boy in a newsboy and shorts thunders past in pursuit of a scruffy terrier which yaps excitedly along in pursuit of a furious tabby cat. The noise of men, Kate thinks – that's what cities are filled with.

'She was ... something,' Mabel answers.

'Something good?'

'Something spectacular,' Mabel says, and they beam at each other. 'Come on,' she says then, hooking her arm into Kate's and pulling her close. 'Let's go and find a real meal. Those pickings won't see me through tonight. Then you can tell me more about this WSPU.'

'Yes,' Kate replies, and immediately she finds herself plotting out how she might voice, as succinctly and readily as Christabel, what she has come to understand. About being a woman. About her responsibility, as a woman with some kind of advantage, to help campaign for change. But how to start? She needs a short, snappy phrase, or she'll persuade no one to listen. She needs a headline! As she and Mabel swerve around window shoppers and delivery boys, she tries out a few thoughts, discards them, tries again. She returns to a thought she had earlier, about London, and smiles as she stumbles across her beginning.

It's not just our stays we must loosen, she will say, but the bindings of our minds.

35.

London, England
1910
THE SERPENTINE

'William,' she murmurs.

A grunt.

'William?'

They are curled into each other on the settee in their front room, Kate with her head in William's lap, William with his arm cupped around her hip. She is balled up, a seashell. Her nose and toes are cold. There is nothing in her ears except the tick of the mantle clock, the weight of silence, and the tidal ebb of William's blood around his body. It is past midnight, but they had not felt ready to retire when they had returned after the evening show. They are doing some weeks at the Canterbury Theatre of Varieties: thus far, the crowds have been easy and Kate and William have practically floated home on the sound of their applause.

'Let's go swimming,' she says.

'It's the middle of the night, Kate.'

'Does it matter?'

He opens his eyes. She can make out their shape but not their detail in the turbid grey light the moon pushes through the gap in the curtains: there is a singular white glint at the centre of each. He always grumbles over her suggestions, but in truth she knows they excite him.

'Where would we go?' he asks.

'The Serpentine.'

'Only men swim in the Serpentine.'

He's right, naturally. Often enough they have walked past the lake to see members of the Serpentine Swimming Club plunging in: gnarled old gents in full woollen bathing suits; muscular young chaps wearing the latest shorts-and-vest-style costumes; barrel-bellied men out to test their weakening, middle-aged limbs; gangling boys on the cusp of manhood, sporting varying evidence of bodily hair and stamina. None amongst them have ever been women.

'There'll be nobody swimming at this time,' she answers. 'So there'll be nobody to stop us.'

'Are you going to allow me to sleep otherwise?'

She smiles. 'Probably not.'

'All right.' He shuffles back against the settee until he is sitting upright, then taps her hip with his flattened palm to indicate that if she wants to go, she ought to stand up. 'I'll find the costumes.'

'No costumes,' Kate replies.

'But it's bitter,' William protests. 'I'll lose my manhood in there if we go in naked.'

Kate laughs. 'I promise to find it for you again.' As they disentangle themselves and rise from the settee, she glances at the clock: twenty minutes past one o'clock. 'If we hurry up,' she says, 'we'll be there for two.'

'You won't make me run, will you?'

'There's nothing wrong with being brisk, is there?'

'You've always proven it to be the case,' William says. 'But wait. First...' He slips an arm around her back and draws her to him. She drops her weight to one side so that she stands two or three inches shorter, as she always does when they are pressed body to body, so that she might better mould the curve of her bust into the dip below his pectorals, easier slide her thigh between his and feel the heat at his groin. He moves his hand up her spine to cradle her head and kisses her, firm and suddenly desperate. She pushes back against him, her lips parting, and that familiar throbbing starts between her legs, and she slaps his chest. That he can still weaken her so! It is infuriating. She takes a deliberate step away from him, smiling and shaking her head.

'I know your game, Roberts!' she says.

He lifts his eyebrows, but cannot keep his moustache from betraying a guilty smirk.

'No chance,' she continues. 'I'm having this my way and that's that.' She spins out of the room, knowing he will follow. It is all he can do, even after all this time, to take his eyes off his Kate.

'Is there any other way?' William asks, but the words are more for himself than for her. He does not want it any other way. He is already chasing her towards the front door and out into the night.

Illuminated by a shy March moon, its waters undisturbed, the Serpentine looks like a lake of ice. Kate stands at its gently lilting edge, inhaling the cold mists which linger over its surface like wraiths. All is white and spectral. On the opposite shore, the trees are dribbled ink lines. A pair of swans sleep on the water, their heads folded into their wings, their feet and feathers as still as origami as they drift without intention towards whatever birds dream of. What it would be, Kate thinks, to exist without constantly striving towards some imagined objective. How peaceful.

'We could be in the Arctic,' she says.

William nods, not knowing how to respond to such a sentiment. Instead of struggling for an appropriate response, as he once would have, he knits his fingers into hers and squeezes.

'I've decided to stay in Bristol for a couple of weeks when we go down,' she says. 'I don't think Alice is well.'

'What makes you say that?'

'She mentioned it in her letter. And she wouldn't have mentioned it, would she, if it was just a cold?'

He releases her hand. 'Why didn't you say anything?'

'To who?'

'Me.' His voice is terse and Kate turns to look at him.

'You're angry with me.'

William huffs, like a child. 'Well...'

'Well, what? I read you the letter, William.'

'But I hadn't thought...'

'And you expect me to do that for you, too, do you?' At some point in the past five seconds, she has crossed her arms tightly over her chest. She hadn't felt herself do it. She lowers them to her sides again, not wanting this flare to become a fully blown argument. So often they catch fire like this, she and William, and flame and burn and spit until one or other of them capitulates and finds some small way to douse the sparks. In the past, she has dedicated long hours to attempting to trouble out how to keep it from happening. But she has come to understand, with age, that it is only their way. That it is their anger or frustration which is turned to ash, and never their love. If an existing marriage, and the denial of their children, and the pressure of touring endlessly from country to country, and the jealousy of competing for their audience's attentions has not lessened their relationship, surely nothing will? With each passing year, Kate feels more certain that her and William's future will be together, always together. She has come to feel safe in that belief.

And yet... How can she be her truest self when she answers to a name which is not her own? And when she can only affirm the constant assumption that she is not a mother? And when she cannot call the man who is, in effect, her husband her husband? 'It is our duty to make this world a better place for women,' Christabel Pankhurst had said. And that is what Kate has been trying to do. *Cast off your corsets*, she has urged. *Strengthen your bodies*. She has led that appeal by example. But she has not shown her audience her whole self. She has concealed her most important facets. And why? For shame? There is something else Christabel says which has been seared into Kate's mind: 'Women have suffered too much from the conspiracy of silence to allow that conspiracy to last one minute longer.'

And oh, hasn't she been silent? Hasn't she suffocated so many longings? There is so, so much privilege she has enjoyed, but she has suffered too. To enjoy privilege in some regards does not mean she has not experienced pain in others. So desperate has she been for her children, on occasion, that she has hallucinated them. The fact had very nearly led her to crawl off a steamship into the raging black depths of the Atlantic.

'Also,' she says, drawing in a deep breath. And then she says something she had never intended saying – not, at least, until this moment. 'When I come back, I'm bringing the girls with me.'

William snaps his head around. 'You can't do that.'

'Why not? They're old enough.'

'They're little girls.'

It has long been their agreement that they will keep the children from the spotlight until they are sixteen and more capable of reaching their own decisions, but Kate cannot wait a minute longer.

'They will soon be ten and fourteen. I was but fifteen when I trained with you. They need to learn the business.'

William's lips grow thinner and thinner as the conversation continues. 'They are learning it well enough where they are. And besides, what of Alice?'

'She will still have Winnie, Arthur, and William at home.'

'We cannot simply pluck the children from her now that we have a use for them.'

Kate stops her gasp in her throat. Their voices have not

risen with their tempers. The night is too still and observant to allow it. 'Is that what you think?' she asks, teeth grinding. 'That I have *use* for them now?'

'Well, don't you?'

'No. I have *need* of them. I have been waiting for them to grow old enough to join the troupe since the first day I left Nora bundled in Alice's arms. I have been waiting resolutely, in silence. And no, I am not going to wait any longer. They are old enough to join the troupe and I shall bring them to London with me when I return from Bristol, and I don't care how much you protest.'

'Whatever Queen Vulcana decrees, I'm sure,' William replies, and fury blushes at Kate's neck and cheeks. William always becomes puerile when they argue. She resists the urge to stamp her heel into the ground like a skittish horse.

'Yes,' Kate snaps. 'Perhaps that's just how it will be from now on. Perhaps that's how it should have been from the start.'

Silence engulfs them after that and they stand, staring out at the lake, arms locked tight across their chests, their breaths coming quick and ragged. The swans have drifted out of sight. Overhead, a neat black creature flits about, its wings the lightest percussion. Kate risks a glance at William. An angry pulse trembles beside his ear. He stares straight ahead, but the glint of tears is visible along his lower lashes and they make her heart swell. She sidles closer and nudges him with her shoulder.

'Why do we do that?' she asks quietly.

He sighs. 'Because we're too full of passion, I suppose.'

'Do you hate me for it?'

'Not at all. Do you hate me?'

'Not at all.'

'Good.' He nods slowly, as though his head is suddenly intolerably heavy. 'That's good.' His chest loosens and Kate puts her hands to his crossed arms and eases him about so that they are standing face to face. William remains a little stiff, but he allows her to direct his body as she takes hold of his coat and pulls it off his shoulders. He shakes himself free of the heavy wool and, catching it, Kate folds it and lays it down on the ground beside them. Next, she moves to his shirt collar and, finding the top fastening, begins to unbutton it. Cold air spreads over his chest and his skin clenches, but he keeps his limbs loose as Kate opens his shirt and furls that off, too. She puts it neatly down on top of his coat and, edging closer, drops her face into his warmth, then, closing her lips around a nipple, flicks her tongue over it. William breathes out heavily: his most sensitive part.

'Now me,' she says, removing her coat for him.

William takes his time, running his fingertips over her throat before untying the ribboned neck of her blouse. Beneath, she wears a soft cream soutien-gorge. William slips the straps from her shoulders and hooks it off. Her breasts harden and lift with her arousal, and William repeats her movements and teases a nipple with his tongue.

She moves immediately to his trousers and works them down over his buttocks. He stands patiently while she goes slowly about each act, her fingers savouring the smooth sections of his skin and the coarse curls of his hair, and then he echoes her. Soon, they are standing naked on the shore of the lake, cold and moon-pale and excited, and there is nothing else in the world.

'Shall we get in?' Kate asks. She couldn't care less if anyone sees them. They need to do this, the two of them; it has become, to her mind, a sort of declaration of their faith in each other. She can't be sure why.

William nods.

'It's going to hurt,' she adds. It is four, maybe five, degrees Celsius. Their bare skin... Their already numb extremities...

'Yes,' William agrees.

'Together, then.'

'Together.'

36.

Bristol, England
1910
THE WOMEN

Had they been able to foresee what would follow so soon afterwards, they would have travelled west together. As it transpires, however, William stays in London to take some meetings and secure their next booking, while Kate rides the train alone and arrives at the Bristol house synchronously with that variety of rain which turns the windows to waterfalls. April rain. Quicksilver. It pours relentlessly and, by seven o'clock that same evening, Kate is curled into an armchair near the fireplace in the front room, bathed and warm in her nightdress, a soft red and brown striped blanket tucked around her. Gloaming has greyed the room. The floral patterns on the curtains, the spines of the novels in the bookcases, the photographs on the walls, the feathered birds' wings in the wallpaper – all are dulled. Ordinarily, this is Kate's favourite part of the Bristol house because it is so rich in colour. This evening, she loves it because the fire flickers more brightly in the gloom.

In the opposite armchair, Alice is a portrait of motherhood: pillow-bellied and aproned, her hair collected into a neat bun, her hands busy sewing a torn dress collar. An artist would name her 'Idyllic Mother' or somesuch. Rubbish. Kate knows as well as the next person that there is nothing idyllic about squinting over tiny cotton threads fourteen hours after your day began. Kate has a book open on her lap, but she has not turned a page in five minutes or more.

'Are you trying to turn me to stone?' Alice asks quietly, her eyes pinned to her stitching.

Kate snorts with laughter. 'Sorry. I was just ... admiring you.'

It is Alice's turn to laugh, then: a timid sound; a descending major arpeggio. 'Don't be daft,' she says, letting go of Winnie's ripped dress just long enough to flap her hand at Kate.

'Why not?'

'Why not, indeed. No one has admired me since before you were born.'

'William has.'

'Nonsense.'

'He has!' Kate protests. 'He does.'

'Maybe once,' Alice concedes. 'Fleetingly.'

Kate closes her book and sets it down on the floor, then sits back in her chair again, pulls up her legs, and rests her chin on the domes of her kneecaps. 'Did you love him straight away?'

'Who?'

'William! Who else?'

Alice shakes her head, but not unkindly. A small smile shimmers across her lips. 'Do you really want to talk about this?'

'Yes.'

'Why?'

Kate shrugs. 'Curiosity.'

'All right.' Alice lowers her sewing into her lap and slaps her flattened palms lightly against her thighs. 'Yes, I loved him straight away. I doubt very much he'd say the same about me – and no, that's not modesty. He was young, and he thought I was too old for him, and I suppose I looked it and seemed it, too. Seven years is significant when you're twenty.'

'So you set about changing his mind...'

'I can't say that I did really,' Alice answers. 'But William was searching for something. A way out. An escape, perhaps, from his... I don't know... His position in the world. And he tried a lot of different tracks. Marriage was just one of them.'

Kate sits forward. 'You don't believe he loved you?'

Alice looks into the fire's sputtering flames as she considers this question. Kate, waiting, observes the rain spilling down the windowpane behind her: it gleams against the blackening sky like a cascade of shooting stars.

'I believe that he respected me,' she replies, 'in his way. I believe he enjoyed my company. I even believe he wanted to love me...'

'But...'

'But love is not something you can forge to suit your own purposes. You know that better than anyone, Kate. Wouldn't it have been easier for you to fall in love with a man closer to your own age? An unmarried man? You would have become Mrs So-and-so, and read your children bedtime stories in your own home, and it would have been so much simpler, wouldn't it?'

389

'It would,' Kate agrees. 'But then I wouldn't have had you.'

'Pah! Why would you need me?'

Kate reaches forwards and grasps Alice's hand. 'I have always needed you,' she says. She is frowning now, and suddenly desperate to make Alice understand that she is not some nuisance addition to their family but the foundation of it. 'You are my dearest friend, Alice. No. More than that. You're my sister.'

'Is that so?' Alice replies. 'Well I'm glad of it. Truly I am.'

'But not as glad,' Kate begins, picking at a loose loop of wool in the blanket, 'as you would be to have William here all the time...'

Alice releases a deep sigh. 'I used to think so. But now, well, I think it all turned out exactly right. We wouldn't make each other happy, William and I, rattling around this or any house together. It's not what we were meant for.'

'But what were *you* meant for, Alice?' It is only as she frames the question that Kate realises it is what the entire conversation has been angled at. This is what she wants to know. Whether Alice feels happy, fulfilled, disappointed, forgotten, lonely... Loved.

'This,' Alice answers, lifting her hands to indicate their surroundings. 'Sitting down in the evening to remember all the lovely, funny things the children have said during the day. Wrapping them in bandages when they cut themselves. Waking in the night to go into their room and soothe their nightmares. I am exactly where I need to be, Kate. I've told you this before.'

'I know. I know. But...'

'But?'

'There's a woman. There's an organisation, I should say. The WSPU.'

'You're talking about the suffrage campaign,' Alice says.

'Yes!' Kate is surprised Alice knows anything of it, and her voice issues too loudly and betrays her condescension. 'Yes. But there's one woman in particular – the organising secretary – who I've heard speak a handful of times, and she says that it's our duty to make the world – the whole world, Alice – a better place for women. And I'm not sure of whether I've been trying hard enough, whether I've been doing enough to... I don't know. I suppose I feel as though I'm in a position of some privilege and that I should ... use it better.'

'And what makes you think you're not using it well enough?' Alice enquires.

'Well, Christabel Pankhurst...'

'Is not Kate Williams,' Alice interjects. 'For years, Kate, you've spoken about the ill effects of wearing stays and the benefits of callisthenics. Just because this Miss Pankhurst does things differently, that is not to say she's doing more. We can't all stand and preach to a willing audience or organise campaigns, but we can all do something, big or small, and what you do is big, Kate. Talking to the magazines, standing onstage, training and pushing yourself and honing your strength – you're *showing* women how they might use their bodies. And that is no less of a contribution than what the ladies of the WSPU offer.'

'Do you truly think so?'

'I know so,' Alice says. 'And, what's more, your wanting to be here for the children does not diminish what you stand for. Don't you start believing it. You've always considered that you can be anything you want to be, haven't you?' Kate nods. 'Then perhaps your task is to find a way of being a strongwoman *and* a mother. I said before that you had to choose, and I believed it. But that's not necessarily true anymore. Or maybe it would be better to say that it doesn't necessarily need to be true. You might be just the woman to learn to balance the two, to show other women they are capable of doing the same.'

Kate looks down into her lap. Her cupped hands and the shadows in the room deepen the lines of her palms. She traces the tip of her left forefinger along the scoop of her right life line, the bend of her head line, the curve of her heart line. The heart line is in fact two lines, twined around one another, which reach all the way to the base of her finger. The chiromancer she saw once would have had something to say about that, she supposes, but then wouldn't she be forced to draw a different conclusion from the corresponding line on her other hand, which does not reach half so far? Perhaps that was why she had not mentioned it. Perhaps there is always a choice to make.

'How is it you always know what to say?' she asks.

'I've got five daughters,' Alice replies. It pleases Kate's heart that Alice does not distinguish between the three who are her own and the two who are Kate's. They have shared these children for such a long while now: a lifetime for Winnie,

Nora, and Mona. 'My task has been to teach them to be invested in the idea that the world can be a better place for women, and that they should help to make it so. It's not a thought which is strange or new to me.' She catches Kate's eye. 'Believe it or not,' she adds with a smile.

'I believe it,' Kate answers. 'How could I not believe it? Our girls are the most beautiful bunch of ruffians I have ever known. They will surely change the world!'

Alice laughs quietly and picks her sewing up again. 'Let's hope so.'

There follows a spell of silence, during which Kate watches the silver rain hit the windowpane, listens to its percussive attack playing in counterpoint to the friendlier snap and hiss of the fire. She takes a long, deep in-breath – woodsmoke, furniture polish, the sweet perfume of a pair of white peonies wilting in a jar on the windowsill, the stale papery scent of the books, wool – and decides she will sleep in here tonight. The scents are comforting, and she has not been sleeping so well since she realised what Dr Crippen had done. The ghost of Cora Crippen seems always to be standing at the foot of her bed, pleading for her help.

She takes a moment to imagine herself transported across the room and into Alice's body. She feels for Alice's wider, softer edges. She tries to slot Alice's sensibilities – evenness, contentment, generosity – into her own busy mind. She thinks before she speaks.

'One of the ladies in my guild has been murdered,' she says. 'Cora Crippen. Belle Elmore, that is. We knew her as Belle.'

'Murdered!' Alice replies, dropping her sewing again. 'Kate, that's terrible. Are you certain?'

Kate nods. 'I've been to Scotland Yard.'

'And..?'

'I don't think they believed me.'

'Whyever not?'

'For the same reason they don't have women police constables, I imagine.'

'Then what will you do?'

Both women glance up at the ceiling as the floorboards creak above them. One of the children, sneaking into another's bedroom to play or read or whisper together. They share a smile.

'I don't know,' Kate says. 'I'll have to go back. But then, unless I have something new to tell them, real evidence, what would I say?'

'Anything that will make them listen,' Alice replies. 'Never mind the truth of it. Say what might prompt them to investigate and, when you are proved right, no one will worry about what you said in the first place. If you're certain, that is.'

'I am.'

'You're bold enough, Kate. You can make them listen.'

Kate lowers her head and considers her hands again. A deep ache spreads through them now, relentlessly, which she has admitted to no one. She has a new awareness of each slender bone, each knuckled joint. On occasion, her fingers tingle and go numb. She worries that soon the day will come when she will fail to lift the weights, as William has before her. And what then?

Music hall has already led to Belle's death, hasn't it? Were it not for her desperation to be a star, she might never have even been in London, scrabbling around in a loveless marriage and making one bad decision after another. And poor Marie. It might be setting about the task more slowly, but it's evident to Kate that music hall is killing her, too. So exhausted has she been left by the endless performances, her war with the National Vigilance Association, the beatings from those damned lovers and husbands who were so jealous of her celebrity, that Kate has come to fear that Marie will drop down dead onstage one night. Oh, wouldn't the newspapers love that.

Well, Kate won't let music hall have her. She will not work herself to a collapse, or push her body so far past its capabilities that she drops a weight bar onto her own torso or neck and shatters her ribcage or her spine. And for the sake of what... Money? Fame? Admiration? No. She will have to find a new way.

'It's odd,' Kate says. 'I was terribly bold once, wasn't I? But I'm not so sure what I am now. I feel as though the older I get, the less I know about myself.'

'I think perhaps that's true of all the best people,' Alice replies.

'How so?'

'Well, it's not that you're understanding less, is it? It's that you're understanding more...'

The floorboards groan again overhead, snitching on the two sets of footsteps now parading across the landing.

'Arthur and William,' Alice says, rolling her eyes to the ceiling. She pushes herself out of her chair and pauses for a moment, waiting for the sharp pain at her knees to wane. 'Those boys are the only ones I expect to be sleeping yet, being so little still. I'll just go and make sure they know we're keeping an eye on them.' She steps across the front room, her rounding figure etched across the wall by the firelight, and, just for a breath, it is as though some part of her has gone ahead.

Later, when Kate thinks back on this moment, she will persuade herself that she knew. But she doesn't. Not now. She has caught only the faintest glimpse of something too soon to come, something which she cannot yet fathom but which feels impossibly sad.

Alice steps into her shadow at the door and stops.

'What I mean to say,' she explains, 'is that if you're sailing along always looking at the crests of the waves in front of your ship, you might well feel that you know the sea. That she's right there before your eyes, sparking and clear and showing you all her secrets. But if you lean over the side of the ship and look down... True, you might never observe the seabed, as dark and distant as it is, but you'll know more for having tried, won't you?'

And with that, Alice taps her stitch-stiffened hand lightly against the frame of the door, smiles, and is gone.

37.

London, England
1910
THE TOMB OF HERCULES

Kate is inverted into the shape of a crab, her bodyweight supported by her hands and feet, her head thrown back so that she can view her audience, seemingly hanging like bats from their seats. The long, thick plait of her hair rests on the stage floor. Her buttocks ache a little. She should have stretched more thoroughly; the Tomb of Hercules will hurt if she is not properly prepared. She studies the rows of faces which fill the auditorium: some flat with impatience, some opened in anticipation, others indifferent or excited or doubtful. Still, she marvels at how many people visit the theatre intending from the off to disbelieve what is put before them. It is only human nature, she supposes, to question the unknown, but she considers that there are kinder ways to live. When she tires of the faces, she looks to the doors, which, to her, appear to be set against the ceiling. Everything, not just her perspective, is upside down of late.

Through late spring and into this sweltering summer, she had petitioned Inspector Dew to investigate her claims about Dr Crippen. Walter Dew had, at all times, been patient and polite, but he did not act on her information. 'There are more pressing matters just presently,' he'd said. 'There is a list of women murdered in London as long as my leg, and each of them with an attendant murderer who must be tracked down.'

And nothing happened.

William appears with the wooden platform, and Kate tenses her stomach muscles while he positions it evenly across her. It is not heavy, not yet, but it must be made completely flat for the trick to work. William talks to the audience while he goes about securing it in place. Kate does not listen to him. She knows his oratory by rote, but she can keep nothing in mind for more than a moment presently before Belle's ghost comes clattering across her consciousness, her American drawl growing more pronounced as she insists, over and over, that her husband has brought her to a hideous end.

Together, Marie, Lil, Margaret, Melinda, Clara, Bessie, and Kate had had the ships' records checked. They established that nobody going under the name of Cora Crippen or Belle Elmore had crossed the Atlantic Ocean on any steamer sailing from London during this calendar year. When Crippen changed his story and claimed that Belle had not simply run off to America with a man called Bruce Miller, but had in fact died in California, they had a husband of one of the guild ladies use his business contacts to trawl the death announcements in the state. There was no recorded death of a Cora Crippen or a Belle Elmore in California.

Kate reported the same to Inspector Dew. And nothing happened.

'Vulcana,' William intones, 'will now perform the legendary Tomb of Hercules.' The audience murmurs. Some, she supposes, will know what this entails, having seen Eugen Sandow or William 'Apollo' Bankier perform it. 'The first woman ever to manage the feat!' William says, raising his voice to elicit the applause he desires. The audience obliges, and a clap ripples around the auditorium, but it does not last long; they do not want to delay the spectacle.

Kate brings her head up so that her spine is straight. Her blood has started to rush to her cheeks, and besides, she does not want to look into the audience any longer. In every picture hat, in every reddened lip, in every gaping smile, she sees Belle, and she cannot afford to be spooked during the Tomb of Hercules.

'He did it,' she had told William, again and again. Thumping around their kitchen, or half-waking in the drowsy dead of night, or sipping contemplatively at her breakfast tea, she cited the sudden appearance of a new lover, the recognition of that lover as Crippen's typist – at this Kate rolled her eyes exaggeratedly – and their shameless theatre visits, the sapphire and emerald peacock brooch, the earrings and fur coat Miss Ethel Le Neve was subsequently spotted wearing on various shopping trips.

But nothing happened, nothing, until Lil and her husband John Nash appealed to a mutual friend – one Scotland Yard Superintendent Frank Froest – and the man agreed to pressure Inspector Dew into interviewing Dr Hawley Harvey Crippen.

'They will listen to a man,' Kate told William. 'You watch. They'll interview him now.'

'You don't know that,' William replied.

'Wait and see, Mr Roberts.' She whirled past him as he sat to his morning reviews and planted a kiss on the dome of his head. She was caught between not wanting it to be true and needing to be believed. 'I'll be proven right now.'

It rankles her still, that John had only had to ask, once and politely, to be listened to.

Though she cannot yet see them, she soon hears the horses being led to side stage. Their hooves sound comical, like coconut halves banged together, in the confines of the theatre, but she has no desire to laugh. She cannot entirely make her peace with the animals being brought in, though she does ensure proof of their good care before and after their performance, and soothes her conscience with the knowledge that they have only to walk across the stage once before being returned to their stables. Any more and she would not agree to it.

Tonight's pair consist of one grey mare and one liver chestnut gelding. She went out to meet them this afternoon, letting them snuffle her face with their whiskery noses, cupping her hands around their ears and scratching at the warm hair there. Each time she meets the horses chosen for the Tomb of Hercules, she indulges a little dream of buying them and taking them back to Abergavenny, where they might roam the mountains together – Kate, the two horses, William. Sometimes, she invents names for them. *Eira*; snow. *Aderyn*;

bird. Other times, she only pictures the mountains and imagines the easy rocking canter of the horse beneath her. She doesn't know where the imagining comes from – she does not ride – but it is none the less vivid for that.

She steels herself as she hears them approach. The eight-beat of their hooves. Their gentle snorts. Their riders are already in the saddle, easing their mounts expertly towards the ramp, making soothing sounds at the back of their throats. Kate recognises the pressure of a foreleg finding the edge of the ramp and concentrates on practising the breathing she must sustain if she is to allow two horses and riders to walk across her abdomen. She can smell them now, the horses: their sweet, summer-grass breath; the stale whiff from beneath their swished tails. She keeps counting through her inhalations and her exhalations, closes her eyes...

With Superintendent Froest in his ear, Inspector Dew had capitulated and interviewed Hawley Crippen. When Crippen's response to questioning was to clasp Ethel close and flee the country, it became apparent to every genius in the employ of Scotland Yard that the man had something to hide. Specifically, a body. The dismembered body of his poor wife, it transpired, which was duly discovered, in part at least, buried beneath the basement of their Hilldrop Crescent home.

Eventually, just two weeks past, on the 30th of July, the *Illustrated Police News* ran the headline, '*The Camden Town Horror. Dr Crippen and Miss Le Neve Make a Dash for Canada from Antwerp. Inspector Dew in Pursuit*'. Kate had wanted to cry at the sight of it, but she had only folded the newspaper and pinned it beneath a milk jug on the kitchen table, meaning to keep it, for reasons she has not yet examined.

The first horse – the liver chestnut gelding – reaches the middle of the platform and is reined in to stand there while his companion clambers up after him. Kate must hold them both, still, above her abdomen, for a count of five seconds for the performance to be considered complete. She can see nothing of the riders but the scuffed soles of their boots as the grey mare reaches the hind quarters of the gelding and is brought to a halt.

Kate stops breathing.

'One!' William cries.

It will be the hangman's noose for Dr Crippen, once he is caught – everyone knows that.

'Two.'

Perhaps they will be invited to watch.

'Three.'

She cannot imagine wanting to witness death, whatever the cause, but then again, she cannot foresee how the trial at the Old Bailey will play out, take hold of the public's imagination, turn her stomach.

'Four.'

Soon, though she would not have predicted it, she and William will begin to wait for news of a death.

'Five!' William roars, and Kate feels her burden begin to lift as the gelding and then the mare are urged to walk on, down the ramp, and quietly offstage. Soon, she will be made light again. Within moments, the only weight she will be tasked to carry is her own. And yes, despite herself, every time she enters the kitchen and sees that newspaper pinned beneath the milk jug, she will wait for news of a death.

Neither she nor William expect to hear of two.

38.

London, England
1910
NEWS OF A DEATH

The winter that follows is the darkest they have ever known.

Wednesday, 23rd of November, dawns moody-blue and snow-cold. Kate has arranged to meet the other Music Hall Guild ladies on the Caledonian Road so that they might walk together down to the entranceway of Pentonville Prison. The pavement outside the building is as far as they can go, but they want to be nearby when it happens. At nine o'clock, Dr Crippen is to be hung.

It had taken a long while to decide whether or not they should come. It was macabre, Bessie said. It was necessary, Marie claimed. It was respectful, Lil argued. It was futile, Clara thought. They had gone back and forth like weathervanes over tea at the Albion House office, gooseflesh crawling over their arms and necks at the thought that all along Dr Crippen's office had been downstairs in this very building and none of them had so much as suspected what he was capable of. They had thought him a creep, yes – too quiet, too keen to stare – but never a murderer.

'He might have snuck up here and killed us all!' Melinda

declared, when they had pored over the reports of Inspector Dew chasing Dr Crippen and Ethel Le Neve across the Atlantic on the SS *Laurentic*, arriving in Quebec ahead of the slower ship, then boarding the SS *Montrose* to apprehend the pair. It was melodrama, of course. Dr Crippen killed his wife because they had grown to detest one another; he had no reason to commit the crime twice. And neither did the newspapers have any right to paint Belle as an unbearable shrew who drove her poor, gentle husband to madness. Vain. Silly. Wanton. Talentless. Drunken. Delusional. So hideous are the words attributed to a woman who just months earlier had been poisoned, carved up, and buried – in part – under the basement of her own home, that Kate cannot stand to read them. Now, when she wakes in the night, instead of walking London's empty streets, she flattens a clean sheet of paper over the kitchen table and, by moonlight, writes her response to all those ugly articles. She wonders if one of the newspapers might publish it someday, but she has not shown it to anyone yet. She has not found the correct way to say, *This woman was not to blame. This woman was not to blame. This woman was not to blame,* and persuade anyone to care. To proclaim it will not be enough – she knows that much. But she cannot find any other way to construct such an obvious argument. Half of London is looking for Cora Crippen's head, when all Kate wants to do is urge them to take a considered look inside their own and question whether she wasn't worth more, this woman.

She does not imagine for a moment that Dr Crippen might have snuck up and killed them all, but the ease with which

Belle was extinguished haunts her. It fills her with a new fear of disappearing, being forgotten.

True to form, Melinda appears on the Caledonian Road dressed tip to toe in black. She slinks along on narrow heels, her hair rolled up beneath a black beaver hat with a lace veil attached to obscure her tears. Kate cannot imagine where she procured such an item, but she manages to resist the urge to laugh at it as they approach one another, smile, lean in to knock cheekbones and kiss the air.

The others appear one by one in their usual day dresses, winter coats, and gloves, picture hats trembling in the wind, leather boots making their footsteps hollow-sounding. Marie Lloyd, Clara Martinetti, Bessie Brown, Margaret Smythe, Lil Hawthorne. They join Melinda and Kate and gather into a bunch, then go quietly down the road towards the doorway of Pentonville Prison. A troupe of their own. A breathy cloud of floral perfume, tobacco, and good intention.

There is not much to see: the creamy-white plaster of the façade; a tall arched doorway; the small windows set into the dark stone of the various wings which reach out to left and right. The thought of being locked in a single room is not one Kate can bring herself to concentrate on without a concomitant churning sensation troubling her stomach, a clamping pressure arriving at her throat. She, who could not be contained by a country, let alone four walls, would go steadily insane if she were trapped in such a place. She looks up into a sky which is fading from blue to grey-white: a trio of magpies soar and swoop there, quaver beats on a sheet of manuscript paper, teasing each other. Their cries sound eerily over the prison building which, in its vast solidity, seems to emanate silence like a pulse. The women stand on the pavement opposite, unspeaking. It is a vigil, of sorts. For their friend.

'Do you suppose they've granted him a last request?' Bessie says.

Marie nods. 'I'll bet they have.'

'What do you imagine it was?'

'If it was a last meal, I hope they laced it with poison.'

'Margaret!'

'What? Don't tell me you feel otherwise.'

'No, but...'

'When did they stop having public executions?'

'This should be a public execution.'

'I think so. If his precious Ethel can sell her story and make money from the publicity, they should let people in to watch,' Clara says.

Lil grimaces. 'Why would you want to watch?'

'I wouldn't *want* to watch, but how do we know it's really happened if nobody witnesses it.'

'Nobody witnessed him killing Belle, but we know that happened.'

'It was proved. Scotland Yard proved it.'

'We believed it a long time before that.'

'Lucky we did.'

Melinda sniffles from under her veil. 'Perhaps lucky isn't the word.'

'Perhaps not,' Margaret concedes.

Kate does not participate in this chatter. She is too keenly watching the tiny gold minute hand of her wristwatch twitching towards the twelve. It is three minutes to nine o'clock. In three short minutes, a man will be dead.

What must he be thinking? If Kate was inside that building, watching a different clock tick and imploring it simply to stop forever, would she be thinking about the lives the children would go on to lead without her; or how scared she was when she boarded the train out of Abergavenny to chase after William; or the thrill she felt when she drove that De Dion Bouton 'Vis-à-Vis' at Harry Rickards' house, herself, William, and two of Harry's friends crammed onto the bench seats to each side of the central tiller, and Kate insisting she be the one to choose their speed and direction; or the elation she felt the first time William kissed her; or the time she locked herself in the bathroom of the Bristol house and sat on the tiles and sobbed silently because she was pregnant again and she didn't know how to bear being such a horrible mother; or the excitement of sailing away from Britain and not knowing what she would discover when she made harbour in a place which had existed only in her imagination; or the ease of those sunlit Sunday afternoons the troupe used to spend down at Boulter's Lock when it was just William, Kate, Mabel, Seth, Anna, and Abe, all of them dressed in their finest and watching the rich and famous boating down the Thames towards Skindles Hotel, before Kate was torn in two. More likely, she thinks, it would be none of that; it would be sitting in the garden of the Bristol house, talking with Alice as the children shrieked around the lawn, their play punctuated by the occasional thud of William's hammer emanating from the shed he retreats into to knock together birdhouses and picnic benches and rocking chairs. That is true peace.

'This is it,' she says quietly as the minute hand of her watch makes its final shudder towards the twelve. They fall into a hush. Bessie bows her head, as if in prayer. They stand like this for long minutes, interrupted only by the rise and fall of their chests and the creak and jounce of passing cabs. Overhead, the magpies continue to circle and wingbeat for a while, then fall into a three-note chord and glide away as one, leaving the sky empty.

'Five past,' Melinda says. 'It must be done.'

The women hum, affirm, nod.

'What a terrible affair,' Margaret ventures, and that is all that can reasonably be said about it, Kate thinks. Two people are dead. Two people who had, presumably, once thought they could love each other.

One by one, the women clasp hands, call out goodbyes, exchange sad smiles, then drift off into the beginnings of their days. That it is only quarter past nine on a Wednesday morning is quite unbelievable, and Kate is at a loss for what to do next. She would like to take a swim or a run, but would need to return home for a change of clothes for either. A walk doesn't appeal. She might go along to the Guildhall Museum, she supposes, and peer at ancient fragments of rock and bone, but that feels too contemplative. The National Gallery, then;

she enjoys sitting amongst the scattering pigeons on the front steps and watching people go by. She doubts, though, that she will find the patience today. Finally, she decides upon a tearoom, an order of breakfast tea in a china cup and a hot buttered crumpet. She is hungry. She hadn't been able to stomach anything before leaving the house.

As she moves off along the Caledonian Road, however, something – a sense, an inkling – persuades her that she ought to go directly back to the Fulham house. William will be awake by now. She sees him, sitting back and snapping open the newspaper, scanning the pages for his reviews. He likes to read them aloud to her while she stands in the window glow, cradling a teacup and listening. And it's William she wants to be with now, of course. William, who would not hurt her, however badly she might treat him. William, who refused to abandon Alice when he fell so desperately in love with Kate. Her William, who, she realises now, she does not know how to live without.

She throws an arm up to hail a cab. And it is Boulter's Lock, for some reason, that she thinks of as she judders across the city to the steady crotchet beat of the cab horse's hooves. Of one particular Sunday – she was around eighteen – when the river had not been the reserve of the rich and famous, and every man in possession of one had set his little boat upon the water and invited both friends and strangers aboard. She does not recall what the occasion had been. Possibly, she hadn't known. But spectators had thronged the banks of the Thames, skirts swishing against skirts, hat brims bumping, waiting to climb down the steps and hop onboard the small planked rowing boats to sit unmoving upon the river, for so crowded was it that the vessels could not sail one way or another. They simply bobbed there, hulls and bows thumping dully as they rocked restlessly in their hemmed-in positions, the people aboard chatting and sharing sandwiches out of crackling brown-paper parcels. Chaos had kicked up when a swan managed to wedge itself between two vessels and, in its panic, flapped its enormous wings so frantically that it caused a number of people to shriek in fright and knocked one slight young lad backwards off the bow of his boat and into the crowded water. The shrieks had turned to laughter as his hat had drifted through the gaps between the boats, following the river flow in a manner none else could manage. Before many minutes had passed, the swan had freed itself and launched into clumsy flight, hauling its heavy body up, up, until it rediscovered its precarious grace.

Kate was wearing white cotton gloves, she remembers, and carrying a frilly parasol to protect her face from sunburn. She, Anna, and Mabel had posed for photographs on the riverside, and she really had fancied herself something, staring boldly at William as he fiddled with the camera and thrilling at the fact that she had been with him the night before, that no one knew about it but the two of them. Or so she believed. There was still a soreness between her legs, a fresh bruise on her left breast where he had clutched her too tight. She pressed her arm against the purpling nub of pain to make it flare. She was excited by that edge of something brutish in William, the idea that he was only just managing to stay in control. She was making it her business, as she gained in experience and confidence, to find a way to push him beyond it. It was an odd desire, but she wanted to ... she didn't know. Break him? Reduce him to something less strong and capable than he was? Demonstrate her power over him? Their lovemaking had been intense from the start but of late it had grown merciless. Inevitably, when it was over, they would collapse into each other, panting and sweating and aching, and Kate would drop for a time into a sleep so deep even dreams could not wade through it.

Sometimes, she would wake to find herself tearful with the torment of it all. The sin – a word she never could manage to shake, despite her lack of belief in any of the Bible's concepts. The shame. If her parents found out, they would condemn her to hell themselves. But, she would tell herself, if what she and William shared was love, she knew that her parents had never experienced it and could not possibly understand.

You daft girl, she thinks now as the cab draws her through the manicured streets of Chelsea. To think that she and William were the only two people in the whole world to know such urgency. But that was how it had felt. Sometimes, it does still. She has already decided that they will make love the instant she arrives home, and she wills the driver to go faster.

When the cab finally stops, maybe ten purposeful strides from her front door, she fumbles her coins in her haste and loses a shilling to the gutter. She does not bend to lift its glinting edge from the muck. She needs to get inside and kiss William. She needs to press her body to his. She needs to bury her face in his chest and inhale the singular charred scent of him and show him how thankful she is that he is such a good man.

'William,' she calls as she steps through the front door. Ordinarily, she can divine which room he is in without either of them needing to speak, but this morning, something is off. She knows it the moment she closes the door behind her. The air is too still. There isn't a movement inside the Fulham house: not a kettle steaming to a whistle, nor a tap running; not the creak of a chair risen out of, nor the thwump of book covers closing; not even so much as the flutter of a curtain left untied at an open window.

'William?'

Though it is early still, she feels the eerie weight of night-time at her back as she steals down the hallway and puts her head around the doorframe of the front room. Empty. She moves on to the kitchen, surprised to find that her heart is thundering. She is jumpy, suddenly. She might be seeking out an intruder rather than the man she has spent half her life with. The kitchen, too, is empty: no cold teacup; no folded newspaper. He has not eaten breakfast. She retraces her steps along the hallway and, turning around the newel post, pauses momentarily at the foot of the stairs to listen. Nothing. She takes a deep breath and puts her foot to the first tread, and that is when she sees his shadow, at the top of the stairs, hunched and closed. He must be slumped on the landing, just behind the banister. Instantly, she is moving. Up. Up. Two treads at a time. Words she has only a surface understanding

413

of fork like lightning across her mind – a heart attack, a stroke, cerebral haemorrhage – and make her breathless. She does not know what a heart attack would look like. She will not know what she ought to do to help him.

'William?' she calls. 'Answer me.'

But he doesn't. Nor does he move when she rounds the top of the staircase and throws herself to the floor. The landing is the darkest part of the house, a shadow space, and she cannot make out the expression on his lowered face. He is not slumped untidily, as she had envisaged, but curled quite deliberately in on himself, his knees drawn up to his chest, his ankles tucked together, his arms locked around his legs – as though he has been turned off and neatly packed away. There is something clenched in his fist. Something white.

'William. Tell me what's wrong.'

She opens her hands and reaches slowly towards his knees. She is expecting some physical reaction, like an electric shock, but when she touches the cotton of his trousers, she feels only that: cotton; the misshapen mounds of his kneecaps; his bodily heat.

'For God's sake, look at me, William. You're scaring me. What's wrong? What is it?'

When he speaks, it is into the hollow he has made between his thighs and his chest. He does not lift his head. His voice echoes as loudly as though he had just bellowed into a black-deep sea cave, and Kate falls back onto her haunches, winded by it.

'It's Alice.'

Intermission

In this new, warm place, someone has arranged her hands over her stomach and so she begins, with the passing of the hours, the days, to run her fingertips over the lines in her skin. Lines made pale by ground-in talcum and deep by time. Lines bumped by callouses and grooved by cuts: paper slices, knife snicks, the split of dry skin. A lifetime of wounds, scarred into silver dashes. She traces the crags and peaks of the Abergavenny mountains – Skirrid, Blorenge, Sugar Loaf – and the tracks of the underground railway. She crests the rolling waves of her knuckles and sails the sea routes the steamers took from London to France and Africa and Australia. And she does not open her eyes. What waits before them is too white, too clean, too stingingly chemical. The inside of her nose burns. The column of her throat scratches. Her eyes, if she were to open them, would smart, and so she keeps them tightly closed, closed, closed. But the light, insistent and rude, shines through her lids and paints maps inside them. Her veins are a network of interlocking roads – London streets, perhaps – or the indicative directions of the tidal currents, or a chart of the wind. Maps, all, which she might follow until she found her way back to herself, if only she had the strength. If only she could move something more than her fingertips. But she knows she cannot. That she has been moved from a morgue to a hospital doesn't mean she is healed. She is trapped on her back, pinned there by so many dropped barbells. And she must wait for William to arrive, so that he might help her lift them off – for what they have achieved they have always striven for together, Kate and William. Atlas and Vulcana. And she would not be alone now, in this, the final bout of the fight. Her closing performance. Her last feat.

1915
Act Five

39.

Algiers, Africa
1915
THE STRONG GIRL AND THE COMEDIENNE

On their opening night in Algiers, the Atlas-Vulcana Troupe is headlined by two different performers: in place of the eponymous Atlas and Vulcana are Mona Eve, the World's Champion Strong Girl, and Nora Althea, Comedienne. The girls have been travelling with the troupe this past two years, but Mona has been performing on-and-off for only around six months, and Kate is nervous for her.

It is not that she doubts her abilities: Mona is almost as strong as her mother was at that age; she has trained hard with William. But a crowd of soldiers, packed close and sweaty and smoke-stale, is a tough audience for anyone to face. Kate is only grateful, secretly, that they are not in full health, for then they will have less energy for teasing. They are due to leave the field hospital soon enough, return to the front, but that is not to say they are well, strong, ready. She can tell as much from their eyes, as she peers out past the curtains at the edge of the makeshift stage and watches them settle for the show. They are a ragged collection of unspeakable experiences, the French, British, and Algerian troops they have come to entertain.

Naturally, each man is entirely different from his immediate neighbour – some tall, some wiry, some blond-haired, others square-set, or thick-jawed, or pale-skinned, some stocky, some broad, some dark-cheeked and smiling, others quiet and brooding, some ragging their chums with simple japes – but their eyes... Their eyes are identical. Whether sunk deep in the skull or starved into protrusion, they are all empty. Brown, grey, blue, green, hazel – it makes no difference. They have dimmed, those eyes. They have dulled into similitude. They are the colour of war.

'Those poor souls,' she breathes.

At her side, William nods.

'What do you suppose they think of?'

'I couldn't begin to say,' William replies.

'They must find this so very asinine. Watching people parading around on a stage, pretending at strength.'

'I don't know. I wouldn't mind betting that pretending is exactly what they need just now.'

'Maybe,' Kate concedes. She drags the back of her hand across her brow. The heat is thick and weighty as a good stew and she has been perspiring steadily since before breakfast, which they had taken on the balcony of their hotel, the four of them sipping coffee and letting the sea air salt-rough their skin and marvelling at how a war could possibly look like this: the hotchpotch of bright white houses and hotels – all sharp corners, and disordered roof tiles, and steep shadows – angling down to the sand-drowned cusp of the land; the shy inward shush of the sea; the diamond glint of the sun off the water;

the friendly braying of the mules being trotted up and down the tree-lined esplanade.

Afterwards, they had been driven to the field hospital in carts dragged by a sorry-looking pair of those selfsame mules, and Kate had felt she might well lose her teeth to the jolting: their pinched gait was quite removed from that of a horse; their smell, though, was musty and familiar and welcoming.

'Do you think she'll be all right,' William asks, 'with that many men...?'

'I doubt she'll think of it,' Kate replies, though he is only voicing her very own worries. 'She's too young to tempt any whistling.'

'Some of those boys are hardly any older.'

Technically, he is right. A great percentage of the recruits currently battling across the Continent are boys of an age somewhere between that of Nora's eighteen and Mona's recent fourteen. At home, in flat caps instead of battle bowlers, their faces slapped by clean winds and their hands muddied with farm work rather than trench muck, they might look just the age to come courting Mona. But they have been accelerated out of their boyhoods, and Kate is certain they will find nothing to ogle in a fourteen-year-old girl with bosoms flattened by muscle and biceps to challenge their own.

The stage is sequestered in a central octagon, created by the positioning of the numberless medical tents which have been pegged into the dusty African soil. Just visible above the bright white peaks of those canvas tents, dusk is beginning to scud inland, cantaloupe and apricot ripe.

421

'Perhaps I should go on with her,' William burbles. He always speaks faster when he is fretting. 'Perhaps, if there's a man there, they might not...'

'What? Give a whistle? It won't hurt her, William. Gosh, she's tough enough to handle a bit of male attention. And if not, we'll be here, close enough to help.'

'But...'

'If she's not managing,' Kate assures him, 'I will go straight on. I promise.'

She turns into him and, catching the ends of his moustache between her first and second fingers, gives it a tug. The bristly hair is equal parts blond and grey now. William opens his mouth in feigned shock, then juts his head suddenly forward to trap Kate's fingers between his lips. The inside of his mouth is hot and strange. Only her tongue tip knows its curves and ridges.

William pops his eyes wide and Kate's laughter erupts and goes bouncing across the stage, causing the gathered troops to fall quiet.

Mona, appearing from nowhere, takes this as her opportunity to push past her parents and stride onto the stage. Her repulsion at this rare moment of outward affection – the limit of which Kate has been lately investigating since only she, William, and the girls have come to Algiers – is implicit. She is fourteen, and her parents are old and disgusting, and if she were not irritated by them, she would have looked over her shoulder for reassurance. Kate raises her eyebrows and clamps her mouth shut, but she cannot suppress her smile. She has always wanted her girls to feel able to stand alone.

She turns her back to William and nestles against him, spine to breastbone, so that they can watch Mona's performance together. He slots his chin over her shoulder, where he has so often rested his burden.

Onstage, Mona has arranged herself in a slant of dwindling sunlight, so that she appears golden as she stands before the barbell and dusts her hand in preparation for her first lift. Joan of Arc, Kate thinks. My very own. And when Mona hoists the bar above her head, and the gathered soldiers whoop in appreciation, Kate feels her heart might stop with the pride of it.

Between lifts and poses, William steps onstage to bellow about Mona's unparalleled feats of strength and whip up applause, but largely she holds the audience alone, and when she skips offstage to allow her sister on, she cannot conceal her joy.

'It was brilliant!' she whispers to Kate when they meet behind the flimsy stage panels.

'*You* were brilliant,' Kate replies.

Nora – who had, in truth, been too nervous to watch from the wings – appears now in her khaki fatigues and stands to attention wordlessly alongside them. She has, in London, appeared as a dandy, but this is her first performance in military garb and she looks just the part. Her short-cropped hair has disappeared beneath the stiff-peaked cap. The wool tunic – neatly fastened, its brass buttons polished to a gleam – gives her a boxier shape than her true figure. Puttees are wound tight around her calves and ankles, disguising what

Kate knows to be shapely legs, and her narrow feet are bulked out by a pair of hobnail boots, which are, perhaps, a size or two too big. Nora is quite the soldier. Her only flaw is that she is clean as spring rain. She gives off a scent of violet, soap, and fresh talcum powder.

Mona laughs lightly. 'I might not have known you,' she says.

Nora, suppressing a grin, answers the compliment with a clumsy salute.

'Ready?' Kate asks.

'Yes, sir!'

She is singing three Vesta Tilley songs, beginning with 'The Army of Today's All Right', followed by 'Six Days' Leave', and, to close, 'Jolly Good Luck to the Girl Who Loves a Soldier'. Afterwards, another troupe will take the stage and the Robertses will rest up and change ready for a finale all the performers will share. In this, Kate and William will appear, too. But Nora is determined not to be outshone and, the moment the brasses blare out, she marches promptly onto the stage and, arms swinging in even time, starts to sing.

Her voice is rich and steady – a natural Welsh alto – and altogether more appealing than Vesta Tilley's more tremulous, bird-like soprano. She stomps out the beat in her hobnails and salutes – not clumsily, as she had for her sister, but with perfect precision. She has practised this routine again and again, bouncing the floorboards of the house they have taken in London, Gosford Lodge, until the cabinets and the doors shook and Kate could not set down a cup of tea safely. She must have practised it with a measuring tape, for she knows the dimensions of her stage exactly as she about-turns, and as she lifts her cap from her head to toss, catch, and replace it, and as she resumes her flawless four-four march.

William, Kate knows, would like to believe that Nora's commitment to her role is the reason she so frequently disappears of an evening, but Kate has long since been convinced that their daughter has taken up with a dancer: a tall, fox-boned girl called Agnieszka, with endless blonde hair, skin like cream, and flashing almond eyes. Kate knows that she is beautiful enough to be dangerous, but she has asked Nora nothing of the affair. Had Eleanor Williams known anything of Kate and William's early relationship, she would have reached a thousand conclusions about it, and every one of them would have been wrong. No, Kate will let Nora have her privacy. She will come to her mother should she need her. She must, she supposes, now that Alice is gone.

Besides, there is a part of Kate which believes that Nora – and each of the children after her, as they grow old enough – ought to experience the feverish black nights and secret strolls, the impossibly bright moons and clamouring jealousy of a love affair. She would not deny them that, even if it does lead them to a broken heart. It is too beautiful a thing not to live.

Nora grows less stern and more expansive for the better known 'Jolly Good Luck to the Girl Who Loves a Soldier', with its gambolling melody and cheering rhythm. The audience laughs and whoops, evidently enjoying the hinting innuendo of the last line.

'Girls, if you'd like to love a soldier,' Nora sings, throwing

425

her arms wide. 'You can all love me!' She jabs a thumb towards her own strapped-down chest and with the downward *bomb bomb* of the brass, the song finishes. She snaps into a final salute, then turns crisply on her heel, and marches offstage to thunderous clapping and bawled appeals for an encore.

She arrives in the wings breathless and beaming.

'They loved you!' Mona squeals, peering coyly around the curtain. Onstage, she is a professional. Offstage, she is a fourteen-year-old girl again, and the sight of all those uniformed men whistling and whooping for her sister no doubt excites romantic notions in her. Probably, she is already envisaging herself and Nora sneaking out of their hotel room and tottering along the esplanade to meet a couple of soldiers for drinks. It is what Kate would have been imagining at her age: a smoky bar, a chilled glass, a warm hand, a cool night, a ready mouth. But she feels reassured that Nora will not indulge her younger sister in such an adventure, given what she believes about Agnieszka.

'They *really* loved you,' Mona goes on. What torture it must be, to be only fourteen and find yourself in possession of an eighteen-year-old sister. 'Do you think one of them might ask you out to dinner, Nora? Do you?' And this time, Kate sees Nora's smile falter. She is certain, however, that she knows how to steady it.

'I'm afraid you're booked for dinner already,' Kate says. 'Your old mother needs an escort, and you, young man...' Nora's smile widens again '...are just the chap for the job.' She hooks an arm through Mona's, then shuffles around to do the same with Nora, and with her girls pinned one to either side of her, where she has always wanted them to be, she swivels their backs to the stage and mischiefs them away. The smile she feels building from her stomach, however, doesn't touch her face. How could it? She has always wanted her girls beside her, yes, but not like this. Never like this. Oh, what they have had to lose to get here.

40.

Algiers, Africa
1915
HER WINGS

Hours afterwards, Kate stands before the open window of her hotel room, looking out at a seemingly monochrome sea: black waves peaked by strewn white moonlight. Soon, she will call on William to come and play that game of theirs, where she coaxes him to look and look until he sees something more than he had at first expected. The game is more than twenty years old and she knows that they have time. First, she wants to listen to the unfamiliar sounds of the strange Mediterranean seaport where the war has happened to deposit them.

It has grown late, and the tinny hiss of the locusts has given way to the tuneless trill of a lonely nightjar; it puts Kate in mind of the clacking of a typewriter, and she is pleased when it is interrupted by the occasional swoop of a true owl's *woohooo*. Beyond the birds is the heavier insistence of the swaying sea and, on it, a small boat which has been anchored and abandoned and from which a bell clangs with eerie regularity. There are the echoes, too, of soldiers entrenched in a bar: their laughter, their arguments, their mumbled words, their sighs. And, just once, the clatter and ghastly grunt of a wild boar, discovered perhaps in his snuffling for stolen food and chased away through the streets.

At the window, the thin silk drapes flutter, though there is hardly a breath of wind, and Kate leans past them and against the railings of the little balcony, set just an inch or two beyond the window frame, so that she can inhale the briny hot smell of the place. She is more careful now, at thirty-nine, to commit these places to memory. It is increasingly doubtful that she will ever come back. Even with her girls in tow, she cannot go on forever. Music hall is a younger woman's game. Who or what she will become next, she cannot say.

On the air, she catches the sounds of Nora and Mona gossiping three rooms along; their laughter, melodic and easy, floats through the open window to join the night music. That she has given these two girls to the world is a constant surprise. She only hopes it will provide them with as much love and beauty in return as they will offer to it.

'William,' she says. 'Come and watch the sea with me.'

William has been lying on their bed, a book in hand. He is stripped to only his underpants, a pair of socks, and his secret reading glasses – which he removes and sets down with the book on top of the bedsheets. He groans as he rises, and Kate wonders if he realises that he always does that now. She will not tell him. She had hardly noticed herself until recently that this man, who had so often boomed and barked, has turned in on himself, quieted. Once, he had been built from all the clatter and grind of Welsh industry. Now, he is chapel song echoing down a valley. But still he is of that country; of home; of the place she had thought she needed to escape but which, in fact, she had only needed to bring with her.

'I never expected we'd come to Africa,' she says, as he wedges himself against the window frame beside her.

'Nor did I.'

'Do you think we'll ever go further again?'

'I don't know. I'm tired, Kate.'

She settles her cheekbone against his shoulder and exhales. 'Me too.'

William slips a hand around her back and finds the nook of her waist. It is, she thinks, more defined on that side, where he most often holds her.

'What should I look for?' he asks.

'The colours, of course,' she answers. 'To begin with.'

'All right.' He hums, low in his throat, as he contemplates the view. 'Well, there's the black of the water,' he begins. 'Tar black,' he adds, quickly, before she can push for the detail. 'And the white of the moonlight where it catches the waves. But there are also veins of green opal and, around the moon, a halo of faded turquoise.'

Kate has closed her eyes for this. His voice is a lullaby. 'You get better every time,' she murmurs.

The owl emits another ghost cry and William puts his lips to Kate's hair. The contact makes her shiver.

'Do you think its Blodeuwedd?' he asks. It is a story they have passed back and forth over the years. Blodeuwedd of the Mabinogi, hewn from flowers to make a wife for a mortal man and punished when she fails to love him as she is expected to. Kate has made certain not to recount it to their children, lest the girls, or indeed the boys, think Blodeuwedd's banishment was deserved. She suspects, though, that William might have told it to them once or twice, thinking nothing of its message.

'I hope so,' Kate laughs. 'It would be nice for her to have the whole world under her wings.'

'Is that what you think she did, flew the world?'

'I do.' Kate is growing somnolent; her words are heavy. 'Those idiots thought they were punishing her, transforming her into an owl and casting her out. But transforming her into a woman in the first place – that was the punishment.'

'How so?' William asks. She has not revealed this take, her take, on the story to him before.

'How would you like to be plucked from nature, given a cumbersome new form, and then immediately bound to a man, a stranger, for the rest of your life? No one asked her whether she wanted it, William. No one even wondered whether she was willing. She could never have loved him.'

'Perhaps not.'

'Definitely not,' Kate insists. 'And then, to turn her into an owl and believe they were banishing her. I don't think so. Look at what she had then, instead of a body and a man she didn't want: the night; her wings. Don't you think it would be glorious, to be made up of just a few nearly weightless bones and all those feathers?'

Kate sees her then: Blodeuwedd, made visible by a slant of moonlight, sweeping across the night in her feathered form.

And perhaps, Kate thinks, that is what she has been seeking all along – not a geographical place or the adulation of an audience or even the approval of her family and colleagues and friends, but her own true form. Perhaps this is it: a broad-shouldered, quite ordinary woman, her skin lined by worry and laughter, her ears full of her children's playful voices, and her love at her back, holding her steady while she glares out at the world in admiration and challenge. She has it all now, everything she ever hoped for, but it is not perfect, this life of hers. It is made heavier than she ever anticipated by the guilt she feels that Alice is not here to live it with them, that after all it is Kate who will watch the children grow. And that guilt is no more than she deserves. She has been selfish, sometimes. She is paying the price.

'You've always wanted to fly,' William whispers. Kate's breathing is slowing. She is drifting towards sleep.

'No,' she says. 'I just didn't want not to be able to.'

41.

Algiers, Africa
1915
CAMEL BOULEVARD

The street is wide and immaculately kept, but for the unavoidable clouds of dust kicked up by travelling feet or hooves, to bloom and wilt and settle. Kate had read the sign: *Boulevard de* ... something; she had not managed to internalise the French. In any case, the boulevard is impressive indeed. It is flanked by vast buildings of sandstone or white stucco, which display their elaborately carved arches and battlements demurely. Despite their size, they are not showy but calming somehow. They make her want to whisper. The pavements are lined with full green palm trees. Sunlight sharpens between the pillars and domes and archways, crowding the boulevard with perfect shadows. Kate pauses to put the toe of her shoe to the fronds of a palm tree, printed in exact replica on the swept clean walkway. If she had a week to spare, she could count every one of its fingers.

'What's their proper name?' she asks, her head still lowered in study of the shadow.

The others, a step or two ahead of her, stop to look back.

'What?'

'Palm trees. They can't just be called palm trees. It's never so plain. Did any of us learn even half of what Alice knew?'

'Arecaceae,' Nora answers. 'But, no. Not even half.'

When Kate looks up, Nora is wearing a fragment of a smile.

'I wish I'd listened to her more,' Kate says.

'Me too,' Mona agrees.

Locking his hands at the small of his back, William begins parading about beneath the nearest tree, making a show of looking up the stem as though engaged in a serious inspection of it. Kate is not sure whether this is because he wants to allow the girls a private moment, or because he does not want them to see his tears.

'Do you miss her horribly?'

It has been five years. But five years is no time at all to grief.

'Of course.' It is Nora. 'Don't you?'

'I do,' Kate admits. 'But I wasn't as much with her as you. We were used to being apart for long stretches.'

Nora shrugs, then glances at her father's back. 'It hasn't been such a long time,' she says. 'At least, it doesn't seem so. Sometimes, I still feel as though she's here. Or there, rather. At home. And that when we get back, she'll be waiting for us.'

Kate reaches out to clasp her eldest daughter's hand; the skin is hot and dry as just baked bread.

'It doesn't make me sad,' Nora continues. 'It's getting less and less, but now and then, I see a flower or I put on a good show and I think, "I can't wait to tell Alice about that". So I pretend that I will. That we're only separated by the sea or a train journey. That is... It doesn't upset you, does it?'

Kate shakes her head quickly.

'Good. I mean, I know it's daft, but on occasion, it seems better to pretend than to properly miss her.'

'I don't think that's daft,' Kate replies. 'Mona...'

She thinks it prudent to ask if Mona feels similarly before they leave this conversation behind. They have lost their mother, after all, these girls. One of them, at least. The one who tucked them into bed, and filled their dreams with stories, and explained to them about their courses, and held them through their earliest weeping disappointments. Alice, with her soft stomach and her neat hair. Alice, always gently spoken. Alice was a proper mother. She will never be lost to crumpled newspaper articles and theatre gossip. She is within these girls.

'Mona,' Kate begins, but she gets no further than speaking Mona's name before they are interrupted by a rapidly approaching din. They turn towards it. Padded feet scud up huge plumes of dust, which, at first, make the animals appear to have no legs whatsoever – only huge, tremulous, sandy bodies and long, angry faces. Their nostrils are flared black holes. Their humps flop from side to side, making an uncomfortable thwacking sound. They snort and rumble and growl. They toss their heads against their leather harnesses and swivel their ears. They pucker their lips and peel them open to reveal enormous crooked teeth.

'A camel train,' William breathes, having abandoned his inspection of the palm and stepped closer. 'I hoped we'd see one.'

The stink of the beasts reaches the Robertses ahead of the beasts themselves. It is a warm smell, which hits the back of the throat and nose and clings there. Urine. Must. Damp straw. It is reminiscent of the stale air trapped inside an unoccupied house, but stronger. Thicker. As though, if Kate were to reach out and brush her fingertips through the animals' coarse hair, they would come away coated with something she would not be able to wash off. Fat flies swarm around their nub-like ears as they honk-honk-honk down the middle of the boulevard. The Robertses stand back to watch them pass. Many have cloth-wrapped bundles strapped to their backs. Others carry saddles stacked with boxes. Canteens hung from their leathers jangle cacophonously. The lead camel is the only one which carries a rider: a small, tan-cheeked man with a straggly grey beard. He holds a bamboo whip, but he does not smack it against his mount's hide. He only waves it around: an empty threat.

'Aren't they wonderful?' Mona says, laughing. 'I want to ride one.' And Kate cannot help but be put in mind of that girl who had stood on the bank of the Thames and watched the policemen skating across the frozen river, and said with such wistfulness, 'I want to try it'.

'So do I,' William answers. His smile is wide and silly. He is as enchanted as his daughter by these cumbersome creatures. And later, they will ride on the back of a camel – all four of them. Before they leave Algiers, they will seek out the owner of a caravan and pay him handsomely to parade them along the esplanade, each of them laughing and wobbling and letting out the occasional shriek. 'Arthur would love this,' Nora will say, and Kate will nod and wonder how much longer it will be

436

before all of her children can join the troupe and they can set about exploring this big, beautiful world together.

But this morning they are only out to find breakfast. The other people on the boulevard do not so much as glance at the riotous camel train. They stride purposefully along or linger in chattered conversation or barter over goods concealed about the seller's person, their flowing white djellabas billowing, their heads draped in thin cotton to protect them from the sun. Kate, Nora, and Mona are not half so wise. They carry parasols, which soon grows tiresome. They have belts fastened around their middles, cinching their skirts in at their waists and causing them to sweat. What a relief it would be, to feel the air sweeping up under a clean white djellaba, like wind dancing through a bedsheet on a washing line. By the end of the week, Kate decides, she will have one.

The camel train trundles away around a corner, canteens echoing behind like cowbells. They are replaced by a fist of soldiers, already down to their vests, bellowing towards the harbour on bare feet. The Robertses stroll a little further, passing a hotel where four women are sitting to tea at an outdoor table. They pause in the shade of a palm tree and watch a trader wheel a cart piled with bags of nuts and spices down the middle of the boulevard, dodging mounds of camel mess and whistling to himself.

'I didn't know war could feel like this,' Kate says.

'I don't suppose it does,' William replies.

'Do you think we'll see anything of it?'

William shakes his head. 'I doubt it. Except in them,

perhaps.' He nods in the direction the wild bunch of would-be swimmers have disappeared. 'The soldiers. Their injuries. Their expressions.'

'I'm glad we're here, doing something,' Mona says, and Kate understands the sentiment exactly. To be idle now would be impossible.

'I would have liked to have been a soldier,' Nora puts in.

'Would you?' William asks. 'Why?'

'For the adventure.'

For the camaraderie, Kate thinks. For the uniform. For the women. William's temper will burst like a firework when he learns about Agnieszka, but Kate has already prepared what she will say to calm him, when the occasion arises, and she knows that he will be all right in the end. She knows everything she need know about this man, who is hooking his arm around Nora's shoulder now and giving her a squeeze. Their daughter is as tall as her father, and Kate knows that this niggles at William, who only becomes more embarrassed by his diminutive height as he grows older and his musculature weakens. He has always feared being a small man. And that, she supposes, is what has driven him across countries and oceans – the longing to make himself larger. Her drive has not been the same. She has not been collecting material with which to build herself along the way; she has been shedding it. *Don't bind your body up in stays. Be yourself. Seek strength.* These messages she has littered the newspapers with in an attempt to leave something great behind her, while William, inversely, has been aiming to leave each city a fuller man. She does not think his endeavour any less admirable than her own, but she does think it more near-sighted. Surely he would have become a greater man by trailing greatness behind him, where it might live in people's memories? The story of a man is almost always grander than the man himself. And that is when she sees it clearly for the first time: the rhetoric he has wrapped Vulcana up in; the poses and the posters; the endless newspaper interviews. *The most beautiful, symmetrical and physically perfect woman on earth. The only known woman of absolutely correct measurements. The world's strongest woman.* She is the story he has left behind.

And perhaps that would matter, on some other day. Perhaps, if she were already inclined towards a dark mood, she would think she'd been the subject of one big manipulation – though the years to come will prove her wrong. Perhaps, if she were feeling irritable, she would conclude that William had been cowardly in appointing her the protagonist in this tale; that he should have plucked up the courage to fulfil the role himself. In any case, she knows perspective to be a thing too readily influenced by that which is exterior to it to be trustworthy. Alice's death had taught her that. In the shock of it, Kate had thought the older woman selfish – for leaving them all behind too soon. And that vicious thought had led her to others: jealousy when William sobbed over the loss of her; the vague and ugly notion that somehow Alice had kept Kate from her own children. It was all nonsense. Time softened her grief and it became clear that she felt angry towards Alice only because she missed her. She was glad then, immeasurably so, that she had not put voice to any of the thoughts that plagued her in the days and weeks that followed the funeral. Just as she will be glad one day – standing before a rain-spotted window, when William tells her the end of their story – that she did not doubt his motives on this easy morning, as they walk together through the strange, musical streets of Algiers and listen to their daughters' nattered observations and hold hands like an old married couple.

At Nora's insistence, they follow the curve of the boulevard, seeking out what she had called, 'A sweet little seafood café, with tables outside and pale silks hanging in the windows'. Kate is too hot. A slick of perspiration gathers down her spine, between her thighs, behind each knee, but she does not complain. She wants Nora to find her café. She wants to sit outside it, under the shade of a huge white umbrella, and have a waiter serve her lobster or crab or mussels. She does not know what the delicacy is here, but she will look forward to finding out. Hasn't discovery always been one of her greatest joys?

Her attention is drawn towards a clapping sound overhead and she tilts back her head. Not wings; it is too noisy for that. She scans the high blue arcade of sky between the buildings on the nameless boulevard until she sights, gliding into view, a kite. Someone is flying a kite. Enormous and diamond-shaped, it has a wooden frame and pure white sails. It soars above them, silent now that it has found its pocket of air, and majestic in its calm precision. It is, Kate thinks, other-worldly. A sigil of some kind, though she cannot say what.

Perhaps, when they get home, she will take Arthur and

William out to fly a kite. She'll drag Mabel along with them, and they'll stop and buy ice cream from a cart afterwards. They'll enjoy that. She has already decided that she's going to take some weeks off once they are home. She is going to refuse theatre appearances and instead take the children to Boulter's Lock to watch the boats, and to picnics in Victoria Park, and for swims in the lido. They'll go to the zoo, and stand outside Buckingham Palace to see the changing of the guard, and one long, warm day they might ride the train to Abergavenny and climb up into the hills and look down the slate-roofed streets and pick out the chimney stack of their old house. She'll take the girls to the WSPU meetings she had neglected after Alice's death, when the children, ready for such a change or not, came to London, and let them decide for themselves whether or not they want to join the fight...

She stumbles over that last thought. The fight. Is the opportunity to fight all she has to offer Nora and Mona? She thinks back over the stories she has told them – the stories she has told herself – in hopes of inspiring them, and she realises that they have almost all featured fighting women: Gwenllian, fighting with her army; Alice of Abergavenny, fighting to avenge her lost love; Jemima Nicholas, fighting to protect herself from invaders; Christabel Pankhurst, fighting to secure votes for women; Marie Lloyd, fighting the National Vigilance Association for the right to express herself just as she pleased. Fighting women, all. Even Kate has been enticed to it, in her quest to ensure it becomes acceptable for women to wear clothes which do not physically injure them. What a

441

ridiculous stance to need to take. If men's waistcoats had hindered the function of their lungs, they would have thrown them off immediately. But still she has to speak against corsetry in her newspaper interviews, still she has to defend her views, still she has to coax and persuade.

She wonders whether it will be within her own lifetime or within her daughters', or their possible daughters' even, that they will be able to stop fighting. For doesn't Kate still have a battle ahead of her, for her good name, when it becomes known that she and William are not, after all, brother and sister? And Nora will surely face a war if she is to defend her attachment to Agnieszka. She will teach her girls, then, to grit their teeth and clench their fists. That is her task. She will teach them to be ferocious.

'Look!' Nora says. 'There.' And Kate thinks she must be talking about the kite, until she drags at her mother's arm and points diagonally into the distance. She must have found the café: the brawny scent of grilled seafood does waft between the palm trees here. But Kate could hardly say where it is coming from, because when she lowers her chin to follow Nora's pointed finger, she can see nothing. The sun, still only just crowning the buildings, has blinded her. The end of the boulevard is a blank white space, which she feels she might step through and find herself somewhere else entirely, and she hesitates momentarily. She is not sure she's ready yet to leave this life behind.

'I can't see where we're going,' she says. She gropes for a hand and finds William's – rough and snagged and familiar. His voice reaches her ear almost immediately, tilting with laughter.

'Neither can I,' he replies. 'It's exciting, isn't it?'

Final Act

London, England
1946
A LOVE STORY

The rain pesters the windowpane. *Tap-tap-tap*. *Tap-tap-tap*. February, the meanest month, leaches all the colour from the city and Kate looks out from the first floor of Gosford Lodge at the grey concrete river below, the black bones of the sugar maple trees, the silver sheen of the roof tiles on the house opposite. It is early, perhaps seven o'clock, and the lamps have not yet turned off. Wind drags their light diagonally away, leaving tunnels of blackness behind. It ought all to be brighter, given that the war is over. Not the war – another war. A second war. She gets them mixed up sometimes.

She is holding a cup of tea. The porcelain is pleasantly warm beneath her palms as she runs them around the flowered surface, trying to ease the pain that bulges at every joint. Her fingers, these days, look like rough kindling: all knots and bumps and nicks. The flesh is ruddy, where it is slack enough to retain colour, and white where it grips too tight to her skeleton. She could not slip a wedding ring on even if she were in possession of one. They never married, of course; it wouldn't have seemed right, after Alice.

443

She lifts the cup to her chin but does not drink from it. She wants only to feel the steam skim over her skin. The heat is a reassuring counterpoint to the view from the window.

At her back, a man is talking steadily: a welcome melody over the rain's accompanying percussion. He might be reading from a book, so evenly does he tell his story, but Kate does not turn around to find out. She wants only to listen to this voice, a good voice, snagged by age, as it describes a young woman, strong in the shoulder and buttocks and thighs, barefooting along a pier – Morecambe Pier – on an early summer's morning. She is wearing a swimming costume – blue, Kate decides, a deep royal blue – and her hair flags loose behind her, long and curled and glinting copper strands in the sunshine. The pier is quiet, it being so early, but there are a few couples walking, arm in arm, looking out to sea. They stop to gape as the young woman thunders past, laughing as she runs towards the pier's end, pursued by a man in a striped costume of his own. Occasionally, she spins around to check he is keeping up with her, then, satisfied that he is, increases her pace. *Wait*, he calls. But she does not. She knows he will follow her. Stretching along the length of the pier, the man tells Kate, is a huge banner. *Diving and Merry Japes*, it reads. *Vulcana, Most Beautiful Woman on Earth, Brothers Redmond, Great Stars, 6D*. At the description, Kate hears it billowing and cracking against the railings in the sea breeze as that young woman rushes past it. She feels the chill morning air on that woman's exposed shoulders and stocking-less legs and the slight give of the wood beneath her feet. She knows this story.

The young woman runs past the pavilion, where another banner declares *Dancing Free*, and continues along the stilted pier. The sea peaks and glimmers beneath the slatted wood. Further back, where the rollers peel back to reveal the shingle, small fishing boats sit wedged into the stony sand. On the foreshore, a suited man is laying out a crescent of chairs, where spectators will sit later, the tides at their backs, to watch a chaotic Punch and Judy show. Only two people stand between the young woman and the end of the pier now: two ladies, in their late sixties perhaps, companions, or sisters, leaning over the railings to watch the slap of the water against the pier's legs. They turn at the approaching sound of her and, rearranging their mouths into matching hollows of shock, move apart to clear the way. The young woman does not break stride. She rushes to the railings, climbs deftly up and over them, then, hooking her toes around the edge of the pier, links her hands above her head, and dives.

Kate feels her go. The rushing sensation. The deep plummet of her stomach. The air against her, spitting salt. And then, in one smooth ripple, the water. It clamps around her, murky dark and cold, and she imagines herself a ship, wrecked in drift ice in some unnameable far north place. But she is a powerful swimmer. Practised. Confident. And she kicks her legs and ribbons her body and hauls with her arms, and the shuddering which might otherwise have taken control of her subsides, and she begins to thaw.

Kate recognises that feeling. The young woman, then, in the blue swimming costume... It was her – before she sailed far enough out to sea to fear it. She had always loved swimming: in lakes, in the lidos, on the coast. She never doubted her own ability. It was never water that she feared, but... The sea. The bottomless black of deepest sea. The immense, unflinching power of her.

'It was me, wasn't it?' she says quietly. 'I was the young woman who dived off the pier.'

'That's right,' says the man at her back. 'We were at the Alhambra Palace. Do you recall?'

But Kate does not. Not presently in any case. All she remembers is the pier, the beautiful emptiness of leaping free of it, the suck of the water. They had spent all morning there, she and William: diving and jumping; drawing crowds. By eleven, they were teaching themselves to perform tumble tosses and eliciting shrieks and gasps from their impromptu audience.

'Would you like to see a photograph?' the man asks from his wing chair. She finds his reflection in the windowpane. His hair is wispy white, combed into fullness. His chin is angled down, so that he can look at her over the top of his glasses. His right leg is crossed over his left knee. There is a book in his lap, but it is not a novel: it is larger; the pages thicker. It is, she thinks, an album packed beyond the limits of its spine with photographs. Of her? Of William? Of the children? All, she supposes. She cannot remember ever seeing the photograph album before.

'No, thank you,' she replies. She has the image well enough in her mind. She does not want to spoil it with a photograph – flat and grey and lifeless by comparison.

446

She wonders how many of this old man's stories are about her. Rotating through her mind, as though she is sitting at the centre of a cinéorama, are glamorous names and far-off places, impossible birds and exotic creatures, nightmare steamship journeys and cheering crowds and panoramas so vast that she could not imagine how the world could accommodate them. The names slip forever just out of reach – Rhiannon, Jemima Nicholas, Gwenllian ferch Gruffydd – sounds to which she cannot attach the correct narratives. But so often, spot-lit and centre stage, there is a beautiful girl, with sparking cinnamon-brown eyes, and luxuriously long hair, and an impressively straight back and a chin held high, and a story of her own.

Kate thinks that perhaps she knows everything and nothing about her.

She drains the last of her tea and, setting down the cup, lifts a hand to her hairline. A scar bumps down the side of her forehead and disappears behind her ear. As she runs her fingers over it, Kate sees it – silver-white and tight – though she can discern no such detail in the fairground mirror of the window.

'There was a fire, wasn't there?' she says.

'Yes,' the old man replies. 'But that was at The Garrick, in Edinburgh.'

The Garrick Theatre, Grove Street, Edinburgh, she replies, *I know*. But for reasons unknown to her, those words seem reluctant to travel to her tongue. She can only nod.

'It was June,' he says. 'A beautiful summer's eve. The sky was the colour of...' He thinks for a moment. 'Periwinkles. There was to be a big Society Athlete's performance, the night The

447

Garrick burned down. We heard about the blaze and rushed down from the hotel, to see if we might save some of your medals. All those medals we lost, Kate. Do you remember? One-hundred-and-twenty at least. Though it was the horses you went in for.'

She nods again. Yes, she remembers. Rushing through the black heat, one arm held up across her face, and hearing the building's timbers groan above her. The overwhelming smoky stink of the auditorium as the seats and the stage and the orchestra's instruments burned, and then, more immediate, the crackle and scorch of her own hair as it caught and singed and she slapped it out with her palms. And then the horses, in silhouette, rearing up against the flames as though they were models on a carousel. They had, thankfully, been wearing headcollars, and Kate was able to hook her fingers through that of the calmest animal and lead it out into the street, where she spun on her heel and returned through the fire for the next. There were four in all: two bays, one blue roan, and a white. Though the last escaped the theatre with its mane ablaze, each followed her out without incident. As though they knew. As though she had been intended to save them. As though those very horses had been galloping through her dreams all along, to prepare her, to remind her.

'Of course it was for the horses,' she says. Then, shrugging: 'What's the worth of a medal?'

He has read her a thousand books while she has stood at this window, looking out and listening, and not one of them has been about the acquisition of medals or trophies. What they have all been about is the maintenance of a life – that precious, unbearable battle.

She ought, she thinks now, to have written about her own life. As Vesta Tilley did. She does not like to think of ending her days, like Marie Lloyd, unexpectedly, and having no say in what might come after. Poor, kind Marie, who had stumbled offstage at the Alhambra Theatre in agony and died, just days later, when her broken heart finally gave up. She was fifty-two years old. Much younger than Kate is now. Kate had attended the funeral in Hampstead Cemetery, where, it was afterwards said, she was joined by fifty thousand mourners. Kate could well believe it. Hampstead was a sea of black hats and black coats that day. And if only one, Kate thought, if just one of those fifty thousand people had loved Marie the way William loved her, she might have lived yet. Cruel men and music hall – that's what Marie died of. And, when she went, poor soul, it was cruel men and music hall who were left to tell her story.

What would she have said, Kate wonders now, if she had known that performance would be her last? She smiles as she remembers Marie's words that night they took drinks together at the Savoy: 'Give the bastards just enough, and let them yearn for the rest.'

That, she supposes, is as good a mantra as any. But it would not be Kate's. What Kate most regrets are the moments when she did not give everything: when she failed to commit to a performance; when she refused to reveal her truths or her fears to William; when she was only a partially present mother.

449

There were times, though, when she got it right. At least, she thinks there were.

Like that day, walking through the dream-white streets of Algiers with her husband and her daughters, laughing at the absurdity of a passing camel train, and believing that soon, very soon now, it would all be as it should be. Nora and Mona would continue to tour with them and, when they grew old enough, Arthur and William would leave their Auntie Mabel's spare bedroom behind and join the troupe, and they would gad about the world together, The Atlases. There would be arguments, naturally, and bad tempers and misunderstandings, but there would be laughter, too. So much laughter. And adventure. And love. And they would be together.

After all, Kate sees now that all she ever truly needed was for them to be together as they set about exploring the world. And they were, for a time. She remembers. In glorious bright flashes and hazy daydreams, she remembers. Despite the accident with the cab. Despite being laid up like a corpse. Despite the long recovery after they discovered that she was breathing still, that Kate Roberts was not ready to leave her life behind just yet, and rushed her to the hospital where the doctors declared that she had been starved of oxygen, that her brain might not recover, that she would not be quite Kate again... Oh, she remembers. How could she forget the sight of her daughter, sneaking into the London night, hand in hand with her dancer, her eyes made bright by adoration? Or the children, all of them, running down the garden of the

Bristol house in pursuit of their father and laughing until they dropped? Sitting in the kitchen dark with Alice and trying to stifle their laughter. The white ibis rising out of Darling Harbour as the storm approached. The distant view of misted painterly mountains from the window of an Australian train. Arthur and William huddled in her lap, silent and perfect, after Alice died. Standing beneath the Rotterdam windmills and grinning into each whoosh of air from the rotating sails. Mona, rushing offstage and throwing her arms around her mother in glee at a successful performance. Making love to William in a sumptuous Paris hotel room.

Oh, all of that. Nothing could steal so much from her. She remembers.

'William,' she says, and the old man rises from his wing chair and steps towards her. His spine remains as erect as ever, but he hasn't much left to give to this life now. He is eighty-three. He is tired. And when he decides to go to sleep, she thinks, she will go with him. The two of them together. As they have been all these years.

Reaching her, William slips his arms around her middle and slots his chin into the groove it has made in her shoulder.

'What is it?' he asks, and Kate does not answer for a minute, more than a minute, because she wants to concentrate on the thud of his heart against her back, and the sweet talcum and pipe-smoke scent of his skin, and the hush of his breath against her ear. She wants to savour him, this spectacular man.

'William,' she says again.

'Kate,' he replies, and it is all she wants to hear – his

grumbling voice, the reassurance of it, reminding her of who she is. Kate Williams, the Reverend's tomboyish daughter. Kate Roberts, who time claimed as a wife. Vulcana, the strongest woman to grace the stages. In the window now is reflected a younger figure, with a straight back and sparking cinnamon eyes and a story of her own, and she is smiling. Ah, yes. There she is. She remembers. Kate, the strongwoman.

'Come and watch the world with me,' she says.

AUTHOR'S NOTE:

In 2018, while researching another story, I happened upon a blog detailing the life of a Victorian strongwoman known as Vulcana. It was a fascinating account, written by Vulcana's great granddaughter, Jane Vanderstay Hunt. I was immediately inspired by Vulcana's story and strength and felt that I must write about her.

In the summer of 2019, I met with Jane and asked for her blessing to write this novel. She was kind enough not only to greet my proposal with enthusiasm, but to spend some hours talking with me at her kitchen table, and later to furnish me with many years of research. This research was invaluable. I could not have told this story without Jane's help.

Miriam Kate Williams (who went by her middle name, Kate), aka Vulcana, is still known in some circles, though, in my opinion, not nearly widely enough. Kate Williams was born in Abergavenny in 1874, according to some sources, or 1876, according to others. It is Jane's belief, based on her extensive research, including primary sources, that 1876 was Kate's true date of birth, and so that is the date I have used in this novel. Both Jane and myself have searched for Kate's birth certificate without success.

In telling this story, I have remained as faithful to the facts (as I know them) as I have been able, relying on various sources

– including family stories, photographs, and newspaper and magazine articles – in my research. The truth does not always slot neatly into a pleasing narrative structure, however, and so there are some events I have had to disregard and some moments I have imagined. The wider troupe members are invented. As is Alice's end. There is also some speculation as to whether Kate had four children or six; in this regard, again, I have deferred to Jane's belief that it is most likely that four of William's children were also Kate's. Despite my necessary inventions, the dates, locations, and events surrounding Kate and William are largely based in documented reality.

My aim in writing this novel was to draw attention to the life of a woman whose boldness and bravery have captivated me, and whose story I believe remains important to women today. Kate was a trailblazer, an inspiration, and a strong woman in every sense of the word. I hope my admiration for her will outweigh any mistakes I may have made.

ACKNOWLEDGEMENTS

I owe my sincerest thanks to...

Jane Vanderstay Hunt, for her passion. Jane – I hope this novel fulfils a few of your expectations.

Janet Thomas, Lynzie Fitzpatrick, and all of the Honno team, for believing in me and supporting me always, and for being champions of women.

Rukhsana Yasmin, for loving Kate's story and for her enthusiasm.

My mother and father, Keith and Louise, for their endless support.

My wonderful friends, too numerous to list, for listening to me talk and talk about Vulcana since the moment I discovered her.

Liz Hyder, for friendship and support which surpasses all expectation.

My dogs, Betsy and Teddy, for the unwavering love and the walks.

Matthew, for the moans and the tea.

And my son, Phinneas, for making me so very happy and reminding me to meet every day with curiosity and joy.

Rebecca F. John is the author of five previous titles. Her first novel, *The Haunting of Henry Twist* (Serpent's Tail, 2017) was shortlisted for the Costa First Novel Award. She won the PEN International New Voices Award 2015. In 2017 she was on the Hay Festival's 'The Hay 30' list. Her stories have been broadcast on Radio 4. She lives in Swansea with her partner, their son, and their dogs. Her previous book for Honno, *Fannie,* was published in January 2022 and was Waterstones Book of the Month for Wales, the BCW Book of the Month, and the Wales Arts Review's Novel of the Year 2022.

ABOUT HONNO

Honno Welsh Women's Press was set up in 1986 by a group of women who felt strongly that women in Wales needed wider opportunities to see their writing in print and to become involved in the publishing process. Our aim is to develop the writing talents of women in Wales, give them new and exciting opportunities to see their work published and often to give them their first 'break' as a writer.

Honno is registered as a community co-operative. Any profit that Honno makes is invested in the publishing programme. Women from Wales and around the world have expressed their support for Honno. Each supporter has a vote at the Annual General Meeting. For more information and to buy our publications, please visit our website www.honno.co.uk or email us on post@honno.co.uk.

Honno
D41, Hugh Owen Building,
Aberystwyth University,
Aberystwyth,
Ceredigion,
SY23 3DY.

We are very grateful for the support of all our Honno Friends.